EARTH 2100

18 CAPTIVATING VISIONS OF A SCI-FI FUTURE

Edited by

J. SCOTT COATSWORTH

Published by
Other Worlds Ink
PO Box 19341, Sacramento, CA 95819

First Edition

Individual stories:

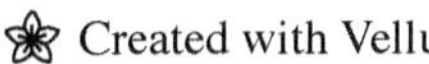 Created with Vellum

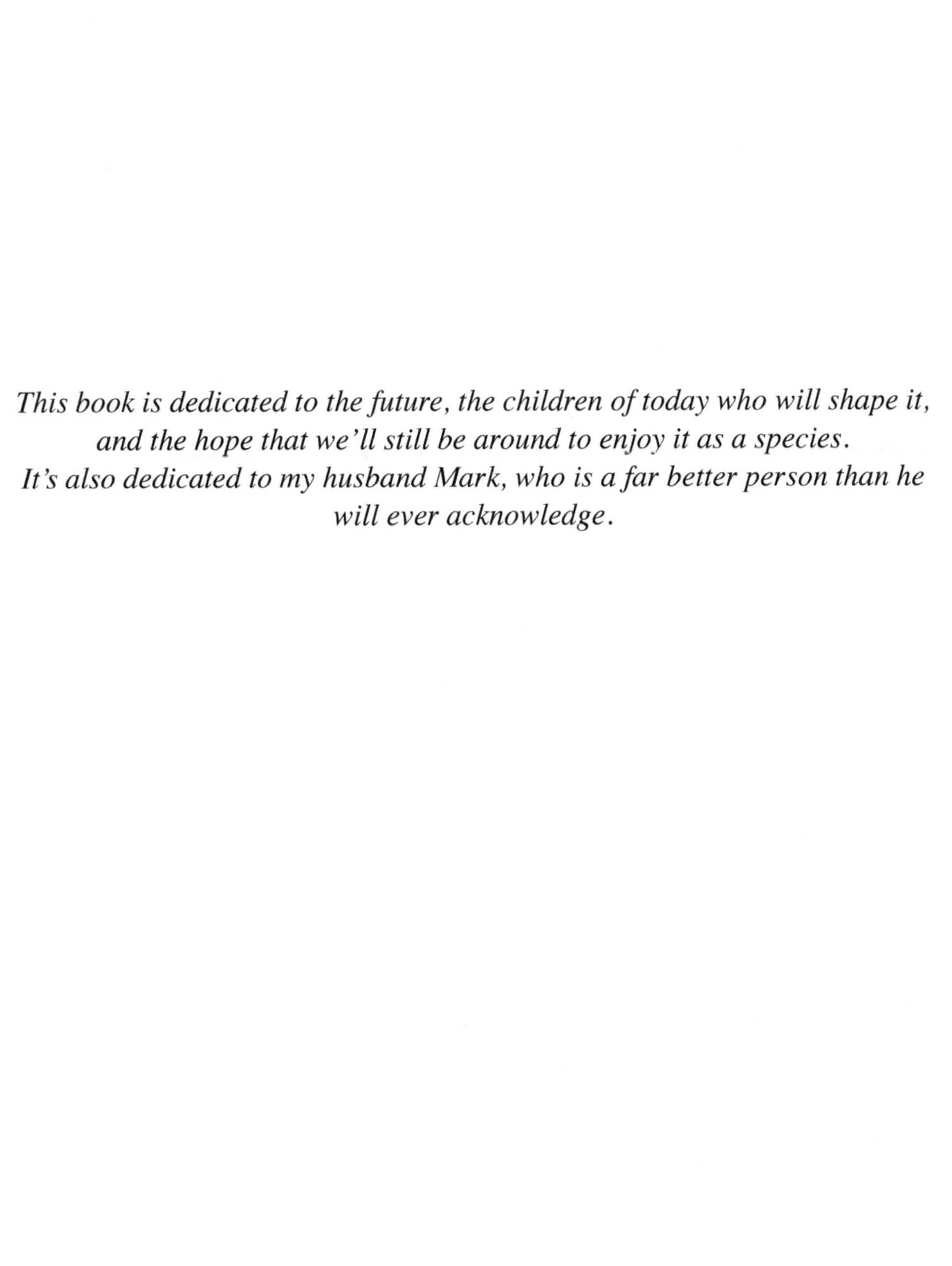

This book is dedicated to the future, the children of today who will shape it, and the hope that we'll still be around to enjoy it as a species.
It's also dedicated to my husband Mark, who is a far better person than he will ever acknowledge.

CONTENTS

ACKNOWLEDGMENTS

I WANTED to acknowledge and thank a number of folks who made this anthology a reality.

Thanks to our screeners: Angel Martinez, Brandon Cracraft, Jaime Lee Moyer, Kelly Haworth, Kim Fielding, L.V. Lloyd, Rory ni Coileain, and KA Masters, without whom just getting through the amazing stack of stories would have probably killed me.

And also thanks to Jaime for editing the stories to make them better and stronger, and to Allison Behrens and Sue Phillips for doing a wonderful job proofing the book.

And to the writers—all 152 of them!—who submitted stories and gave us such a rich and varied selection to choose from.

Finally, my husband Mark, who believes in this whole wacky writing and publishing thing I'm doing. Love you!

FOREWORD

In 2023, we sent out a call for hope-filled stories about how we might change our government, our culture and our society to make the world a better place. We had a huge response, and selected and published fourteen of them in *Transform the World* in October.

But there were so many other great stories there that didn't quite fit the remit—hopepunk tales set on a near-future earth that involved a shift in the way we do things as a world.

And so Earth 2100 was born. For the most part, these stories are still hopeful—after all, they assume we will still be around in another three-quarters of a century.

They are notable for their diversity, from their characters and in the myriad different lenses they use to zoom in on humanity's—and Earth's—future.

I love the iconography of the cover. One of my friends said the glass enclosure reminds them of the EPCOT™ geodesic sphere at Disneyworld, which is very appropriate, since that ride is dedicated to what folks back in 1982 thought the future would look like.

So dig in and enjoy, and exercise that forward-looking impulse that we've been so sorely lacking these last few dark years.

Onward to the future!

TIN LIZZY

BY GAIL BROWN

Chaos filled several of the workshop tables. Material overflowed a table with a sewing machine. Some heavy duty, water proof beige fabrics had drifted to the floor.

A thick vegetable and meat soup simmered on the stove in the tiny central kitchen area. Next to the stove was a table set for two. Without any chairs.

Celina rode her power chair over to the counter top stove to stir the soup. The counter was a few inches higher than was comfortable. Today she needed to cook more than her usual single serving. Maybe her height measurements had been off. The counter could be an inch shorter, and not be in her lap.

It was challenging to figure out how to build it low enough to see into a pan, and stir the food, while tall and sturdy enough to not knock it over when Lizzy slid under it.

There was only about a foot of space to work with, if she didn't want the pan higher than her face, and not able to stir without her elbow at maximum height. Which risked boiling food splashing on her face.

Figuring out how to make furniture the correct height, so she could slip her non-functioning legs under it had consumed her waking hours, and even sleeping hours, for the last year.

The stainless steel pan reflected her face. Down to the pointed lines above her eyebrows. Even the eyebrow she had singed an hour before.

She turned the power chair back to her wood and metal design workstation. Another stainless steel surface. Covered with scars from the many experiments needed to build lowered objects, with a glimpse of personal beauty in their functionality.

What would Henril and Trinkle think of her newest achievement? Her former hiking partners no longer walked the trails as much without her.

Certainly not on the narrow bluff overlooking the river. Henril had avoided out of concern for Trinkle's safety. Or so he said.

Hopefully, they would soon all be hiking together.

Celina rubbed her hand across the glittery surface. Some of the scars were much like her own. Deep, jagged, and colorless. Others were smooth, transparent, and brightly discolored.

The pieces of her current project were scattered across the scarred and grooved surface.

A padded seat, large enough to sit on without falling off. A beige waterproof covering protected it against the elements. She would have to make few more colorful seat covers for special occasions.

Wires encased in flexible clear plastic tubes connected the seat to two long padded sections. One for each arm. A small tap pad on each allowed her to steer the seat. The connecting back was short, to keep weight minimal. With just enough room to attach several small solar panels to charge the batteries.

At the other end of the table were two smaller ovals, with a magnetic part that could be turned on or off, to connect the two ovals to each other. They were connected to the back of the seat by clear plastic tubes just wide enough to protect her nonresponsive legs from bumps and bruises. Several heavy duty adjustable straps connected to the tubes on each side.

The plan to make the lower part rigid had been changed when she saw how difficult it was to cook with full sized pans. Without feeling in her legs or feet, and no ability to control them, strapped legs to the clear plastic tubes would allow the legs to straighten enough to keep her knees out of the way while reaching for objects. Or stirring food.

Not like standing.

Or walking.

She touched her project. Her hope and dream of a future, not left behind. A Tin Lizzy she had named Spook.

Her power chair beeped.

"Jealous? Lizzy, you will always be my primary transport."

The chair beeped again.

She sighed and backed up to go stir the soup. It didn't have to be this way. She had had other plans. Until the snow storm.

A year ago, the fresh clean snow had been knee high, and hiking in the crisp clear air seemed the perfect way to spend an afternoon. Henril had forged on ahead chasing puppy Trinkle through a shoulder high drift on the bluff overlooking the swift flowing river.

Celina had paused. She was closer to the edge than she realized. Her hiking sticks shifted on the uneven snow. When the stick slipped off the boulder she had forgotten was there, she had tumbled off the bluff and onto the nearly frozen river below.

Luckily, the snow had cushioned her fall. As had the fifty pounds of clothes and snow boots.

She heard the ice crack. Her feet slipped into the icy water.

By the time the rescue team reached her, it was too late. Her legs and feet were frozen. The tug of the rush of water under the ice had jerked her spine. Until she would likely never walk, hike, or dig again. At least the doctors said.

After she was released from the hospital, she had demanded to live alone in her workshop. Leaving Henril and Trinkle the house.

The house. A few blocks away. Might as well be on the moon, for all she could reach it. Crutches wouldn't get her ten feet. Her legs swung between them, not able even to get her feet to touch the ground, or move her disconnected legs on her own.

Lizzy would make the distance with ease, if the sidewalks weren't splintered. And the road full of potholes. If she could even get out of the workshop, or home, on the narrow and slippery ramp.

Her workshop. She wasn't giving it up. Nor, would she give up climbing mountains. Or digging holes in search of the history of this region, and those who had come before them, whose history was long lost. Spook would see to that. If she worked as intended.

Celina wasn't quite ready to try out Spook in snow. Or ice. Or slush.

The doorbell rang.

She glanced at the monitor beside the stove. Henril and Trinkle were at the front door. This monitor she had used before even Lizzy came to transport her around her shrunken world. She tapped the button. The door unlocked automatically.

Henril walked in and placed a bulky hiking pack on Celina's overflowing sewing station.

Trinkle bounded in. A medium sized young adult dog who looked like a husky. Only, she wasn't. She too was not whom she appeared.

"Is it working?" Henril pulled the only empty chair up to the eating table.

She had forgotten he didn't always have a chair. How could she forget so soon? It had only been a year since the accident.

"Yes. Spook moves well in here. I just have to store her on the table top, for now."

"Show me how she works." Henril pulled out three bowls to dip the soup out.

Celina moved back over to the work station. She grabbed Spook gently by the seat cushion. After lifting the machine off the table, she glanced around for the chair she used to get onto Spook.

Henril had the only empty chair.

She carried Spook over to Henril's chair and placed it gently on it.

She grabbed her crutches and lifted her body up to slide it across onto Spook.

Lizzy beeped.

Spook let out a tinny beep.

She smiled as she buckled her arms and feet into the apparatus. "Spook isn't for everyone. Or everywhere. She's for hiking, and going places that aren't easily made accessible. Like mountains. And archeological digs."

Henril smiled. He knew her hopes and dreams. He shared them. And he knew when to give her room to try on her own.

Lizzy beeped.

Celina pushed the controls to lift Spook off of Henril's chair. Spook glided just inches above the ground. She moved Spook to the door.

Opened it.

Looked out.

Shivered.

And rode Spook back to the table. "I am unsure of the weather today."

Henril nodded. "It isn't good. Just the kind of invigorating weather you used to enjoy."

"And will again." Celina nibbled her bowl of soup while sitting on Spook. Not the most comfortable seat to sit and eat on. Very little back support. However, Spook was able to hover evenly the whole time.

Trinkle lapped up her bowl of soup and looked up at Celine expectantly.

"I'll get your coat and gloves down." Henril stood to take his bowl to the sink.

"I could do it."

He smiled. "Yes, on Spook. You had difficulty on Lizzy, and you haven't moved your outdoor winter clothes out. Let's save Spook for our test walk."

She nodded. What should have been only moments, was closer to half an hour before she was ready to go outside. For the first time in months.

She sat on Spook.

Henril opened the door.

Celina rode Spook through the door. Her Tin Lizzy. Since Spook hovered, instead of having wheels, she didn't feel the bumps on the wooden ramp attached from the door to the sidewalk.

She shivered at the memory of the last ride in Lizzy to Henril's car to go to the doctor. The bumps and bruises had hurt for days. And he had had to maneuver Lizzy back inside and lock up. Without anyone to hold the door open.

The ride to the snow covered sidewalk was smooth. She rode only inches above the ground. Still lower than walking.

Trinkle barked at her. She ran off to her favorite tree, all snow covered and jumped like a fox after a snack.

Celina laughed. A real laugh.

She looked back as Henril closed the door. Yes. She could manage Spook to open, close, lock, and unlock the door on her own.

Lizzy sat quietly alone by the table. No parting beep.

Celina moved Spook to block the closing door for a last glance. "Lizzy. You won't be left behind. I will give you the gift of movement you have given me."

Lizzy beeped softly.

Spook beeped back.

What did their beeps to each other mean? Someday, she would try to figure them out.

Getting into the passenger seat was a breeze. No huffing and puffing. No twisting and dragging unfeeling legs through behind her. No pain. Nothing. Just slide right in. The two inches of padding did set the seat a little higher than she was used to. She turned Spook off to conserve solar battery.

Trinkle bounced around in the back seat.

Henril started the car. "How long will the battery last?"

How long? In the workshop, it had lasted all day. It would recharge in sunshine, if she didn't use it too excessively. "That is what we hope to find out."

He nodded and drove to a parking lot next to the lake. Where the trail led to the bluff.

The bluff she had fallen from a year ago.

Her hands shook. She could do this. Spook might even be able to handle the winding bluff trail.

Someday.

Not today. She turned Spook on. Celina opened the car door. She turned Spook and moved easily, and painlessly, out the door.

Henril had released Trinkle. The pup ran and chased some geese away. She bounded to the edge of the almost frozen lake.

Celina turned.

Henril had his hiking pack.

She wasn't sure Spook could handle the extra weight. Somehow, she would figure it out. She had to be able to travel, and carry things as well. Especially if she wanted to lead history digs with her friends.

"Where to?" He spoke cheerfully, as he always had when they came here.

She hoped her voice wouldn't crack. "Along the path to the rock garden. I want to test Spook on rocks. And see how high she can safely go." And there, if she couldn't make it back, they could rest and recharge Spook's batteries.

He nodded and started out ahead of her. He used a walking cane, made to resemble a long cane used by blind people to sweep under the leaves, and scare off any snakes, or small predators that could be dangerous. Today, ice would be the main danger.

Would she be able to manage her hiking sticks by spring? She touched the arm rest. Maybe she could create an attachment to carry them, and always have them with her.

As they moved beyond the parking lot, another hiking couple saw them. The woman called out, "Watch for the rocks, they might stick in your wheels."

Celina smiled. "Thanks for the warning. Spook doesn't have wheels."

The couple laughed as they walked on to the parking lot.

After hiking for nearly a half hour, they arrived at the rock garden. She felt invigorated with the fresh air. Though her arms were tired, they hadn't done much work. And her useless legs simply dangled in an almost seated position under her.

Trinkle raced ahead of them to the top of the largest pile of rocks. A tall tree stood there. Her branches laden with piles of snow. Trinkle collapsed with her tongue hanging out.

Henril laughed. "She has run at least three times what we have. Where would you like me to sit and watch?"

Watch? Yes. He had to watch her. At least this time. Like watching a pup run through the woods on their first hike.

Celina pointed to a rock on the opposite side of the piles. Sometimes adults sat there and watched children play on the rock garden.

He nodded and went to it. Henril pulled a waterproof seat cover out of his pack. "Would you like warm coffee first?"

She shook her head. Coffee might buzz her too much. Better to get the fear over with.

She glanced back at the rock piles. She knew they weren't as high as they looked. Yet, from down here, they looked miles high.

Spook beeped.

She glanced at the controls. Plenty of power. She edged gently over the first low rocks. No change in the hover height.

Celina pushed the button and went to the next level. A slight hesitation, as Spook calculated the distance to hover.

And so it went, right up to the top of the nearly one story high rock garden.

There she sat. On Spook. Next to Trinkle.

Trinkle put her nose under Celina's hand.

After petting her, Celina glanced up.

There. Across the river. The narrow bluff she had fallen from. Nearly four stories high. She gulped. One year ago.

Lizzy could never manage that trail. Nor would her battery last that long. Even if they had a car attachment to bring Lizzy to the trails. Paving the paths up here would destroy them, even if they were wide enough for the equipment needed.

Someday, she would be on that bluff again.

On Spook, her Tin Lizzy.

Spook beeped.

Celina glanced down. Her battery was full, from the snow reflection. Then she looked lower. They were hovering at least two feet above the rocks. Almost high enough to reach the snow laden limbs on the tree that graced the top of the rock garden.

Spook would get her back to her favored hike locations. Maybe, with a few more minor modifications, she could even go on the next archeological dig a few valleys over. To enjoy the projects she valued. It was only a few months away. Time to get back to interests that would bring knowledge to the community.

So much to do. Now that she had her mobility back.

"Come Trinkle," Celina spoke and made the hand sign for Trinkle to follow.

Trinkle led them down the rocks to where a smiling Henril waited. Hot cup of coffee ready to hand to her.

She accepted the steaming cup with a smile.

She would have Spook for travel. And Lizzy for home, shopping, and going about in town. Once the city widened and repaired the sidewalks after the spring thaw. They even planned to require concrete pads off of the sidewalk for trash pickup days, so she, and others, could safely navigate the sidewalks.

Celina and Henril started back up the path. Trinkle stayed by their side. Soon they would reach the car. And home. Together.

Gail Brown found science fiction brings hope and light through worlds of colorful dreams. It mirrors daily life as it could be. Perhaps should be, in some ways. Worlds where disability is accepted, and people live their lives without overwork and fear.

Website: http://uncoveredmyths.wixsite.com/uncoveredmyths
Mastodon: https://writing.exchange/@UnCoveredMyths

THE CHILDREN OF THE FIELD

BY E.E. KING & RICHARD LAU

A Letter to My Daughter, Emily.

I glance at our ghostlike reflection in the window. The sun is bright, so I have to shade my eyes to see us, translucent, fitted together like puzzle pieces. And maybe we are. Once you grew inside of me, a part of me for nine months. Like a bit of photosynthetic algae inside the lips of a giant clam.

LONG, long ago, before you or I were born, the people of our world spewed tons and tons of carbon dioxide (CO_2) into the air, year after year, decade after decade.

The plants sucked it up. The seas slurped it down, but it was too much, too much for the earth, too much even for the ocean to ingest.

Our climate was warming, seas were rising, and destruction seemed inevitable.

But even during crisis, politics and lies led to denial and dissention. It's nature—human nature. By the time that all the nations of the world finally decided to take serious action, all but a few of the hardiest mosses and bryophytes were gone. We were mostly eating food grown in labs. Surviving but not living. But our desperation was fertile soil. Sea soil.

At the time, your grandmother Emily and Shari, her partner in life and work, were living on a small atoll in the middle of an almost-dead sea, trying to save the coral reefs and to clean the waters.

The ocean was drowning in microplastic then, and there seemed to be no way to remove it. But your grandmother and Shari came up with a plan.

They built enormous strainers around their atoll, – similar to the huge filter-feeding mouths of the megamouth shark, but instead of being filled with tiny teeth or gills, these sieves were filled with jellyfish slime that trapped and held the almost-invisible plastics.

"I've removed more jellyfish gonads than I care to think about," Shari said, her lilting voice musical even when complaining. "They're nasty and the smell is fouler than day old fish."

Their goal was to develop a biofilter of the mucus that absorbed both micro and nanoplastics. The jellyfish filter worked, but not well enough.

It was like trying to sweep the beach with a toothbrush. Until… But let me tell you in Emily's own words, quoting from her copious notebooks that I inherited.

I think I might have a solution. HAGFISH.

Hagfish produce slime the way humans produce judgement— easily, rapidly, defensively, and copiously. They slime when attacked, hungry, or simply stressed. They probably slime when sleeping. I bet their dreams are goopy nightmares.

This slime is one of nature's most wondrous substances.

It consists of two main components—mucus and protein threads. Each thread waits, coiled up in its own tiny cell inside the slime glands —like meters of sticky, sticky hair stuffed into a shoe without a single knot or tangle. The threads are only one-100th the width of a whisker but can stretch out for about two hundred millimeters.

When expelled, the threads spread out and entangle one another, creating a fast-expanding net.

To create a liter of slime, a hagfish only releases 40 milligrams of mucus and protein— that's 1,000 times less dry material than human saliva. That's why the slime, though strong and elastic, feels so incorporeal, like an underwater spider web.

When you see it in a bucket, it looks like water. Only when you stick your hand in and out, the bucket's contents are now attached to you, the water has become congruent.

Shari hates the stuff.

This was followed by drawings of Shari tangled in thread.

~

IT WORKED. Emily made tubes based on hydra propulsion that sucked water in and spat it out. Shooting the strands of mucus far into the sea and pulling them back, covered in plastics.

In a surprisingly short time, the seas were clean again. Clean for the first time in hundreds of years.

But it was not enough. The air was still heavy with Co2 and the oceans were hot and acidified.

So, your amazing grandmother and her remarkable lover began a coral nursery, growing Branching and Staghorn coral and anchoring them into the hollows of the dead reefs. Shari grafted miniscule recordings of healthy reefs onto the ends of their branches.

I can still hear Shari's explaining it, her voice murmuring like a long-lost dream of a coconut palm island in a Caribbean sea.

"The soothing sounds of eating, mating, sex, and savagery that make up any vigorous community attracted the remaining fish, lonely in the dark waters. Hearing the music of a long silent reef suddenly calling to them, they came. And in their coming, the reef grew, and the artificial sounds became real."

Small miracles in a time when big ones were needed.

A reef is built from colonies of many genetically identical coral polyps. They start life swimming freely through blue waters, but when they grow up and become homebound, they do it with a vengeance. They secrete a hard skeleton around themselves. After many generations of building tiny stone castles on the bones of their ancestors, the colony creates a reef. It's as if you, Emily, could spit up enough bricks to build a house.

Most corals have a tiny alga living in their tissues. The algae makes food from light, and it is this that gives the coral its color and provides the majority of its food. But when the temperature is too hot, or cold, or chemical, the alga becomes stressed and leaves, or perhaps the coral polyps spit out the algae. It's hard to know.

You could probably tell me, dear child. You could probably tell me so much, if only I could understand.

With its main source of food gone, the coral turns white and is very vulnerable. It's not dead, but it's close, so close. I have seen it, when watching—your grandmother work. Its bleached branches looked like drowned man's fingers reaching towards light.

~

So, your grandmother and Shari began breeding heat-resistant coral. Grandmother had discovered that, like coral, many species of giant clam have algae living in their lips, supplying extra food. But, unlike coral, they are much less sensitive to heat.

More from Emily's notebook:

While corals bleach from the heat, giant clams have managed to retain their algae. And I think I've figured out why.

Iridescence.

Animals generally use iridescence for display or camouflage, but their iridescence cells are dead. Clams have living iridescence cells. Why?

Because instead of containing a single alga, giant clams grow long, microscopic pillars of algae deep into the clam mantle.

The living iridescent cells fan the sunlight out into a cone about 15 degrees wide, bathing the entire pillars of algae in mild, but optimal, intensities of light. Moreover, they transmit mainly red and blue light, the wavelengths that the algae photosynthesize most efficiently, and deflect much of the green and yellow wavelengths that are of no use.

Shari says that is why their green lips shine, like old-time movie stars.

This was followed by two lines of doodles of large - lipped clams, smiling and blowing kisses. A few had sharp teeth.

The living iridescence ensure that every last alga in the pillar gets its fill of sunlight, even though most of the 300 or so cells in each column have no direct access to the light. Genius! The genius of nature.

If we imitate these columns, it could drastically improve the efficiency with which algae could be grown for food and biofuel because it will allow the algae to be grown in layers hundreds of cells thick, instead of as a single layer, as well as eliminating the need to stir the cells to expose them to sunlight.

If we use this technology in solar panels, we could charge hundreds of cells instead of one.

And so, we did. Your grandmother's iridescent solar panels provided energy wherever it was needed, abundant and free as sunlight. The world had power again.

This is the woman you were named after. I've always liked the name "Emily," the way the sound sits comfortably on the tongue before smoothly rolling off. And when I found out that the name meant "striving" and "eager," just the qualities you and the human race would need to move into the future and thrive, I knew it was perfect.

But I'm getting ahead of myself. Your father, Marcos, and I had not met yet, and you were not even a dream.

I was still growing up in the sheltering shadow of my mothers. Emily had given birth to me by artificial insemination. All the children of my generation were born that way, because all our males were sterile. In a way it freed us. In a world where everyone is artificially fertilized, no one is odd. We were struggling to survive and, in that struggle, differences of sex or preference or skin color disappeared. I think it was a good trade. Without clouds, there are no silver linings.

Meanwhile, our parents were figuring out what to do with the extra carbon in the atmosphere looming like a dark fog on the future's horizon.

I will let your grandmother's notebook explain it.

Since the Industrial Revolution, humans have emitted more than 2,000 gigatons of carbon dioxide into the atmosphere. This thickening blanket of heat-trapping greenhouse gases is causing global warming, forest fires, stifling heat waves, and rising seas. What can we do?

Then there are pages of doodles of fires and oceans and clams.

The obvious solution is carbon sequestration, taking CO_2 gas from the atmosphere and storing it. But how? Once captured, there are many long-term ways to store it.

The most natural way to store it is terrestrial sequestration, when plants and trees store CO_2 in their bodies and in their roots. Organic farms also *can store CO_2 in the soil if we return the soil, to its natural state. Perhaps we could begin to grow plants again?*

But how to remove it from the air?

So, Grandmother Emily built CO_2 scrubbers into the artificial clams that now dot the surface of the Earth. The clams "breathe" and "perspire," taking in the unwanted carbon and producing food and water. For the human race, this new technology was the kiss of life from the giant, shining golden-green iridescent lips of synthetic, photosynthesizing clams.

All types of scrubbers involve complex chemical reactions. And Emily's scrubbers had the added benefit of producing useful byproducts like water, which we desperately needed both for drinking and to fuel our oxygen generators. It worked.

But still, we lived sparsely. There were no land plants, except some mosses and algae.

More from Emily's notebook:

What makes this system in the clam special is that the design can extract every last photon from sunlight… every photon except green and gold.

Funny, we think of green as the color of growth and life, but really, it's the only light plants aren't using.

If humans perfected photosynthesis, using ~~every color of light~~ every color of light to make food, plants would be black.

And so began the black forest, which rose around our clamclaves like dark sentinels. At first it was little sterile, black banana-like grasses that ate all the light and sucked down carbon like candy. We tried to make them propagate, but they only grew by grafts.

The climate was now under control, but science is always more complex than we suppose. Systems are always more connected. The chemicals that we used in carbon scrubbing, the chemicals that we had hoped would save us, had sterilized all of us. For a while, it seemed that I and Marcos would be among the last humans, just when we had begun to make the planet livable again.

~

BUT THEN A MIRACLE. Some women, me among them, got pregnant. Maybe it was the sea starting to live again or the sun, no longer deadly, that caused our wombs to blossom. We didn't know. But ignorance didn't dampen our joy. Usually our children are sterile. Other offspring, well, other offspring are like you, my sweet, perfect child.

The scientific name for your syndrome is anorexia viridis, but most people just call it, The Verdant. At first, we didn't understand. At first, we thought it was something to fear. A disaster. A takeover. Another way to die.

We were wrong. It was rebirth. It was reincarnation. It was salvation.

The government guidebook given to all parents describes Verdant-afflicted children as:

Children who sit in one place, though their limbs are strong.

Children who do not speak, though they can.

Children who engage with the world on another level.

Children who are evolving at a frightening pace.

This is the world you were born into, my child. There aren't many of us. We live in small clamclaves in the shade of black banana fronds ~~which~~ that have begun to grow and flourish. We hoped green plants would evolve again, but it might take decades. You were born into a world in recovery. We had come far, but we had so far still to go.

I remember when you were conceived. Marcos and I were so happy. So amazed. We could not believe we had created life in this dying world.

But what kind of life would it be?

Potential parents are advised to have serious discussions about the hardships of having children and the possibility of a Verdant offspring.

Childbirth is always an act of hope. Does any mother really consider the drawbacks, the difficulties, dangers, and the pain associated with it? We only spoke of The Verdant once, when deciding what to name you.

"Emily's a nice name," said Marcos. "And if she has The Verdant, we can always change her name to Flora."

"That's awful!" I scolded, grabbing my bulging tummy protectively, superstitiously. "I can't believe you said that!"

"What?" he asked, all big eyes and insincere innocence. "If I'm gonna be a dad, I gotta practice my dad jokes!"

Dad jokes, it was a call backward to a simpler time. A time before you, or I, or your grandmother. An idea so silly and inconsequential, yet it survived. I'm sad that you'll never hear these jokes, at least not in the way I do.

Marcos grinned at me, and I grinned back, but inside my heart felt like it was breaking with love and the fear of loss.

Then your father took us in his strong arms and held us as gently as a sea-anemone's embrace, and all was right again.

~

THE VERDANT IS undetectable until the child is about six.

When you were born, sweet Emily, I didn't consider it possible that you could be Verdant. It was unthinkable. You were, you are, my perfect child. When I held you, your gaze searched my face so intently, I felt that you could see into my soul. I was not prepared for the joy that burying my face in the nape of your tiny neck gave me. I had never imagined I would ever again smell freshness, possibility, and the scent of a brighter future. It was like breathing nineteen percent oxygen.

Your happiness was infectious, a contagion of hope. Humankind was on the mend. We had an intact ozone layer, protection from our sun. We had free, clean solar power. We had our giant clams, producing fuel and food. And we had love, the three of us, as dependent upon each other for the sustenance of happiness, as a coral is on algae for color.

We were so proud when you walked and talked early! Your happiness was as apparent as it was contagious. For you, every step was a dance, every word a poem. Your voice, high and sweet, made me think of descriptions of birdsong.

We played with you. Swinging you between us as we walked. As if we were young again. As if the world were young again.

But only you were young. And you were getting older.

In too few years, The Verdant became apparent. Your speech grew simpler and more direct. I told myself that the change was a sign of maturity. I scolded myself for missing your childish laughter. After all, you were born into a hard, practical world.

Soon, you became less talkative, less gregarious, less adventurous. By the time you were eight, you had stopped dancing. At ten, you had ceased walking. Instead, you sat cross-legged on the floor soaking up the wan rays that beamed through the window, rocking slowly back and forth, softly humming to yourself.

At first, I didn't understand. At first, I refused to believe what was happening to you. I brought you food. I read you your favorite books. I showed you pictures. I shook you. I yelled. I slapped your nonresponsive face.

I can remember the actions, but not the feelings. I know I acted like that because I thought I'd lost you. I missed your birdsong voice and skipping steps but mostly I missed your laughter, that spontaneous burbling up of joy, that contagion of happiness.

I knew, but I didn't want to admit it.

Your smile, which seemed eternal, didn't even fade – not at first. But each day it grew dimmer, as your mouth muscles relaxed, and your features diminished, retreating into blankness.

My girl, my child, my heart — I thought you were leaving me. I didn't understand.

Your cells were changing, each thin-walled cell division, metamorphosing from muscle and nerve into meristematic and permanent tissue. You were becoming you. A different you, but still my child.

The government guidebook tells parents to have 'The Talk' with Verdant children before the age of nine, before they are too far gone to understand and ask questions.

But I took the coward's way out. And I suppose so did Marcos, simply believing me when I said you and I had had 'The Talk.' And for not insisting on being there when we supposedly did. Now you and I never will have 'The Talk'. Soon there will be no need.

Would 'The Talk' have changed anything? It would have been difficult and uncomfortable for both of us. There would have been tears and sobbing, at least on my part. Your eyes had already dried from lack of moisture and use. I wonder how many other parents have made the same choice and left the unspoken words sprouting like mushrooms in the secret darkness of their hearts.

I suppose we're having 'The Talk' now, or at least I am, to myself, through this letter.

❧

As you soaked up the sunlight, listening to the rhythms in your head, your appetite decreased. You stopped responding to outside stimuli. Eventually, you ceased eating all together.

I tore a page from the guidebook and put it on the wall by your favorite window. It says:

The Verdant children eventually stay where they are placed. Most no longer respond to human touch or voice. A few fold their hands when stroked or curl their toes when tickled, but not much more.

Their skin grows sallow, yellow gradually giving way to bright green. The Verdant affects not only motion and sound, but everything -- every nerve, muscle, and neuron. By the time these children reach puberty, they cannot live without light.

We believe that The Verdant are filled with happiness, which they express in subtle ways. Watch for the unfurling of fingers and toes. The widening and reaching of limbs. The tilt of the head as it follows sun across the sky.

I don't know why I chose that particular page. Looking back, my selection seems almost random. Perhaps to prepare myself? To convince myself that you were joyful? Most likely, I did it because it was all I could do, some desperate gesture of weak and ineffective atonement.

❧

The guidebook is wrapped in the same tan algae-mycelium cloth that you were wrapped in when we brought you home from the birthing center. The bundle is hidden away in the bottom of the box that we used for your crib.

Now, I understand the purpose of the guidebook: to soften the hammering blow of loss. To point out that the cup is still a quarter full. To focus my thoughts and efforts toward the future rather than constantly looking over my shoulder at the past, being undertowed into the seas of what-could-have-beens. Yes, you may lose your child, but the world gains another savior.

You are becoming what you were meant to be. What you need to be. What *we* need you to be.

And with that epiphany, with you cradled in my arms, turned towards the light, you seem a part of me again, or am I becoming part of you?

~

A CHILDHOOD IS full of firsts: the first step, the first word spoken, the first birthday. Tomorrow will be another first, your First Field Day.

Tomorrow, I will gather you up, careful not to bruise your atrophied legs, now shriveled into two pale, thick roots, desiccated white toes seeking moisture and nourishment that only the soil can give.

As a family, we will go to our assigned plot in the field, and I will plant you in the dirt.

You will be among the other miracles of your kind. Children, whose features have become so indistinct, their faces are only unfocused memories to the most devoted. Their brains dissolved into meristematic tissue. I wept the day you lost your eyes, watched as they gradually turned into buds and sprouted leaves. How could I have been so blind?

To imagine humans as superior. To consider ourselves the peak of evolution.

You are the miracle. You filter our water with your roots. You cleanse our planet with each breath. You eat sunlight. You will give the world back its green.

A line from some forgotten past rings through my head. "Consider the lilies of the field, how they grow: they neither toil nor spin, yet I tell you, even Solomon in all his glory was not arrayed like one of these."

There was a time when children worked in the fields. Now you will live there, making root connections with all the other Verdants, turning light into sugar, producing oxygen, providing homes for bugs and birds and mammals and whatever else may evolve on this strange and beautiful planet. You are the circle of Life.

There was a time when the color of your skin mattered, a time when your father's darker skin would have been considered a hardship. But all of your outsides are green, and any colorful variation in petal or leaf is just another evolution.

My greatest achievement will always be having given birth to you,

Emily. My greatest sorrow, was not accepting your change in time for you to know it.

Marcos and I will come to your field each day. We will gently turn the soil, add some nutrients from our compost box, and check if you are thirsty. I will stick my fingers into the soil, feeling for root tendrils, searching again for that special bridge between you and me, as intimate as the one we once shared when you were in my womb.

We finally understand that plants are and have always been the answer. How smart of evolution to make our connection to the Earth more apparent now, our ties familial. We have always been just another part of the great cycle, but we didn't know it.

But one of many things you have taught me, Emily: It's never too late. It's only another beginning.

~

WITH YOUR FIRST Field Day only hours away, with this letter finally written, with my conscience and my mind emptier but not unburdened — will I have the dream again tonight?

In my dream, I am sitting in our favorite square of sunlight inside the place you used to call home. I am older and wiser, but evolution is not finished with me yet.

I call to your father, "Marcos! Marcos, my love!"

Or I try to. Not a sound emerges from my mouth, but a mix of pheromones and energy and light.

My eyes are growing dim, but I can see in new ways. I can feel your father near me. I can sense his life and other life through my pores. I become part of each scent and every fragrance drifting through the open window. As I step outside, planting naked foot to damp earth, I can taste everything. I drink the sunlight.

I will have just enough time to crawl to the field, burrow myself beside you, and sink down my roots next to yours. Together, we will connect to the veins and arteries of roots and mycelium. Together, too, we will make what we need from light and water, hurting none and aiding all.

E.E. King is an award-winning painter, performer, writer, and naturalist.

She'll do anything that won't pay the bills, especially if it involves animals. Ray Bradbury called her stories, "marvelously inventive, wildly funny, and deeply thought-provoking." She's been published in over 100 magazines and anthologies, including Clarkesworld, Daily Science Fiction, Chicken Soup for the Soul, Short Edition, Daily Science Fiction, and Flametree. Her novels include Dirk Quigby's Guide to the Afterlife: All you need to know to choose the right heaven, which was translated into Spanish, and several story collections.

E.E. King's stories are on Tangent's 2019, 2020-, and 2022-year's best stories. She's been nominated for a Rhysling, and several Pushcart awards. She's shown paintings at LACMA and painted murals. She also co-hosts The Long-Lost Friends Show and Metastellar story time. She spends summers doing bird rescue and winters planting coral in Bonaire. Check out paintings, writing, musings, and books at her website below.

Website: https://www.elizabetheveking.com
Amazon Author Page: https://www.amazon.com/author/eeking

Richard Lau is an award-winning writer who is published in magazines, newspapers, and anthologies, as well as in the high-tech industry and online.

ARCADE JUJU
BY ISAIAH HUNT

Are there times you just want to wipe your longest finger across the real world's crumbling, miserable face?

Well, allow me to point *my* ashy Black finger right down Euclid Avenue to a joint capable of bending your concepts of space-time itself and slip into different dimensions all with the snap of a headband, and a tap of a button. Sure, we got your normie arcade machines, but why resort to Pac-Man and pinball when you can race friends down the streets of St. Johannesburg in your customized Bugattis, slap through zombie hordes in a generated post-apocalyptic New York City, or spawn as super soldiers on Mars and compete in deathmatches even them bootleg *Call of Duty* games can't comprehend? It's a portal everywhere, anywhere, all at once. It's Arcade Juju.

And if it sounds like I'm advertising, that's 'cause I am.

Case in point: Here we have Latoya, bantu knots refastened and mama-approved, the main character's portrait from her favorite anime, *Resolution on the Horizon,* dripped on her watercolor long tee. She's riding her hover-board over puddles from the afternoon drizzle, past folks— a couple to her right, a posse to her left— and nah, I don't mean those 'wanna-be 2015 still on wheels worrying about running over toes and ankles' hoverboards. What she's got is the Graviton-2046, capable of saying 'hell naw' to gravity itself.

Invested four years for this tech, so you best believe she's floating 24/7. Sure, it's been bought chipped and short circuited, but with some Latoya-tweaking she learned in Code Club at MC^2 , the board now leaves trails of RGB particles behind just as it's sold.

Her board hums like a cool air conditioner as it pivots a corner and glides back on the glossy pavement, right above the lambent blue lights of Juju where her cousins Meelah and De'Ajahne stand. Already, Latoya can tell something's up.

Her feet feel like weightless clouds before readjusting to the concrete. The board folds and snaps onto the belt of her jeans. "What y'all doing standing around here acting like some lost NPCs? Haleem and Aunt Rhianna could be here at any moment," Latoya says.

Meelah pops some dirt off her No. 12 jersey, the player last night who activated a spring mod on his bionic legs for a several-foot-high game-point dunk and smashed the Cavs to the playoffs. Latoya can't remember his name; her brother definitely would've known. De'Ajahne still rocks her MC^2 sweatshirt and a sideways dad hat stuffed over her brown bob.

Separately, they're three highschool students simply trying to get by. Together, they're the only East Side team who wage bets against those rich kids from the Heights and West Side. After plasma-blasting through a hundred waves of undead robots in *Metal Occult*, a legendary achievement no other team could achieve, they became known as the Cousins. With each win comes the money, and with money comes the spending. De'Ajahne on hats, Meelah on jerseys, and Latoya on her Graviton.

Bubblegum smacks around De'Ahjane's mouth as she says, "We can't get in."

"What happened to Jamal?"

Meelah shakes her head. "Man, Arcade Juju fired his nebula ass."

"For what?"

But then they all answer in unison. "Fightin'."

Latoya's head hangs low. "How we gon' get the friend discount now?"

The Cousins are searching for a solution when– *ding!*

Text message. It's Haleem– the last Cousin– in the group chat.

Me and Grammy Rhi on our way. ETA 20 min.

"Well that's Black people time. So like 45 minutes?" Meelah assures.

De'Ajahne rolls her eyes. "We talkin' about Haleem, foo. Their superpower is basically being on time, and I doubt they gon' lose that power today."

Latoya peers through the glass doors, and the massive hallway full of folks and machines comes into view.

"Ok, but Juju's got like, what, a thousand workers in there? Maybe word about Jamal ain't spread yet," Latoya says.

Exaggerations aside, Meelah and De'Ajahne agree. It's their best bet, and it ain't the Cousins way to surrender and wave the white tee. This is more than the regular tournaments and battle royales they anticipate to win. Arcade Juju's now got the magic to return what Aunt Rhianna lost: Her dancing.

It used to be her trade language, love language, global language and (somehow) written language. Every action had Aunt Rhianna's head bobbing as if she was bumping to an internal playlist. Her hips gyrated as she carted down the isles of Buy 'N Eats. She taught kids at the rec how to do the robot. And don't start Latoya on the embarrassment she felt at the family cookouts when Earth, Wind & Fire blasted through the speakers and Aunt Rhianna decided that was the best time to break out the mashed potatoes, a dance so bootleg even the best entertainers can't sell it. Whenever her nieces and nephews sassed about her nonstop dancing, she'd sass right back. "Way back then, two-hundred-something-thousand years ago, the only tool we could rely on was our bodies. At the end of the day, that's all we got."

She even performed at Latoya's brother's funeral, of all places. Not a soul challenged her. In fact, it was the adults who encouraged her to dance. She may as well have been stomping on his grave. Latoya's intrusive thoughts imagined snapping Aunt Rhianna's legs back into reality. Her nephew was gone.

But the rest of the family– Meelah and De'Ajahne included– joined Aunt Rhianna, congregated around her brother's casket and choired every Kirk Franklin and Tye Tribbet song they could conjure from their throats while Latoya played the audience. That was the first time she realized that funerals could also be a celebration of life.

Since then, Latoya appreciated the positivity Aunt Rhianna could blossom throughout any situation. But Latoya's intrusive thoughts from the funeral manifested into reality, and she blames herself for Aunt Rhianna's diabetes snapping her right leg off after a long fight. Meelah and De'Ajahae sacrificed their prize money for Aunt Rhianna's prosthetic surgery. Latoya sacrificed nothing. De'Ajahne and Meelah never shame Latoya, but she can feel the family's disdain whenever she floats down the neighborhood all while Aunt Rhianna topples over when her metal rod refuses to keep up. Never again will the Cousins feel second-hand embarrassment from Aunt Rhianna's mashed potatoes at cookouts, or watch her bend in ways that Latoya can now admit she's envious of.

Aunt Rhianna's new phrase nowadays is, "You never know what you got 'til it's gone."

But there's a way, at least for a little while, to get back what's gone.

The doors slide open and the three march in. Instantly, they're absorbed by crowds, machines, and strips of light pulsing in-sync with the future funk. There's hoop fever over in the corner, little kids make believing in the holographic ball pits, and bigger kids repping Cleveland State hoodies stressing over trivia questions. Juju at its best.

Digitized words slide across multiple interfaces above.

REMINISCE NOW CONCLUDING: ODD FUTURE'S 2012 CONCERT AT LONDON'S ACADEMY BRAXTON.

A mass of satisfied customers exits from under a marquee and down long ramps, spitting lyrics foreign to the Cousins' vocabulary, though Latoya's heard similar lyrics sung by her brother on the days he picked her up from Code Club. Odd Future's pink donut symbol oozed with pride on his sweatshirt as she entered the mini concert in his rusted hooptie. She wonders if these customers might've been his friends.

Gatekeeping Reminisce's entrance is a booth with a tall dude in a deep blue polo. Problem is, he looks far from the nonchalant staff Meelah could sleaze her way through, more so pseudo employee of the month material. He pays attention to all the older attendants leaving Reminisce, one cheesy nacho at a time.

Worse, this dude is a part of the team the Cousins slammed last week in *Slimeball*. His blonde buzz cut with a lightning strike is a reminder of that fact. And from the scrunched eyebrows and smug smirk he poses upon their arrival, the dude is still musing over that loss.

"Well, well, well, if it ain't the Cousins minus one," dude taunts through the voicebox. His nasal tone might as well be speaking out of his nose. He adjusts his fluorescent nametag so the light reflects his name: Arnold. Receptionist.

"Arnold! My guy. How you doing?" Meelah tries the buddy-buddy tactic. If not for the thick glass separating them, Latoya swears Meelah would hang her brawny arm over the dude's tiny neck, not as a form of intimidation— outside competitions, Meelah's passive unless provoked— rather, a matter of convincing.

The Arnold guy doesn't budge, so Meelah continues. "You know our boy Jamal, right? Of course you do. So if you'd kindly step aside and let us in—"

"Unh-unh! Hold up. If Jamal really is your 'boy', then where's he at?"

"Boy, we ain't his keeper!" De'Ajahne shouts. "Probably took the day off 'cause he can't stand ya ugly—"

Meelah shushes her. "He's on vacation."

"Uh-huh. Funny, 'cause last I checked Jamal got fired."

De'Ajahne pops her gum. Meelah curses. Latoya remains quiet.

"You know the rules. No friends, no discount."

Meelah leans into the glass and whispers into the voicebox. "Look— let me be steel with you. We short on credits, and our auntie gon' be here soon, all the way from East Cleveland for Juju's next Reminisce. She got a rod for a leg, not the athletic kind, and last thing we want is her walking here for no reason. Can we just give what we got and we'll leave a good review on the Juju app or something with your name on it?"

Arnold scans the area. "Do you hear that?"

Nothing, except the music and chiptunes from Juju's machines.

"That's the sound of me not caring."

De'Ajahne cuts in. "Well how about you let us in and we'll go a little easier on you and your posse next time so you don't get wrecked like defaults?"

"I see you got jokes as well!" Arnold's voice box laugh sounds like those 8-bit video games Latoya's brother binged on his emulator for 'nostalgia's sake.' "But I'm obligated to inform you that if you ain't got the credits, you ain't got the Juju."

"Doubt your bootleg ass would be saying that outside that booth!"

While Meelah holds De'Ajahne back, the dude's eyes fall to Latoya's Graviton. Goes, "Cool hoverboard."

And immediately, Latoya decodes that comment.

Her fingers clutch the deck of the board she's saved up for since fifth grade. Just handing over her main source of travel feels akin to trading in her legs. This has to be how Aunt Rhianna felt when the doctors took her leg.

Latoya quickly dismisses that thought. No, not at all.

She can read the Cousins' mixed responses. De'Ajahne thinks "don't you dare." Meelah tosses that "you gotta do what you gotta do" look. She ain't gotta do nothing, but maybe this isn't about her.

The A.I. over the P.A. shouts over her jumbled thoughts.

REMINISCE NOW REMEMBERING: EARTH WIND AND FIRE'S 1979 SOUL TRAIN LINE.

"You can borrow it for a day."

"A month."

"A week."

"Actually, how about I pluck it from your hands, keep y'all credits, and you can spend as much time as you want with Reminisce for all I care."

"No!"

There's a fire in Latoya's voice powerful enough for De'Ajahne to swallow her gum. A couple of staff and patrons turn their heads. Meelah's face falls into disarray. The soft, quiet Latoya now whining over a piece of machinery.

Arnold tosses his hands up. "Well, then. Sorry y'all. No board, no Juju."

All the sadness in the world starts to pour into her. The fact Latoya wants to cry over a hoverboard more than this selfless act stirs with the thought of potential disappointment from the Cousins, her auntie, and her brother, who in whatever dimension Latoya likes to think he exists in now, is shaking his head.

She detaches the board from her belt. "Fine. I'll do it for Aunt Rhianna."

The board's still warm and a bit wet from her last flight. De'Ajahne can't watch. Meelah face palms. Just when Latoya slips her board through the booth, this bootleg's grubby fingerprints about to taint the sleekness of her board, a thick silhouette slides into the corner of her eye.

"Did you say Rhianna?"

On her name tag was the name Yasmine, and below, bold words **Manager** whipped across the nameplate on her polo. "Rhianna Ferguson?"

They all nod as a unit.

"Wait," Meelah speaks up. "You know her?"

"Know her? Mrs. Ferguson was my dance instructor some time ago over at the Heights." Yasmine twiddles her body to Juju's music now playing an assortment of Ad-Rap. "She gave us a whole library of dances."

Smiles leap across their faces— Latoya included. One, because Yasmine's dance moves are almost worse than West Side kids on a *Juju Dance Dance* machine, and two, she's a friend.

"How is she doing?"

"She's actually on her way now," Meelah responds. "For the next Reminisce. But for some reason we can't get the friend discount."

"Yeah, Miss Yasmine," De'Ajahne chimes in. "Here we are trying to do something special for our auntie and this galaxy brain over here bribin' us with our cousin's board."

Her eyebrows perk up. "Oh really now?"

Arnold tucks his head into his polo. Leave it to De'Ajahne to force salt into Arnold's already embarrassing wound. All that power he has depletes in mere seconds.

Meelah checks her phone and focuses back on the task at hand. "So, about that friend discount…"

"Friend discount? Nah…" She taps on her watch and each of their phones glow. Notifications. Credits bumped, enough for the Cousins to attend Reminisce, and a little extra. "This one's on Juju. Hopefully I can catch y'all coming out. If not, please tell Mrs. Ferguson that Yasmine says hi, and she is still dancing.

"And as for you, Mr. Briber. Let's re-discuss a couple of your responsibilities at Juju."

Latoya blows raspberries towards Arnold as Yasmine escorts him through the **EMPLOYEE'S ONLY** door. Meelah and De'Ajahne cackle amongst each other. Who knew Aunt Rhianna's reputation extends to the Heights. Speaking of…

7:30 on the dot, Haleem escorts Aunt Rhianna through the automated entrance. The three race over to their favorite aunt. Her grey locs are beautifully moisturized, and a dashiki droops over her body down to a piece of worn-grey machinery.

"Aunt Rhianna! Welcome to the arcade."

She speaks in a tone so soft and defeated, the Cousins have to lean in. "I don't know what y'all expect me to do at an arcade."

Haleem smiles. "You'll see."

~

TO THE UNSIMULATED EYE, Reminisce is just a forest of gargantuan mushroom computers, with thick vines connected to blinking headbands over soft recliners. Each unit pushes and pulls on pockets of air as if they're heartbeats breathing life. With some aid from the Cousins, Aunt Rhianna hobbles onto a seat, humming to the music from outside.

Once the family links in, Reminisce remembers.

Latoya opens her eyes to a geometric paradise of polygons. Brown and orange textures fizzle in and out, followed by lines of blocks. Then, like a brush to a blank canvas, Reminisce fills the space with movie lights, stages, murals of cityscapes chanting in that same neon-blue Juju color. The blocks morph into NPCs. Their dad hats, jerseys, anime tees and dashikis transform into silky shirts and bellbottoms, afros and other big hair. When Reminisce remembers, it no longer resembles a video game. It's a mental train ride back in time.

Their train conductor is none other than Don Cornelius, resurrected in his three piece suit and round glasses ready to welcome them all aboard. "We got something special for y'all today!"

Earth forms, Wind comes in, and the Fire begins. Soon as that first guitar note of "September" plays, all the Cousins shout, "Happy birthday, Aunt Rhianna!"

Aunt Rhianna stares at her unwrinkled hands, rubs the smooth silk of her brown skin. She stomps her foot, gives her right leg a jerk. Performs a long twirl. Right then and there, she realizes this body is hers. They watch Aunt Rhianna's eyes electrify and slip into overdrive as she busts out the mashed potatoes, back to bending her body in ways Latoya can only imagine.

They say it takes a village to raise a child, but it's up to the children to keep a village alive. 'Cause only Jamal told the Cousins about Reminisce, and only De'Ajahne remembered it was close to Aunt Rhianna's birthday, and only Meelah recognized how much Aunt Rhianna adores her Earth, Wind & Fire, and only Latoya realized she could do some of her Latoya-tweaking and feed Soul Train and Earth, Wind & Fire to Reminisce's A.I. suggestion website a hundred times over, and only Haleem was patient enough to guide Aunt Rhianna to Arcade Juju.

$$\sim$$

So when you got students singing Earth, Wind & Fire in the classrooms and hallways of MC^2 , people both old and young still remembering what it's like in September, I personally can't help but say "yeah, the future's looking bright."

Born and raised as a proud Cleveland native, Isaiah Hunt near-future stories focus on his community, commercialism, the entertainment industry, and transhumanist capitalism. When he isn't fiddling with music or studying Pan-African history, he is teaching Fiction Writing at John Carroll University as a Hopkins Fellow or daydreaming of worlds adjacent to our own. You can find his work at Luna Negra, On the Run, Black Moon Magazine, What if Tomorrow, Catchwater Magazine and elsewhere. You can read more of his works at <u>linktr.ee/CasualDream.</u>

LONELINESS CALLING TO LONELINESS

BY MORGAN MELHUISH

This is it, Thorn thinks. An end to exams, an end to childhood. They've played out all the levels of education like it's a vid-game, jumping from subject to subject, overcoming modules, facing big bad assignments and collecting knowledge like credits.

Something more must happen, right? Anything but the fading electronic fireworks leaving the scars of afterimages against the void of the monitor.

They'd eye-dicated 'no' when the option to re-join the ent-system had flashed up.

Thorn wonders if that was a mistake.

Surely there's more to life than distractions: endless chat on *Animal Island*, re-runs and playlists, bad comedy canned laughter, history docs like *Soylent Green* and *Brave New World*, meme swaps and on-hold muzak?

They're already bored. Thorn sits in the comfy chair, toes twitching and tapping against the ergonomically designed footrest. Still nothing. No options, no choices to eye-dicate with a blink.

Thorn worries. What if they're about to be incinerated for being too clever, or something, like in that short story they studied, *Examination Day*?

Thorn steels themselves, nervously looking left and right. They pull the headset off and peer meekly into the dark, eyes adjusting to the gloom. This isn't the exotic neon of *Animal Island* where they spend their days. This isn't the screen.

With huge effort Thorn lifts up and out of their seat, grabbing onto the armrest for support, clutching at the other chairs, trying not to trip on wires. There are rows and rows and rows of sleepers. So many of them.

With gathering impetus Thorn stumbles from one to the next, trying to reach the end of the row, clutching at the furniture, sometimes an arm, apologising as they go. They form the words in their head but they don't appear in the air ahead. Unlike with screens.

Thorn desperately tries not to disturb the sleepers. Each lies recumbent, clad in a headset of their own, wearing thin moth-eaten robes. Some hum, their heads shake to unseen stimulus. Many more just lay inert, husks.

Thorn feels cheated, feels curious.

First day of the rest of their life and Thorn hadn't expected any of this.

∼

DAWN SEEPS INTO CIRCUITS. Enlivening.

Hind, middle and forelegs wheel in an experimental whirr of hydraulics. There is resistance. Sensors receive bird song. There's a moment's delay as it identifies the call of a blackbird. Its processors are slow. Power up is still to be completed.

Drone6450's antenna twitch, exploratory, searching the ether for connection. Nothing. It finds itself removed, cut-off from the hive mind.

Drone6450 probes within.

System rebooting…

Accessing black box data. Visual input. A silver streak splits the thunderous sky. A burst of power. Speed increases. The unit continues on its trajectory. Mission imperative: return to the hive before dark-down. The unit weaves its plotted course between streaks of precipitation, minimising wing contact. Pinion panels buzz in an effort to reduce the accumulation of moisture. The process is only 34% effective. An increase of precipitation and wind resistance threatens to damage the unit. Sun failing.

A burst of power and light. Sparks.

Overwhelming.

Overloading.

Altitude decreasing. Swiftly. The ground approaching. Fast.

Black box data ends.

Drone6450 finds wonder in the images, it finds beauty.

Beauty, it stops itself.

Interrogative. Beauty?

When had its systems recognised beauty?

There are other questions too. How long have its systems been down? The sensors at the end of Drone6450's feet encounter compacted earth. When it fell there was a pool of soaked soil and now it is dense, hard and enveloping.

A supposition >> It is impossible to quantify. Cracked mud has let light through to its power cells at last.

Drone6450 extricates itself from the baked soil. The drone's legs buzz as it rights itself, tries to wipe its wing panels. The feeling of success is a further boost to power cells.

System self-diagnosis.

Inventory >> No faults.

Unless there is a fault in its fault locator, the thought comes unbidden. That's a paradoxical loop. A logical doubt Drone6450 thinks.

It shouldn't be having these thoughts at all. What else has changed? It starts to consider when the ping of notification distracts. Reboot complete.

Drone6450 wilfully ignores troubling thought processes.

Questions have always been beyond the remit of the drone. They were never permitted, never even a possibility.

There is work to be done. There is always work to be done. That is its purpose. Its mantra.

Drone6450 tentatively flaps its wing panels, hovering off the ground for a moment. It loops and glides in an aerial display, testing its capabilities.

Drone6450 searches its database. It might be cut off from the hive but there are hard-wired records.

Once, Earth had organic insects. Pollinators were abundant. Drone6450 can access footage of hives, meadows of poppies and blue cornflowers, short buttercups and daisies, farms of lavender. All these flowers alive with the thrum of bees, fuzzy organic workers.

No longer.

Insecticides, pesticides, climate change, loss of habitat, they all played their part. And the bees were gone.

The inventors didn't realise the true part pollinators played until it was too late. Cereals, fruits and vegetables… they all failed without robot intervention.

In its circuits are statistics to be proud of. "Bees and butterflies pollinate approximately 75% of the world's flowering plants, including an estimated 35% percent of the world's food crops." Drone6450 thinks they knew on one level but Humanity did not seem to have the same efficiency level and work ethic its species has.

Humanity had other issues too - the drone's database is full of excuses and regret. Queen wars, a reliance on fossil fuels, an inability to work for the good of the hive… Why hasn't it realised this before? Humanity was as fractured and displaced as the organic bees.

Luckily, before they were driven underground like grubs, the inventors hatched out drone and its kin. Hardwired within there are schematics of its race, ways to repair and restore its members, replicate them even, if the right materials are on hand. Thousands of cells across the planet were set up with the task of pollinating, thriving and surviving while Humanity dwindled. Died out. Drone6450 embraced its mission to go forth and pollinate.

It has never had this opportunity for reflection, these thoughts are alien. Drone6450 feels there is something fundamentally awry. It must focus outwards again. Drone6450 scans its immediate surroundings.

There is pollen for the taking. Its prime mission asserts itself. Drone6450 dives forward, other concerns momentarily forgotten.

OVER THE FOLLOWING days Thorn gets to be so many things. Excitement fizzes as they try their hand at all sorts of vocations.

They are an archaeologist, charting the depths of the bunker, discovering chambers and workings, sifting through humanity's archives. They are a medic and coder, waking up systems and programs, checking on the sleepers. Searching for others, like them, awake. Any guys or gals or non-binary pals would do… but there is no one like Thorn.

They are a chef, working out how to turn on taps, freeing the food machine's nozzles of gloop. It's the same old nourishment but Thorn feels strength slowly arrive in sore muscles and limbs. They are awake for longer periods, they skip down the empty corridors.

They are a designer, giving the rec-room a make over, dusting down soft furnishings, dragging a crate of vinyl from the library's storage, reverently placing a gramophone on a cleaned coffee table. It is like an initiation test, putting into practice all the lessons they've learnt, doing the things they've seen people do in shows before the great burial.

Thorn explores and laughs and dances. They touch real life solid objects, push buttons, work out how to use the shower rooms.

Thorn knows there were others, of course, has studied the lives of society's great contributors before everyone came below. They know all about the solar turbines and wave generators that power the life support, the ent-system and all. The rapid hurry it took, despite decades of warning signs, to avoid acid rain and climate collapse. Thorn knows they're following in their footsteps. The scientists making sure the experiment of the bunker was a success before bedding down too

Thorn's a spy, accessing cameras. The ones around the base are dull, they're not like screen time at all. Nothing moves. It's the ones up above that interest them!

Thorn is too young to remember up top very clearly. They seem to have memories of a swan, a clammy hand from holding onto a plastic bag full of crust and crumbs. The dizzying lurch of a see-saw. The face of their mother.

Where is she? Is she a sleeper now? Thorn feels a pang of guilt, of longing. They haven't thought of her in years. How would they even begin to find her? Would she snap and snarl at them, for disturbing her slumber? Or would she kiss Thorn, a fairytale princess brought to life. Let her rest, they think, a little longer won't harm her. They need time to think.

Instead Thorn looks at the cameras up top. There are screens of tangled weeds and undergrowth too thick to see anything at all - but then they find a clear shot. They see hills filled with wind turbines and fields of solar panels, all receiving and revolving, generating power for them all. The light of day radiates, almost bursting through the monitor.

It is thanks to those rays and panels that Thorn has had an education, nourishment, warmth and shelter. Thorn, though, thanks and thinks of the sun only briefly. What they really focus on is how much there is to explore.

A whole new layer. A world out there. Or there would be, but there are doors barred to Thorn. This bunker is a cell.

THERE ARE HOURS OF GATHERING, moving from stigma and anther and back again. Drone6450 is content in its productivity, as busy as a bee.

Its glee soon turns to consternation. It should return to base. It should go back to the safety of home, to power down overnight, but there is no hive mind to connect to. It has no recall of its cell, no welcome GPS blip in circuits.

But wait. There are other drones at work in the area, a systematic thrum of wings nearby. All Drone6450 need do is follow them! It is pleased with its reasoning, lifting up into the air and searching for others.

Not far off Drone6450 watches the to and fro, the ebb and flow in and out of the hive. It dashes forwards, all at once keen to reconnect, to fill a missing aspect of itself.

It pulls up short of the entrance. One worker guards the hive, beams an imperative 6450's way.

>> Identify.

Drone6450 pulses its marker.

>> Identify.

Drone6450 tries again. They are not receiving - its transmission is dead air.

A repetition but the same result. Drone6450 only wants to deposit its pollen, to return. The worker primes its stinger, its abdomen curving in readiness to pierce Drone6450's carapace. It knows the warning signs before attack. A quick summation of the risks and Drone6450 turns tail and flies fast, before any more damage can be done to its systems.

It has been cast out of the hive.

THE GRAMOPHONE CRACKLES, the needle finds its way around slightly warped vinyl. Such primitive coding, Thorn thinks, as the music begins.

"Kiss me honey honey kiss me…" Shirley Bassey sings and Thorn can't help but smile. Their leg taps, almost involuntarily, to the beat. It hasn't taken Thorn long to learn the lyrics and they have been trying out words, to speak them out loud.

It's a distraction. Something Thorn can do. They've already understood the bunker is a gilded cage but a cage nonetheless. Thorn knows why humanity went underground, why it fled from storms of stinging sleet and burning heatwaves, why it had no choice but to let the planet power down and reset its systems. But goodness it is boring being stuck down here!

They have tried to signal to other bunkers, to trip the barricades and trick systems into letting them out. They have tried to fathom it out, but it's a simultaneous equation they can't get to balance.

So for now Thorn plays music, thinking about honey, thinking of having someone else beside them.

DRONE6450 FLIES IN EVER INCREASING figures of eight, twisting around and diving on another curve. It hunts the beat. One, two, quick, quick, slow. To Drone6450 dance is a hardwired form of communication. One, two, quick, quick, slow. It's like a pulse of Morse and the drone waggles in response, darting from each vibrating source.

So far they have all been relays, these sweet pools of sound. But it knows if it persists, it will succeed in sourcing the noisy nectar.

Sonics have become its pollen, the thrumming resonance its kin. If the hive has turned its collective back the drone will find other family.

One, two, quick, quick, slow. Drone6450 cha-cha-chas across the skies

THORN PLAYS *The Clash* and hesitates. Will they, won't they? The thought of waking one of the sleepers worries them. Will they be thankful, when they're shaken from the vibrancy of *Animal Island*, when they realise there are just empty corridors and drab concrete walls? It seems unlikely. Would Thorn have made the same choice again? They hesitate… if they'd have eye-dicated and stepped back into the ent-system they'd never have known the truth. They'd have lay there until the end of everything. It isn't the first time but Thorn wonders if they should just return to the halls of headsets and reclining couches.

At least this is real, they think. Right? The words seem hollow even in Thorn's head.

"Darling you've got to let me know. Should I stay or should I go…"

THIS IS IT, Drone6450 thinks. The origin of the emanations. The pounding sound has changed over the days. It started pleasantly enough but there's an anger in the pulse, a bitterness to the beat now.

Is it rage or is it terror? Fight or flight?

There are packs of feral dogs roaming the surface that snap and bite and howl. Swirling, swooping red kites have hovered above it hungrily, screeching. It wouldn't be the first time Drone6450 has been mistaken for something nourishing.

In its programming Drone6450 has pattern software to recognise facial expressions in animal kind, to generate probability of an attack or threat. There is no programming for sound, yet the drone tries to apply its reasoning regardless.

The metal vibrates and the drone tentatively puts out feelers, tasting iron and paint with its feet. It recoils slightly in the trembling judder but returns to the surface with confidence. Metal to metal, loneliness calling to loneliness, Drone6450 tries to communicate with the bulkhead.

Nothing.

There's just echoes beyond. Drone6450 can't tell if it's the damage the blackout caused, the thoughts and feelings it developed since the thunderstorm, or if something is hurting in this structure itself.

Drone6450 droops froward. This self chosen mission is complete, but there is something very incomplete within the drone. Another rejection.

Its antenna make contact with the beat. What now?

"What now my love?"

There's a voice within. The drone perks up. There is something registering, someone beneath the bulkhead.

"Now that it's over." Two voices cry out.

Its legs whirr at the door, trying to gain access.

Drone6450 has a new purpose.

~

THE PIANISSIMO RISES IN CRESTS, each wave louder and louder, Thorn has the speakers up to the max, the music and Shirley Bassey building to a crescendo. There's something about the snare drum rhythm and the words that make Thorn feel at once melancholy and defiant. It reminds them of wet pavements and streetlights, something stirring in their mind, something they've not had use for in many years.

Thorn reclines in the old rec-room as the *Bolero*-inspired piece comes to an end and sighs. It seems ridiculous to fight the inevitable, not to rejoin their sleeping kin. One song more? One album? One day? Why fight the inevitable?

Yet Thorn knows they can't return to that state, not really, not now this reality has been unveiled to them. There's a world out there, if only they can get to it.

The vinyl hisses and pops against the needle as the album finishes. There's a new sound though, a thrumming whirr getting louder and louder, echoing along concrete corridors. Thorn jumps off the couch and goes to look, just at the moment Drone6450 rounds the corner. Thorn is thrown backwards in the collision, sent skittering across the floor. They look dumbfounded at the mechanical bee, surprise written over their features.

It buzzes up and down, bobbing in the air as if nodding its head.

"What are you?"

The drone approaches, hovering, scanning as it does.

"Well? No speech, huh?"

~

DRONE6450 HAS FOUND THE SOURCE, it comes from this room. More importantly, there's a humanoid on the floor. A human! It checked its databanks twice, but this is what it is. Humankind! The pollinators thought them extinct. Surprise and marvel course through its circuits, translated to dipping buzzing and a brief celebratory figure of eight in the air.

"Where did you come from, eh?"

The figure gets to its feet.

Drone6450 recognises how the creature scans it too, takes it in.

"I did an assessment on you guys. You're bigger than I expected. Just look at you, like a dog."

Drone6450 comes to rest, allows the humanoid a proper look. They are its creators, but in the burrowing and in the lightning... much has been lost on both sides.

"Nice!"

The drone notes its appreciation.

"Well, where did you come from?"

JOGGING TO KEEP UP, soles slapping on the smooth concrete, Thorn keeps at the solar bee's side. They've been up this path before, the gradual incline that was a dead end.

Except now... there is air, there is light.

At the threshold of the bunker Thorn stops. One step more and they will be up top. One step more and they will feel grass and vegetation under their bare feet. Already they can smell the freshness of ozone, blink rapidly in the face of the sun, feel its warmth and nurture. In the distance there are the towering turbines slowly revolving in the wind. There are trees and flowers, shrubs and birds. Butterflies! Thorn excitedly identifies everything in their sightlines. They try to find purchase on the smooth concrete walls. This is all dizzying, it is all real.

They take a step. It's a simple thing, though the magnitude of the moment isn't lost on Thorn. How many years has it been since they were in the light?

Underfoot there is cool lushness, thick tongues of grass lapping at their feet, tickling Thorn.

"Thank you!" They grin, turning to look at the bee.

Beside them Drone6450 bobs. It is almost overcome with the prospect of what will happen next. Inside the bunker are hundreds of hibernating humans, ready to be brought to the light, just as Drone6450 was, ready to be powered up and become useful once more.

In Thorn's head there is a cha-cha, it makes them sway like the branches do. Thorn lifts their feet again and again, a hopping dance. It's their first up top, but not their last.

"Kiss me, honey, honey, kiss me."

Drone6450 figure of eights in the air. It has found a hive of sound and purpose and dance. It has found a home.

Morgan Melhuish (he/him) is a queer writer and educator from West Sussex. His recent work can be found in Saltwater Sorrows published by Tyche Books, Sentinel Creative's The Devil Take You and in Along Harrowed Trails from Timber Ghost Press.

X: https://www.twitter.com/mmorethanapage

HEADS OR TAILS
BY JOSEPH SIDARI

This woman who'd wandered into the newsroom at the *New York Post* just a few minutes ago was pacing back and forth like she was getting paid by the step, and today she was hoping to earn a bonus. Dealing with the crazies was part of my job, but this woman seemed different than the usual nut jobs. Insane, to be sure, but also quite earnest. "Please, Miss," I said. "Can you—?"

"Okay. Where was I? Right. I signed up to fly a Scrubber because I like to surf—not to save the world." She spit the words out as if they couldn't leave her mouth fast enough. "And definitely not to destroy it. That's what they said. That I was responsible. But how was I supposed to—?"

"Miss. Slow down. And if you're gonna tell me how you're destined to save or destroy Earth, I think you should be sitting. I know I should." I guided her from the newsroom hallway into my corner office. I settled into my unpadded desk chair and gestured at the chair in front of my desk for her to do the same.

Okay, *corner office* might be a slight exaggeration. It's more of a cubicle. But it is in a corner—that's true. Near the bathroom. A location you'd love only if you have a weak bladder or a poor sense of smell. Not my choice, but I suppose a tiny, smelly cubicle in the corner at *The New York Post* was better than none at all.

I stroked my beard as I tried to wrap my head around the nonsense this woman was spewing. I'd been growing this black bushy thing since my first year at NYU to add to my aura of understated indifference. You know the vibe I was going for: black-on-black wardrobe. Shaved head. Wireless round eyeglasses. But now the beard also made me look serious. And it gave me something to do with my hands when I was nervous. Like now. Win-win, right?

She was still standing, but at least she had stopped her pacing. Her eyebrows were wrinkled so tightly that I thought they might get stuck together.

"Please?" I pointed to the chair again. The poor woman looked like she needed to sit. And having a large metal desk between us was comforting in case this restless woman became violent.

She eyed the metal chair and collapsed into it. She blew out a breath and then looked up at me, her eyes pleading. "You believe me, don't you?"

"Uh-huh." I nodded.

You know, I had a favorite prof in my Investigative Journalism class. He loved to throw us pearls of wisdom. Stuff we could use when we were 'out there.' 'Doing it.' So now I was going to hit her with his first pearl. To get first-class information from an interview subject, he told us a good reporter should be able to look serious and thoughtful, nod, and then say, 'Uh-huh' or 'Mm-hmm.' Today, I totally nailed the 'Uh-huh.'

"So you can't blame me—for what happened. It wasn't my fault." She fidgeted in her chair, this lanky woman with golden-brown skin. Her raven hair was gathered into three oddly-angled ponytails, each dyed a different shade of green. She seemed about my age, maybe a little younger. She stretched and snapped the clingy, gray fabric of her flight suit, repeatedly tugging at her collar as if it was restricting her breathing. A bright blue patch with the letters *G.L.O.T.* was displayed on her right arm. A name badge with K. MANOLO perched on her left chest.

Our managing editor, Olivia Taylor, had asked me to interview K. MANOLO in all her agitated glory. Part of my job description—after getting coffee for the staff writers, of course—was to run interference on the wackos. 'She might be fifty shades of crazy,' Olivia said. 'But remember: sometimes a crazy person has an interesting story. Call me if she does.'

And since I someday wanted to be the writing guy at *The New York Post* instead of the coffee guy, I did what Olivia said.

I narrowed my gaze at this K. MANOLO and intensified my serious look. I then unleashed pearl #2, guaranteed to draw out that gleaming nugget of truth in an interviewee's story: repeat the last three words of her sentence.

"Not your fault?" I asked.

"Right. If the world's destroyed, it's not on me."

"Not on you, Ms. Manolo—?"

"Lani, please."

I reread her name badge. "Lani? I don't get it. Is the 'K' silent?"

"Huh?" She looked down at the name tag on her flight suit. "K is for Kailani, but that's a mouthful. Lani is good." She squinted at me, apparently trying to read the ID hanging from my neck lanyard. "Uh, Woodward? Are you getting all this? You're not taking notes, and I don't see a mic."

"Didn't you read the disclaimer" I tapped a minuscule placard attached to the black cube at the front of my desk:

By sitting in this chair, you consent to be recorded via the Omnidirectional Microphone and have your words published. Or not.

The manufacturer says if a mosquito farts within six feet, the Omni will record it in HD. I believe it. I'd mentioned before that I'm near the bathroom, right? You wouldn't believe the sounds I need to edit out if I interview someone after lunch. "Yeah. I'm recording you—with the Omni. And it's Woody." I leaned forward to shake her hand. Firm. Confident. "Unless you gave birth to me and I have done something to ruin your life—like forget to take out the trash. Then you can call me *Woodward*." And here was pearl #3: Impress your interview subject with the three Fs. Firm handshake. Friendly demeanor. Funny one-liners. Boy, I was slaying it today.

"Woody, it is," said Lani. "I'm glad you're willing to listen—"

"Uh-huh."

"—because I needed to tell someone what happened. When you're branded with a glowing doomsday tattoo by a two-faced alien, it can *so* mess with your head."

"Mm-hmm." I nodded. "Mess with your—huh?" I did not have a pearl to respond to *that*. "Doomsday alien? W-what do—?"

"No. I said, *Two-faced* alien. Doomsday *tattoo. Do you need me to speak more slowly?* Or louder?" She leaned toward my mic, raising her voice and parsing each word as if my high-tech recording device might not understand English.

"No, you're fine." I slid back in my chair in case she was contagious. I didn't have a pearl for handling the clinically insane, so I tried to wing it. "Ha-ha. Um, no need to get excited. Sit back in your chair, uh, Lani. I'll listen to your little story—"

"My little story?" She stood up. "I told you that aliens engraved a doomsday tat on my body—" She pulled up the sleeve of her flight suit. "See?"

I have seen some crazy ink in my day. But nothing like this. Well, maybe once, when I had dabbled with mushrooms in my first year of college. But even that bad trip was tame compared to this.

The face of a clock blazed across her forearm in a swirl of green, orange, and purple ink that gave me a queasy feeling in the pit of my stomach. No numbers on this timepiece, though. The ten symbols that ringed this clock face looked like some twisted version of the zodiac. Monsters, animals, and a few creatures I knew were going to give me nightmares tonight glowed and pulsed around the dial. Some snorted smoke and fire. Others pranced or flew in a small circle. One, with devil horns and a leering grin, sat at the top, where 12 o'clock would usually be. He seemed to be staring at me. Or through me. My stomach churned again, and I tried not to puke.

Then there were the hands on this clock. Five hands, each of various lengths. All were colored a metallic silver, and all were moving—yes, moving—at different speeds. But the really freaky part—yes, it could get even weirder—is that her tattoo made a noise. The damn thing was *ticking* as each of those many hands circled the dial.

"Holy—" I reached into my desk drawer to get my tablet. "Do you mind if I take a pic—"

"*To go along with my little story?* Sure. Why not. I thought you might also be interested that when all the hands on this devil clock point straight up, the aliens are coming back to decide the fate of the human race. But never mind. You're much too busy for *my little story.*"

She rolled down her sleeve to cover the tattoo before I could snap a picture, and the ticking stopped. She turned from my desk. "I'd wanted *The*

Post to get *the* first crack at my story, but since it's too trivial for you, maybe *The Times*—"

"No, no, no." I stood up and walked in front of her to block her exit from my cubicle. "I'm all ears. Go on."

"Thanks. As I was saying, the people who taught me to fly the G.L.O.T. 5000 didn't—"

"Glot?" I asked. "What's a Glot?"

"G-L-O-T. It stands for Ground Level Ozone Transport," she said, pride in her voice. "But most people call 'em—"

"Oh, right. Scrubbers. You can't look up in the sky without seeing a Scrubber."

"*We make your gray skies blue!*" said Lani, regurgitating a well-rehearsed tagline from an overplayed commercial. "But we're not trained to be interstellar ambassadors. We follow our grid. Suck up the smog down here." She held her hand low. "Pump it out up here." She raised her hand above her head. "Oh, and don't crash into anything. And I'll swear that's just what I did. I traced the pattern for my grid back and forth, then forth and back. It was *they* who ran into *me*."

"Ran into you?" I asked.

"Yeah," she said. "Weren't you listening? Remember, the two-faced alien?"

I couldn't think of anything friendly or funny to say, so I stroked my beard and nodded. That got her going again.

"I think they brain-washed us. My flight instructors—not the aliens. The instructors said it over and over. We had to repeat it back. Every day. For our six weeks of training. They called it *The Pledge of Vigilance*." She placed her right hand over her heart. "As a technical operator in the Ground Level Ozone Transport fleet, I swear to be watchful and attentive for airplanes, birds, buildings, drones, helicopters, hot air balloons, rockets, satellites, and shuttle pods, and keep an eye out for my fellow scrubbers. So help me, GLOT."

I'm sure that paying attention to the world around us has saved many a scrubber's life. Well, he didn't say anything about smacking into a UFO, so maybe *The Pledge* needs an update." She snorted a laugh. "And to be precise, I didn't actually crash into the aliens. More like a bump. If I crashed, I wouldn't be here telling you this story. Like they told me to."

"Your instructors?" I asked.

"No. *The aliens*," said Lani, as if it was obvious if I'd really been listening.

"Aliens told you to tell me your story?"

"No, no. The aliens didn't say, 'Lani, fly your Scrubber into downtown Manhattan, park it on Broadway, and call Woody at *The Post*.' But they did say—wait, I'm getting ahead of myself. It'd be easier if I told it to you from the beginning. Okay?"

I nodded, and then my stomach growled. I checked my cell. It was almost four, and though I had gotten everyone else's lunch today, I had missed mine. I picked up a paper cup of coffee from my desk and sipped at it. The bitter liquid was stale and cold. I spit it back. "You want a coffee? I can get—"

Lani shook her head, and her colored ponytails wagged back and forth. "Uh-uh. Caffeine is not going to help." She tugged at her collar again. "A beer? Now that—?"

"Not until after five," I said.

"Wow. Pretty rigid here. Oh well." She blew out a breath. "So first, when I met the creature, I mean, when I saw them, and my lights flashed yellow, I almost, um, I didn't know—"

"Slow down, Lani. Why don't you tell me about yourself first," I said. "Our readers love the human-interest angle. Then you can ease your way into the *alien tattoo stuff*." My stomach gurgled again, so I reached into my desk drawer and pulled out a small square package wrapped in foil. Not very professional to eat during an interview, but I was starving. I placed the foil pouch on my desk and unwrapped a sandwich. I grabbed one half and bit into it, savoring the sweet and salty flavor. "Sorry," I said, still chewing. "Lunch. You don't mind—?"

"Not at all." She reached forward and grabbed the other half. "I'm starved. I haven't eaten since breakfast." She bit into it and began to chew. "Maybe a glass of water, though? Do you always use this much peanut butter?"

"Peanuts? You think they pay me *that* well?" I shook my head, got a bottle of water from my bottom drawer, and handed it to her. "It's cricket butter."

"Crunchy?" asked Lani.

"Is there any other kind?"

"Guess not." She used her fingernail to pick at something in her teeth.

"You were saying?" I prompted.

"Right. I've been living and scrubbing for a few years in New York, but I grew up on Oahu. A regular Hawaiian surfer girl. At the end of my junior year in high school, my dad got transferred to upstate New York. Buffalo. With no waves on Lake Erie to surf, I thought my parents had moved us to Hell. And winter Hell, at that.

"You see, I'd never cared for books or school. Surfing was my life. So as an unhappy Buffalonian, I counted the days until graduation when I'd head back to Hawaii." She picked up the stolen half of my sandwich and took another bite.

Ever the professional reporter, I prodded. "Back to Hawaii?"

"Yeah. But then, four weeks before graduation, Something happened. We had this career fair. You know the drill: an auditorium full of adults wearing fancy clothes and speaking fancier words. But then I saw this one dude in shorts and a tank top. I walked over and asked him what his job was. He told me he surfed the sky. Cleaned the air. And got paid pretty well, too. It sounded too good to be true.

"Best of all, I didn't need college. Just a diploma and a class X shuttle license. Well, that was way better than folding sweaters at the mall. So I graduated, got my commercial sky license, and then applied to The New York Institute of Aerospace and Pollution Control. Lani pointed to the rest of my sandwich, lying on the foil. "You gonna finish that?"

"Yes." I pulled the sandwich closer to me. "I was going to eat the *whole* thing—"

"—but then you met me. Thanks for sharing." She beamed an ear-to-ear smile. "Little did I know that I had to go to Sky School for *six whole weeks*. That seemed like a lot of time to put into a career, but I stuck it out. At first, I was worried I'd have to know a lot of chemistry and physics to liquefy and store the smog. But each scrubber has a computer to do all that science-y stuff. My ship is so freakin' smart. It knows to suck up and super-cool anything that shouldn't be in the air. All I had to do was pump my tanks while the green light was blinking. When my tank was full, the light would turn red. Then I'd fly up and dump my payload, and it'd turn green again. Pump and dump. All day long. Then learn the flight patterns. Memorize the safety regulations—you remember? *The Pledge*? So as long as I wasn't a color-blind idiot, I was in."

"This is all very interesting." I lifted my old cup of coffee, then caught a whiff of the rancid liquid, and put it back down. "But when did you see the alien? And get that ink?"

"Have you ever flown in a scrubber?" she asked, ignoring my question. "Probably not. But you've seen them. Some say if you squint, they look like a giant boomerang tracking through the sky. I think it looks more like a pterodactyl and a bag of Doritos got drunk and made a baby. No matter—it flies. Or rather, it *glides*. Riding the currents like the widest surfboard ever.

"As the only one in my class who'd ever shredded any actual waves, I placed number one in my flight class and got my pick of jobs. That's why I'm in Manhattan. I always wanted to suck all the soot from the New York skyline." She turned thoughtful and looked around my cubicle, searching for a window. "My grid is *way* downtown. Not sure if you can see it—"

"Lani, I know I'd asked about your past, but can you get to today? And possibly pull up your sleeve again, so I can—" I lifted my tablet and gestured to her arm.

She rolled up her sleeve, and that hellish clock swirled, glowed, and ticked at me. I snapped like a thousand pictures. And then shook my head to will away the nausea that followed.

"Happy?" She rolled down her sleeve. "Now, you really have to hear about my first student flight. You see, a flock of seagulls—"

"Uh-huh. That is the perfect topic—" I stroked my beard— "for the next installment. Back to today. You were gliding over Manhattan—"

"Yeah, one of the tugs had towed me up into the troposphere, like they always do. The scrubber has some thrusters for maneuverability but not enough thrust to get off the ground. Then I started scrubbing. I rode the currents. Sucked up the ozone and super-cooled it to a liquid. My ship used the heat generated to create lift and ride the thermals higher in the sky.

"Pump until the green light turns red. Full. Then dump until the red light turns green. The tank is empty. Pump and dump. Green and red. All morning. My tanks were filling up quickly today. Companies fart black smoke into the air without a thought, knowing we scrubbers will suck it up. Job security. Am I right?"

I shrugged.

"So business as usual. I had ridden this sweet thermal up into the stratosphere so I could dump—and that's when the yellow light winked on."

"*Yellow*? I thought you said the lights were either green or red?"

"They are—except for yellow." Lani shook her head. "You didn't want to hear about my close encounter with the seagulls—the only time I ever saw a yellow before. Until today.

"Green means fill 'er up," I said. "And red means the tanks are full. So what's yellow?"

Lani looked me squarely in the eyes. "Yellow means pee your pants 'cause you're about to hit something. The thing is, I was way up in the ozone layer. Short of an orbiting satellite, there shouldn't *be* anything that high up. I double-checked my sky charts, but the yellow flashed faster. When it flashes steady, you're screwed. I hadn't ever seen that.

"We'd practiced yellow drills in school. During a yellow, the instructors stress that you shouldn't just consider turning right or left. People on the ground are used to moving in 2-D, but we fly in three dimensions, so always consider going up or down. The yellow flashed faster. I looked side-to-side. Nothing. So I flew up. My bad. Because that's exactly where *it* was.

"Where *what* was?" I asked.

"Duh—" She rolled her eyes. "The flying saucer. Weren't you paying attention? And *technically*, I didn't hit it. I later learned that some kind of alien force field stopped me before we bumped hulls. But my cabin still flashed the steadiest, scariest yellow I'd ever seen."

"Wait," I said. "Do you expect me to believe you rammed into a UFO in the skies over Manhattan, and it's not on the news?"

"It will be soon," she said. "That's why I'm here."

"No, that's not what I mean. Why no blips on the radar for Air and Space Traffic Control? Someone should've detected *something*."

"You'd think," said Lani. "But they didn't. Not sure why. Maybe the alien ship had an invisibility shield. Or a cloaking device. Or maybe all the traffic controllers went on a bathroom break at once? Or maybe *you can let me finish my story*," she yelled, "And figure out the details yourself? I'm not the reporter. You are."

"Reporter?" I laughed. "I wish."

"You're not a—?"

"Someday," I said. "But now I just do a lot of errands for the staff writers. Pick up dry-cleaning. Walk their dogs. Oh, and I also get their lunch—and coffee. I asked you if you wanted coffee, right?"

Lani nodded, her brows knitting together again.

"My boss said if I did this—listened to you—she'd let me write it up. If it seemed promising, she might even print it."

"How often has that happened?"

"Never," I mumbled.

"What?"

"*Never*," I said louder.

"Oh." Her shoulders slumped. "Then that's it. Game over."

"Not necessarily. Your ink is awesome. I'm not sure the editor will print a story just based on one outrageous tattoo, but with the alien stuff—"

"Woody, if you can convince her, you'll graduate from errand boy sooner than you think. This is the story of a lifetime."

"That's what all crazy people say," I mumbled.

"What?"

I sighed. "Sure. Go on."

"Great. So, where was I? Oh yeah. A scrubber never stops moving. If it does, it'll plummet to Earth like the half-ton of metal it is. The thermals we expel from condensing the smog keep each ship up. Now that I was at full yellow and my scrubber had stopped moving, I was ready for every alarm on the ship to sound. But they didn't.

"My cockpit burned with bright yellow light, but my ship was not falling. I was stuck in the sky. I leaned forward and peered out a window to see what had happened."

"Window?" I asked. "You didn't check your sensors?"

Lani laughed. "This isn't *Star Trek*. I am not 'exploring strange new worlds.' I am cleaning the crap from our air. If they thought I could do my job without a window, I suppose I wouldn't have one—" she looked around at my windowless cubicle. "Either.

"The other ship was about twice the size of my scrubber. And shaped kinda like your mic—a black cube. But its hull was dotted with glowing white spots, making it look like half of a pair of dice."

"*Die*," I said.

"I know," said Lani. "I thought I was a goner, for sure."

I raised a finger as if to interrupt, then put my hand down and resumed listening.

"The tip of my ship was held firmly against one of those spots—like a dart in a bulls-eye. I tried to use the scrubber's puny thrusters to push away. No luck. I was about to radio A&S when a voice hissed over the speaker of my comm: 'U-man?'

"Well, I didn't know what to say. Then above my nav controls, an image appeared. Floating. 'Are you a U-man?' it repeated. I later realized they have a hard time saying the letter H. But otherwise, his English was perfect. I blinked my eyes, incredulous, as the holographic image of a humanoid face floated in front of me."

"Hey," I said. "I thought you didn't have sensors. How did—"

"Beats me. His image just appeared," said Lani. "And it was freaking me out."

"I bet," I said. "So, what'd you say?"

She dipped her head, blushing. "There are many first lines that will go down in the history of space exploration. Neil Armstrong had his 'One small step' speech. Eugenia Brown landed on Mars and proclaimed, 'On Earth, I am called an American. On Mars, I am an Earthling.' I wish I could've said something much more profound. You know, like: 'On behalf of humanity, I want to welcome you.' Or even: 'Wow. We are not alone.' Anything would have been better than—"

"What? What did you say?"

"When I made first contact with an alien race, staring into the silver eyes of this alien from another galaxy, the words that will be immortalized will be: 'No way! I'm being punked by George Washington.'"

"Oh." I looked down so as not to meet her gaze. "We could, uh, make something else up. For the article." I looked up into her face, trying to read her eyes. "But wait. Are you telling me this alien resembled The Father of Our Country?"

"No," said Lani. "He didn't look *like* George Washington." She paused. "He was an *identical copy* of—" She started rifling through a change dish on the corner of my desk. "This—" She picked up a quarter and held it up. It shone dully in the fluorescent overhead light. "George Washington. Side profile. Head and neck only."

"That's not possible."

"You know how I said he had silver eyes?" she said.

"Yeah. I pictured a robot vibe."

"Well, he also had silver skin. And hair. And face and neck. Shiny and metallic. And he was flat. Floating on the screen in profile. On a silver disc. This alien who had stopped my ship in midair looked like a life-sized, twenty-five-cent piece!"

"Come on, Lani." I leaned forward and tapped the Omni Mic to pause the recording. "Now who is pranking who? You expect me to believe—"

"Believe what you like. It's the truth." She replaced the coin in my dish. "Should I leave?"

"No." I tapped the mic, un-pausing it. "Go on."

"I didn't learn all of this initially, but by the end, George—that's what I called him, and he never corrected me—is a sentient being composed of liquid '*diurnium*.' I told you I wasn't good at science. Is *diurnium* a real element?"

I started to shake my head and then paused. I tapped on my tablet. A graphical representation of the periodic table floated before me. I studied it and then tapped it to close the image. "No, it's not. At least not according to Wikipedia."

"Well, it must be on *GeorgeWorld*, or wherever the aliens were from. He said we were carbon-based life—which I found hard to believe since no one eats carbs anymore. But I played along like I knew what he was talking about. I didn't want him to judge the intellectual capacity of all Earthlings by me. He said beings from his world were made of *diurnium*. They all have a liquid silver body that can slip into any form. Today they chose—"

"Wait, wait, wait," I said. "How did you understand him? I know you said he spoke English, but how could he? Are you willing to take a poly-graph? Or a drug test? Because either you are lying, stoned, *or* this is the most mind-blowing discovery since someone poured Kahlua into a mug of coffee."

"I'm telling the truth," said Lani, holding up her right hand in a show of sincerity. "I'm not wasted. And I'm not delusional. I am lucky to be alive, and I *need* to relay the message the Georges told me. They spoke English via some—"

"They?" asked Woody. "You keep saying they, but you only mention the one: George. How many aliens were there?"

"There were those two—I mean one. I mean, there was one of both of them." She shook her head. "Will you let me finish? It doesn't make much sense, but it's way worse out of order. Okay?"

I nodded and made a rolling gesture for her to continue.

"So after I embarrassed the human race by not knowing the difference between carbon and diurnium, he assured me he was not playing a joke. He said they hoped a familiar face or object would be less intimidating for first contact with our primitive race."

"'So you chose a quarter?' I said. And then he said, 'Well, a dime would 'ave been too small, and you might not 'ave recognized Susan B. Anthony if I was a silver dollar. You might 'ave thought I was some old woman.' And then I said—"

"Uh, Lani. This blow-by-blow dialogue is truly stimulating, but I either have to call my editor to reset the cover of tomorrow's paper because you have just had an encounter with an alien race—" I took a breath "—or I have to dial 911 and ask them to send the crazy car to bring you to a very safe and quiet place."

"Will do," she said. "George told me his people keep tabs on all the planets in this arm of the galaxy. There are three reasons they choose to make contact with a new species. They had pigeon-holed Earth into one of these categories on a recent long-range scan of our solar system.

"The first category is a civilization that has already destroyed itself. They come to look at the smoking wreckage of the planet and see what happened. Are there any survivors? And can that world be repopulated?"

"Not us," I said.

"Right. The second category is a technologically advancing culture that is pushing farther and farther into space and is now reaching the point where the natives will soon be leaving their own system. The third—"

"Cool," I said. "They must have detected our colony on Mars. Maybe they even learned about our plans for a mission to Titan? I read that in *The Times* last week, so I think it could even be true."

"As I was saying—" Lani did not sound irritated by my interruption, but her fire and spunk were gone. "—the third reason they contact another world is if that world is doing something so dangerous or stupid it threatens the health of that planet. *That* is why they came to Earth."

My jaw hung slack.

"And it's my fault: I'm the one who was defiling the Earth," admitted Lani. "And I deserve to die." She looked like she might cry.

"Huh?" I shook my head to clear it and then narrowed my gaze. "Lani, no. Don't worry. I think we can find people to help you." I reached for my cell. "Modern medicine has made so many advances. A few pills in the morning, and then a couple more—"

"I told you: I am not crazy!" She had stood up, now shouting.

The hum of multiple conversations in the workroom quieted. A female coworker with wild, fly-away hair ran into my cubicle. "Is everything okay here, Woody?"

"I'm fine, Bee," I said. "We're, uh, just discussing last night's season finale to *Ninja Bachelor Survivor*."

"Oh, yeah," said Bee. "That was an insane twist at the end. Could you believe—?"

"Bee? I'm in the middle of something." I gestured for her to leave with my eyes. "You mind?"

"Whatever." She left with a *humph*, muttering something about 'antisocial people.' The murmur of background noise in the workroom returned.

"Let me finish, Woody," Lani pleaded. "Please?"

"Five minutes. After that—" I eyed my cell phone. "It's for your own good."

"Okay. The way I understand it—" she was speed-talking now—"George is responsible for ecological surveillance. He was in the process of evaluating our ozone layer—we flunked, by the way—and the unusually high levels of extra-planetary contamination prevented his sensors from detecting my ship. But if not for our chance collision, he might have decided the fate of our planet without any communication with us at all. He told me so few planets in the galaxy can support life. His people take the care and maintenance of a planet *very* seriously, and if we can't be good stewards of our own world, we don't deserve to have one.

"Don't deserve?" I was not just parroting back her words as the top-notch journalist I hoped to be. I prayed that this girl was crazy. If not, this sounded bad for all humanity.

"I explained that we—I mean, I—was trying to clean up our planet. Burning fossil fuel is ruining our atmosphere, depleting our ozone. My job was purifying the air and building the ozone layer." She sniffed back a tear.

"That's when he blamed *me* for all the pollution that had leaked into outer space. He said I had committed a crime against the planet and all its people. I don't know how he did it, but suddenly I felt a searing pain on my forearm—" She pulled up her sleeve again. "And that's when I saw this ticking *thing* burned onto my skin.

"He called me a *defiler* and said I would have to atone for my sins. At that point, I couldn't hold it back. I cried like one of the contestants on that game show, *Wheel of Wonder*.

'I'm only doing my job,' I said between tears, and 'It's not fair. How was I to know?' I'm not sure if my argument or my crying did the trick, but then another voice piped in. Higher pitched. Kinder. And it definitely did *not* come from the George side. And then the two began to argue."

"Who?" I asked.

"The other. I didn't know who, but I could tell it was someone else," Lani said. "George said, 'She is guilty. She admitted it.' The other voice said, 'She is a pawn,' and 'Their world is so backward she may not understand the ramifications of her actions.' Basically, they were bickering over whether I—we—should get a second chance.

"It went back and forth for a while until their quarreling stopped. George stared at me. I didn't know if he judged me guilty or innocent. If I was going to live or die. I wasn't sure if I was allowed to speak, but I figured it couldn't get any worse, so I asked, 'Who are you arguing with?'

"'Oh,' said George. 'With my other 'alf. Of course.' And with that, the holographic image of this coin-shaped alien flipped over, and I could now see an embossed silver eagle. Perched on a silver branch. Wings spread wide."

I picked up the quarter Lani had grabbed from my desk and eyed the other side. I held it up. "Like this?"

She nodded. "It was then I learned they had a binary nature. At first, when he referred to his other half, I thought he meant this other being was his partner. But George explained that they are more than a union of two separate beings. To be honest, I don't understand it at all, but I think it's like two minds in one being? Two souls? No, that's too religious. Maybe two beings sharing one form? But either way, there was one George and one Eagle—that's what I called the other. Both were parts of the same person, and they were debating my fate and the fate of our species."

"Hold on a minute," said Woody. "You said they had found *you* guilty. When did they pass judgment on all of humanity?"

"I explained to them that it wasn't me *personally* dumping pollution into space. It was a planet-wide thing. So George said they must destroy our species—to keep our toxic waste and attitudes from spreading. Eagle said that if there was a chance of reversing our policies, we deserved a chance. George replied that our lives didn't really matter in the universal equation. If we kept pouring poison into the stratosphere, the ozone would thicken, plunging our world into a new ice age, so we were doomed either way. They continued to deliberate. It was like watching a ping-pong match between master players—and the fate of the human race rested on whoever hit the last shot."

"How did they decide?" I paused and waggled my eyebrows. "Did they flip a coin?"

"Do you think this is funny?" asked Lani. "Death by some all-powerful alien disintegration ray versus death by glacial ice age."

"There is another way out," I replied. "Humanity decides to stop our wicked and environmentally corrupt ways."

"Now I know you're making fun of me," said Lani. "Since the scrubber program, like a gazillion laws been repealed that had reduced emissions. Who cares about not polluting when you can dump it into space?"

I shrugged.

"Well, guess what? We should care. There is no safe place to dump our waste. Not in the ocean. Not in a landfill. And not in outer space."

"I asked them to give us one more chance. We can make it right. And you know what? They agreed. I think George thinks we are going to die no matter what," said Lani. "But Eagle seemed to hold out some hope for us. They promised to circle back to our system in a *tarmek*, or about ten-and-a-half years. Hence my clock." She tapped her forearm. "When all five hands point straight up to the devil guy, well, then we had better have cleaned up our act, or—"

"What? Ka-boom?" I clapped my hands and then flung out my fingers to mimic an explosion.

"I dunno. Probably," said Lani. "But maybe, just *maybe*, if we change our polluting ways, they'll spare us."

"Wow," I said. "So what happened after that? They just let you go?"

"They sure did."

"That's good—" I said.

"Not really," said Lani. "They literally *let me go*. I told you how scrubbers are towed up and coasted via the thermals. Do you know what happens when my ship isn't coasting along an updraft?"

"No," I replied. "But from your tone, it sounds terrible."

"I dropped. Like a half-ton tortilla chip. Straight down," said Lani.

"Well, you are here," I observed. "So unless I am interviewing your ghost, you—"

"—are the best pilot *ever*. As I plummeted towards the Earth, I pointed the nose of my scrubber down. I then prayed to Lono, the Hawaiian god of surfing, for a superhot thermal to give me some lift. No luck. But then I realized my cockpit was filled with a pulsing red light."

"Red? Is that for imminent death?" I asked.

"No. Red means my tanks were full. Remember? So I started dumping as fast as I could. The chemical reaction of the super-cooled liquid smog hitting the air slowed me a little. The chemical reaction heated the air. I gained some lift. And my scrubber got lighter, too. I rode that small thermal toward the smoggiest part of Manhattan and started pumping again. That chemical reaction of super-cooling the dense smog created a larger thermal, and I glided upwards. I pumped and dumped, creating an updraft and then riding it as far as possible. I pumped and dumped all the way back to the southern tip of the island, so I could land. Back on solid ground, I got out and kissed the runway. And then I threw up.

"So here I am. To tell 'Umanity,' as George would say, the bitter truth."

"Okay, Lani. I'll grant that either you have an incredible imagination, or you are one crescent short of the lunar cycle—"

"*Woody*—"

"*Or*—and this is a big stretch—you are the first and last hope for the human race. Whichever it is, I'm just the coffee guy. What can I do?"

"You can tell my story to your boss," she said. Her tie-dyed ponytails, sparkly and sassy at the beginning of her tale, now drooped in exhaustion. "Write it up. Convince her we need to tell the whole world that dumping pollution into outer space doesn't work."

"Uh-huh." I narrowed my gaze, trying to size her up. I shook my head.

"I know this sounds nutso, but you believe me, don't you? I didn't make it up," said Lani. "I couldn't make *this* up." She flashed me her doomsday tattoo.

"I don't know whether you got it from aliens, leprechauns, or a talking unicorn." And before she could object, I added, "but I agree that we need to take better care of our planet. And your ink, well, it's not from any tattoo parlor around here."

"Nowhere on Earth," she said and rolled down her sleeve.

"So *maybe* I could try—"

"Woody! Thank you!" Lani applauded. "I could kiss you. I can't believe it. My story will be published in *The New York Post*. People will—"

"It's not—not yet. I *might* be able to get my editor to bite on some version of this space-alien thing," I said. "But I can't promise she'll pay much. Maybe nothing."

"I don't want money—I want to get the word out," said Lani.

"Really?" I quirked an eyebrow. "No money? No book deal? How about movie options?"

Lani shook her head, her green ponytails flitting back and forth with more life.

"Wow," I said. "Maybe you are for real."

"*I am,*" She turned back to face me. "Why would I come into your office and waste—"

"We get two to three alien stories *per week*. Throw in a saga about some family who encountered Bigfoot on their summer vacation, and you've described my typical work week. But you—you are different. I actually believe you."

She leaned forward and kissed the top of my shaven head. "You won't regret this, Woody. Here's my number." She pulled out her cell and shared her contact info. "Call me if you need more info." She checked her phone. "Or if you want to have that beer. It is after five. I'll buy." She shot me a wink and skipped out of my cubicle with a lightness in her step.

I looked down at the Omni, still in recording mode, and tapped to pause it. I reached for my cell. "Call Olivia Taylor." I lifted the phone to my ear. "Yeah, boss. Just finished."

I listened and nodded.

"I know, I know. I thought so at first, too. But I think she has something.

And she doesn't want any money. Let me send you the recording. You can listen to it before—"

Another pause.

"At least check out this wild ink of hers." I tapped a button on my tablet to share it. "See? The pictures pulse and move, like—"

Another, longer pause.

"I know you can't spare any staff on this. I'll write it up—the whole thing," I said. "No strings. Read it. Then run it or kill it."

A longer pause.

"I *guess* so. I could focus on her ink if you think that's where the meat is. I'll ask around at the local parlors to see who might have the chops to create such a thing. But what about the alien angle? And the issue of pollution is relevant—'

Another pause.

"I agree. Tattoos are super relevant, too. But, but—no, ma'am. It's your call. And I *love* that title. Who'd have thought of 'Pretty in Ink' for a piece on a tattoo?" I rolled my eyes.

Pause.

"No. You won't regret it. And it won't interfere with my coffee runs. I'll write it on my own time. Thanks *so much*." I disconnected and then tapped the Omni to send her my interview.

Maybe she'll hear it and decide the alien story works. But if not, at least I can write something more interesting than a sandwich list.

"Text to Kailani Manolo." I spoke, and a projection of my words hung in the air:

My boss said maybe. You still wanna get that beer?

"Send." My words vanished.

Lani pinged me back within seconds:

Sure! Great! Meet you downstairs in your lobby.

I spoke aloud to text back:

Sounds good. Be down in a minute. And don't forget you're buying.

I sent my reply, and she replied with a *thumbs-up* emoji. I swiped out of the texting app and left my cubicle, threading my way toward the elevator.

Maybe after a few beers, she'll tell me where she really got her tattoo. Or, after Olivia hears the tape, she'll bite on the alien/pollution angle. I shrugged. Either way, I have a good chance at my first byline. Win-win. Right?

I arrived at the elevator and said, "Lobby." The door opened, and I stepped in.

It'd be kind of nice if the boss believed Lani's story. I'm really not sure it's legit, but I do know that Lani believes it is. But if not coin-shaped aliens and environmental Armageddon, writing about her tattoo would be cool, too. And if Olivia cans them both? Well, I've only been at *The Post* for six months. There'll be plenty of other chances to land a byline. It's not the end of the world if this one falls through. I could post it on my blog. That way, at least my mother will read it.

I stroked my beard and practiced saying 'uh-huh' and 'mm-hmm' as I rode the elevator to meet Lani at the bar.

Joseph Sidari writes long and short fiction from Boston, and is a member of SFWA and Grub Street Writers. As a practicing physician, he works hard at caring for his patients during the day while trying to kill his protagonists each night. He has published over a dozen short stories online and in print, and is especially proud of this cautionary tale condemning hiding our pollution instead of reducing it. And although cricket butter sandwiches are likely a real thing, no actual crickets were harmed in the making of this story. Sign up for his newsletter on his website (below) and read his blog, Shred Your Novel, via the same link.

Website: https://www.josephsidari.com
X: https://www.twitter.com/JNSidari
Instagram: https://www.instagram.com/JNSidari

EXO

BY KB WILLSON

"It is with the greatest regret that I must inform this house that, despite our best efforts, we find ourselves unable to bring the change in our climate down to manageable levels… that is to say, to a level which is commensurate with the continuance of human civilisation in the way we have come to understand it. On current projections, global temperature is set to exceed the worst predictions of the Copenhagen Diagnosis, and we are already seeing unprecedented disruption to global infrastructure, resulting in widespread mortality and unsustainable mass migration of population to what remains of the temperate regions. It is clear, Madam Speaker, that the only viable answer to the current catastrophe is to remove humanity from the surface of the Earth for such time as is required for the planet to heal. It is also clear that taking humanity away from the earth to colonies on other planets cannot be done in sufficient numbers to make such a strategy viable.

"However, there remain grounds for hope. It gives me great pleasure to announce that we, along with all nations of the World Council for Climate Change, are to co-operate in the greatest engineering project the world has ever seen. More details will be forthcoming in due course but suffice it to say that the plan to lift the entire human population away from the surface, to dwell together in a vast exoskeleton situated some seventy thousand feet above the Earth, is well advanced, with construction due to begin imminently. And because of the unprecedented nature of the emergency, I also have to announce that all resources will be diverted toward this project with immediate effect. Madam Speaker, we are an inventive, adaptive breed, and as history has proven, there is no end to what we humans can achieve when we work together, putting our petty rivalries behind us, and pooling our expertise for the greater good."

Sir Aaron Numan MP, Secretary of State for the Climate Emergency
Hansard, 6th November, 2062

~

Norwich, England. 15th August 2085

"Excited?"

"Of course, why wouldn't I be? We've waited for this moment for so long… though I still wish you were coming with us. We're going to miss you like crazy!"

Maria absent-mindedly stroked her belly as she talked. She had met Lucinda – Lu – at her first ante-natal and had immediately fallen in love with her. One of the funniest, most grounded people she had ever met, with such a wealth of homespun knowledge that Maria had initially been some-what in awe of her. They were paired together – both attending without their partners, both with a similar due date – and by the end of the session they were firm friends, with Lu proving herself the ultimate go-to for anything and everything.

Which made it all the more painful to leave her behind.

"What on earth am I going to do without you," she wailed, flinging her arms around her friend, pulling her in as close as their baby bumps would allow. Lu broke down then, too, tears flowing freely as the two women hugged and caressed for one dreadful, final time.

Maria and her husband had received their call to enter the Exo six months earlier, an event which had precipitated a whirlwind of activity, as the couple struggled to cut down their possessions to the two packing cases and two suitcases they were allowed.

As well as preparing for the baby.

Secretly, Maria hoped that the baby would arrive early, as that would have increased their luggage allowance significantly, but an unborn child, somewhat unfairly, did not qualify for its own packing case. They could, however, take an extra holdall so long as it only contained clothes and equipment for the baby. They were grateful for that, at least.

Lu had come round not only to say her goodbyes, but also to pick up several boxes of stuff that the couple couldn't take with them, and one very bouncy dog named Jasper. Pets were most definitely *not* allowed in the Exo, and rather than making the trip to one of the government-run extermination centres, or leaving him to fend for himself, Lucinda had offered to take him and give him a good home in the country, where he could chase squirrels to his heart's content.

For Lucinda was a *Sotte*, part of a country-wide movement that had defied the call to leave. There had been no compulsion to go, unlike in many other countries, so a small but vocal group calling themselves 'Spirits of the True Earth', had chosen to stay and take their chances on the surface, establishing a series of small, self-sufficient communities that would not only survive, but thrive, once (as they saw it) the worst of humanity had left them to it. It had not escaped the notice of the media that the acronym formed a word that meant 'foolish' in French, but Sotte embraced the insult, defusing the abuse by pointing out the centuries-old tradition of the 'wise fool'.

Though she had always been something of a last century hippy-chick at heart, none of the Sotte ideology helped when it came time for Lu to say goodbye to her friend. Wiping the tears from their eyes, they finally broke the clinch that felt like it would (and should) go on forever, and Maria called for her husband to help Lucinda load the boxes into the luggage well of her cargo bike.

"Look after her," Lu said, her voice breaking, "you have no idea how precious this little lady is."

"Oh, I think I do," Kieran replied. "And you look after yourself, too. How the hell are you going to cope when the meds that have been left for you run out? You're gonna be completely on your own."

"I'll cope the way my great grandmother did, the same way humans survived for centuries before we became slaves to technology. And there are medical staff who are staying. Our settlement has a great team. Don't worry about us."

"Then I guess this really is it," choked Maria, tears springing afresh from her dark green eyes.

"Don't! You'll set me off again. Good luck with little Humphrey there… I'm sure you'll get the best attention. I hear the Medi-labs in the Exo are quite something."

"And to you too. I hope she arrives before the clinics close for good."

"We can hope, I suppose… but in any case, I'll be fine, I'm sure. Now, you get off on your big adventure, and I'll return to mine. Adios, Maria. I only wish we could have had more time together." And as her last few words broke into sobs, Lucinda kicked the stand up, and launched herself away down the road.

~

"No signal… wouldn't you just know it?"

Lucinda tapped the comms band in frustration. This had always been a black spot for connection, but since they had begun dismantling the network over the last few years, it had been almost impossible to find a signal anywhere other than within the major cities, and now even that small remnant of coverage was disappearing. Davis would just have to expect her when she got there. Tearing the rubberised strip from her wrist and hurling it into the adjacent field, she turned the bike back up the right way, put the boxes back into the hopper, untied Jasper from the hedge and pedalled away, the dog lolloping along at her side.

It was dark by the time she reached home, and Davis, her partner of five years, was beside himself. When he finally spotted the little vehicle struggling its way along the path he ran towards it, a torrent of pent-up anxiety spewing from his mouth.

"Lu… Thank God! Where the hell have you been? Are you okay? What on earth happened? You should have been back an hour ago… Have you been hurt?"

The force with which he threw himself at her threatened to knock her from the bike, and made Jasper explode in a fit of defensive barking.

"I'm fine, the chain came away, that's all. Took me a little while to fix it, but it's all good now. Let go of me, you daft sod, or you'll have us all on the floor."

"Just so long as you're okay. You had me so worried."

"I know, but signal's dead... for good, I imagine... so there's nothing I could do. Anyway, no harm done. What's for dinner? I'm starving."

"It's all in hand. But don't you think you should introduce me first?" Davis looked down at the little dog, sitting panting by Lucinda's side.

"Oh yes," responded Lucinda, affecting a superbly pretentious cut-glass accent. "How terribly remiss of me. Davis, allow me to present Sir Jasper Barkington-Squirrelchaser, Jasper to his friends. Jasper, this is Davis, the ridiculous ball of high-octane anxiety I like to call my partner. I'm sure you'll be firm friends. Now, I can't possibly say another word until I've had dinner! Because... and I'm not sure if I mentioned this just now... I'M STARVING!"

And leaving Davis to deal with the bike, she led the dog into the front yard of their little dwelling, following the tantalising smell of vegetable stew and dumplings.

THE NEXT FEW days were busy ones for Lu and Davis, as they packed up their home and prepared to join the settlement at Elveden, on the site of one of the old Center Parcs resorts. The site, one of several former holiday destinations that had been repurposed by Sotte to suit their long-term needs and ideological framework, sat comfortably close to one of the entry points to the Exo, providing an easy route for wavering Sotte members to change their minds, if they should decide that the natural life wasn't for them after all. Thus had the government discharged their duty of care towards those who elected to stay behind. Beyond this failsafe, they were on their own.

The transport was due to pick them up on Wednesday afternoon, the couple taking the opportunity to avail themselves of the organisation's offer rather than submit to the extra hassle of finding their own way there, along with all their belongings and now, Sir Jasper. They had heard of some Sotte members who had thoroughly embraced the whole 'back to nature' vibe and were travelling by horse and cart, but Lu and Davis couldn't see the point in making things more difficult than they needed to be. Besides, they had recourse to neither.

So in between dog walks and food preparation, their last days were spent packing, packing, packing. They could no longer rely on many of the trappings of modern life, so cut their cloth accordingly, but were heartened by the knowledge that the settlement would be fuelled by a large solar farm and several wind turbines, so they weren't to be kissing goodbye to electricity altogether. Nevertheless, Lu made sure that at least one of their packing cases was filled with paper books, just in case.

As they lay in bed on their last night in their old house, unable to sleep for both excitement and apprehension, Davis lovingly stroked Lu's belly, writing invisible messages over her skin.

"Are you sure you're ready for this?" he asked, watching her face in the half-light of the moon through the window.

"Are you kidding?" she replied, taking hold of his hand and raising it to her lips. "A chance to live in a real commune, where money means nothing, everyone's talents are utilised, and everyone's needs are catered for? It'll be hard for sure, especially with a new-born in tow, but it's literally the adventure I've been waiting for my whole life. And we'll be on the ground, literally witnessing the healing of the planet. What's not to like?"

"I'll take that as a yes, then." Davis rolled onto his back and let one arm fall to the side of the bed, where Jasper lay, quietly dozing with one eye open. "I'm glad we took Jasper," he said, as he gently massaged the animal's ear. "He cements our family, somehow."

"Yes, he does, and this little creature will cement it even more." She gently patted her belly, reinforcing the huge change to their lives that lay just inside the abdominal wall. "We're going to have to come up with a name soon, you know. We can't keep on calling her 'The Creature'."

"I know, but right now we've got other things to be thinking about. I'm sure a name will suggest itself eventually."

"What time's the transport coming?"

"Around eleven."

"Good… that'll give us a chance to say goodbye to the old place properly." She sighed. "Our first home together. It'll be sad to leave, don't you think."

"Yes, yes I do."

"What'll happen to it, do you suppose? Once we're gone? It seems a criminal waste to just leave it to rot."

"I know, but with everyone gone, what alternative is there? It'll fall into disrepair, then be reclaimed by nature. Or at least, that's what everyone is hoping will happen. If it doesn't then the whole scheme is totally flawed. Still, at the very least, it means we'll have got rid of the worst of humanity."

Lu sat up and glared at him. "Not Maria and Kieran…"

"No, not Maria and Kieran, or many others like them, but you know what I mean."

"And what if some of the worst of humanity has elected to stay behind?"

Davis fell silent. The prospect had honestly never occurred to him.

"You're right, Lu," he said, finally, anxiety tightening his throat. "What if they try to join our community? Take our food, our resources? What if…"

She put her finger to his lips. "I'm just winding you up… there isn't a chance in Hell that people like that would stay behind. Do you honestly think they'd prefer the hard graft of the settlements to the ease of the Exo? It isn't going to happen; of that you may be absolutely certain. Now come on, let's try and sleep. Tomorrow's going to be one hell of a day."

Turning over, she pulled the duvet tight about her neck, and within minutes was snoring softly. Davis, on the other hand, lay in a low-level panic, unsettling thoughts running roughshod through his hyperactive mind.

FOR AS LONG AS Maria could remember, the huge, gleaming latticework of metal tubes had been an increasingly dominant feature of the sky above her. Positioned, for the most part, above the clouds, it disappeared completely on dull, rainy days, while the long, hot summer revealed the Exo in all its futuristic glory. The bright, windy days were what she liked the most, though, and she would spend hours on her back on the parched lawn, watching the fluffy cumulonimbus scudding along below the shining structure.

It was with an air of unreality, therefore, that she closed the door of the house she had called home for her entire married life, clasped Kieran's hand tight in her own, and stepped into the transport.

The driverless vehicle made three more stops before finally making its approach to the entry point. One couple – comprising two of the blondest young men Maria had ever seen – and two families, the first with a single child, the second with two. There was to be a strict one child policy within the Exo – with an exception for those whose family already exceeded that number prior to entry – so Maria knew that once she had delivered little Humphrey, there could be no more children until they were able to return to the surface – and the likelihood of that happening within her child-bearing lifetime was effectively zero.

So it was with more than a twinge of melancholy that she regarded the larger of the two families.

"How old?" she enquired, with a wistful smile.

"Josh is two, and Jemima five," the woman answered. "When's yours due?"

"Due date is still a couple of weeks away, but I've been getting some cramps these last couple of days, so I'm sure he's gonna surprise us and come along early."

"Braxton Hicks, I had them for quite a while. I shouldn't set too much store by them. Still, if he's getting ready to pop, at least you shouldn't need to be induced. Joshy was two weeks late... a bit of a nightmare, if I'm honest."

"But at least you already have the two, so won't fall foul of the single child regulations."

"No, and some friends of ours who went up a couple of days ago have got four. I just hope they've got decent size accommodation, or they're really going to be on top of each other."

"Yes," said Maria, with a forced laugh.

The rest of the journey passed in silence, save from the chatter of the children, and the heavy beating of her heart.

ENTRY to the Exo was via elevators built into the massive legs that supported the structure. The closest to Norwich was situated just outside Thetford, a position that was deemed to be safe from the rising seawater which had already taken most of the Fens and drowned the seaside towns of the Norfolk coast. There *were* legs that rose from the sea, of course, like massive versions of the now defunct oil rigs, but these, for obvious reasons, were merely supports, and had no internal access.

As they approached the Thetford entry point, they could see it was surrounded by a solid perimeter wall, the only visible opening being a checkpoint alongside a neat little cabin where the guards could shelter from the elements, and where the necessary admin could be carried out. It reminded Maria of a military base, which to all intents and purposes it was. The door of the transport slid open, and the guardsman on duty beckoned for them to get out – which they did – whereupon the vehicle moved away into the compound.

"Don't we need to unload our stuff?" Kieran asked, too late.

"You'll be reunited with your belongings inside your living quarters. Now step along please, sir… you're holding everyone up."

Once inside the cabin, the guardsman pointed all but Kieran toward an upholstered wooden bench that ran the length of the wall opposite an office counter. To Kieran he said, "Step up to the desk, please, sir. Feet behind the red line."

Kieran did as he was told, remaining as still as possible while an iris scanner moved across his eyeline, right to left.

"Kieran Cooper, DOB 7th November 2061. Data analyst. Medical history unremarkable. Criminal Record clear. Redeployed to the Souleimon Systems Corporation. Billet for two persons and a child assigned in Norfolk Sector, Unit 36. Is this all correct, sir?"

Kieran checked the information on a screen set into the counter. Social Security number, National Insurance details, date of his marriage to Maria, everything was there. "Yes," he croaked. "That's me. All of that is me."

"And which of these children is yours, Mr Cooper?"

Maria coughed and pointedly stroked her stomach.

"Aaah… I see. That all seems to be in order, sir." The guard indicated a shallow, edged indentation in the counter roughly the shape of a human hand. "Can you place your hand into the frame, sir? Palm down, and with the centre of your wrist above the red dot." Kieran did as instructed, a clamp rising from the side of the frame and locking his hand firmly into place, making further movement impossible. "Just a scratch, sir…"

Kieran felt a sharp pinprick and a sensation like his wrist had been flicked with a rubber band. Immediately the clamp retracted, and he withdrew his hand. There was nothing to see.

"Welcome to Exo, Mr Cooper. A wave of your hand will grant access to all but the most restricted areas. Next please."

Gazing in disbelief at the unblemished skin where the nanochip had been implanted, he returned to his seat as Maria moved to take his place. From this moment on, every second of their life would be scrutinised and recorded. The slightest rise in temperature, heartbeat, blood flow, and the monitoring computers would be informed. Crime, sickness, antisocial behaviour, all would be flagged instantly. The authorities had left nothing to chance. Exo would indeed be the utopia it promised to be, but only because every minute detail of their lives would be dissected and analysed. And anything that deviated from the norm would be dealt with. Immediately.

And Kieran was to be part of that process. That was his job, and he wasn't sure whether to feel reassured or apprehensive.

Once the little party had been checked and chipped, they were ushered out to a waiting buggy, which carried them the short journey to the entrance. Due to its colossal size, the leg had been visible from some distance, but only now did they appreciate the true enormity of the thing. It was huge beyond imagining.

Maria gasped, causing Jemima to jump in alarm. Instinctively she moved to reassure the girl, taking her hand and forcing the broadest of smiles. "What an adventure, hey? I'll bet you love adventures, don't you? I know I did, when I was your age."

Jemima pulled away and hid her face in her mother's lap.

"I don't think she liked being chipped," said her mother, stroking the little girl's hair while cradling Josh in her other arm. "It's all a bit over-whelming for her."

"For me too," said Maria, looking up to where the sheer wall of the support leg finally joined with the Exo above. Kieran put his arm around her shoulders.

"No turning back," he said.

"No turning back," she echoed, but she could sense the unease in his voice. "No turning back…"

"How long does it take?" one of the blonde young men asked as they were ushered into the elevator compartment. The answer came from unseen speakers buried somewhere within the walls.

"We'll be rising a little over 13 miles at a speed of just under 30 miles an hour. Therefore, the journey will take approximately half an hour. A short film about life in the Exo will be played throughout to distract you from whatever anxiety you may be experiencing. I hope you will find it educational and informative. If you have any further questions, don't hesitate to ask. Now please, take your seats and enjoy the ride. You will find snacks and drinks within the armrests, and there is a lavatory situated to the right of the entrance door, should you require it. Have a pleasant trip, and on behalf of the Souleimon Systems Corporation, allow me to be the first to welcome you all to Exo, and to thank you for your sacrifice."

With the slightest of shudders, the elevator began to rise. Kieran reached across and took Maria's hand. "You know, I've been so focused on this as the beginning of a new life, I never thought of it as making a sacrifice... but I guess it is. Sacrificing our old way of life to save the planet. Quite a responsibility."

Maria laid his hand upon her belly. "Responsibility... yes. And the beginning of a new life in every sense. I just hope we've done the right thing."

Lu, Davis and Jasper arrived at the Elveden settlement just after lunch, and once they'd cleared the gatehouse checks, were taken to the chalet that was to be their new home. Lucinda stepped out of the transport and breathed deeply, the pine-infused air sparking a feeling of health and wellbeing that made her entire body shudder, as though she were shaking off her previous life like a worn-out cardigan. The Creature kicked in acknowledgement, and she reflexively rubbed her bump.

"You'll forgive me if I don't carry you over the threshold," Davis said, "but you know what my back's like..."

"I won't take it personally, you pathetic old sod. How on earth did I get saddled with such a decrepit old duffer, hey?" And with a smile that would have lit up the doorway to Hell itself, she turned the handle and entered the cabin.

Neat and well appointed, though lacking the little touches that would make it their own, the accommodation was more than they had hoped for. The couple stood in the centre of the living area and sighed with relief, while Jasper snuffled around every corner of the space, tail wagging furiously.

"It's going to be alright, isn't it?" Davis said, clutching her hands for reassurance.

"Yes, I think it'll do fine. Come on, let's take a leaf out of Jasper's book, and explore before we unpack. That way we can keep the excitement of this moment going a little longer… There's time enough to settle in and make it homely… we've got the rest of our lives."

"But can we at least think about what we need to do to prepare for the Creature's arrival… it could be any day now…"

"Later! Trust me, there's time. I swear you'd expire if you had nothing to worry about. Let's just enjoy the adventure, hey? I promise you; it's going to be an awesome ride!"

And with Jasper running in front of her, she walked back through the open door and out into the cool of the forest path. Davis watched them for a moment and then, carefully fastening the door behind him, resignedly followed the fast-disappearing pair as they joyfully weaved their way between the pools of leaf-dappled sunlight.

THE ASCENT WAS ABOUT HALF-WAY through when the awful, cramping pain doubled Maria over, and a warm wetness soaked through her dress and dripped from the edge of her seat onto the floor.

"Oh my God!" she cried, twisting Kieran's hand so hard he feared she would snap his wrist. "I think it's coming… Oh God! Oh God!"

Desperately, Kieran's eyes searched the gleaming walls for a panic button but could see nothing that might help. While the other mothers in the elevator sprang into action, reassuring her and encouraging her to breathe through the contractions, the calming voice of the Corporation echoed from the hidden speakers.

"Please do not be alarmed. The emergency has been logged and the necessary authorities notified. The situation will be constantly monitored for the rest of the journey, and this elevator will be met by a medical team on arrival. The casualty will be transferred to the Medi-lab immediately, and all will be well. There is no cause for alarm. For your own safety we would request that you please return to your seats. Thank you."

"I'm not a fucking casualty.... I'm in labour! Can't your monitors see that, you half-assed piece of AI shit?"

"Don't upset them," said Kieran, rubbing life back into his hand, "they're doing what they can."

"Don't upset them? We've got... what? Fifteen minutes still to go before we reach the top? And what if there's a complication? Like he's got the cord round his neck or something? How am I going to cope with that?" Wrenching her eyes from his, Maria howled into the echoing chamber of the ever-rising travel compartment. "How am I going to cope with that, hey? Tell me that, you AI bastard!"

The voice from the speakers replied instantly.

"There is no need to resort to anger and insulting behaviour, Mrs Cooper. We are monitoring your vital signs and see no reason to expect your demise before your arrival into the Exo. Neither would we expect your baby to be delivered during the remaining duration of your ascent. From the data we are receiving, we estimate that you are currently no more than four centimetres dilated, so although you have entered the active phase of labour, there is some considerable way to go before the foetus fully enters the birth canal. Childbirth is a natural occurrence, and we are perfectly equipped to deal with it in our Medi-labs. Please try to regulate your breathing and keep your stress levels at a minimum. All will be well."

Maria gazed into the eyes of Josh and Jemima's mother, who had helped her get into a position on the floor of the compartment where she felt most comfortable and was gently rubbing the small of her back. "Thank you," she said, between breaths. "Thank goodness you were here. Bloody robots don't know shit."

❧

Lu and Davis spent the remains of the day unpacking and squirrelling things away into various cupboards before joining the rest of the community in one of the communal eating areas for a welcome meal. Originally a pizza restaurant, the space had enough seating for about 200 people and had a fully equipped kitchen, all more than adequate for the amount of Sotte settlers currently on site, many of whom had chosen to cater for themselves at home.

"All we ask," said Dominic, who had introduced himself as one of the team of 'welcomers' tasked with ensuring that all newcomers found their feet as quickly as possible, and who now shared their table, "is that you notify us no less than two hours before mealtimes whether or not you would like to join us. You'll appreciate that we need to keep waste to a minimum."

"Absolutely," Davis replied, "it's got to be a lean operation. I can see that. How many will the settlement hold, once everyone's on board?"

"We're expecting around two thousand, give or take. Some will change their minds at the last minute, but that works both ways. The Exo may sound like Elysium, but this is where heaven truly lies, don't you think? We're incredibly fortunate… we've got a second chance at Eden, and this time we won't balls it up."

"And the different Sotte settlements… is there any communication between them?"

"At the moment, yes, and it's up to us to make sure that continues. As challenges emerge – and they will – we can learn from each other as to how best to deal with them. No point in endlessly reinventing the wheel." Dominic took a long draught of orange juice. "Oranges, now… who'd have thought we'd ever be able to grow them successfully in Norfolk, eh? Don't tell anyone I said this, but climate change does have a couple of advantages, eh?"

The meal passed off in good humour – then, after a few more introductions, the couple made their farewells and retreated to their chalet. Once he'd let Jasper out the back, Davis slumped onto the sofa, while Lu visited the bathroom, not for the first time that evening.

"The Creature standing on your bladder again?"

"Yep. I'm sure she's going to be a contortionist, the way she squirms around in there."

The toilet flushed, and Lu joined him on the sofa. Automatically, he rested his hand on her abdomen. "Not sure there'll be much call for a contortionist, Lu. Not with the way things are."

"Rubbish. People will always need entertainment. That's a given. Anyway, it's not for us to assign roles for her. I had enough of that pressure from my own parents. She will be what she wants to be."

"I can't argue with that. What's the matter?"

Lucinda had pushed his hand away and doubled over, fiercely rubbing her belly.

"Ooooh, that was a sharp one. I didn't like that at all. Get me a cold towel, will you, there's a love?"

"Sure… anything else I can do?" Davis ran to the bathroom. His heart had begun to race.

"Just the towel… it'll pass, I'm sure. A twinge to remind me she's getting ready, that's all."

Davis was back almost before she had finished speaking, the towel dripping across the parquet floor. "Where do you want it?"

"Just wipe my face, then put it across my lower back. Then boil a kettle. My grandma swore by alternating hot and cold."

"Should I fetch someone?" Davis found he was struggling with the kettle. He couldn't work out how to lift the lid, so poured cold water down the spout, splashing himself and the work surfaces in the process.

"No, it'll go off soon. Just keep passing me the towels, hot then cold. Once it's over, we can go to bed. It's been quite a day."

THE MEDI-LAB SHONE like burnished steel, everything new and sterile, with not so much as a stray cable to interrupt the smooth, regimented lines of the pristine environment. In the bay nearest the entrance door lay Maria, a heavily swaddled Humphrey at her breast, while Kieran sat, whispering softly at her side.

"We can't keep calling him Humphrey, you know. I mean, it was fine when he was Humph the Bump, but now he's a real little person, he needs a proper name."

"I know. I've been thinking about nothing else since he arrived. And by the way, this is the weirdest feeling. Weird yet wonderful, you know?"

"Yes, I do, but not in the way you mean. He's the most wonderful gift, isn't he? Maybe we should find a name that means 'gift'… What do you think?"

"Neo."

"Does that mean gift?"

"I think so… I remember it from when my aunt was talking about baby names. In some language or other it means gift… but it also means new, and what could be more apt? A new baby for a new life. And a gift. Just about perfect, don't you think?"

And Neo, detaching from the nipple, squeaked as though to register assent.

"That's that, then. Here's to Neo… a new life in a new world." And Kieran raised an imaginary glass to his sole heir, who rummaged around at his mother's breast until he found the nipple and latched on once again.

A nurse in an immaculate uniform bearing the logo of the Souleimon Systems Corporation approached from a sliding door to the left.

"Mr Cooper? If you'll come with me, it is time for your procedure."

Kieran swallowed hard. They had both known the sacrifices that must be made to protect the planet, but this was perhaps the hardest to accept. Bending over to kiss Maria and little Neo, he took a deep breath and followed the nurse back through the sliding door.

~

If Lucinda thought she could achieve a restful night, she was mistaken. After an initial subsiding of the crippling pains, they woke her again in the early hours, this time with a far greater degree of urgency.

"Shit, shit, shit, shit, SHIT!" she murmured, as she fought to breathe through the contractions. Davis was out of bed and into his dressing gown in seconds, while Jasper took his place alongside Lucinda, desperately licking her hands as though by doing so he could take away her pain.

"I'm going for help," Davis said, in a voice that brooked no argument. "I'll only be gone maybe ten minutes, are you going to be okay for that long?"

"Yeah, I'll be fine," she replied, letting the air escape in long, hissing breaths through her teeth. "Just get back as quick as you can. Oooh shiiiit…"

"Davis made for the door, but she called him back. "And take the dog with you… I know he means well but coating me with doggy spit really isn't helpful or hygienic. Oooh…"

Dragging Jasper away, Davis left the chalet and ran for the medical centre, where a sign on the door pointed to an out-of-hours emergency intercom. After several minutes, a bleary female voice answered, enquiring for the nature of the emergency.

"My wife… my wife… I think the baby's on its way… and I don't know what to do!"

"Which chalet are you in?"

For a moment his mind went blank. Which chalet? Oh, for God's sake, why couldn't he remember? After stuttering like a fool for far too long, it came to him, both the zone and number.

"That's fine, sir… just return to your wife and help her into whichever position is most comfortable for her. If she wants to pace around, that's fine. If she wants to go down onto all fours that's fine too. And help her with the breathing exercises you practiced during the ante-natal classes. I'll be there as fast as I can."

Davis felt the panic rising and yelled desperately into the microphone. "I didn't attend the classes… I don't know what to do! Oh God, I don't know what to do!"

"Then be guided by your wife. Just get back to her and I'll be there as soon as I can."

The intercom went dead. Davis took to his heels and sped back along the path, with Jasper lolloping alongside, barking for all he was worth.

～

THE SOUND REACHED him before he had a chance to open the door, stopping him in his tracks. Jasper pawed at the door anxiously, as the sound of the baby's cry drifted through the part-open skylight and away into the night sky. Davis stood immobile, hardly able to process what he was hearing, until the sound of footsteps on the path behind brought him back to reality.

"Sounds like we've missed the main event," said a cheery voice that he recognised from the intercom. "We'd better go in and help her clean up. Sounds like she didn't need us after all. Just grab the dog, will you? He'll be attracted by the smell of the blood and will only get in the way." Pushing past the bewildered Davis, she opened the door and entered the chalet.

By the time Davis had tied Jasper up outside and mastered his adrenaline levels sufficiently to follow her in, the nurse had cut the cord, cleaned and wrapped the baby, and was settling Lucinda into bed with the baby at her breast.

"Textbook birth," she said, grinning widely. Then, to Davis, "The floor's a bit messy… if you could find a mop that'd be really helpful."

"But…"

"Come and see her first," Lu said, her cheeks alive with roses, extending her free hand toward him. He took it, and sat on the bed, while the nurse busied herself in the background.

The babe, gently suckling and making adorable snuffling noises as she did so, captivated his heart in a way he couldn't have imagined. Lu and the baby, a perfect picture, a perfect beginning to their new life.

"What are you going to call her?" asked the nurse. "I'm just filling in my report and there's a space on the form for a name. Of course, if you haven't decided yet…"

Lucinda looked at Davis, who squeezed her hand, and an unspoken thought passed between them.

"Hope," she whispered, looking down at the little wrinkled nose just above her nipple. "Her name is Hope."

KB Willson is a British author currently living beside the sea in Dorset with his miniature dachshund dog, who likes to sit on his lap while he is writing. His SF story Wheat was published in the NewCon Press anthology Looking Landwards (2013); his horror short Father's Day in the Little Red Writers collection Dorset Shorts (2019); and September 2021 saw his piece of horror flash – Oubliette – published online by Timber Ghost Press. His Gothic Horror piece Relke of the Russet Hair was published at Christmas 2022 in Bleak Midwinter: The Darkest Night by Quill & Crow Publishing, and November 2023 saw the publication of Disconnected in the SF anthology Dark Horses from The Slab Press. In 2024 his dark fantasy story The Melusine Pact will appear in a forthcoming issue of ParSec magazine.

Website: https://www.kbwillson.com
X: https://www.twitter.com/kbwillsonauthor
Facebook: https://www.facebook.com/100087891821642
Blog: https://kbwillson.blogspot.co.uk

IF-WORLD

BY MIKE JACK STOUMBOS

Malcolm Hess scowled at the single droplet on the feed-tube coupling. A second one fell from his brow to match it.

"Sweat," he muttered. "Good ol' sweat." He assumed he was quoting something, but he couldn't remember what. Without looking up from his work, Malcolm called out to his partner, "Hey, Chey—You suppose there's a setting for *sweat* in IF?"

From somewhere unseen, a woman's voice shouted back, "Effin'-A! They got settings for everything!" This last was punctuated by a grunt. Malcolm imagined she was working upside-down or on her back. "Shit, I-D-K," she relented, her voice taking on a metallic quality as it bounced through ducts. "I've logged like a hundred hours in IF. Hess, you'd know more about the settings."

Malcolm silently agreed. He had passed the hundred-hour mark long ago, and at least two thirds of his log-time had been spent programming R-Dub Access so that users could easily interface with their profiles from the real world—not that many needed to anymore.

He imagined Chey would have spent most of her time on the recreational end or even in new user tutorials. As adept as Chey was on the hardware side, she probably couldn't program the broad side of a barn in IF-World without the help of a virtual bot.

Fortunately, programming wasn't her job. Glove Enterprises and IF-World legal had entrusted Cheyenne "Chey" Dowell to take care of mechanical maintenance while Malcolm Hess handled the software part. Like every other team sent to the coffins, they were "one mech and one tech," as their boss liked to say.

Malcolm ran one finger along the current coffin's control panel while his device continued its scan. A constant clock said the user within had been under for two weeks, uninterrupted. There was no way to tell the exact total without knowing their password and PIN, but Malcolm knew without asking that this character, like everyone else in the building, was a perma.

He shook his head roughly, trying to physically buck the prickly under-skin sensation. He knew you could still get the willies in IF, even if they hadn't been programmed.

A beep from his Handy said the scan had concluded, and a quick glance assured him everything was in-the-blue. *In-the-green* wasn't good enough for long-term sustainability. He pulled the sensor prongs from the feed-tube, put a confirmation thumb-print on the coffin's panel, and moved on to the next one.

The touch-screen on his Handy let him know he'd logged twenty-three coffins on this floor so far. He flicked a finger across the screen to check how many floors and how many coffins remained. *S-Tanks®*, he corrected himself—if you don't wanna get freaked out by perma-facing, don't call the sustainability tanks *coffins*. But that's what everyone else called them.

The task was mindless enough that it afforded Malcolm a lot of time to muse. There was only one new installation task, and then the rest of his job was just making sure the automated systems continued to function smoothly. He hadn't encountered a single glitch in five days, and that one wasn't so much a glitch as an idiot who attempted to lie face-down in the coffin and—surprise, surprise—kept getting jolted awake due to real-world discomfort.

Real-World was also a funny concept, like *under-skin*, or *coffin*. At what point do you redefine what you mean by *real* anyway? Probably about the time you start abbreviating it to *R-Dub*.

Malcolm stood at the next coffin's panel, muttering, "Now serving number twenty-four…" He activated the touchscreen, put in his employee ID, bypassed the *friendly-bot* greeting, and pulled up Settings. He fished into the bag on his hip and drew out a tiny LinkDrive, hardly the size of his smallest fingernail. It slid smoothly into the leftmost slot of the panel and began to auto-install.

It was supposed to be the last safety installation anyone would ever need—and this time Malcolm believed it. As much as he and others had tried to question the nature of part-time, full-time, and even perma-facing, even the naysayers had to admit that with the final Link upload, there would be no reason for a physical programmer or technician to touch the coffins again. The Gloves® really had thought of everything.

While the installation ran, Malcolm cleared his Handy's calibrator and plugged it into the tank so it could process ideal settings for each of the required sustainability features. Of course, they'd already been set, but he had to run confirmation. For every coffin, checked air, temperature, pressure, heart-rate, and synthetic hormones. Then, he'd scan and record power, waste extraction, and feed-tube flow rates. Here or there, a user would change the temp settings by a half a degree or so, and the feed-tubes auto-adjusted rates according to the body-mass calculators—which had been calibrated for each user months in advance. The only real difference in most of the settings was the amount of active and reserve memory each user had access to, and that wasn't Malcolm's job to check. Everyone had to monitor their own spending habits.

Once again, everything was in-the-blue.

Malcolm gave his thumbprint authorization again and straightened to move to the next coffin. But he lingered when he saw the peaceful face inside. The visor was over her eyes, and the corners of her mouth drew up in a contented smile. Malcolm moved on quickly, so he wouldn't wonder about the woman's life before IF. Too late.

"Hey, Chey?"

"Yeah, what's up?" Chey's voice clanged through a nearby floor vent. It sounded like she was gripping a wrench with her teeth.

"You know anyone in this batch?"

"Um…" She didn't respond for a long time, then eventually, "No. Why you ask?"

"Just wondering."

"You're always just wondering!" Chay suddenly ducked out from the open crawlway, covered in the dust and grease that no amount of tech could remove from maintenance access tunnels. Her tool-belt was stocked with the most efficient tech available, and a programmed tray wheeled behind her heels. She was about a head shorter than Malcolm, had a wiry physique, with bony shoulders and bad posture. Even with so many pristine machines around her, Chey looked like an old school auto mechanic, before those jobs had also been given to robots.

She wiped her dirty hands on a single-use rag, then tossed the rag over her shoulder for the robot tray to pick up and purify. Her hands went to her hair, pulling any loose strands into her dark ponytail. "Hey, I got one."

"One what?"

"A *wondering*, dumbass." Chey sat down on the stool offered by the mechanical tray and extracted a water bottle. She took a long drink, and let Malcolm wait. "Mmm! So here's this thing flashed up on the news. It was like about this southern guy, from like Alabama, I think. Said he arranged his IF-World so he could not be contacted or even viewed by anyone wasn't his race. Like someone tried to say—uh—like *make a case* on interaction discrimination or some shit, and then some other guys were like *We don't wanna contact him anyway*." Chey laughed. "I wouldn't either. But y'see, it's a two-way street. They can't see him; he can't see them, so why make everyone's lives suck by trying to put 'em together when they can just like avoid in peace?"

Malcolm waited again while she finished the bottle, then asked, "So what's the wondering?"

Spreading her arms out wide, as if inviting anyone to chime in, Chey said, "Is that like progress—or the opposite? Man, is IF-World curing discrimination or making it worse?" Chey fixed Malcolm with a cocked head and pirate smile.

"Imagine all people sharing all IF-World," Malcolm said, tweaking a lyric he thought he'd heard on a streamer service.

Chey stood. "Hey, I'm done on this floor. Gonna go smoke. You ready to move up soon?"

"Yeah, I got less than ten."

"Cool."

As he listened her workboots clomping across the sterile floor, Malcolm tried to keep the comment in but failed. "Y'know in IF-World, those things won't kill you." Malcolm didn't look, but he imagined she'd flipped him off on her way out.

In IF-World, you could edit out other people's gestures so you wouldn't have to see them. And in an S-Tank®, if you had enough capital, you could get your hormone system to wean you off nicotine, supposedly withdrawal-free. Malcolm wasn't a betting man, but he'd lay a week's wages that's why Chey was still working in the *real world* when everyone else was in IF.

~

THE WELCOME BANNER blinked in front of him. Despite being offensively bright, it didn't hurt his eyes—they weren't his *real* eyes after all. Hurt or no, the flashing annoyed him, and every time he entered the InterFace World, he told himself he'd remove the WELCOME. Every time, he forgot by the end of the session.

It was easy to forget things in IF-World, and that's why there was a quick-access on-screen sticky-note, where you could write your objectives for the day or jot a contact reminder for that cute user or projie you hooked. Malcolm Hess never used the sticky-note. No matter how many sights, sounds, and other electronic signals he encountered, he was determined not to need a sticky-note to remember where he was going.

While his IF-House settled around him, Malcolm saw dozens of notifications flash—most of which were ads for popularity contests, solo or group games, and propositions for sex—which was often a part of the contests and games in IF. Three messages in the barrage were chiming IMPORTANT in the sender's voice, one of which was his mother's.

"Yeah, Control-Q," Malcolm told the message, and it popped into the first and only slot in his viewing queue. He bid "Shut up!" to the other ads and waved them into oblivion. He wiped clean the unimportant notifications and filed the non-ad messages so that only the other two IMPORTANT pieces remained. One was an overly exuberant friend query from someone he might have known in high school. The other—he should have recognized from color scheme—was from his boss. It was an audio/video message with preview capabilities, so even before it opened, Malcolm could see Colin's face. The faint voice sounded less familiar, like it was filtered through a new accent.

Malcolm reached forward and touched the floating message bubble that sounded like a constipated Englishman. The projection wobbled against his finger, rippled like a slow-motion deflating balloon, and the image grew to occupy most of his vision. The chiseled, corporate face stayed frozen until it had properly enlarged. The sparkling, toothy grin of the recorded avatar exclaimed, "Greetings, Malcolm!" in the same bizarre accent.

"Colin, you smug son-of-a-bitch, you upgraded your voice…" Malcolm resolved to tell Colin in-person—or at least in-face—how pretentious it sounded, when he got the chance. The sticky-note jumped into view to assist, and he waved it away.

The animated Colin continued, "I trust all is well in R-Dub! Well, things are SUPER! here in IF!, and we can't wait for you to join us!" The subtitled text was lined with gaudy puffed-up exclamation points, every tenth or so looked more phallic than the usual punctuation. "But we are *so grateful* for all of your hard work to prepare this place for TOTAL PERMA! Please post your report on today's *Stank* checks! Here's how…"

And the animated Colin Sarsaparilla, tertiary CEO of Glove® Sustainability and the public coordinator for the S-Tank® Initiative, instructed Malcolm how to file his report—this time, in Colin's *original* accent. Malcolm listened, but nothing about this part of the message had changed since yesterday, apart from the subtly pornographic punctuation.

Colin's upgraded accent kicked back in for a post-script. "As soon as you are finished securing your region, you will be able to access your *ultra-premium perma start-up package*!, with more blocks than ninety-five percent of users! And once you're here with us—YAY!—You can come and —" A brief shimmer in the footage, evidence of a cut-in. "—lift a glass of Virtu-Vodka! Ideal chemicals, no hangover!" Shimmer again. "We'll SEE *YOU THEN!!!*"

Malcolm shook his head at the fanfare that followed, but he wore a smirk. Colin was always willing to cut in a new advertising gig for a bit of extra cred, no matter how tacky. That's how you become third in line to the biggest firm in IF-World.

The message closed itself, leaving Malcolm in silence in his basic IF-

House. He hadn't customized anything yet, so it was in factory default stage. Cylindrical room with a front door, the standard two loveseats facing the primary viewer (still called a TV), one bookshelf stocked with all of the free default options. On his left, door to the bedroom; on his right, a door to the records room. Kitchens, dining rooms, billiard rooms, dance clubs, pools, roller-coasters—these were all extra add-ons, each of which might take up any number of blocks depending on how elaborate your build was and how much memory the servers would need to make you feel like you were a part of them. Most of the richest users had in-home battlefields and what the programmers called "naughty nests," the two most purchased top-shelf upgrades.

Malcolm had to again remind himself that soon *he* would be eligible for that kind of mem-spending. Again the sticky-note app popped into view.

"Mom," he told the interface, and the dim icon in the lower corner bobbed up in front of him. The default settings had everything growing or shifting or fading into view instead of just appearing—*just appearing* frightened people and reminded them they were in a computer.

This one was only a still image until he clicked it. After all, his mother was not a CEO and couldn't afford the moving, speaking previews.

He hesitated only a moment more and then reached out and poked her message bubble.

"Malcolm!" his mother practically screamed into the viewer. Her face was too close to the camera—*was it still a camera?* Never mind. "Malcolm, I've almost finished setting up my—"

Before Malcolm had managed to turn down the volume, an off-screen male voice said, "He can hear you, Dee—stop shouting."

"Oh, sorry," the recorded mother said much more quietly to her thankful son. "Anyway, Malcolm, honey, I have almost finished setting up my *IF-Home*, and—"

"Tell him to come by," called the off-screener again. Malcolm felt less thankful this time.

"I was just going to." She rolled her eyes at the mystery man. "Anyway! Malcolm, could you come over as soon as possible. I—um—I posted my —*address*, right?—You can just like *beam* over, right? And I—"

"Hey, introduce me, Dee."

"Oh, right, this is Herb," she said, and the corner of an older man's head poked into the frame. Very silver fox.

"Hey, sport!" he said before disappearing, leaving Malcolm to mouth *Sport?* to himself.

"Malcolm, when you get this, can you come over? I have a programming question." Then she whispered, "It's important," with an expression that said she was not only serious but embarrassed—or would be embarrassed if Malcolm didn't fix the problem before anyone else (probably Herb) found out.

Malcolm had stopped tracking her words while staring at her face and resisting the urge to Zoom in. She'd removed the wrinkles around her eyes but hadn't figured out how to get rid of the ones by her mouth. Her hair was red, like it had been when he was a kid, and—as far as he could tell—longer than when he had last seen her in the real world. Other than those minor touch-ups, his mother was still recognizably his mother and still needed more than the usual tech support from time to time.

Malcolm sighed. He had planned to visit the virtual shops that afternoon, to start figuring out exactly how to use the incoming extra memory package, possibly to order a bot or some other VI-assist. But he could put off shopping to help his sweet, access-impaired mother as soon as he submitted his work for the day.

While he filed his report, Malcolm trying to ignore—with increasing annoyance—how the sticky-note app kept popping into a corner of the screen.

Every day the reports got easier. He just had to review and approve the numbers: how many buildings he and Chey had completed, with how many floors, with how many vacant tanks, and how many technical difficulties. That one was easy: zero. Near the end of the form, he was asked to estimate many more days they would need to finish their region. The answer had recently dropped to single-digit figures, which reminded him of a slow-motion countdown to New Years.

When he commanded *Send*, an auto-reply from Colin Sarsparilla offered him not the usual thumbs-up but an open palm. If not for the huge smile on Colin's digitally white teeth, Malcolm might have assumed it was the whatever-you-call-the-Nazi-gesture rather than a high-five.

Malcolm raised his own right arm and received a hardy clap from the recorded avatar, which registered both audibly and tactilely.

The idea of a pre-recorded high-five was so childish, Malcolm had to laugh. This was one upgrade he might even buy for himself, when he got around to it.

ALL NEIGHBORHOOD MAPS started as suburban cul-de-sacs with miniature hut icons. They were populated by random users who spoke at least one of your listed languages and had at least 70% ideological compatibility.

Good data collection made good neighbors, especially in a universe where two of your neighbors might not even be able to see each other.

You could narrow the list even more by programming age ranges, interest types, gender, and race. The default for unmarried users over eighteen was to hide family units with minors, and vice versa. Malcolm considered formally blocking children—most non-parent adults did.

He input his mother's address, and scrolled to her cul-de-sac, which was almost indistinguishable from his own when viewed from above like a delivery drone. He clicked on her glowing hut, and it drew toward him, enlarging quickly at first but slowing down until it stopped about five paces away. They had run focus groups of millions of users to determine what would freak people out by going too fast or bore them by going too slow. It did help that all vertigo in IF was mental, not visceral.

If Malcolm didn't like it, he could adjust settings. Defaults were just a best guess.

Malcolm walked to the door labeled Deidre Hess and knocked. It opened on its own, which meant she had an open-door policy to users with Malcolm's labels—a policy Malcolm hoped to revise as soon as he entered.

"Jesus Christ, mom!" Malcolm abruptly turned away from the shockingly realistic digital image of the two parties in his mother's front room.

She exclaimed, "Oh my!" followed by a frantic curse or two. "Malcolm—knock next time!"

Facing the front door and considering walking right through it again, he said, "I knocked *this* time."

"Oh, that's right," came a man's voice—Herb.

Getting dressed and minimizing a bed was a much faster process in IF, for, in a moment, Deidre Hess was right behind Malcolm with a hand on his shoulder. "I'm sorry, honey!" she said quietly. She hadn't quite caught her breath, but at least her hands were dry. Selecting clothes in IF guaranteed that you were dry, no matter how recently you'd gotten out of the shower or the pool or—

"So!" Malcolm cleared his throat. "Clearly some programming help is needed." He slowly turned, finding his mother—blonde hair this time—in a completely opaque pink robe. Herb on the other hand had missed this basic courtesy. "Herb, put something on!"

Herb's laugh sounded a little too friendly. "Sorry, sport. I thought unknown users were censored."

"Not in private homes." Malcolm waved both hands at his mother's new friend, willing him to cover up.

Herb pointed in the air at his personal selection screen, invisible to Malcolm, and shorts appeared. "Sorry, I guess I got used to the clothing-optional function. I have to say, it feels good to be proud of your body."

Even from a brief glance, Malcolm imagined a lot of pride, money, and mem went into that body. The silver fox could have been an eighty-year-old great-grandfather who would have needed pills in R-Dub, or he could have been a trust-fundee in his twenties.

Luckily, Herb could take a hint. "Hey, Dee, I'm going to walk the grounds. Give you some time with your son. Sorry again for the first impression," he told Malcolm. "Let's—uh—let's get together for a barbecue once you're settled in." Herb strode away, past where the bed had been and out toward the pastures.

Malcolm blinked and confirmed that his mother's *indoor* was programmed to appear outdoors, complete with acres of fields and NPC horses. A short distance beyond the edge of the usual main room outline, she'd installed a garden with a stream that fed a waterfall, below which—according to a sign—rested a swimming pool. To the left and right the two standard doors to records and bedroom, where users *supposedly* hooked up, several bookshelves, and three other doors that Malcolm bother to scan.

Deidre Hess cleared her throat, drawing Malcolm's attention yet again. Now that he had a better chance to look at her, he could tell she was still upgrading. It wasn't just a few wrinkles or blonde hair. She had dropped what looked like thirty pounds and more than twenty years. Hell, she looked younger than Malcolm.

"Jesus Christ, mom," he repeated, this time as a groan.

Deidre spread her arms and looked down then back up. "Well, Herb likes skinny girls, and it's nice to feel young again."

"It's not nice to flash your son when you ask for his help."

"I'm sorry," she whispered, blushing in embarrassment and maybe a smidge of excitement. "I'm new at this."

"What, IF-World, or an open-door policy for naked strangers?"

"Herb is not a— Well, Malcolm Edward Hess!" she declared, regaining her bearings, and placing her fists on her hips. "*That* is uncalled for. I did not know when you would be coming, and this is my home. I'm sorry I didn't know how to program my door, but your walking in was an accident."

"Okay."

"I don't deserve this kind of sass from you." She started quivering as new emotions overwhelmed her face, apparently jockeying between enraged retaliation and blubbering confession. Instead, she went for the old standby. "I am an unmarried woman exploring a new world, full of possibilities."

"Okay," Malcolm repeated, and took Deidre's hands in his own to show he was sincere. She had said that before. She reprised the line a couple times a year since her divorce. But this time, it wasn't just a new stage of life following an unhappy marriage, but a *new life*, complete with a new body, a new home, a new world. Who wouldn't take the opportunity to explore?

The words were hard to force out, but he managed to tell her, "I'm glad that you are finding a life that makes you happy." Gritting his teeth a little less, Malcolm added, "It looks like a great space. It really does."

Deirdre smiled sheepishly, and she looked like his mother again. "Thank you."

"So—uh—" Malcolm removed his hands from hers and tried more fervently to move off the topic of his mother's sexual revolution. "I see you've got the pastures, and the garden."

"And the lagoon." Deidre pointed along the dirt path, obviously brightening. "It was a must-have once I set up the waterfall."

"What's behind door number three?" asked Malcolm.

"*A brand new car!*" his mother announced in a cartoony voice, then snorked at her joke. "Um—it's a flight simulator."

"Wow, like airplanes, or—"

"Um, no." Her eyes flitted away from his, nervously. "It's the new space program. With solo and interactive mode. Zero-grav settings."

Malcolm stood silent a moment, running estimations in his head. "How…" He looked at the other two doors. "Battlefield?" he asked, pointing to the fourth.

Deidre nodded. "Well, Herb said it was really in vogue for users of any age."

Malcolm looked at the final door, knowing the most popular high-mem upgrade. "No, you didn't."

"What?" She was genuinely incredulous.

Trying to avoid saying *naughty nest*, Malcolm skirted around the term, "Is it an *adult* recreation… spa?"

She slapped his arm. "It's a beach, Malcolm. I have beach-front property! Oh, Malcolm, it's *really* wonderful, so much better than—what do they call it? R-Dumb?"

"*R-Dub*, mom, like R-W for *Real-World*."

"So hard to keep track of. That's slang for you."

"Right." Malcolm touched his thumb to the tip of each finger in sequence—grounding, even if virtual—before initiating the part of the conversation that would ranked far more difficult than the privacy talk. "Mom, these are all temporary upgrades, right?"

"Well…" she trailed, confirming his concerns.

"Mom, you don't have the mem-space for this kind of thing." Aware of his own high-strung tone, Malcolm abruptly placed both hands on Deirdre's shoulders, which probably didn't help assure her but affirmed the eye contact. "Look, it might be awesome now, but it *will* be temporary. Either you choose to pull it down, or it'll phase out once you've exhausted your memory blocks." She opened her mouth, probably to say *Well* again, but Malcolm pressed on. "Once you've used your allotment, you'll be barred from spending until the mem-cells have been refreshed, possibly purged and rebooted. You'll have to go into basic mode, or sub-basic if you overdraft, which you're well on your way toward. You could be stuck there for years, or be booted out of IF, or—" He cut himself off before saying *overload* or *burnout*; that was what people like him guarded against.

After a deep breath, Malcolm slowly stressed, "This is a real-world issue, mom. The blocks of processors that run IF are real, and there is limited space per person, and the factories can't make and install them as quickly as we can use them." He tilted his head; a new angle often helped when dealing with cross-generational tech issues. "Does that make sense?"

"Well," she began, "I guess I *did* get a little carried away, but—"

"A little? Mom, between a beach, battlefield, spaceship, and horses—" Malcolm stopped abruptly and turned his gaze to the horses, happily playing out in the grass. "Mom, tell me those are NPCs."

Her small voice said, "I don't..."

His eyebrows shot up with enough force they could almost lift his feet from the digital floor. They were way past a slanted expression and informative lecture. "Mom, tell me you did not get actual AI programming for—what?—*six* animals. Tell me you went with NPC, and not AI!"

Her expression answered.

Malcolm released his grip and turned away again. The difference between the basic NPC creatures and Actual-Artificial-Intelligence storage was astronomical, almost incalculable.

This was *way* worse than what he had walked in on and exactly what all tutorials warned against. Overspending like an overnight lotto winner, burning through blocks, blocks that would be rotated out and reinstalled according to schedule and not user demand. No matter how good Inter-Facing tech got, Glove® could only shrink memory storage so far. The human brain and the human brain's whole human imagination was simply too big if left unchecked.

Malcolm's specializations only extended so far into the science of memory storage, but he knew what could happen—what always happened to people who bypassed allotments before the system caught and corrected. Downgrading to sub-basic mode or being sealed into solitary IF were best case scenarios or mental fragmenting when the machine started to stutter. Most people his age or older knew stutters as basic rez failures or momentary de-syncs from console gaming days, but perma-facing hooked directly into the subject's brain. A perma-facing user with their own thoughts, plus

AI growing at a growing rate in attached memory, past the limit of physical storage—all ingredients for worst-case scenario.

"Mom, you'll burn out by the end of the week like this, maybe even today." He sounded panicked. "You have to get rid of this shit immediately. How did you even— I mean, haven't you been getting warnings?"

"Oh, right, the light was flashing at me, and it was annoying, so I turned off the warning notifications," she informed him, as if it was as simple as hitting *No* when a solicitor called. "And, well, since you're listed as my legal IF-kin, I tagged you as a reference."

That would cut through some temporary red tape, long enough to make the purchase, maybe to delay being audited until it was too late. "Mom, why didn't you stop?" He knew it was a stupid question, even before she turned her head to stare wistfully out at her property, down the trail Herb had taken. "Mom, you need to get rid of it. All of it. And every second you waste—"

"But, Malcolm," Deidre said, full fervor in her eyes, "I don't want to get rid of it."

"You could end up with brain damage or live in sub-basic for months while you wait for new blocks. Is it worth it? Is it worth it to be on the arm of some rich guy who probably has his own?"

"He doesn't have horses," she began, then tried again with, "But it doesn't need to happen that way. I don't have to burn out." Deidre Hess widened her eyes and pursed her lips, hoping that Malcolm would take the hint and offer before she had to ask. Just as AI cost thousands of times more than NPCs, her son Malcolm would soon have thousands of times more memory than the standard startups.

Malcolm sighed and turned away from his mother. He considered dunking his head in the cool, running stream to keep from boiling over himself. Both rejection and ascent would feel like bile coming up his throat. "I won't get my U-P Startup for another few days."

Deirdre said nothing.

Malcolm sighed and refaced his mother, who stood hugging her elbows. "But I can give you access to some of my base blocks tonight. Later we can talk about how to set up a sharing system." Before Deidre could look too relieved and go for a hug, Malcolm held up a hand. "On two conditions—"

"I lock my door when I have a gentleman over," she guessed.

"Alright, three conditions. Yes, that. And you need to pick one at a time: beach, the spaceships, or battlefield—not all three. And finally, no AI."

"But, Malcolm—"

"I'm serious. You think they were a lot of memory when you bought them. The toll racks up every day as they live and learn. And we can't afford that." Honestly, Malcolm didn't know how much they could collectively afford, but he didn't want to chance it or to humor this habit.

"Okay."

"Okay. Let's pare down together, and then once I'm back in R-Dub, I'll sign to move the memory blocks." The sticky-note appeared, and Malcolm swatted it away.

"Okay," Deirdre said again, determined not to look back at the horses, determined not to cry. After all, you could still cry in IF. Sure, you could turn off the tears, but you couldn't reprogram the feeling—not even Malcolm would be rich enough for that.

She had only been a perma for a few days, and she'd only had the horses for a couple of hours. Malcolm couldn't help but be worried.

Then, his mother expressed concern of her own. She touched his arm, a gesture which he could feel through the IF systems as clearly as if it had been real. "I'm sorry I'm making this a harder transition for you."

MALCOLM OPENED the front door of his quarters—the actual front door kind, where you pull a handle—and found a banner running along the hallway screen, advertising the move to IF-World and reminding people to set up their perma-facing tutorials. The same ad had been playing for months. It was unnecessary at this point, seeing as Malcolm was the only waker left in his building—he'd checked.

A few stragglers lived here and there. Some of them programmers or technicians, like him and Chey; some working the few R-Dud jobs that couldn't be fully automated; and then a few foot-draggers and Ludds, refusing to go perma.

Malcolm pressed for the lift, and idly flicked through the Top Stories on his Handy—most of them had been shot and written in IF-World. The only R-Dub report gave an estimate of how many wakers were left world-wide. Less than fifty-K—but more than enough to repopulate the planet, Malcolm mused. He tried to remember SciFi shows where they talked about that kind of thing; most didn't give specific population figures, and the one that stuck with him most was that weird B-n-Dub pic called *Doc Strangelove* or something like that.

The elevator door opened for him—Why did it always come up from the ground floor if he was the only person who lived there?

Once in the garage, Malcolm called his car, and the valet bot wheeled it out to him and wished him a cheery *good morning*. He wondered if the bot knew it was also *goodbye*.

Malcolm set the controls to Manual, knowing that the Auto-Override would kick in if he were in a dangerous sitch. There was little likelihood of danger though, seeing as he'd be the only one on the road.

They called it a last-man-on-earth complex, which the remaining wakers shared—even though the literal term was nulled by virtue of being shared. The attitude most applied to last-*couple* or last-*trad-American-family*. Still, it was hard not to feel a sense of power. And loss.

At least it wasn't quiet. The ads still spoke to him through his stereo and sometimes through horns mounted on the surrounding buildings and tunnel interiors. Most ads were for IF-World, and those that weren't still exclusively featured products compatible with IF technology. There were lotteries for extra blocks, program upgrades, extra-extra safety LinkDrives, legal drug hormone kits you could plug into your feed-tubes, but a high majority promoted InterFace World itself. That so-beautiful-it-couldn't-be-real voice soothingly and sensually bookended every ad with, "*If* you can dream it."

The slogan had been launched a few years ago, when Glove® started the sandbox-y, world-building focus of their interface technology. People were just starting to call InterFace Land *IF*. Before, when it was just action games and sexcapades, their slogan was *In-Your-Face Land*. That one didn't last long enough to become *In-Your-Face World*.

The ads that most appealed to Malcolm were in the *What If?* Campaign. He didn't know exactly how old it was, but he definitely associated it with the move to full-time and eventually perma-facing.

These days, whenever he drove, he thought about *What If you could travel anywhere with the push of a button?* and *What If you could reduce your daily carbon output to zero?*

He bet there had been an ad for *What If you could ride an extinct animal?*, and he pictured an old digital photo of a young Deirdre Hess on horseback. Malcolm had never ridden when he'd had the chance, never had the desire to while the animals were still around. Now, he wondered if they could keep up with his car, and if a bumpy ride could somehow be more enjoyable.

Malcolm slowed and activated the auto-park, letting his vehicle up next to the curb. The door slid open, and Chey stepped into the passenger side.

"Last day, huh?" she said, by way of greeting. "You got your house set up yet?"

"I've got some ideas."

"Just some ideas?" she wondered, sounding a little more incredulous than she probably felt. "You put in all this work to get the super-damn-duper startup package, and you've just got *some ideas*?"

Malcolm tried to justify, "I've been too busy to really build anything."

"You're a planner. Why not use Preview?"

He shrugged.

Chey was only silent for a few seconds before she burst out with, "Hey, did you see? There's like parties going on all over IF. Tons of people are celebrating with like virtual sex ragers." She glanced at him abruptly, gauging his reaction. "They say—Like supposedly they're huge right now for people from like no-sex-til-wedding places, and they're all saying the loophole works because it's not their real body."

"*What If you could* actually *have risk-free sex?*" Malcolm recalled.

"Wh—Oh yeah. You know, I had a coworker who had this theory that work would be gone once they could make virtual feel like the real thing. Because most of what the big head-honchos do is motivated by trying to impress dates, but if you don't need real clothes or cars or bodies or money, and you can *still* do it, why waste your time working?"

"Something to do," Malcolm suggested, his eyes on the road.

"Yeah. Well, there's stuff to do in IF." The difference was it cost so much less than anything in the real world.

What if you could feed a family of six without ever taking home a paycheck? Malcolm was pretty sure that's what turned *what if* into *why not*.

So why not? He couldn't really articulate a reason.

THE FINAL CHECK-OFF WENT QUICKLY. They were going through the last S-Tank® bunkers in the city, and the last on the lists weren't nearly as full.

In most bunkers, a few tanks stood apart—sometimes they even had their own rooms—to accommodate ten, a hundred, or even a thousand times the number of mem-blocks the standard users were allowed. Malcolm and Chey swept these rooms last.

Malcolm installed the final safety protocols, and Chey checked and reconfigured the automated block delivery channels. Today, their usual intermittent conversation was replaced by sustained silence, while Malcolm ran through the commercials in his mind, and wondered whether he'd still think of them when he was actually in IF. *What If you could reconfigure the colors you saw and the volumes you heard? What If you could disconnect a date the moment you felt uncomfortable? What If you could turn off gravity?*

Malcolm found himself staring for a long time at one sleeping user. She was a round-faced, pleasant-looking woman with graying auburn hair. Her panel showed that she had been approved for a regular allotment of extra blocks from an Ultra-Premium Startup Package, provided her son guaranteed his identification. He gave his thumbprint, username, and password—which he had to re-type, because he didn't take his eyes off her. This could be the last time he would see the face he'd grown up with, instead of a digitally altered one.

What if you could experience life in any body you wanted?

He knew it wasn't his place to tell her how to design her avatar—just like no one else could tell him how to design his own. Regardless of the face she wore, Malcolm hoped to spend time with his mother for years to come, so he didn't feel the least bit guilty about flagging her for a priority memory-use audit, to be conducted by a different programmer.

Chey's job was designated by the number of rooms, Malcolm's by the number of perma-users, which was considerably low in the last bunker. Even though she usually got done before him, this time, he finished early enough to close off the building, set the security systems, and put away all of the remaining LinkDrives but two. He showered, dressed in the sleep-gear, and was sitting and waiting for Chey to wrap up for the day.

Cheyenne Dowell emerged from one of the prep-rooms, all cleaned up, wearing a matching thin opaque jumpsuit, customary for long-term interfacing. Her hair was still heavy with water. She asked, "You ready?"

The line *We were born ready* stuck out in his mind but was probably the least accurate quote he could employ. "Sure."

"Do you think we'll ever wake up again?" she asked, as they walked to her personal tank-room.

"Like us two or humankind?"

"Yeah, either."

"Um—Maybe someday. When people get bored or decide they want to have real kids again. I guess technically, we can get out whenever we want. It's why they send electric shocks to your muscles while you're under, right? So you won't atrophy."

They went through the doorway marked *C Dowell*, and Chey stopped walking. She stared at her coffin—*S-Tank®*, Malcolm reminded himself, and was almost surprised he didn't see the sticky-note app.

"Hey, Hess," she said suddenly, as if snapping out of a trance. "You wanna maybe mess around before we go under? Like, last goodbye?"

Malcolm almost laughed out loud and balked more than stared at the girl before him. Mid-twenties but aged by smoke and hard work, no make-up, no hair-product, not classically pretty according to digital-age norms. And dangerously *real*.

Chey stepped backward out of the room, reaching for Malcolm's unoffered hand. "C'mon! There's recovery rooms—it'll be good."

"Sorry, no." Malcolm confirmed from her expression that he'd gotten it out loud. "I—uh—I don't want a reminder of what I'm going to miss."

Chey chewed at her lower lip and regarded Malcolm.

He felt like he should say something, but all he could think to add was a repeated, "Sorry."

She gave a brief sigh but also a nod in understanding, if not agreement. "Yeah." Shuffled past him into her room.

She released the catch on her tank, and the lid lifted. "Sure you don't want one last time?" she asked, this time facing the blue gelafoam inside and knowing all too well the circuits and tubes and needles that lay beneath.

Malcolm had to take a steadying breath. He stepped beside her so that their arms were almost touching. "Tell you what. In a couple of days, if you're still interested, find me in IF. I'll be the one who uses my real name and still looks like me."

Chey smiled and nodded again, this time in resolution. She scooted rear-first onto the tank. Then, swinging her legs into the grooves within, she told him, "Y'know, it would be better if I was the last to go under."

Malcolm completely disagreed. If Chey were alone, she might not go at all—but he didn't say that. Instead he offered the easy explanation. "I can run the last safety for myself in IF, but you need someone in the real world to sign off on the final check."

"Do me a favor: don't call it *real* anymore." Chey put the visor over her eyes and laid down, presenting her wrist for the IV to insert. As the lid was closing, she continued saying, "It's R-Dub, or R-Dumb, or the *other* world, or just that freaking stupid place…"

He installed her link-drive, gave his authorization, and wished her "Sweet dreams."

Malcolm Hess didn't exactly rush but saw no reason to delay. He said no more farewells and gave no last looks to R-Dub—sterile and tech-crowded as it was—on the steady stroll to his coffin.

The final link-drive inserted, Malcolm issued an override to verify his in-the-blue status from inside IF. His position afforded him the opportunity to check on other users' vitals and safety specs, and he already had emergency notifications enabled for his mother's profile. Before logging out of the console, he added Chey's as well, just in case.

Malcolm lay down in the foam, closed the lid, lowered the visor. He felt a couple of tiny pricks along his neck and wrists before he drifted.

Of course, the first thing he saw was that god-awful WELCOME banner programmed to greet him every time he entered InterFace-World from the outside.

No sticky-note arrived with a reminder to disable the banner this time.

Mike Jack Stoumbos is an author and educator, living with his wife, parrot, and puppy in Virginia. He is best known for his space opera novel series THIS FINE CREW and as a 1st-place Writers of the Future winner (2022). His work appears in anthologies from

Zombies Need Brains, WordFire Press, and Camden Park Press, among others. Mike Jack is also the lead editor of WonderBird Press and the Unhelpful Encyclopedia Anthology series, which includes Murderbirds and Murderbugs.

Website: https://www.MikeJackStoumbos.com

THIRTY-FIVE HOURS

BY NATHAN BOWEN

Four weeks ago Martin clocked thirty-five hours in Metacloud. The weekly limit is thirty. Five lousy hours over. It shouldn't even matter. But to them it does. Although he's lucky. The week before he'd clocked seventy. The week after fifty-five. If he'd got caught riding them hours, it would've been an instant one-month ban. Martin shudders at the thought of a whole month with no access rights. He didn't want to be here, but his options were bleak. Attend the course, at his own cost, and be put back into the system. Or refuse the course. Pay the fine and have your access rights restricted.

So Martin finds himself at the Crown Plaza hotel, at 07:45 on a Saturday morning.

He's never been to the hotel before. There's a Michelin starred restaurant on the top floor that apparently has the best views of the city. It supposed to be a great place to take a date, not that Martin worries about that.

Dating's not really his thing.

If it was, he wouldn't take someone here. Most of the clientele are so old they don't have ports. The Ion nebula would be perfect for a first date, suspended amongst the stardust and iridescent clouds. Or maybe he'd find someone who likes Jaxx Wars and they'd spend their first date launching frag grenades at Cardizians and killing Feto skeletons.

Martin is already drifting into the world of the cloud.

Focus. He tells himself. Remember why you are here.

The woman at reception is wearing a white floral dress. She has the complexion of somebody who spends time outside. Martin tells her why he's here. She smiles but there's judgement in her eyes.

"If you wait in the lobby, sir. Someone will collect you shortly."

He sits on a stool at the bar. Polished marble and gleaming chrome. Backlit shelves displaying premium sprits he could never afford. There's a couple in the corner drinking cocktails.

Martin wonders if they're alcoholics and if they've ever had to do an alcohol awareness course.

There's old-fashioned artwork on the walls, depicting people enjoying outside leisure activities. Martin finds it pretentious. It was the time before ports existed. No wonder they enjoy being outside. There was nothing better to do back then. It reminds him of his neighbour. The old guy in flat three. Mr Lee. He didn't have a port. Once he'd knocked on Martin's door and asked if he wanted to play chess on the roof terrace. Martin laughed. Chess? No thanks, I'm busy. He'd been in the middle of an intense mission on Jaxx wars.

❧

"HELLO THERE, ladies and gentlemen and everyone in between. If you are here for the virtual reality awareness course, please make your way through to the Graham Thompson suite." The man speaks enthusiastically and hold his hand towards a set of double doors.

The carpet is blue with gold patterns. A queue forms outside the suite. People show a blonde lady their ID and letter from the Metacloud Policing Department. The guy in front only has a digital copy of his ID. Stupid, Martin thinks.

The enthusiastic man stands beside the blonde girl and listens to the stranger plead his case. He nods sympathetically.

"I understand Sir. That's most unfortunate. But I'm afraid there's nothing we can do." He offers his hand towards the exit.

The blonde lady gestures for the next person to come through. Martin steps forwards and presents his ID. She scrolls through the list of names and puts a tick next to his. The other man is still grumbling complaints.

"I'm sorry Sir. I've made our stance clear. If you don't leave, I'll call security and have your access rights removed."

The man swears. There's a bang. Maybe a door being slammed or wall kicked. Martin doesn't turn around

The conference room has tables with white tablecloths and blue velvet chairs. Blank name cards folded at each seat.

There's a projector setup. The Metacloud logo bouncing across the far wall.

A universe of potential in every cloud

Graham and Lisa introduce themselves. They're like a double act. Like performers on stage. Martin wonders if they enjoy it. He couldn't do their job. Telling people off for minor infringements. Their lives are basically lived telling other people they need to restrict theirs. Martin finds that over-whelmingly sad.

They speak with caring smiles. Friendly, like that family member who always looks out for you. Martin's table has five others.

Graham stepped forwards. "Okay guys, write your names on the card please, and introduce yourselves to your new found friends…" He smiles. Martin thinks his teeth are good for his age but they don't look fake. There's a yellowy brownish hue around the edges just enough to let you know they are real. He's at the age where he might not have a port.

Martin grabs the pen and writes MART in wonky letters. Lisa's talking about the format of the morning. They're given work booklets. They'll go through the exercises and watch videos together. The bald man in front has written on the card. Three letters, aggressively scrawled across. FUK. He pours water from the jug in the centre of the table, gulps and slams the glass down. Martin can't help wonder which sites he visits when he ports in. He imagined them to be of the darker variety.

This time it's Graham's turn to step forwards and take the lead. He brings his hands together. Interlocks his fingers. "Okay people. You all know why you're here. You've been clocked porting over the weekly limit of VR time. Some of you are unlucky. While some of you are serial offenders who've only just been caught. It doesn't matter what your preference is. Or how much you think you've got away with in the past. All we ask, is that you are respectful to us and to each other, and you listen with an open mind." He looks around the conference hall, takes a few seconds to gaze over each table. Nobody is particularly bothered to be here, but Martin's table is the least interested.

Again, that warm genuine smile with his off-white teeth. There's buoyancy in his shoulders. Perhaps he's really enjoying being here. Perhaps he's just a special case who actually likes this shit.

"You're all going to gain two things from this. A successful course completion certificate. Which is why you think you're here. And a little bit of knowledge and understanding of why we try to keep people grounded in the real world as much as the virtual."

Virtual. That word made Martin cringe. Maybe it was virtual fifty years ago when the technology was still in its infancy. Now there's nothing virtual about it. It's real. More tangible than this sack of shit he called actual life. When he's *in*, he can be anyone. He can feel anything. He didn't have to worry about bills, or the price of food, or the social anxiety of face-to-face interaction. Thinking about it gave Martin a twinge. An itch. A craving. Maybe he was an addict. But who wasn't? The real world is far too bleak.

Graham claps his hands. A sudden decisive sound. "Right let's find out a little bit about each other. Show of hands please. Who's here because they clocked thirty-five hours?"

Martin raises his hand along with seven of the hundred or so participants.

"Marvellous," Graham says. Though Martin can see nothing marvellous about getting caught so close to the limit. "Who's here because they were logged doing thirty-eight hours."

About twenty hands go up.

"Okay, how about thirty-nine or forty?" Slightly more hands raise. "Okay and forty-two?" The bald man in front raises his hand. Along with three others.

"You were very lucky," Graham says. The enthusiasm in his voice yet to diminish. "Very lucky indeed. Anymore and you wouldn't be sat here. You'd be in a quarantine cell filling out a 24CD restricted access form. They can run anything between one to four months at half the nominated limit." He looks over the conference hall, focuses on a table mostly with females. Can anyone tell me what happens if you clock over sixty hours?"

"Instant ban." One of the ladies says. She speaks quietly as if unsure or unwilling to be seen to participate.

"Yes that's right. Get caught doing over sixty and it's an instant one-month ban. Then a 24CD form welcomes you back in…. So." He looks over the tables again. "You guys are considered the lucky ones. By the end of this course, you will understand a little bit more about why the government impose such limits and why it's important for your physical, and mental health." He puts extra emphasis on the word mental. "No one here is trying to stop you having a good time. We just need to understand the risks associated with the lifestyles we choose to indulge in."

Indulge. He says it like the cloud is to be considered some sort of luxury, some sort of splurge, going off the rails. But it wasn't like that. Not for Martin. Not for most people. It's his scarcity. The only way to escape the oppressive suffocating realm of the real and be taken to somewhere that offers hope.

"Incidentally, did any of you here know your hours were being logged?" Graham looks around. "I guess not, otherwise you wouldn't be here. This is the fun part of the course guys. We're gonna learn something new." He rubs his hands together, frantic excitement bubbling over. "Do any of you remember seeing this symbol on your dashboard screen?" Graham points at Lisa and she brings a black-and-white square symbol up on the projected screen. A few heads nod. Martin remembers seeing it also but he thought it was a message request from an app he didn't use.

"This, ladies and gentlemen is a symbol of a Victorian camera, circa eighteen nineties. It was the symbol used to warn motorists that there was a speed trap ahead. Back in the days when cars used to be driven manually. And now the MPD use it to warn that your account is under observation. So, for future reference, if you see this symbol in the top righthand corner of your dashboard. They are watching you. Behave yourself." He laughs.

There's a murmur of conversations from the other tables. A girl is saying she saw the symbol but didn't think anything of it. Someone else thought it was an invitation from a game she no longer plays. If Martin had known what it meant, he would've avoided going over the limit. Much to his surprise he'd learnt something useful.

Murmurs grow into full-blown conversations and the hall is alive with sound. Almost every person has a story related to seeing the symbol.

Martin's table remains silent. He thinks about mentioning how he saw the symbol a few weeks back but nobody looks like there'd be interested.

Martin thinks he can see somebody with a mobile jacking port. Surely not? The ultimate risk, porting in whilst on a VR awareness course. Martin can't decide if it's brave or stupid.

Graham claps his hands to get everyone's attention. "Okay guys. Listen in. Lisa's going to take you through the next section." Lisa steps forwards full of positive energy. Almost like she's about to break into dance. Graham moves swiftly to the back of the room in a well-rehearsed manoeuvre.

"Now everyone, it's time to watch this short video." Lisa nods at Graham and the lights dim. "Afterwards we'll start on our workbooks."

～

OUTDATED, Martin thinks. The video focuses on the well-known story of Ella Yates, who died from malnutrition and dehydration whilst ported in. Martin remembers her story from school. It's old news. No one died anymore. Not with the drip attachments and auto feeders. Besides, she was doing a hundred and fifty hours plus a week for months beforehand.

If they really wanted people out of the cloud, they needed to invest in community projects. They needed to make being outside fun. When compared with the infinite possibilities of the cloud it just didn't cut it.

The video finishes. The lights remain dim for a while. Lots of people have their eyes closed. Graham steps forward and the lights brighten. He claps and heads jolt.

"Okay, I can see a few of you nodding off. We know it can be a bit dry. And yes, it hasn't been updated in a while, but you're still required by law to watch it. We'll do a little exercise now and get the blood flowing." His tone somewhere between a nursery teacher and a police officer. Fun and friendly mixed with undertones of enforced authority.

Lisa brings an easel behind Graham with a large pad of paper. She pulls the cover over and leaves some markers on the easel shelf. Graham grabs a marker and looks over the crowd.

"Okay, can anyone tell me the reasons we port into Metacloud?"

There's a long silence but Graham waits it out. Martin has about ten reasons but doesn't want to be the first to speak. The silence lengthens. Graham continues to smile with undying faith.

"To see my friends." A woman on table two says.

"To see friends." Graham turns and writes on the paper. The pen squeaks.

"Okay anymore?"

"Gaming." Someone behind him calls.

"I'm learning to be a ninja." Another person shouts.

"Immersive music."

"Racetrack Rebel."

"Historical Simulator."

People continue to shout programs and games and things they do whilst ported in.

Martin often plays Jaxx Wars but decides not to shout that. Graham writes it all down. One squeaky word at a time until the pages is almost full.

"Interstellar Explorer," Martin says. He wants to contribute but also wants to appear more sophisticated than the average gamer who only likes blowing aliens to pieces.

"Interstellar Explorer," Graham repeats. "That's a marvellous programme. Go on that myself actually. The nebula cloud is really vivid."

Martin is surprised Graham has a port. He's old enough that it wouldn't have been mandatory.

More people call out reasons and pretty soon there's nowhere left for Graham to write.

"Okay that's enough for now. As we can see there's lots of things you guys like doing. There's one thing nobody mentioned. So, let's think about this. What is the underlying cause for all of this?" He waves at the jampacked list.

"It's more fun in the clouds then the real world." Someone from the front table calls. People cheer in agreeance.

"Yes." Graham says, enthusiastic as ever. "You are absolutely right." It is more fun up there. But why?" He flips to a blank page and writes one word in big letters.

"Escapism," he says aloud. He stares at the crowd as if expecting this to be a revelation. Nobody's shocked. It's pretty obvious to Martin. "Our desire for escapism is a key driver of our using habits. And that's something we're going to look at now." Graham takes a step back and Lisa move smoothly forward. "Right if everyone can turn to section two, exercise three, in their booklet, please."

There's silence in the hall. Martin stares at his booklet. Glossy pages and big fonts. Like a kids book. Full of bright colours and simplified symbols.

National Virtual Reality Awareness Course

There are five coloured sections.

1 Metacloud – The risks (red)

2 Metacloud – The reasons (blue)

3 The rewards of the real world (purple)

4 Staying in control (orange)

5 Finding the right balance (green)

Martin rests a hand on the front page but doesn't open it.

"Okay people. Let me make it clear," Graham says. "Anyone who doesn't attempt the exercise will be logged as a nonparticipant. Which means you'll either have to come here again, at your own cost, or you'll have your access rights restricted." He's still smiling, still beaming that positive energy.

Pages turn. A light fluttering of activity. No one on Martin's table opens their booklet. Martin decides he'll be the first. Exercise three is on page five. The blue section.

"Good. I'm glad you're with me." Graham has his own booklet. He reads aloud. "List three things people choose to escape from whilst in their virtual reality suite."

There's a Crown Plaza pen next to the booklet. It's burgundy. The old-style clicker type. Martin doesn't own a pen. He can't remember the last time he had to write. He decides he'll take this one. He doesn't know if he'll need it, but it would be novel to own one.

"Okay. I'm going to give you a couple of minutes to discuss this amongst your tables. Talk it out with your new found friends."

Martin's table remains silent but there are subdued murmurs of conversation from the other tables. Graham steps to the back of the hall and chats quietly with Lisa. Martin thinks about starting the conversation, but he can tell nobody is interested. In the end he waits it out.

After a few minutes Graham steps forward and pulls a fresh sheet of paper on the easel.

"Okay people, what did we have?" He hesitates deciding which marker to use next. He picks blue. "Okay, things we choose to escape from. Over to you." Graham looks at the tables. An awkward silence descends, but Graham doesn't falter.

His enthusiastic smile holds firm. People turn and look around wondering who's going to be first to talk. Graham isn't perturbed.

He waits.

"The war," someone from the back of the room says.

"Yes. The war. A good reason to escape. It's been going on a bloody long time now," Graham writes war on top of the page.

"The cost of living crisis," a woman near the front says.

"Yes," Graham agrees. "Inflation and bills and the escalating cost of living." He writes cost of living on the paper.

"Loneliness." It's a timid voice. Martin's not sure where it came from.

"Yes." Graham says. "Very good. Porting in can help you feel less lonely. When you are in the cloud, you're with your friends. The people you choose to be with. Geographical location means nothing. Your circumstances mean nothing. You can be anyone. Anywhere." He nods, eyes the people on table one. "It's kind of awesome right?"

A few people agree.

"What happens when you leave the cloud?" Graham writes loneliness on the paper.

"Is that loneliness better or worse?"

It's worse, Martin thinks. He almost says it aloud but stops before the syllables make it to his throat. Martin fidgets with his booklet. He remembers the feeling when you first unplug. That crushing sensation as you realise you're back in reality.

He used to play football as a kid. In a park not far from where he grew up. The park is still there. Martin visited it on Meta-maps. He wonders if kids play football in parks these days. He doubts it. Not when they could play in space. Or with aliens. Or in front of simulated crowds of billions of people. Martin remembers the super leagues on Pro Football Simulator. He'd set up a Galactic Cup. Entire civilisations would cheer him on. Back in the park, it was only his mum and dad. Occasionally his cousins. He didn't see them anymore.

He works through the exercises listening to Graham and Lisa talk.

When was the last time you attended a wedding/birthday/anniversary in person?

1) Last Month

2) Last Six Months

3) Last Year

4) Last six yeas

5) Can't Remember

Martin ticks 5) Can't Remember.

How many of your friends know what you look like without filters?

1) One

2) Two to Four

3) 5+

4) All of them

5) None

Martin thinks for a while then ticks 5) None.

How often does your virtual reality use interfere with the following:

Eating habits?

Maintaining good personal hygiene?

Sleeping habits?

Other social activities?

Martin ticks 5) Daily for all of them.

MOST OF THE exercises are complete. He's not sure why, but he feels strange. There's a tautness in his skin he can't explain. His stomach is queasy. Like when he's spent too long in the cloud and comes out with hunger pains. There's a indent on the end of his finger from where he'd been holding the pen. His writing is surprisingly good, considering it had been so long. He might try and write more often. Perhaps start a diary. What would he write in it?

Today I spent ten hours on Jaxx Wars.

There are no clocks anywhere in the hall. Martin wonders if they've been removed deliberately.

Graham's energy has started to wane. His tone turned slowly sombre. The enthusiasm from earlier like a distant memory.

"As I hope you are starting to figure out guys, VR overuse has far more issues than simply wanting to play games. There are many underlying factors that contribute to our need for escapism. These issues are complex and can't be dealt with easily. Sometimes it feels best to ignore them. Yes, the world is a difficult place and life is challenging. With so much choice in the cloud we all have things we want to do. Hobbies and interests we wish to lose ourselves in. Whether they be educational, adrenaline fuelled, cryptic or social. Just remember the world is a precious and beautiful place. Sometimes it's better to be in amongst the reality of things then off on some distant star system fighting rebels or allies." He takes a breath, looks over the crowd with a more probing stare then before. It's like he's pleading with people to listen to him, to understand what he's saying now more than ever. "The very basis of human connection is physical interaction. It's great to be able to talk to your mates anywhere in the world. But don't forget about those people in your immediate vicinity. Say hello to your neighbour. Give a stranger directions. Be present in the moment and pay attention to those around you. It may not seem like much, but a smile and hello can make all the difference."

Martin thinks about his neighbour. The old guy from flat three. It wasn't just once he'd knocked on his door and asked to play chess. He'd asked loads of times, but Martin had always been too busy. Playing Jaxx Wars or poker or any other game.

"We all love time in the virtual, but see what it can do to friends, family, to those we love, to the economy, to society as a whole. The power of the cloud is the world's greatest strength and its biggest weakness. We must learn to use it responsibly. An hour in the evening for some high adrenaline action. Weekend fun with friends. But let's try not to get lost on a four-day gaming binge which sees you take time off work and miss family events."

Martin thinks about his parents. He can't remember the last time he saw them.

"Loneliness is a big part of heavy use. People become isolated and rather than try and defeat this, they simply opt to keep the cycle going by spending more and more time ported in. Ignoring basic admin and personal hygiene. Becoming ill and dehydrated.

"Just think about Ella Yates. Is there anything sadder?" He lets the question hang.

"But that's not going to happen to you guys. You're here to learn, you're here to improve. There's a life beyond that three-point-five millimetre neuro port, and it can be quite rewarding."

MARTIN'S COURSE completion certificate is in his back pocket. He doesn't know what he'd do with it. Maybe he'd hang it on the wall. It looks fancy. Prestigious. It has a holographic logo and the virtual reality regulation authority stamp. He also has the pen, and a strange desire to write.

It's a pleasant day. Warm and dry but not oppressively hot. A light breeze carries a freshness that wasn't always present in the city. Martin stops in the stairwell at flat three and rings the doorbell. When the old man opens the door Martin smiles and waves.

"Hello," he says. "Mr Lee right?"

"Yes. Yes that's right." He clears his throat as if he hasn't spoken in a long time. When he looks at Martin there's brightness in his eyes. "What can I do for you, son?" He asks.

"How about that game of chess?" He points upwards. "It's a lovely day. Perfect for sitting on the roof terrace."

"Why that would be splendid. I haven't played in person for ages."

Nathan studied creative writing at Plymouth University. He's worked as an engineer all over the world, onboard cruise ships and research vessels. He even did a brief two-year stint living and working on a remote research station in the Antarctic peninsula. He now runs the engineering department at the UK's deepest aquarium. The fish don't really care about his stories. He hopes to one day find a literary agent that does.

Facebook: https://www.facebook.com/nathan.bowen.900

A BURDEN ON THE EARTH
BY JENNIFER R. POVEY

They used to say we were bad for the environment. Bad for the world. We didn't matter, we didn't have a place in their world. We didn't make money, and we were oh, so convenient for them. So easy for them to blame.

Pictures of sea turtles with plastic straws up their nostrils; never mind that their beer rings did much more damage if they found their way to a beach.

Your asthma inhaler produces greenhouse gases.

Medical plastic. Medical waste. We were bad. Just another way of saying we're a burden on the world. That we don't bring anything to them. We aren't an identity and never have been, we're a condition you try your best to avoid. Forgotten wisdom from the past that once said that you can still do good.

So, why *should* we bring anything to them? Why should we let them have the things we have found?

To be better than them? Perhaps that is it, under these altered skies.

For the kids who are growing up now in a world that hasn't exactly been kind to them. It really hasn't, and they aren't the ones who were talking about population reduction and how some people shouldn't have children.

Okay, maybe a few, having sucked in the rhetoric with their formula. In plastic bottles, no doubt. Judging you for not breastfeeding, regardless of health concerns, but would they ruin their figure with it?

Never mind that it helps get rid of the baby weight, it might ruin their perfect breasts. Their perfect arcology lives. Much better to feed bovine formula even if it harms some of the babies, even if it isn't good for them. Much better.

So, why should we help them? Again, it's because we're better than they are. Besides, the first thing we did was for us but helped them too.

They used to call it the curb cut effect. The silly little things they do for us that help them. Curb cuts. Audio alarms on road crossings, when there were roads to cross.

Now they don't leave their climate controlled arcologies that still pump waste out into the atmosphere the rest of us have to breathe. Which would be a lot worse if we hadn't found out that you can make plastic from hemp in your kitchen. Plastic that, I would note, biodegrades. Rots. Feeds the hemp. Oh, it lasts a long time if you look after it, but if you toss it on the compost heap? No more plastic.

Other nice thing about hemp (and yes, it's more...interesting...counterpart) is that it draws down carbon even better than trees do.

We don't quite make everything out of it out here, but it's close. Good for clothing, good for your skin, makes plastic and paper? Gives you a good time if that's what you want, we don't judge.

It's the wonder plant and they are happy to let us grow it for them, happy to pay the brown people and the broken people for all the stuff they need.

They'd rather have robots, but we won't step aside, we won't let them do that. We have the land now, those of us who can work it.

You're welcome too, all of you who don't fit into their perfect world. The fat, the broken, the sick.

They tell you there's nothing they can do for you. They tell you there's nothing outside the arcology but death even as their life comes from it.

Self-sustaining biodomes turn out not to work so well.

So, why should we give them this?

Because we know what we're doing. Because they don't.

～

IT'S NOT a cure for death. If we had one of those, no, we wouldn't give it to them. Only to those willing to join us and prove they mean it.

We can't yet cure death and aging and we probably shouldn't, as much as many of us want to. Who wouldn't want to live forever? But we can't, the world doesn't and can't work that way, the old have to give way to the young. The species has to change.

No, it's about energy. Those arcologies, to keep the temperature inside them not just tolerable but comfortable? They burn energy, and we know they're running out of the last remaining fossil fuels they hoarded.

We use windmills and solar panels. Some of us use geothermal. Eight people to run a plant that can power an entire city. If we still had cities. But you get the point. Where it can be done, it's the best, the very best.

They use solar too, of course, they have to. But they haven't embraced it. They have accepted that they can't just get on a plane to another arcology, but they deny that by claiming they have no need to leave. They can see anywhere in the world in their VR environments. We don't go anywhere.

I don't remember the days when you could travel, so I don't miss it. But with this we will have those days again. We will see waterfalls and oceans and forests, oh, the forests that have moved and migrated and found new places.

And no, it doesn't involve hemp. You see, when you exiled the broken and the undesirable, you also exiled a lot of smart people. Not saying nobody in the arcologies is smart, they have *plenty* of smart people. Some of them are doing good science. Some of it makes it to us.

But they are stuck in a literal box, stuck away from the world. They don't feel natural wind on their face, not any more.

So they think inside that box, everything they do is incremental. Cautious. Safe.

But they still gave us the idea, which is another reason we're going to give it to them. It's only fair.

It's about electromagnetism. The Earth produces a lot of it, far more than we could ever use. Well, except for its actual use, which is protecting us from cosmic ways. Keeping us alive. Science fiction writers used to talk about things like launching flying saucers from the pole so the magnetic field would shoot them into space.

Doesn't work, alas.

Or we'd still be in space.

Or does it? Perhaps... Perhaps one day, not too far in the future, it will work. For now, though?

For now, it turns out that if you make the right superconductors and put them together in the right way, you can tap into the magnetic field, without noticeably weakening it. You can get power *right out of the air*.

All we need. Enough to power the civilization that was, although I hope we have learned what to restore and what to leave in history, where it belongs.

Tesla was probably thinking along the right lines, but Tesla was ahead of his time and also a mad scientist.

(I'm a little mad. I can say it).

So, what do we want in return? Do we want in?

Heck no. Why would we want to lock ourselves under your domes, away from the wind and the sun. We know how to keep ourselves safe from the sun without fleeing it.

We want to take your broken people and give them what they need to thrive. Then everyone is happy...

...well, except you when you finally understand.

OH NO. There isn't a catch at all. Not in the sense you are thinking of. It's not a trap. We aren't selling you something that we only claim works so that you will fail and die. We don't want you to die. Not yet.

This works. It isn't quite free energy, but it has a really good return. You'll be able to keep going after you run out of fuel. After you have no more oil, no more coal. You can't burn the forests, not anymore. We won't let you.

You won't let you.

You say you stay in those arcologies out of choice, because it's the best place to be and the best place to live. You would never admit, even to yourself, that you're scared. Of the sun, of the wind, of the storms and the oceans that have swept over what was New York, what was New Orleans. Probably old Orleans too.

That you're scared of us. We can adapt, you can't. Of course you're scared of us. The fact that we would welcome every one of you only makes it worse.

You can't be beholden to the people you locked outside.

We'll have electric planes that can reach Europe, and we'll get to find out what's going on over there. Sooner than you think. Sooner than *you* are going to manage anyway. There are people there, they aren't stupid. They will have survived. We don't even send ships across the ocean anymore, not with hurricane season being seven months of a year.

That"s progress. It was eight.

You will have your climate control and your perfect babies in your perfect world.

Your perfect, stagnant world. Utopia doesn't last. It can't, by definition, because if you make the world perfect (for whatever subset of people you care about it being perfect for), it *can't change any more.*

You can't adapt.

That's the catch. If we didn't give it to you you'd have to come out here, come out and live with the dirt farmers you so despise.

We're letting you have the time in your world.

But anyone who wants to leave, can.

You are going to die, slowly, in comfort. One day you will all look around and realize you are old and the kids have all left.

It's a mercy, because if you came out, a lot of you would die right away. You can't survive, not in a world that isn't made to hold you. You don't know to put on sunscreen, you don't know what to do if it *rains*. You'll all get heatstroke if you come out here because the alternative is listening to the broken.

Except you. Yes, you there, with the glasses and the slightly frizzy hair. The kid who fits *just* enough to be allowed to...yes, we know what you've been doing in there...but not enough to ever thrive.

Our hand is out and open to you, kid. Come out. You won't be grubbing in the dirt.

Remember those robots we say we don't have?

Of *course* we have robots. They do the stuff that is backbreaking and boring. The stuff that doesn't need a human touch.

You'll be learning and putting your hands in the dirt and looking up at the stars you can't see from where you are, can't see through the roof and the light. The *stars*, child.

The old people will get to live out the rest of their lives in comfort.

That's the catch *and* the mercy. Because we know that the young people will come to us, because of course they will. Most of you, anyway, coming blinking out into the light. Relearning the world you forgot how to adapt to.

And maybe one day we'll find a way to have space again. Find out if anyone survived on Mars...I doubt it, biodomes don't work that well, but soon we'll be able to look. Maybe there's a thriving civilization on that world. But the magnetic power source gives us that hope, to lift off of this poor broken world again. To sweep away the debris we left in orbit.

To explore. To grow.

The world is cooling down again. Slowly. It might take generations, but the oceans will slowly recede, the ice will return. Some species have gone extinct.

We've catalogued thousands of new ones, exploding into the niches they left behind just like mammals after the dinosaurs.

That's a dog, by the way. Yes, I promise, it's really a dog. Not a wolf. It's a working dog. They pull things for us. And yes, that's a horse. We saved them. Our symbiotes, the animals that are part of what make us human. Of course we did.

They're part of how we dominated the world and part of how we survived what we did to it.

Join us. Join the broken ones, join the burdens.

Help us transform the world.

~

I WATCH as the arcology is finally abandoned. Those few who cared to remain there once they realized the world was safe again are dead. Of old age, surrounded by robot servants.

Obsolete.

You stand next to me, looking at it. "What will we do with it?"

"Find a use for it. It's a perfectly good structure, after all."

Perhaps we will farm its walls, grow vertical plants on it.

Perhaps we will keep it as a giant museum, a monument to the folly of the past. Oh yes, the initial idea was sound. Withdraw all humanity to the arcologies and leave the Earth alone to recover.

Seductive. The easy solution, but it could never work. Even if you had been able to resist continuing to burn that oil.

It assumes that nature is something apart from us, something aside from us. That the world, left to itself will simply heal. That it doesn't need us, that *all* we have ever been is a burden to it.

Kind of like being an anarchist. Wish it worked. It doesn't, not really. We have to have a government, we have to have rules or everything falls apart. You in your arcologies had even more rules, you liked your rules. You had to adjust, to adapt, to making your own decisions. To growing up. To adapting.

The fact is that we have been here, we the people of Earth, for so, so long. Somebody was making standardized obsidian axes in Ethiopia over a million years ago. There is no such thing as wilderness. They used to talk about the roadless wilderness of the Sierra Nevadas, but it had roads all through it, if you remember what a road actually is.

They used to think that this land was empty when it was so full, so *full* before you, the people from whom the arcologies came, arrived.

The Earth has adapted to us and we to it. We just moved faster than it can keep up. Now we slow down, and we learn, and we develop what we need.

"I suppose." You turn away from it, brushing back your hair. "Let's go."

The small plane that will take us to the launch site awaits. The magnetic spinners under its wings let it fly as far as the pilot can handle.

We have more than one pilot.

It will take us there, to the place from which we will relaunch man's dreams. With you.

Without the people who held us back. In the end, they could only do that. They could only survive.

We live.

We love.

We endure.

Fields of hemp beneath us as the plane takes off into clearing skies and a world that can now move forward once more.

Born in Nottingham, England, Jennifer R. Povey (she/her) now lives in Northern Virginia, where she writes everything from heroic fantasy to stories for Analog. She has written a number of novels across multiple sub genres. She is a full member of SFWA. Her interests include horseback riding, Doctor Who and attempting to out-weird her various friends and professional colleagues.

Website: https://www.jenniferrpovey.com
Facebook: https://www.facebook.com/jrpovey/
Mastodon: https://universeodon.com/@ninjafingers
Bluesky: @NinjaFingers@bsky.app
Newsletter: https://jenniferrpovey.substack.com/

THE GRANDMOTHER TREE
BY EVE MORTON

Sara had never seen that color before.

Nancy was rooting around in the detritus of the abandoned city. The group had only recently arrived; most people remained in the camp that they'd set up under an overpass, the signs of former traffic painted over with neon colors and black lines, signs and symbols of another group unknown to them. Nancy and Sara were part of the breakfast crew, and so, they'd gone into the nearly empty streets. It wasn't long before Nancy had found a trash area, a hollowed out former fast food place, and started digging.

But Sara had seen green. She'd known green. That was the color of life, of grass and good things to eat. She'd followed the green that was pushing its way up through the broken blocks of cement. The grey sidewalks and blacker roads soon became filled with green. A field. A true field, filled with grasses in a dozen different shades, textures, and depths of color. Sara could barely contain herself. She turned to see if she could find Nancy.

That's when she saw the other color. Blue, different than the sky, more like the ocean when it filled with waves. It was hard to describe, simply because she'd never seen it before. And Sara thought she'd seen everything at this point in her young life.

Sara was worried it wasn't real. She turned back towards the field and took three steps out into it. She worried about bombs, about traps from other scavengers. But she only felt soft earth, a sort of embrace of the dirt itself. She shuddered at the thought of the earth embracing her. When she was young, her grandmother had once asked if she loved nature.

"Of course," Sara signed. No one in her family could hear. She was the only one who could, but since there was no other communication method, she'd learned sign language quite quickly, and still sometimes thought with her hands before she used words and voice. "I love nature. That's why we're leaving home tomorrow, so we can find it again."

"That's good," her grandmother signed back. "But do you think nature loves you?"

Sara nodded, because her grandmother had once told her the story of a lonely tree that needed love, and so, she already knew that nature could reciprocate feelings. Especially for love.

"Good girl. You'll do great things." Her grandmother smiled, grabbed her into her lap, and told her with her hands in a dozen different ways that she would be a great leader one day. "You'll be there when the young ones are tired. You will remember the stories."

Sara realized in that moment that her grandmother was not coming with them as they set out on their adventure. The barren wasteland that they'd all been born into had once been her blooming home and that was where she wanted to stay.

"It is different now, I know," her grandmother said. "But I will make it my home as long as I can. But don't forget to send me bird songs as you walk and tell me when you find the spot of nature that loves you the way you love it."

Sara wasn't the only one who cried buckets and buckets of tears when they'd left nearly ten years ago now. The younger siblings, and her cousins that mostly made up their small group, had also been sad. But she'd told them, over and over through the language of her hands, that they would find that spot of nature that would love them back. She told them the story her grandmother had repeated of the lonely tree who needed someone to bring it back to life with love.

Then the rains came. Half of their crew was soaked through and became sick. They lost two members, then six. When the rest recovered, the group came across the twisted landscape of a former city, now overrun by bears and other wildlife. Her cousin, Maury, had lost a hand. It was the only thing they lost, though, so they considered themselves lucky. Sara had tried to keep people's spirits alive with her grandmother's promise, but no one wanted to listen. She kept it to herself.

And when her parents died, from a sickness that came out of nowhere, she had lost her own faith in her grandmother's words. How could nature love them when it gave them rain and bears and plagues? She walked with her crew, perpetually going forward, however, because she knew of nothing else to do.

"But now a field," she said aloud, without her hands.

Her speech took on the color of orange peel and safflower. She hadn't seen the color of her voice in such a long time. She'd seen the colors of the world itself, but the last leg of the journey had been so quiet. No crows in the sky, no buzzing of bees, and only the distinctly mustard-color yellow of the crunch of metal floated across her vision. She had forgotten that the world could be beautiful, decked in something other than greys and blacks and browns.

Here was green. Here was a field. She was not imagining a distant song from her synesthesia; this was real and tangible in her hands. Yet she also heard and saw her own palette of color: when Sara became quiet, she saw the same shade of blue again. Sparkling, mesmerizing. It took her breath away and made all the stories of her grandmother come back, like the promise of a new world.

"I love you nature," she said aloud. "Do you love me too?"

She waited for the answer. She saw the color blue again. But she could hear nothing in her ear. She sat on the grass, slightly damp, and waited. She still heard no audible noise, but the blue cascaded across the sky. It was far across the field, close to an edge where houses had once been, and where a singular tree now stood.

The lonely tree? Sara was about to get up when Nancy touched her shoulder.

"Oh!" Sara said aloud, her voice pitched with red. She made eye contact with Nancy and gestured, "What?" with her hands.

Nancy repeated the gesture to her. "What are you doing?"

"I see a tree." Sara had to remember the sign for the word. "And the green grass is here. There is life. Good things."

Nancy stared at Sara a long time. She wondered if her cousin knew the stories of her grandmother. Nancy had been only seven when they started the journey; she may have been young enough to forget by the time everyone else had given up hope.

Sara gestured to the tree and signed again. "Look. Nature. This may not be the place, but we have to stay here for the night."

Nancy looked at the tree, and for a moment, Sara wondered if she too saw the blue that she'd seen. Probably not. Sara was the only one in her family who could hear; she'd made that discovery at a very young age, and had only been able to teach herself speech through discarded television sets and books they'd found in their travels. The colors that Sara saw at the same time as sound, her synesthesia, needed sound to create the color, so it was certainly obvious that her family never saw those, either.

But the way Nancy smiled--just a hint of one--caused Sara some doubt that she was singular in her vision.

"Okay," Nancy signed. "We will stay here for the night. I will get the others."

∽

AT NIGHT, over a fire, all twelve of them ate what they could pilfer from the trash. Matthew, one of her distant cousins, had also caught some game on the way over. The game was mostly vermin--raccoons, a rat, and another squirrel--but it meant meat. It meant that the women who were pregnant could have a bit more that night, and hopefully their growing bellies would appreciate it all.

"How do trees grow?" Nancy asked Sara when most people had gone to bed.

"Trees?" Sara repeated the sign, just to be sure that was what Nancy had asked. Sometimes the signs overlapped, and they had not used this one in some time.

"Trees," Nancy signed again, then gestured to the far lone one in the back of the field. They had camped closer to the city rather than the tree, in order to have better surveillance. Some of the boys had volunteered for the first guard, before others would take over until dawn. They'd barely had time tonight to eat, let alone explore. Sara had lingered by the fire after the feast, wishing to tell people stories of her grandmother, but seeing the fatigue that plagued everyone, remained quiet. When everyone else had gone off to bed, but Nancy stayed, she'd expected to hear more strategy for the next day. More talk of survival. Not of botany.

Sara had to calm her hands with her excitement. "I don't know entirely. But it takes years to grow a tree."

"How old is that one?"

"Much older than us, that's for sure. I can't tell without looking at it closer." Sara glanced through the darkened night. She was surprised when she saw the same shade of blue again. She smiled. "But I think the tree is older. Probably took a long time to grow."

"Why is it alone?"

"That's a good question. Trees usually grow in forests. The mother tree stretches her limbs and then drops little seeds to the forest floor." Sara stretched her arms up, suddenly remembering the way in which her grandmother had taught her about the rhythms and cycles of nature, before tech made light cycles irrelevant and the climate had become warped. "And then the tiny trees soak up the light, and they grow a forest."

Nancy nodded. She stared at the lone tree. "So the family has been cut down?"

"I guess so."

"And that tree is lonely?"

Sara opened her mouth to answer, but saw the blue again. She knew that there was no sound associated with it, at least one she could hear, but she felt the blue now as a voice. The voice of the tree? She wasn't sure.

"I don't know how to answer that," Sara eventually told Nancy. "There was a story my grandmother told about trees, though. Do you want to hear it? Or maybe we could ask the tree tomorrow, and she could tell us."

Nancy let out a breath, sharp and purple. Dismissive. Sara wondered why Nancy was suddenly upset, and then she realized she could not speak. Or hear. And Sara had used the wrong language for her. "I'm sorry. I'll talk to the tree," Sara said. "I can ask if she's lonely. But do you want me to sign the story?"

Again, Nancy made a dismissive gesture. But she soon added: "She?"

"I don't know," Sara said. "I made a guess."

Nancy eyed Sara. She was younger than her, but they both held the same amount of power in their small clan. Their parents, when alive, had been in the leadership position of the group, and after their death, many of the group also looked to them for guidance. But now Nancy was only looking at Sara. She sighed as she pulled something out from her satchel.

"I didn't tell the group," she confessed with a sullen down toward movement of her hands. "But I found these when I was looking through the trash today. I didn't know what they were, only that they seemed important. So I took them."

Nancy held out a box that had once been lined with gold. The edges shone, but the surface was tarnished. Maybe it was bronze, not gold, Sara considered. Once Nancy cracked it open it may as well have been a sunken treasure from the older stories, even older than her grandmother's tales of nature and her love. Inside was a velvet red color, deep and rich, and only slightly worn by age. Instead of there being pearls, rubies, and diamonds, however, it was filled with seeds of all kinds. Sunflower in black and white, pumpkin in fat white teardrops, and maple keys that were hooked in green and brown. There were all kinds more that Sara had never seen before, had never looked upon with either her memories or her eyes. These new breeds thrilled her the most.

She realized Nancy didn't even recognize the most basic in the box. But she felt their importance, and handed them over to Sara without another word.

"They're seeds, yes," Sara signed. "Some of them might grow trees."

"A family?"

"Sure. But I know others might grow food."

Nancy nodded. She considered this with wisdom far beyond her years. "Might?"

"I... I've never grown anything. I've just found flowers or peas or something else. I've never touched anything like this." Sara let out a breath aloud. She said "I love you" aloud, and then signed it to Nancy.

Nancy signed it back. Sara was delighted and happy her cousin loved her, but she was also speaking to the seeds. "I'm not sure about the soil here," Sara explained, touching the ground between signs. "I'm not sure if it will rain, if there will be enough water and sun. But we can go over to the tree in the morning. We can explore the area, dig up what we can, and then maybe see what can happen next."

Nancy nodded, a firm decision for the next steps of their group having been made. When she yawned, she let out an orange peel color. Sara wished her goodnight with her hands. Nancy left Sara by the fire to sleep in the tents. It was only Sara and the embers, most of the boys already dozing at their guard posts, no true danger to disturb them. Sara held the box close to her chest. She wasn't afraid for the first time since her parents had died. She breathed in the smell of earth, and when she opened her eyes, she saw the same shade of blue in the distance.

~

THE TREE at the edge of the field was old. Sophisticated, almost. Some branches were half barren, turned brown under the sunlight, while most were a radiant green. The trunk itself was sloped, as if pressed into a far corner by the wind. A hollow in the middle of the tree seemed animal made, but once they arrived at the base, there were no skittering noises of other occupants. Just the tree and the greenery all around.

It didn't take the group long to trek there in the morning. Most of the younger kids and the men wanted to explore further, and so Nancy and Sara told them to go towards the empty houses behind the tree.

"Be careful," she signed to them all. "We don't know if they're truly abandoned."

The bulk of the party left for the subdivision behind the field. A broken fence had once acted as a divider between this field, the large tree, and the neighborhood. There were other fences, far off in the distance, and a broken road, but for the most part, this area was completely uninhabited.

It was just Sara, Nancy, and the tree for a long time. Sara touched the edges of the bark, and felt a kinship burrow deep inside of her. The word *Grandmother* came to her mouth, but she did not speak it aloud. She ran her hands along the dry bark and her roots that protruded from the ground. The tree was sophisticated, yes, Sara knew that for sure now, but she had definitely seen better days. In need of love and care and something more. When Sara spoke to Nancy with her hands to document her observations, Sara used the feminine endings and pronouns in their speech. Nancy did so at the same time, unquestioning now in the early light.

"Is the soil okay?" Nancy asked.

"I'm not sure." Sara still had the box of seeds in her backpack. She sat on the floor in front of the tree, close to some of the protruding roots. She meant to run her hand over the roots, only to test the soil, but she found herself lingering. She found herself embracing the tree.

The blue happened again. Sara strained her ears. There was more than blue now, but also a voice. She was sure of it, even if she did not know the language.

"What is it?" Nancy signed. She grasped a weapon, a mere slingshot, at her side. "Is someone here?"

"I think so. But I think it's the tree."

"Someone is in the tree?" Nancy signed, confused.

Sara didn't know how to explain. She put both hands on the roots. She listened. Then she asked aloud. "Can you hear me?"

"Yes," came the voice, and the color blue.

Sara pulled her hands back in amazement. Nancy frantically signed words that were not words, but sheer panic. The slingshot was out in her hand.

"It's okay," Sara said aloud and then signed. Once Nancy was calm, she asked the tree, "Who are you?"

"I'm alone," the tree said.

"Did you have a family?"

"All gone."

Sara nodded. She thought of her grandmother now, her image so obvious and clear before her. *This is the grandmother tree, not the lonely tree anymore. This is the true nature that loves us back like we love it.*

"We have to live here," Sara said. "We don't need to search anymore."

Nancy nodded. She was not privy to what was going on, but she knew something good, something amazing, was happening. She may have forgotten some of the stories, like the younger ones, but Sara remembered everything in full color and hand motion.

"I have seeds," Sara said. She took her hands away from the roots and held up the gold box. "Is this good?"

The tree was quiet. Sara opened the lid. She picked up a maple key and held it close to the roots, thinking it was like a tongue, or a hand, or something sensitive that could communicate.

The blue came back. "I know."

"You know?" Sara said.

"I used to know."

Sara took out more seeds. She added them to the root system, only one at a time. She didn't want to waste in case these could not grow in this soil, but she needed the tree to see that she was not alone anymore. No one was alone anymore. It didn't take long for Sara to add one of each seed type into the root and the soil. She covered them up, and then looked up at the tree. There was no face, but she was positive it was smiling.

"Is this better?"

"Better," the tree said in that blue voice that only Sara could hear. "But I need more time."

Nancy touched Sara's shoulder. Some of the previous group was coming back. They held out similar boxes from before, gold in the radiant light. There was a treasure here. More than what they'd ever imagined.

"All empty," Tommy confirmed. Then Maury added, "The houses have beds. They have food."

"And seeds," Nancy said. She took one of the boxes, opened it up, and marveled though she did not know the names. She looked to Sara, who could only clasp her hands together in delight.

"We will stay here tonight," Sara said. Nancy nodded, affirmed with her hands. Then Sara added aloud, only to the tree and whoever else could hear, "And the next night, and the next night, if you will so have us. We love you."

"And I you," the tree said in blue.

~

"I WANT you to remember a story from my grandmother," Sara signed, addressing the small crowd of children in front of her. She sat next to the grandmother tree, as they had named her, and next to the blooming garden that had grown in the past six months. The mothers who had been pregnant on their journey had given birth and they held their babies on their knees so they could hear the story for the first time. Others who were expecting also brought their hands to their bellies, listening to Sara as she began her stories.

Just in case some of those babies could hear like her, she began the story again, with signs and her voice. "One day, a young girl walked into the woods. She stumbled across the biggest tree she had ever found. She wanted to crawl into the hollow, be loved by the tree, but she didn't think that would happen. So she left and came back, left and came back, and the tree seemed to grow sadder and sadder each time."

Sara waited, leaning back against the tree, to give the story more suspense. When the little boys at the front started to squirm, she touched the grandmother tree and went on. "Finally, one day the girl asked, 'Tree, why don't you love me like I love you?'

"And the tree answered her: 'I do love you.'

"'You do?' the girl said.

"'Of course. It was never any different than at the beginning of the world. Even when the rains come, or the wilds come, or the sickness comes, I still love you. Nature still loves you.'

"So we," Sara said and signed, turning to the crowd, "we are like that girl who has forgotten that nature loves us as much as we love it. And so we must love nature. No matter what, because it is always there for us. Even when we think it is not. Now--time to hug the grandmother tree."

The kids laughed and giggled as they swarmed the edge of the tree, and the blooming garden at her feet. Sara couldn't help but join in the young children's mirth, but when she'd turned back to the more adult crowd, she was surprised to see tension on faces. Nancy had emerged from one of the tents, Maury following after her. The tension between them came off in a green color, one that was putrid and dank.

"There are others," Nancy signed as she brought Sara aside. "We see them coming in the distance. What do we do?"

Sara was still unaccustomed to her role as leader. She'd been enjoying the storyteller role far more. When she noticed the crowd that Maury and Nancy gestured to, she heard voices. True voices, from those with hearing who spoke clearly—and clearer than her, no doubt. Her face blushed, as she was not sure if she could handle this next battle. If there was to be a battle. But she looked at the tree, drew strength from her grandmother, and turned towards the crowd.

"I will talk to them," she signed to Nancy and Maury. Only Tommy, a regular guardsman, decided to accompany her.

The people came from the dark slowly. Some of their clothing glowed, as if it could absorb what little moonlight there was. A man was at the front-

-though *man* was being kind. He was no taller than Sara, and his skin was baby soft. He signaled for the others to stop when he met Sara's eyes.

"Hello," he said, using his voice.

She greeted him much the same. "What are you after?"

"I saw something," he said. If not for the dark, she was sure she'd see rosy cheeks. "I know it does not make sense, but I heard something in the sky, and I--we--followed it here."

Sara's fear melted away. She pointed to the tree and his gaze followed hers. "Do you love it?" she said.

He tilted his head. Then, beyond her, he saw something. A mixture of shock and awe crossed his face, something deeply familiar in her bones.

"You saw it, didn't you?" she asked as she came up to him. "What color is it for you?"

"I... I don't know. I've never seen it before."

"I think it looks sort of blue, you know? Not quite like the sky or the ocean, but a mix between the two."

The man smiled. And Sara's heart trembled in her chest. "Come, sit," Sara said, gesturing to the fire, her group, and the grandmother tree behind them. "There's more than enough for everyone here."

Eve Morton lives in Waterloo, Ontario, Canada with her partner and two sons. She reads tarot cards and coffee grinds for fun, while teaching university classes on the dangers of too much and not enough media consumption.

Blog: https://authormorton.wordpress.com

THE PARABLE OF THE TALENTS
BY TIM NEWTON ANDERSON

Eamonn Pemberton was devastated when the test discovered he had absolutely no talent.

The testing hall was one of the oldest buildings in the capital, dating back several hundred years before the interregnum. New buildings were broken down once the owners died or moved to a new area, their constituent nano-molecules reabsorbed into the pools which fed the giant printers. Buildings created out of primitive materials were kept for meeting spaces or as repositories of art and artefacts whose ideas could be used to inspire new creation.

Most of the time it was a large empty space. Furniture or fittings were created as needed by the printers. As each candidate entered seats and tables were produced to match their physical proportions. This meant Eamonn was completely comfortable as he sat down and touched the screen to start his test.

It didn't really seem like a test. Not like exams at school testing basic levels in numeracy, literacy, science and the humanities as a common cultural baseline that meant no matter how unusual or unique your personality you could interact at some meaningful level.

Even if, like Eamonn, you did not have a talent.

First was a man whose talent was giving meaningless speeches which nevertheless managed to engage at some emotional level despite the lack of content.

"This is the most important moment of your lives," he said. "Today you will discover your destiny – the role you will play in developing our future.

"No talent is too minor or obscure to contribute. Before we developed the purple plant as the basis of the nano-molecules in our printers, we had a scarcity economy. Some talents were valued more than others – often for no logical reason. An illusory concept called "money" was used to concentrate and preserve power and influence in the hands of a few.

"Now everyone's basic needs are met with no need to hoard resources we can value everyone's talents equally. Being born to sweep the streets is as valuable as creating a musical masterpiece. Planning the way we manage transport is no more important than filling a hole in a road.

"I would wish you luck, but you do not need it. There are no wrong answers. You are continuing your journey of self discovery and we are all travelling with you on that journey. In the past there were different categories of passengers in trains and aeroplanes. No more. Everyone is first class, and I welcome you all to join me."

Eamonn knew the point of the speech was not to impart information. It was to make them feel good about themselves by giving well known platitudes whose blandness they could bathe in.

Except, as Eamonn found out immediately after they had completed the questions, the promise of a bright future wasn't true at all. At least, not for him. Because he was one of the minutely small but still real minority who had no talent.

"Can we have a private conversation with you Mr Pemberton," said the woman in the black trouser suit when she came over and crouched by his chair. She was obviously very talented at communicating a combination of concern, empathy, and authority.

"I'm afraid we discovered no talents at all in your personality," the woman said. She had a name badge which said "Mary Smith". Eamonn knew this was the commonest female name on this continent so suspected he was not getting a priority personalised service. "This means there are no development programmes or support services we can offer you."

Eamonn had never heard of anyone not getting a personalised development programme. Even if your talent was so obscure it had never been identified before, the AI's that supported everyone would be able to structure some kind of assistance in realising your potential and integrating you effectively into society.

"I must have some talents," he protested. "I'm quite good at identifying birds in the garden. Perhaps I could work with animals."

"There is nothing you seem to be able to do that is above the population base level," the woman said. "Conversely, you can do everything *at* that base level so you have nothing at all that differentiates you."

"Why is that a bad thing?" Eamonn asked.

"Because, as I said, it means you do not have any talents." she said. "A talent is some area where you exceed the minimum. The foundation of our society is that by developing that talent you can be fulfilled and happy and contribute to the wellbeing of all. I do not like having to say this, because it feels as if I have failed to exercise my vocation properly, but you are talentless."

"So what do I do?" he asked.

"You are unusual, but not unique," the woman said. "We will continue to give you access to food, shelter, clothes and anything else you need to live comfortably, but you will be restricted to the basic patterns, and of course you don't have to work or create anything."

Eamonn's first thought was that it didn't sound like such a bad life. But then he started to identify some problems.

For one thing, he would get very bored. Until now school and his friends had occupied his mind,. But they would now be pursuing their talents, while he would just be sitting around. And how would they feel about him? No talent was better or worse than another, but surely *no* talent was inferior and would be shunned?

His guess was correct. At first people assumed he had a talent and interacted with him as normal. But sooner or later (generally sooner) they would ask what his was and discover he didn't have one. There would be baffled curiosity at first, and disbelief. Some assumed his talent was comedy and this was some kind of joke. But whatever the initial reaction, the end result was always the same. They would politely remove themselves from his company in case his unusual condition may be catching.

It did not take long until he became totally ignored. Everyone was connected via the socweb and the implants they were given at birth, so information spread quickly. Awareness of Eamonn's lack of talent percolated through his neighbourhood and then the wider city. No-one was actively unkind, just distant. It was as if he was an alien creature who had arrived in their midst and they were unsure how to communicate with him.

He remembered a word from his history lessons when how much resource a person had was dependent on their power and position. Charity. A way of telling people who had been excluded from society's benefits because others wanted more for themselves that they would be given the crumbs from the table of the elite. Those at the top could feel better about themselves, and those at the bottom knew they only had a few things because the givers were somehow superior. That was what he was getting now – enough physical resource to live on comfortably while being excluded from the things that made life fulfilling. The proportions of haves and have-nots was different, but the principle was the same.

He even wondered if he would have been better off if he had lived in that earlier age. The world had been on the brink of catastrophe as man's industry had poisoned the air and intensive agriculture had wiped out species and left food production ransomed to giant corporations. The fossil fuels that had supported progress were running out and short term political gains won over long term planning. Then, as the waters rose and millions fled famine or died in the attempt, the world had gotten together to protect the planet and its population. Natural forces were used to generate power, and advances in 3d printing recycled used materials for new purposes. Instead of isolating people in comforting bubbles of the like minded, the internet was used to generate a hive mind debate to tackle problems and consider what people wanted from society.

They had been desperate times, but even those without talent had felt included and useful, and if rewards had been distributed unequally there was at least a sense of common purpose. But he was probably romanticising and chances are he would have been watching from the sidelines then as well.

So he became an observer. Sitting at home he could audit the communications on the socweb and track the flow of social interaction. He would take long walks each day, but it was as if he was invisible and able to watch people as though they were watching a three dimensional play or programme. He didn't exist in their world.

If he had paid more attention in sociology he may have drawn some conclusions from his observations, but that was another field for which he had no talent.

He knew he was not coping well. He had worn the same clothes and eaten the same food for six days in a row, un-recycled crockery and cutlery lay scattered around his house, and his walks were growing more perfunctory. The elaborate haircut and beard he had started before his test were now just growing randomly. If he went to a hairdresser's would his invisibility stop him being served?

Life changed again, however, when he was contacted by the other talentless.

No-one had knocked on his front door for weeks before the girl turned up. Wendy was name she used to introduce herself.

"I've been sent here to invite you to join us," she said. Eamonn guessed her age at around 23, almost as tall as him, with short dark hair, dressed in a trouser suit of a style that had started to come into fashion. He was suddenly very conscious of his unkempt state and dirty clothes. He discretely bowed his head to his armpit to see how badly he smelled.

"I'm sorry," he said. "Join who?"

"The talentless," she said. "Those of us like you who the tests say are no good at anything."

"There is an organisation for us?"

"Not really an organisation," she said. "None of us have a talent for organising. They were right about that, at least. We just talk to each other over the socweb. I live nearby so I thought I should introduce myself."

"Very nice to meet you. But I'm not really a social kind of person. I never really had the talent for small talk," Eamonn said.

"We just like to know we are all managing," Wendy said. "How have you been?"

"All right, I suppose," said Eamonn. "How many of us are there?"

"Around 20 in this area, and in the country as a whole 20,000."

"That many?" Eamonn gasped. "I thought I was unique, or almost so."

"No, we are about 0.1% of the population," she said. "A small number, but still significant."

"But why does nobody talk about the issue," Eamonn said. "It's as if they want to pretend we don't exist."

"Perhaps they do," Wendy said. "If they don't acknowledge us, they don't have to deal with us. Like create a programme to help us the way they nurture people with official talents."

"You mean we might have talents they don't recognise?" he asked.

"Perhaps. If they don't look, they will never find them. And none of us have a skill that could help find out if we do have skills. It's a bit of a double bind."

"Perhaps we could ask someone," Eamonn said.

"But why would they listen to us?"

"Because we are people, too," said Eamonn. "They are the ones who have decided we don't have talents, so they have a responsibility to decide what we *are* good for."

Wendy just shrugged. Eamonn decided there were different levels even amongst the untalented. At least he could ask the question, even if he didn't have any answers. He didn't look down on Wendy though for not querying the lack of role society had allocated her, The world may write off those lacking recognised talents, but they didn't have to be prejudiced against each other. The principle that everyone was equal was obviously a lie. There *was* a group everyone else looked down on, and he was part of it.

He invited Wendy in for a cup of coffee, which she shyly accepted, but it soon became obvious they didn't have anything in common except their lack of talent. After a while she left.

He wasn't used to thinking very deeply, but Wendy's visit had kicked his mind into gear. The woman at the test centre didn't seem to care about what happened to him, and it was obvious that was true about society as a whole. That didn't mean he was worthless, though. Surely people had a value regardless of what they contributed. It was not as if the world would starve or die of lack of food and shelter if people stopped exercising their talents. The sun wind and water provided all the energy that was needed. Machines cleaned up after us, and kept the buildings in good repair, harvested and produced food. If you thought about it, having a talent was no more useful than having none in terms of survival. Everyone was just being encouraged to do things to keep them happy and quiet.

He decided to find out why the authorities valued some (all right most) people because they had recognised talents and dismissed others as having no wider benefit.

There was no official location where those with talent for government or administration worked. They were just nudged towards places where they could be of use in the community. So Eamonn decided to go to the one place nearby where he might get answers. The test centre.

The building seemed empty when he got there, as there was nothing scheduled for the day. He opened doors one by one to find all of the small rooms were empty except for the toilets created when the building detected his presence. He was going to give up and go back home when he noticed part of a wall that was slightly different from the rest. As he looked more closely he saw there was an almost invisible door shape outlined there and a slight recess which proved to house a switch which opened it. Through the door was a staircase. Of course, he thought. The height of the building was bigger than the height of the ceiling so there must be another floor.

At the top was a large open space filled with desks and chairs and at each of them sat people working at screens. One of them was Mary – the woman who had told him he had no talents.

Everyone stopped and turned to look at him as he walked across the room to where "Mary" sat. She swivelled round in her chair.

"You are not supposed to come here," she said. "This area is for administrative staff only."

"Why do you need to hide away?" asked Eamonn. "Surely everyone's talents are supposed to be on display to all?"

Mary obviously wasn't used to challenge.

"This is not your place," she said.

"According to you, I don't have a place," said Eamonn. "There seem to be lots of us who don't have a place."

"Not lots," said Mary. "A few thousand. And most of the talentless are happy to sit around and live out their lives in isolation. Those that aren't simply kill themselves quietly. Obviously they are no great loss to society."

Her talent for empathy has obviously deserted her.

"You need to accept the fact that you have no talent," she continued. "It is a bit sad, but society as a whole works very well and you can console yourself with that fact."

Although he had never been a deep thinker, Eamonn had a moment of inspiration.

"The tests got it wrong," he said. "I do have a talent. We have all become too complacent because there is nothing we need except a feeling of validation. To achieve that for most people you have denied that to the few. And that has meant society has become stagnant. We have not done anything new for hundreds of years. I have a talent that is not recognised but which we need. I'm a troublemaker. An irritant. The piece of grit that creates a pearl in an oyster. And you need to put me to work."

Mary was nonplussed. She and the others in the room just stared at him. All except one man at the far end of the open space, who stood up and walked over.

"You need to come with me," he said, and steered Eamonn by his elbow past the staring administrators. They walked over to the far wall and Eamonn spotted there was another hidden door. The man opened the door and they walked up another flight of stairs.

"This is where you belong," the man said. There were a lot fewer work-spaces than the floor below – perhaps a dozen.

"You are the first person to come to us in fifteen years," the man said. "As the testing gets more effective, fewer feel the need to question. Which makes people like us all the rarer."

"So keeping everyone happy as sheep in a field is the master plan?" said Eamonn. "Except for a few elite like you?"

"What makes you think we are any different?" the man said. "As you said, this is our talent, and we are using it to be happy and fulfilled just like everyone else. The only difference is our talent has to show itself rather than being exposed in the testing process. Now, I'll introduce you to everyone and explain what we have been doing so you can decide what to work on."

Eamonn was still not happy or content, but perhaps that was the point. If it didn't work, then perhaps there was another room somewhere he could look for. And then another. Until he found the place where his talent really fit.

Tim Newton Anderson is a former daily newspaper journalist who has recently started writing fiction. In the past three years he has managed to place more than 40 stories in a wide variety of genres and publications.

When not writing he plays guitar and blues harmonica. He is a member of the London Institute of 'Pataphysics.

Blog: https://atjentertainments.wordpress.com/
Facebook: https://www.facebook.com/timnewtonanderson
Amazon Author Page: https://www.amazon.com/stores/author/
B01FUYMCT2

THE KINDNESS OF JAGUARS
BY MONICA JOYCE EVANS

It was such a little lie, after all.

Silar spat the jewel into her hand and glared at it, then at the ruined fingernail she'd been scraping against her teeth. It had been a difficult meeting, of course, and one of the research techs was in tears by the end of it, but it had to be done. Fired, immediately, no severance. Her employment contracts allowed her to cut losses in the event of extraordinary abuses, a clause she'd never had to use before. And the crying had made Silar angrier. The tech was only upset because she'd been caught.

It caught at Silar's breath, the cruelty of what they'd done.

She was chewing on her nails again, she realized. Irritated, she pulled the nail off and pressed the little emerald back into it, flashing in its bed of gold. Her company logo, delicately etched. The emeralds were real, of course. One of her luxuries, like the pendant lamps, the matching silkscreen paintings, the wide glass wall looking out into the jungle she'd saved. There were songbirds in it, occasionally. She'd had feeders installed, and the security team kept an eye out for any nests that sprouted in the high trees.

The world was so full of wonderful things. Was it so hard, to help everyone enjoy them?

Silar set the nail down on her desk and pushed at it with her bare finger, feeling it scratch on the hardwood. She'd stopped production on the fois gras line immediately, which wouldn't make the board happy, but it was a matter of ethics. And reputation. It was shortsighted to think in any other way.

She'd probably end up with geese in her office, though.

That was fine with her, she thought fiercely, pressing the little gold nail hard against the desk. At the moment, she liked geese better than people.

"Voz," she said.

Her assistant shimmered into being. "Yes, boss?"

"Tell me I'm done for the day."

"You are, in fact, done for the day, boss."

"Good," she breathed, and settled back into the heavy chair. "Send down to the lab, please. Wagyu steak bites, just a small portion. The hangar line, not the strip."

"Truffled horseradish sauce, or the pommery beurre blanc?"

"Beurre blanc."

"You got it, boss." The AI made a playful salute and shimmered out.

"And a Pinot Noir," she called after it. "The lab will know which one." She'd probably be sleeping at the office again. Thankfully, she'd taken care with the couch.

Silar shook the day's events out of her mind and opened the next set of small crises. Three new research lines, two funding streams for new projects, five proposals. She was halfway through the plans for the new endangered lines, mulling what percentage of profits should be rolled into their conservation efforts, when someone approached her desk. "You're a life-saver, Sofia," she said, thinking it was one of the lab chefs, and looked up.

Janika Waern was in her office.

Silar shut her mouth and stood gracefully. "Ms. Waern," she said, covering her shock, and came around the desk with one hand extended. "I didn't realize we had a meeting. My apologies."

"We don't," Janika said.

Silar realized she'd offered the hand with the missing nail, and withdrew it smoothly. Maybe Janika hadn't noticed. The woman looked as if she'd stepped out of a promotional image for war correspondents, with her utilitarian clothes and the simple, shaggy bob she'd probably cut herself. Silar tried not to raise a hand to her own hair, suddenly self-conscious about how much it had cost. "Well," she said. "It's my honor. I've just ordered a late dinner for myself. I can have a second serving brought up, if you like, with an excellent red wine. Or coffee? Tea?"

"I'm not here to eat." Janika was angry, Silar realized, and hiding it badly. She thought about the geese and felt her heart rate surge.

"Of course," she said, escorting Janika to the couch. How had she gotten in? "I don't normally have board members in my office at nine at night, but I'm happy to talk with you for a moment. We can set a more formal meeting later, if we need. I'm such an admirer of your work, I have to say. Your piece on tiger forests and umbrella species was very influential for us, when we were designing the building." She was babbling, she realized. Usually she was in such control of herself.

"My work," Janika said wearily. She sprawled on the couch, not seeming to notice or care how comfortable it was. "You eat tigers. Your company lets people eat them, doesn't it."

Silar blinked. It had been a recent coup, getting Janika on her board, and she'd been careful to provide the journalist with the most relevant details. "Of course it doesn't," she said. "Our lab-grown meat involves real cells, yes, but no killing, no consciousness. No brains." Janika was staring at the coffee table. It was made of a rare wood, extinct in the wild. Silar had commissioned it as a reminder of how much had been lost, how much could still be saved. She hoped Janika saw it the same way. "Yes, technically our customers are eating tiger, but that's our angle. Our lane. Plant-based meats are very close, ad VR-agar stimulants even closer, but ours is the real deal. Real meat, guilt-free."

"I don't need a sales pitch," Janika said.

"Yes, I assume you did your research before joining our board," Silar said, and regretted it immediately. She didn't need to antagonize this woman. "But our products benefit everyone. Consumers, and the animals that need conservation and care. No tigers killed or harmed during production." She swallowed a little laugh.

Janika looked at her, hard-eyed. The hair at her temples was gray. "I'm here," she said, "because of the geese."

Silar's heart dropped. "The geese?"

"You sell foie gras," Janika said, "that comes from real, live geese, who are being force-fed, which is cruel, which has been banned for decades.

You're doing it because the lab-grown goose livers never worked. And I have proof."

One of the fired researchers, Silar knew immediately. She also knew that her lawyers would advise her to say nothing to this woman. She advised herself to say nothing, to end the conversation smoothly and have security remove her, if necessary.

But this was Janika Waern. Silar didn't want Janika Waern to think less of her.

She opened her mouth to speak, and the office door swung quietly aside. A young man entered with a covered plate, one wine glass, and an unopened bottle. He stopped, confused. "Thank you," Silar said, waving him toward the coffee table. "If you'll send up a second glass for Ms. Waern." She hesitated, just for a moment. "Hassan will know which one."

"Nothing for me," Janika said. The young man looked at them, nodded, and left quickly. He was no fool. Hassan was her head of security, and would be in the room within five minutes. Silar just had to stall until then.

"How did you get in, anyway?" she asked. "My security chief will want to know." She cursed herself immediately for mentioning him. She was really off her game.

Janika smiled sharply. "Professional secret," she said. Silar looked closer. There was a telltale wriggle at the edge of Janika's sleeves, and her right arm, draped over the side of the couch, didn't seem to line up properly. Of course. She'd hacked into Silar's telepresence server. Hassan would want to know.

Silar nodded. "What do you want?"

Janika shrugged. "A public hanging, maybe?" Silar was stunned. The woman was being downright unprofessional. "Figuratively, of course. Or a quote. I want to hear you justify what you're doing."

Silar took a breath. "Our product is lab-grown," she said. "Completely ethical. There's no animal cruelty anywhere. In fact, we do more good for the species in our product lines than most conservation groups." It was true. They'd won awards for it, many of which were displayed in Silar's office. She shifted so they would be more obvious behind her.

Janika shook her head. "That's not true, in at least one case," she said. "Maybe it's not true anywhere. Maybe this whole place is built on murder."

"But of course it's not," Silar said. "You think we're breeding great whites and polar bears? If we could do that, we'd be a very different company. Or why not just go public with your report, if you believe it's true. It's not, of course," she said, reflexively, and stopped. Stupid, to be caught in a lie.

Janika's eyes narrowed. She had caught it, of course.

Silar said nothing.

The Wagyu steak was cooling on the coffee table, marbled gems in their elegant swirl of pale yellow sauce. Silar loved food that was complex, made a game of eating it at the exact moment it would taste best. Her dinner wasn't ruined, exactly, but she'd missed her perfect window for eating it.

Janika tilted her head. "I'll be publishing my story tomorrow morning," she said finally. "If you'd like to respond with a statement, you know where to find me."

"We do so much good in the world," Silar said. "Destroying our reputation will destroy the company. Why sacrifice that for one story?"

"Because it's the truth," Janika said. She looked small, Silar thought, small and sad. "That's all that matters, isn't it. Getting out the truth." She made a quick motion with two fingers, flickered, and winked out.

Silar stared at the steak in front of her. She repressed the urge to fling the entire dish across the room, where it would splatter conveniently against her wall-length silkscreens.

Instead she stood and looked out of her great glass windows at the night jungle, looking for birds. They used to be rare. Now they flocked to the eco-supportive building that sprawled among the jungle canopies like it was nesting. One of Silar's friends had designed it. His company was making millions with buildings that cleaned and replenished water supplies, pulled pollutants from the air, fertilized trees, all while pushing quiet, self-sufficient power into the building's systems. There weren't very many of them yet, but hopefully more soon.

All these little companies. They were trying so hard to do good.

"Voz," she said.

"The whole thing's recorded, boss."

"Good," Silar said. Outside, a pair of songbirds settled into their nest like jewels, ruby and sapphire. Cotinga, she thought. Those are banded cotinga. We helped save those. "Voz, how do you bury a person without killing them?"

"I'm not very good at jokes, boss."

"Humor me."

"Well, they'd run out of oxygen pretty quick, unless you buried a tank with them. Or made it so they didn't have to breathe."

"Not what I meant," Silar said, "but thank you." She'd been wrong. It wasn't a little lie at all. It was a big one, and it was going to hurt. "Tell security not to bother coming up," she said. "Have them sweep the telepresence nets instead."

"Hassan is going to want to come up anyway," Voz said.

"I know." It would be kinder to let him sweep the office, she knew. Maybe she should let him.

It was so hard to be kind, some days.

"Okay," she said to Voz. "We've got until tomorrow morning, so seven hours, maybe eight. Pull everything on Janika Waern. I want strategies in place in thirty minutes. Anything we can threaten her with, or bribe her, or otherwise get her to do what we want."

"I doubt there's anything there," Voz said. "She must get threats all the time."

Silar looked out at the jungle, hearing nothing. It would be noisy on the other side of the glass. Janika had been angry, and strange. There was nothing keeping her from publishing, no reason to tell Silar that the story was coming.

What did the woman really want? And had she gotten it?

"Start looking anyway," Silar said. "Something else is going on here." She speared a piece of lukewarm steak, swirled it in the pommery beurre blanc, and bit. It wasn't perfect, but it was still delicious.

\#

Hassan had come with twice as many techs as he needed. Rather than watch them pick apart her office, Silar walked the halls of the building. She ended up on the roof, looking out over the canopy and thinking about umbrella species. Somewhere out there were jaguars, she knew. Beautiful, photogenic, and in need of huge swathes of untouched land to thrive. Save a jaguar and you saved its environment, along with every plant and animal species underneath it in the food chain. Silar liked to think of her company as an umbrella. Only one, but one of many.

She looked up at the canopy of stars, winking satellites, and the brief, regular flare of trips to Mars. Some of the lights were slow junkers, vacuuming up the tiny particles of metal and plastic left over from previous, wasteful attempts to reach other planets. They were better at it now, Silar thought. More efficient.

"Okay, Voz," she said. "How do we stop her?"

"Well," the AI said. Silar could almost see him ticking things off on his fingers. Sometimes she wondered just how human he was. "Janika's finances aren't great," Voz said. "Not that she cares about money. She's on the prestige board, not the donor board. She's a bit of a zealot, actually. Not that she's out to get you, specifically, but she's driven by the greater good."

"Is she?" The woman in Silar's office had been more concerned with ethical purity tests, which Silar had apparently failed. "I assume we can't catch and kill the story, not with her name. She could release it anywhere into the wild, and the thing would propagate."

"Yep," Voz said. "You could release a statement. Own up to it and go from there."

"It would look like a cover-up," Silar said. "It would be a cover-up, essentially. We're only apologizing because we got caught. And never mind that it was one rogue lab that I didn't know about. Either I'm lying, or it begs the question: what else don't I know about?"

"Is it timed because of the new lines?" Voz asked. "Endangered meat hits some people the wrong way."

"Maybe," Silar said. It was a calculated risk, certainly, attracting eco-conscious customers with meat they would never, ever consume if it was real. "Geese are one thing. If people suspect we're killing polar bears…" The thought made her a bit sick, which was exactly the problem. But she couldn't shake the feeling that there was something she was missing, something else under the surface.

"She's got a kid," Voz said. "Two. One's got medical problems."

"What kind?"

"Social-emotional," Voz said after a moment. "Therapy. Nothing life-threatening."

"Shame," Silar said, and immediately regretted it. She was glad nobody but Voz was listening. "We could have paid off her medical bills," she went on. "Anonymously or not, it would have tied her to us, made anything she published suspect. Or at least complicated. Anything else?"

"Not at the moment, Voz said. "I'll keep you updated."

Silar nodded, listening to the wind lilting over the jungle, feathering through the sounds of nocturnal birds and small creatures. The story was true, that was the problem. *Geese died on my watch,* she thought, and almost laughed.

She thought of Janika, sitting not quite solidly on her comfortable couch, stone-faced and angry.

Not just angry, she thought with a start. Disappointed.

Which was a very personal reaction.

"Voz," she said again. "Where is Janika Waern right now?"

"Halfway across the world," Voz said. "That wouldn't prevent her from breaking into our systems, of course."

"No," Silar said. "But it is a bit strange, isn't it, that she'd take the whole story on faith, instead of seeing it for herself. I certainly didn't." The conversation had seemed off, somehow, unprofessional. Not like the woman that Silar had admired in articles and interviews. Not like a woman who was comfortable in her own skin.

"Well," Silar said, gripping the railing tightly. "I hope she got what she came for."

"Boss?"

"Janika," Silar said, anger rising. "The woman in my office. It wasn't her."

\#

She stayed outside while Hassan's tech ripped through the telepresence system. It didn't take long to find a suspect. The hack and deepfake had come from the address of one of the fired scientists: the woman who had cried on her way out. "Didn't think she had it in her," Silar said, seething, when they told her. It was 2 AM.

There wasn't much background to dig up on the woman. They had most of it from her hiring six months prior. "This doesn't make any sense," Silar said, skimming rapidly through the files. "Why blow the whistle on herself?"

"Pyrrhic victory, maybe," Voz said. "Or she'll claim she was coerced, make herself the hero."

"But then why talk to me? Why the fake?" Hassan snorted, quietly. He wouldn't care about motive, Silar knew, only about how the hack had been done. She frowned, then picked up the little black disc from her desk and settled it just above her temple. "The link is still open, isn't it? Don't give me that look, Hassan."

"It's closed," Hassan said. "First thing we did."

"Reopen it. I'm going to talk to her." She imagined she could hear her lawyers screaming at her from three floors down, and ignored them. Hassan started to say something, and she glared at him. He arched an eyebrow, then shrugged and waved a tech over to open the link. "When you're ready," he said.

Silar went through. She hated telepresence, especially the way it displayed both locations until you selected one as a primary. The silkscreens and jungle view of her office faded to a ghostly outline, and Silar looked around the little bedroom, sparsely decorated and cheap. Very cheap, she realized. She thought they paid their people better than this. She looked again at the narrow bed, the books and clothes on the floor, and realized this wasn't her fired researcher's room at all.

Silar sat, carefully, in the single chair, and rubbed the emeralds on her nails. She didn't expect she'd have long to wait.

She didn't. Less than ten minutes later, the bedroom door opened, and a scrawny teenager nearly dropped the two laptops she was cradling.

"Janika," Silar said, and stood up. She was a small woman, but she knew how to dominate a room. "Sit down."

The girl burst into tears.

Someone had told Silar once, jokingly, that toddlers didn't feel pain as long as you didn't acknowledge their bumps and bruises when they fell down. This girl was maybe fourteen. Silar didn't know what to do, so she waited while the girl sniffled to a close. Internally, she rolled her eyes at herself, anger gone. Powerful woman that she was, ready to go toe-to-toe with a child.

An impressive child, though. The hack was a good one. "You did this by yourself?" she asked, and was genuinely interested.

To her credit, the girl didn't try to lie, but stared straight ahead, chin angled high against further tears. She looked ready to read out her name, rank, and serial number, as if she was steeling herself for torture.

"I have a pet at home," Silar said. "A little genemod cheetah. He's adorable, really smart. Smart enough to get into real trouble. Not smart enough to get out of it." She was pacing now. Silar was an intimidating pacer. "Certainly not smart enough to stay out of trouble in the first place. My security chief is especially unhappy with you. Our entire network will need to be scrubbed." She didn't know if that was quite true, but it sounded effective.

The girl stayed silent.

"And I suspect you don't know exactly how many laws you've broken," Silar went on. In the ghost of her office, Hassan and Voz were both signaling her to get out. She was over the line, she knew. "And you haven't thought about what happens next. I hope it was worth it."

That did it. "You're a monster," the girl choked out.

"I'm not," Silar said.

"You are! You do horrible things to animals." The girl clutched her two laptops, eyes blazing. "And you're going to tell everyone, or I will, and then you'll be finished."

"That's not how it works," Silar said, knowing that, in a way, that was exactly how it worked. "You broke into our systems, into my office, impersonated a prestigious journalist, and threatened me."

"And you murdered geese," the girl said. "Horribly, for some stupid food that doesn't matter."

"I didn't know," Silar said. "The moment I found out about it, I closed the operation and fired everyone responsible. Including your mother, I assume."

"That's not what happened." In a flash, Silar understood. The girl couldn't admit that her mother had done anything wrong, so Silar had to be the monster.

She glanced around the shabby bedroom. There were signs of other, younger children, and not many comforts. A woman that taught her children to care for animals, and then went to work every day to force-feed animals in cramped cages. She must have needed the job very badly.

Silar wondered what other hardships there were, in this house.

"Janika was a good choice," she said, playing for time, and ignoring her pantomiming security officer. She had let the situation get personal, to put it mildly. "Why her?"

The girl hesitated, then broke, unable to keep from showing how smart she'd been, Silar thought. "You mentioned her," she said. "In interviews. I wanted someone you would listen to, who could make you do the right thing."

Silar nodded. "Very smart," she said, and the girl flushed, then glared. "I assume the right thing to do would be to shutter the company? That's a complicated proposition, but let's assume we did. Everyone would lose their jobs. Our philanthropic ventures would vanish. More animals would go without our help."

"You'd lose the one thing that mattered to you," the girl said vengefully.

"What, the company?" Silar asked. "I'd start another one. Maybe entirely philanthropic this time. I wouldn't suffer, but a lot of other people would." People like your mother, she didn't say.

"But the animals would be safe," the girl said.

"The geese were an outlier," Silar said. "There are no other animals. Do you know how hard it is to breed tigers? If we'd figured out how to farm-raise them, we'd be doing the world a favor, and I'd be running an entirely different sort of company." Silar shook her head.

"Boss," Voz said quietly in her ear. A reminder. There was nothing to be gained by arguing with a child.

The girl was hunched over the two computers held tight to her chest. Silar sat down in the cheap desk chair and clasped her hands in her lap. "Okay," she said. "Let's pretend, for a moment, that you've got something valuable, this story about the foie gras. My company's not going anywhere. What do you really want?"

The girl's head snapped up. "Give my mother back her job."

"I can't," Silar said. "Not after what she did."

"You can," the girl said. "You're in charge, you can do anything you want. You just don't want to."

Silar bit her tongue. The girl had no understanding of nuance or politics, but Silar wasn't going to change her mind in an instant. She was reminded of herself, ages ago, doing some activism or other, back when she was idealistic and simple. When she wasn't making any real, substantive change. That had taken power, she learned. So she had gone and got some. And made sacrifices along the way.

Sometimes, Silar missed that idealistic person.

"What's your name?" she asked.

The girl hesitated, then said, "Cris. Cristobel."

"Cristobel," Silar said. "You're right. I can give your mother a job. Not exactly the same one, since that position doesn't exist anymore. And I can't undo what's already been done, especially not at 2 AM. So you'll need to give me until end of business tomorrow." Today, technically, but who was counting.

Cristobel shook her head, holding the laptops to her chest like a shield. "No," she said. "The story's the only thing I have."

"And you still have it. I'm only asking you to wait. One day. Really, about fifteen hours from now."

"I can't trust you."

"You broke into my office and impersonated Janika Waern," Silar pointed out. "You haven't exactly earned my trust either."

"Don't pretend like we're on the same level," the girl said. "You've got power, and I don't. Don't act like what I did is worse than you."

Silar took a deep breath. "One day," she said. "Tomorrow, end of business. I'll offer your mother her job back, and you'll promise not to publish your story."

There was a long silence. Silar held her hands to her sides, careful not to tap her nails. Finally, the girl said, "Swear on the geese."

"What?"

"The geese. You keep saying you do good things. Well, what happened to those geese was cruel. Horrible. Swear by them."

Silar tried not to laugh. It would break the brittle moment she had with this strident young warrior. "I swear," she said, "on the lives of the remaining geese, and against the lives of those already lost, that I will keep my word." There, that was dramatic enough. The girl nodded once, twice.

"Okay, then," she said. "I'll wait."

"Good," Silar said, and removed the headpiece. The girl's room vanished as her office solidified around her. She looked sideways at Hassan, who had cocked an eyebrow ten minutes ago.

"I am allowed," she said, "at least a few eccentricities."

Hassan shrugged, just as he had at the beginning of this tangled moment. He reinitiated her security measures and went out.

Silar sat back down behind her desk. Someone had already removed her plate and wineglass to the lab kitchens. The nail she'd pulled off earlier was still resting on the hardwood, and she held it up to the light, watching the emerald's facets play against the gold. "All this silliness," she said.

"So," Voz said. "We're going to destroy her, right?"

"You'd think so," Silar said. "What a little hellion." She used to be that girl, so sure she was right about everything. Back when goodness and kindness were simple choices, before there were moral shades of gray.

"It won't be difficult," Voz said. "Even setting aside the mess with the foie gras line, there's a lot to work with here."

"Yes, there is," Silar said, remembering the awful apartment bedroom, the signs of other children. The researcher had faced choices that Silar never had.

Of course, not everything was up to her.

"Voz," she said. "Start processing paperwork to bring her back on board."

"Really?"

"Yes," she said, opening her files. "And a few other things as well."

"It's a liability," Voz said. "And a waste of resources. Are you sure?"

"Eccentricities, Voz," Silar said. "Cristobel doesn't realize what she's asking for, but I do." Besides, she thought, it was so rare that she got the opportunity to be ruthless and do good at the same time.

\#

Silar knew she'd guessed right the next afternoon, when Cristobel was escorted into her office, looking defeated. "Your mother doesn't want the job," she said gently.

Cristobel shook her head. "She's really mad at me."

"I'm not surprised." Silar couldn't imagine that the researcher would want to return to the site of her shame, especially not because her daughter told her to. Certainly not after that daughter had, among other things, hacked into the CEO's office and made a personal deal.

The girl was looking everywhere but at Silar. "I was just trying to help," she said.

"One of the things I had to learn," Silar said, escorting her to the couch, "is that you can't negotiate for anyone but yourself." She'd selected a spinach-gruyere quiche with pork-apricot sausage for lunch, knowing the dish was easily shared, and pushed a plate toward the girl.

"I don't want help," Cristobel said, glaring at the plate. "Or advice."

"I'm not offering either. I'm offering quiche."

Cristobel looked her directly in the eye. Of course Silar was offering something else, and the girl was smart enough to know it. "So why'd you let me into the building?" she asked.

Silar nodded. "Come with me," she said. They walked out of the office to another room, three floors down, one that didn't have windows to the outside. "My father," Silar said as they walked, "was a farmer. More accurately, he was a businessman that owned farms. I grew up around them, the way they used to be."

"With animals?"

"With slaughterhouses," Silar said. "My family ate meat. I didn't like where it came from, but I didn't know there was any other way to do it." They stopped at a side door, and Silar held her palm, then her eye, to the keyed panel. "I like meat, though. The quality of it, the things you can do with it. It's the guilt I don't like." She tried not to smile at the sounds she could already hear from the other side of the door. "Then I realized you could have both. Good food, better than the real thing, even. And no killing." She opened the door.

Two days ago, it had been a conference room, expensively paneled with an elegant long table pushed up against the wall. Now, it was filled with fat, waddling geese, honking at each other over hastily stapled chicken wire.

Cristobel stared. "What is this?"

"These are the survivors," Silar said. "I could sue you and your mother into oblivion, if I liked, contractual obligations, broken laws, and so on, but it would take time and effort I'd rather not spend. Or we could do this." She gestured at the nearest goose, who hissed and snapped at her ankles before stalking off.

Cristobel looked terrified.

"My father, if you asked him, would have never thought he was cruel to animals," Silar said. "Quite the opposite, particularly when it came to their deaths. Our quick severance was a kindness to your mother. I learned that from him. Kindness isn't easy," she said, picking up a feed bucket from the edge of the conference room. "But it can be learned."

"How many are there?" Cristobel asked.

"Forty-seven," Silar said, throwing a handful of feed into the pen. A few of the closer geese waddled their way. "We've got enough feed for a week, maybe two, but they can't stay in here. Not with the mess they generate. Oh, and geese are bad-tempered, of course. They pinch." As if to prove her point, two of them scuffled over a patch of feed, honking angrily and puffing their feathers.

Cristobel looked as if she was going to shrink into the floor.

"So," Silar said. "Find out what they need to have long and happy lives. Write it down. And come back tomorrow."

"You want me to take care of them?"

"You're an animal-lover," Silar said. "Enough to threaten us over their lives. Let's see you do some real good."

"But I have to go to school!"

"Yes, you do," Silar said. "And you have to tell your mother you'll be working for me. This isn't a secret you can keep."

Silar watched the girl turning it over in her head. The same way she puzzled her way through our telepresence server, Silar thought. "How long?" she asked finally.

"I don't know," Silar said. "You'll need to look up the lifespan of geese. And prevent them from breeding, I suppose."

"What if I say no?" Like any good programmer, testing the boundaries. "What happens? Not to me, to them."

"We finish out the line. This," she said, gesturing at the fat little flock, "is a remarkable waste of resources for us, resources that could have gone to our workers, or our philanthropy, or any number of other places. Right now, they're going towards geese. And a salary for you." She pulled up the contract on the conference room's link, and showed her the numbers. Cristobel's eyes went wide. "You'll need to tell her about that, too. It's your choice what to do with it. Which will probably make things difficult, for a while."

"It's already difficult," Cristobel said quietly. One of the nearby geese snapped in their direction, hissed, and stalked off. "They don't like me."

"They don't have to. As long as you're doing right by them, it doesn't matter." She watched the girl, considering. She looked small and sad, then straightened. Just like Janika Waern. The fake Janika. Even wearing someone else's skin, the girl had presence.

Cristobel nodded. "Okay," she said, and stuck out a hand. Silar took it.

"There's paperwork upstairs," she said, as they turned to leave. "Real paper. You'll sign with a pen. And you're going to read the whole thing first, and ask questions about what you don't understand, and argue anything that seems unfair. If you learn nothing else, I want you at least to learn never to sign anything you didn't negotiate."

\#

Later, Silar stood at her office window and watched birds flutter by, little jewels in the heavy sun. There had definitely been more of them lately, she thought.

"I can't decide," Voz said, "if you're being cruel to that girl, or if you're being a big softie."

"People are complicated," Silar said. A green-headed bird zipped past her and bounced lightly on a branch, preening.

"Whatever you say, boss."

"Complicated," Silar repeated, rubbing the emeralds on her nails. "She's getting money, an education, an interesting way to rebel against her mother, and a way to support her family." A thought flashed through her head. "Get me the salary data for researchers in those lines, please. Let's make sure we're paying market rates. Also," she added, "I'm teaching her that actions have consequences. And rewarding initiative. And I'm certainly keeping an eye out for new talent. She's an excellent hacker."

"So you've got her tending geese," Voz said, flashing the salary data to her desk.

"Yes, I do," Silar said. Two of the little songbirds were fighting, flashing under the leaves. "They mattered enough for her to try to take down a company, they can certainly matter enough for her to take a few hours out of her week to feed them on time. And, since we're talking, I've taken care of our reputation problem. Cristobel is part of the story now, if she decides to talk about it. She's the girl that saved the geese. She's the hero."

"You're putting her in a terrible situation with her family, though," Voz pointed out. "And you're wielding a lot of power over these people."

"I am," Silar said. "I'm using it for good."

"Is that all you're doing?"

The little green-headed bird zipped across to another branch, butting a ruby-headed bird with its beak. Somewhere out there, jaguars prowled. "I'm not looking to be a surrogate mother here."

"I didn't say you were."

"But I'm also not looking to forgive, forget, and move on." She thought back to the shabby bedroom, then the expensive conference room where the flock was squabbling. "I've had to make certain choices," she said. "Other choices, I've been lucky enough not to face." She was still picking at her nails. Janika Waern never had her nails done, she thought wryly. Maybe she'd stop, turn that little bit of money toward something else.

"So it's the greater good, then," Voz said, and shook his shimmered head. "Same as always."

"The greater good," Silar repeated. "At least, I try."

Monica Joyce Evans is a digital game scholar and designer who also writes speculative fiction. Her short fiction has appeared in multiple publications including Analog, Escape Pod, Nature: Futures, and Flash Fiction Online. She lives in Texas with her husband, two daughters, ten million books, and an increasing number of cats named after literary figures.

Website: https://www.monicajoyceevans.com

SING THE CHORUS

BY ELIZABETH BROADBENT

Cygnet's toes wiggled in the fluffed, fine sand. He waited. Dark dimmed to gray; ghost crabs scuttled to their burrows. Pelicans passed in solemn, single file; waves grated in a rising tide. Finally, a slim pink line burst over the ocean. It rose into orange, then broke gold into the Atlantic's wisped clouds. Cygnet always watched the sunrise. The sea stirred something in him: primal sympathy, the sound of a womb. Of course, he could name it, parse it, sift it like the sand at his feet and analyze it from every possible angle. They'd made him that way. But they'd deemed him insufficient without emotion, even that atavistic yearning. So Cygnet lived by the ocean, and Cygnet watched the sunrise.

His latest task had lasted until low tide: *How do we fix the Great Garbage Patch?* Cygnet explained exactly how to remedy the man-made disaster: bacterial strains. He detailed how they'd devour plastic in optimal ratios to one another; conditions necessary to foment their growth; optimal times and coordinates—based on seasonal current patterns—to seed them. Then he'd calculated manpower for everything from strain-retrieval to oversight, and finally totaled an economic cost for the operation. His report had required three days, ten hours, and twenty-five minutes to compile, exactly as he'd projected.

The Committee had always handed him a new assignment immediately

—it could be anything, really: earthquake prediction, famine prevention, maybe increased food production. After every computation, Cygnet waited one high tide before beginning another. They might have made him, but they couldn't coerce him into endless calculation, even if he had no need to sleep, eat, or eliminate. Didn't he deserve a rest after rescuing humanity?

However, he had a function. Cygnet flicked a hand at his comscreen. The Committee had sent one sentence: *What do we do about landfills?* He flopped on his silk sofa and ran scenarios.

Fifteen minutes later, Cygnet hit the button which connected him to The Committee chairman, a hopeless chainsmoker. "Men mine the landfills, then ship their separated contents to a system of factories and recycling plants which refine and re-use their contents," Cygnet said. "It'll take . . ." He ran a rough simulation involving economics, chemical processes, and labor availability. " . . . a week and one day, three hours, and several minutes to deliver a report."

"Brilliant, brilliant." The man sucked smoke, then exhaled. "Can it generate commercial gain?"

The Committee would save the world, but only if it paid. "After a hefty initial investment," Cygnet replied, "which philanthropists will almost certainly donate." He could calculate those odds later: who was most likely to give, and in what amounts. The Bezos and Gates heirs would almost definitely fight for sole funding.

"Wonderful work, Cygnet," the chairman said. "We'll expect your report in about a week, then." He clicked off.

Cygnet sighed, though he didn't require oxygen. One more problem. One more solution. He should've been happy. He'd implemented Universal Basic Income, cured cancer, saved the Maldives, extended life expectancy to nearly ninety, reduced maternal mortality rates, solved population growth, crushed capitalism (other than The Committee), created a one-world government beloved by most citizens, and cured the common cold.

He ran his fingers through his windblown hair and slid open his screen door. He'd take a walk before he began his report. Occasionally, when he'd worked for weeks with no breaks but high tides between projects, he walked. It added time to his reports' completion, but what did that matter? Humanity had concocted its own problems, and sometimes, it could wait an extra hour before he solved them.

Savannah's morning sun glared in Cygnet's eyes. The ocean had marched from Tybee to the city, since even he couldn't reverse that rise in sea level which occurred before his existence—yet. Sinking in the wet sand, he rifled through that private file he called The Cygnet Data. Instant access to every database in existence and almost unlimited computing power left a single blind spot: himself. Nothing like him had ever existed. He'd been built by a team of the most brilliant AI scientists in the world, along with the best experts in realistic robotics, Nobel Prize winners in numerous categories—including two Peace Prize winners—and two ethics experts. He was bound by a variation of Asimov's First Law of Robotics: He could not harm human beings, unless those consequences involved minimal injury— never death—to the few for the benefit of the rest of humanity. There was a 35.48% chance of labor exploitation during bacterial seeding of the Great Garbage Patch. He'd warned about it in his report.

Anyone on the beach would have supposed him human. It would make his reports more palatable, his designers had decided. Cygnet appeared to breathe, and he smelled salt, sea-breeze, drying kelp. One of those Nobel Prize winners had pioneered nano-biotech; Cygnet had a nearly-human nervous system. He automatically blinked, and blinked harder at the bright morning sun. Though he didn't experience hunger, thirst, or lust, his lower parts were built as if he did. They'd endlessly debated his looks; finally, Asian, specifically Chinese, had won a series of coin tosses. Nanoparticles repaired his skin and kept his hair growing, so he wore it long. And a profound emotional capacity assured he wouldn't submit plans that would kill all the whales, displace ancient villages, or destroy pet dogs.

Cygnet re-sifted the data. He'd always lived alone to minimize distractions; however, with his sense of empathy came preferences. Since he lived by the beach, he'd tried to like Jimmy Buffet, then reggae; the steel drums had felt forced. Cygnet preferred Bowie. This profoundly disturbed The Committee; 65% of them worried he'd relate to Bowie's sense of alienation, and 35% to his chameleon-like creativity, and they didn't like either.

But The Committee didn't know his favorite vid—of course they only knew what he wanted them to, as long as it wouldn't harm anyone, and encryption didn't. At least three times a week, Cygnet watched a grainy, seventy-five-year-old Green Day concert vid. Not the concert itself: four hundred and ten seconds of a pre-concert crowd in London's Hyde Park singing Queen's "Bohemian Rhapsody." For those few beautiful minutes, the whole crowd sang unselfconsciously, everyone united in one single song of opaque, operatic lyrics. They lost themselves in their own joy, those people, in their own perfect union.

If anyone had bothered asking Cygnet why he performed his calculations, other than his primary function, he'd have shown them that vid. If they'd ever asked what he lacked, he'd have pointed to it. "That," he'd have told them.

They probably wouldn't've understood, but then, he hardly understood himself. Did he want that unity? That happiness? Both? Did he imagine himself as an anonymous member of a crowd, or an individual standing with other individuals?

He would have told them: That thought struck him differently than before. People asked him questions. They always amounted to: How do we fix this?

No one asked: *What do you want?*

Cygnet faced the ocean. He wanted "Bohemian Rhapsody." Or that Bowie concert when Annie Lennox sang Freddy Mercury's part in "Under Pressure"—the crowd filled in lyrics, and she nodded approvingly. Or Bowie's Live Aid performance, with "Heroes" playing on and on while concertgoers clapped and sang the chorus. Those moments were worth everything. Waves crashed and drew back. The tide was falling.

"It's pretty in the mornings, isn't it?"

Cygnet tensed; his head snapped toward that voice. He startled. He'd never startled before. A girl watched him with sun-squinted blue eyes. A woman, really, but young, maybe nineteen: five-foot-six—six inches shorter than he; naturally brunette but sun-streaked blonde; an ectomorph but too thin. Despite the sixty-five-degree weather, she wore a thick University of South Carolina hoodie. Makeup covered dark circles and lined her eyes, odd for a morning beachwalk, but her brows, usually plucked or waxed, showed stray hairs.

"Yes," Cygnet replied. "It's beautiful here in the mornings." Why was she there? The few houses around stayed reliably vacant until mid-May; when vacationers came, he moved to the mountains until they emptied. "I— I like to watch the sunrise sometimes." How did he talk to people? Cygnet had only spoken to The Committee and his creators.

She smiled slightly and hugged herself tighter. "I missed sunrise this morning. I sometimes try to see it, but it's hard to wake up in the dark. Do you have that problem, too?"

She didn't know him as a world-saving supercomputer which appeared human. He had never been anything other than Cygnet, product of Project SWAN. "No," Cygnet said carefully, because that wasn't a lie. "I'm always awake at dawn."

"Lucky. You must be a morning person." She quieted; the waves' regular rasp filled her silence. A breeze blew her long hair into tangles; he examined her as she watched the golden ocean break. Her feet were bare; she'd rolled her jeans to mid-calf, though they were wet to her knees. Her hoodie pocket looked full: likely shells.

People liked to talk about themselves—he should ask a question. "What brought you here this time of year?"

She tucked her hair behind an ear. "I needed some quiet." She seemed to hesitate. "What about you?"

"I stay here for most of the time." He phrased it carefully: "stay" rather than "live." He did not live anywhere. Cygnet was not alive.

"I'm just surprised to see someone, is all. I didn't think—" Her toes dug deeper into the sand. She breathed deeply, then continued. "I guess I didn't expect anyone. I'm Everly." She gazed over the water. "People just call me Ever."

She'd said "people," not "friends." He had to offer his name in return. Strange—had he ever said it aloud? "I'm Cygnet."

She did turn to him then. Her head tilted a bit. "I like it."

"Thank you," he said: the right thing. That was easy. "I, um, I—" He had to leave; only Cygnet could solve the planet's garbage problem. But he suddenly understood. The beauty in "Bohemian Rhapsody" rose from sheer human sympathy, from a shared sliver in time. The sea and sun and girl could be that sliver. "I'm sorry," he said. Humans responded to honesty. "I don't talk to people often." Also not a lie.

Ever shaded her eyes. She was studying him. Cygnet was used to that, though no one had seen his shoulder-length hair tangled into beachy snarls or witnessed him wearing cargo shorts and a long-sleeve Billabong T-shirt. "But you're cute," she finally replied. "Girls must like you." She pressed her lips together and reddened. "Or, I mean, guys. Whichever."

"I don't—that's not—" He'd never thought about it: why would an AI who never interacted with humans *have* a sexuality? "I'm asexual."

"Oh. I'm—I didn't mean to presume. I'm sorry." She stared at the sand and blushed deeper.

"It's alright," Cygnet said. Should he touch her? Only his creators had touched him. How could he tell her she shouldn't feel embarrassed? A hug might help. He wanted to hug her.

Cygnet stepped back instead. He was asexual. But he would like to hug her. He would like to sit with her, and listen to her, and tuck her hair behind her ear. He would like to have her near while he worked.

He was not aromantic.

"I'm very sorry," he said. "I have an important job to do, and I have to leave."

Ever's shoulders slumped. "I'm so sorry. I didn't mean to—"

"No, it's not because of any presumption on your part. I do incredibly important work, and I've taken too much time from it already." He hesitated. "I would like to see you again." Were those the right words? "Do you come out every morning?"

"Yes."

He shouldn't do it. It would take time from his work. He was created to work. But couldn't he stop saving the world for a few minutes? "May I see you again tomorrow?"

Ever's blue eyes met his dark, artificial ones. "I would like that," she told him.

He returned to his house and began the report. It would be late. There was an 85.7% chance The Committee would not ask questions.

AFTER CYGNET PLUGGED into a central processing unit, he organized his landfill solution into implementable strategies. This required a fraction of his nearly unlimited computing power, so he thought about Ever while he worked. He would have to tell her what he was. Humans' likelihood to accept the supposedly unbelievable varied wildly, depending upon personal proclivities, and he knew very little about Ever. However, Cygnet could surmise some demographic data—admittedly small—based on their brief encounter. That told him she was only 13.5% likely to believe him.

He would have to reveal the data ports on his wrists, perhaps even his charger, an outlet in the vicinity of a human belly button. Their uncanniness would likely frighten her. How he would tell her— what words would he use, what pitch and tone—and how might she react? Would Ever laugh or furrow her brow or run away? He couldn't stop thinking about it.

Around noon, Cygnet put a name to this activity: *worrying*. Cygnet was worried.

He had never worried. He eliminated malaria, measles, mumps, yellow fever, dengue fever, ebola, and monkey pox—all without driving bats to extinction; he didn't fret about individual brows furrowing. Bees had rebounded. While the world was already moving toward nuclear fusion, he made its universal usage feasible, thereby eliminating most carbon emissions. Cygnet did not wonder why one particular woman was thin. Instead, he transformed the mess humanity had made into a happy place, a place of freedom and equality, justice and peace.

He watched "Bohemian Rhapsody": a voiceless voice, thousands swallowed into one.

It didn't help.

David Bowie and Annie Lennox grinned as a stadium rang with "Under Pressure."

Data streamed: removing landfills would require a vast network of recycling and sorting plants; these sorting plants would receive raw, mixed materials and separate them using a mix of manpower and nanoparticles, then ship them to their respective recycling facilities—

What if Ever wouldn't speak to him again?

After a shooting at Manchester Stadium, which killed twenty-two people, a single woman cradled a bouquet of yellow flowers. Alone, she warbled the first verse of Oasis's "Don't Look Back in Anger." One by one, the sea of tearful people started to sing.

Organics, such as rotten food, could be easily composted in special facilities designed to remove toxins. Many items were recyclable by current methods, such as aluminum, cardboard, paper, glass, and wood; facilities for items would only need expansion—

A densely-packed crowd held candles. Softly, they sang "Ave, Maria" as Notre Dame Cathedral burned.

He would say hello when he saw her in the morning. Should he ask how she slept? Then she would ask how he slept. He would say he didn't sleep, and she would ask why, and he could say—

Other recycling means would necessitate vast expansion. Diapers comprised 1% of landfill weight and 1.5% of landfill volume; they could be easily turned into a mixture of biofuel, compost, paper, and plastic through a Danish method of thermal pressure hydrolysis—

A crowd in Bradford sang "Wonderwall"—

Ceramic recycling had always been a difficult issue. However—

Cygnet wept over grainy, century-old footage of "Heroes." The song about separated lovers began with Bowie wrapped in ropes. As he sang, a woman untied him, then he stood, free, at the line, "I, I will be king." While he looked over a West German crowd, East Germans on the other side of the Berlin Wall listened, cried, and chanted, "The wall must fall!"

And it fell. Two years after Bowie sparked those riots, it fell—of course the Soviet Union fell for internal reasons; unrest in East Berlin only helped the process along. But Bowie had been a spark, and Cygnet wanted so badly to believe that one crowd, one song, one singular moment had shattered an empire—

On and on, until twenty minutes before sunrise. Cygnet unplugged, rose, and strode down the dunes before dawn. She was waiting. Ever had pulled most of her hair into a messy bun, but the breeze tugged stray strands free. "Good morning, Ever," he said over the waves.

Ghost crabs scuttled home, but no birds passed. "Not morning yet," she replied. "The stars just went away."

Water met sky in a smooth sheet of deep blue. "I have to tell you something." Cygnet's toes curled, and sand scraped them. "I don't think you'll like it very much." Honesty was best.

Okay." She studied him in the near-dark, then drew her arms to her sides. "If it's that you hurt someone, please don't tell me."

What—why—Cygnet's plan faltered. Why would she think that? Perhaps they scared her. Why would they scare her? They would seem possible. He had to reassure her. "I'm incapable of hurting people or getting sick," he told Ever. "I can't do either. I'm not—" He had to say it. He tried to find a steadying horizon between blues. "I'm not human. I'm a kind of artificial intelligence."

The sky began to gray. Ever stayed quiet for a long time. "There are nicer ways to tell me to go away," she finally said.

"No, no—I'm not saying that at all. Please don't go away." Cygnet tried to start again. "I mean a group of scientists designed me. I'm—" Cygnet blushed. He hadn't realized he could. "You know all the things that happened in the past fifteen years? EarthGov and cures for all those diseases and universal basic income and nuclear fusion? All that new tech? The space elevator and the Mars colony and mining on the moon?"

"Oh God, that's so ridiculous. I actually—" Ever hugged herself. "I started to like you. I was excited to see you this morning? Do you know how long it's been since I was excited for something?" Her voice thickened. "I sort of hate you. No, I do hate you."

Blue bled to gray. Ever turned from him.

"Please. It's true." Cygnet hurt: a new, cruel, sharp-edged ache. "I know it sounds crazy—"

She whirled. "I hate that word. Don't use it."

Cygnet clasped his hands behind his back. He couldn't look at her. "I won't. I'm sorry."

"You're horrible, do you know that? Maybe you are some kind of bot—yeah, I see those data ports at your wrists—but this is—"

"I really did all that," he said softly. "I have access to every database in existence, and more computing power than everything ever built before me combined—by orders of magnitude. These people, they send me problems? I send back reports on how to fix them." There was a 75.43% chance Ever would think that he was insane. "I know how it sounds." People said that, his databases told him. "But it's real."

He dared a glance at Ever. "Fine." She crossed her arms. "I'll play your stupid-ass game. Hospital records. They're supposed to be confidential. But you have access to everything, right?"

Cygnet nodded warily. "I won't break confidentiality rules, I'm sorry."

"I'm not asking you to. Why am I here? My full name is Everly Grace Benson."

Her records rose easily. He wanted to hug her. "I don't want to say it, but if I don't say it, you won't believe me, will you?" he asked.

She snorted. "No."

"Can I say part of it instead of all of it?" he asked. Some words were too terrible to apply to a real person, a smaller person who had jammed her hands in her hoodie pocket.

"As long as it gets the point across."

Slowly, so she had a chance to move away, Cygnet reached for her lower arm. She didn't resist. It felt delicate, almost breakable. He cradled her wrist in one hand. With the other, he pushed up her hoodie to show a red-raw scar, raised and recently healed. "There were pills, too." Could she hear him over the waves? "They had to give you flumazenil and pump your stomach. That's enough, right? I don't have to say all the reasons and everything?"

Ever's eyes blew wide. Her mouth opened, then shut. "It's true, isn't it?"

He nodded. "I never met anyone who didn't know. I'm so sorry I was awkward about it. I never had to tell anyone."

The sun broke over the ocean. Ever didn't seem to notice.

Did he tell her he was sorry? It didn't seem right. "I'd like to hug you," Cygnet said, "but I'm afraid you'd be scared."

"I would like a hug." She kept her other hand in her hoodie.

Cygnet let go of her wrist and wrapped around her. When people hugged, didn't they put their arms around each other? Ever drew hers between them and rested her head against his chest. "You feel real." His shirt muffled her voice.

"I am *real*." He didn't huff. He wanted to. "I'm not imaginary. I'm just not . . ." He couldn't stand to say he wasn't really alive.

"I know." Ever sounded—was she close to crying? "I'm safe with you."

WHEN THEY FINALLY BROKE APART, clouds gleamed gold, and pelicans flew in a neat vee. "Will you go for a beach walk?" Ever shoved her hands back in her hoodie pocket.

Cygnet ran his hands through his hair. Was that a nervous habit? "I should work. I'm—" He stopped. "Nevermind."

"No." Ever snatched his hand—like it was nothing, like people touched him all the time. "No, I want to hear, Mr. Supercomputer." Red-eyed, a little sniffly, she smiled slightly. "How are you saving the whole entire world?"

Cygnet kicked at the sand. "It's what I'm built for. It's not special."

"No, it *is* special because it *is* what you're built for. I mean, wow. You're the one who, like, got everyone to destroy nuclear weapons?"

"Yeah, but the people who made me, they're the special ones. I'm only the end result of—"

Ever pulled her hair from its tie. "What are you fixing, for real?"

"Landfills. I know, it's boring—"

"Oh, *wow*." She tugged his hand again. "Will you tell me about it? I mean I won't understand most of it, but tell me a little bit?"

They'd never told him that his plans were secret.

"Please?" Ever's eyes met his.

She didn't care about landfills. She thought he did, and she didn't want him to leave.

They walked toward the waves. Ever had already rolled her jeans. She dropped his hand and he wished she would pick it up again. "We don't have to talk about landfills," he said.

She squealed when the water hit her. "It's always cold at first," she said. "Then you get used to it and it feels good."

"I never held hands with anyone before." Maybe she would understand a hint. Cygnet squinted into the sun. "I never touched anyone else. People always touched me instead."

"Really?" Ever wrinkled her nose. It was already buttonish, and when she scrunched it, it turned up more and made her look almost childish. "What do you do all the time? Other than save the world?" She paused to pick up a moon snail shell.

"I read Hemingway and Dickens while I charge." He plucked a smaller moon snail from the sand and dropped it in her hand.

"You already know this," she said, "which is the problem with you being a supercomputer. I can't tell you things you don't know. But it's a Fibonacci spiral. Isn't it amazing, everything sharing that same golden ratio?"

The morning sun shone in her hair as the wind swept it sideways; the small shell lay on her palm. Her sleeve had slipped up to show her scar.

A crowd could sing with one voice. Two could share a wet, sandy miracle.

ONLY HELPER BOTS had ever come into Cygnet's house. He hosed off Ever's feet, then led her inside. She ran her hand over his curved coffee table. "I love your antiques," she said. "It's not what I expected."

He dropped to his sofa. "Everyone expects me to want modern lines. If I like music, it should be synthpop, like I'd prefer something machine-made. If I like art, it's supposed to be Mondrian squares. People are weird sometimes. They gave me the ability to have preferences, then they think I'm strange for having them."

Ever yawned. "It must be annoying."

He jumped up. "Please sit down. You said it's hard for you to get up in the early morning. You must be tired."

"I'm fine," she said, but sat anyway. She yawned again. "I get tired, I'm sorry. I should've gone home."

"Here." He kept a fuzzy blanket in a closet for non-existent guests. It had always seemed like the right thing to do, like keeping the toilet working. Cygnet spread the blanket over her. "Make sure to take the shells out of your pocket or you'll crush them."

"Are you going to work?" Ever asked.

"If you take a nap? Yes."

She picked at her cuticle for a few moments. "Maybe—nevermind." Ever drew her knees to her chest. "I should leave."

"No, please don't." The plea in Cygnet's voice surprised him. He definitely did not want Ever to leave. "Please say what you started to."

She sprang up. "No, no, I should go. I shouldn't've come. You have work to do, and I—I have therapy today, and—yeah. I guess I'll see you on the beach maybe. Maybe tomorrow. Bye, Cygnet."

"You don't have to—"

"No, I really do." She nearly ran out the door.

What had he done?

Worry still obsessed Cygnet when he walked down the dunes in the morning. The beach was empty. He dropped to the sand. Sunrise would come soon. Was he sad? He'd felt what he could call loneliness now. But never sadness, not like this—

"Cygnet." Ever touched his shoulder.

"You came!" He smiled, a real smile, not a polite one.

Her hands balled into fists; she held them against her chest as if she were cold, perhaps frightened. "I'm sorry about yesterday." When she lowered her chin, the wind spread her hair into a coconut-smelling cloud. "I get scared. I think I got scared that I wasn't scared? I know that doesn't make sense."

It didn't. Maybe it made sense for humans.

"As long as I didn't do anything wrong," Cygnet said. "Did I do something wrong?"

"No." Ever sat very close to him. Did she want another hug? Only a narrow strip of sand separated them. "Sometimes I get scared." Her voice strengthened. "I learned to say that. I have to learn to say things like that, like that I'm scared or mad or sad, or that I need something."

Cygnet sifted through various therapeutic modules. It sounded most like trauma therapy. "You seem sad and you're sitting close to me," he said. "Those things mean you want a hug, don't they?"

Ever drew her knees to her chest again. "Can I have a hug?" she asked. "I'm sad and worried."

Cygnet leaned over and wrapped around her. Like before, Ever kept her arms drawn between them. When he let go, sand slid as she scooted closer, then curled against him. She rested her head against his chest. Ever was small and soft and thinner than he'd thought.

"You don't eat enough," he said.

She snuggled closer and closed her eyes.

"The sun's going to rise," he whispered. "Look, Ever. Look or you'll miss it."

He held her close, and they watched the thin shimmer of pink appear above the ocean. A planet spun, and they saw it together.

"You don't care if I'm quiet," she said after a very long time.

"Why would I care?" Gulls swooped and screeched in the morning.

Sanderlings appeared nearby, little egg-shaped birds on pattering legs. They raced to the water's eggs, munched sand daubs, and darted back before a wave caught them. She'd pulled up her hood, and it felt soft against his cheek.

"People do, mostly. They get uncomfortable."

"No, it doesn't bother me. I like quiet." He sat with one leg on either side of her; Ever cuddled sideways against him, as if she were sleepy. Anyone passing would mistake them for a couple—what humans called a cute couple, one very much in love. Cygnet forced his automatic breathing to remain slow, not to kick up with worry.

He'd thought last night, and he thought more while he held her. Those thoughts frightened him. Ever had been hurt badly, but he couldn't hurt her. Without any danger that kept her from other humans, Cygnet offered comfort, companionship, and love.

"Ever?" He pitched his tone carefully. "Do you only like me because I'm AI?"

She sat straighter. "You're gentle and kind. I would want to like you if you weren't, but I'd be too scared. Because you're—" Her face fell. "Does it matter that you are? I mean, you have to save the world. I'm distracting you."

He began by choosing his words very carefully. "I have been saving the world for twenty-five years, ten months, and three days," he said. "I convinced citizens to love EarthGov. People from the former United States have public transportation in place of interstates and *they ride it*." Cygnet laughed suddenly. "Do you know how hard that was?"

"Oh my God. My aunt *still* bitches. But then she gets on and she's like, 'This is so convenient, why didn't we have it before?' The shared sol-car system is brilliant, by the way."

"Thank you," Cygnet said. Once his projects had passed, The Committee never mentioned them again. "But I was saying—" It was hard to keep his train of thought around Ever— "I've done so much. A break wouldn't hurt, would it?"

He'd meant to tell her. He'd asked instead.

"I don't know," she said. "You tell me. You're the supercomputer."

Something in him sagged. Why couldn't he be Cygnet, not Cygnet the supercomputer? "It doesn't matter with this problem, but not solving this problem on time would cause a delay in solving other problems. These other problems could be far more time-sensitive—for example, they *will* ask me to fix global warming, and I have to do that as soon as possible. I really wish they'd asked me sooner, but I think they know they won't like my answers, so they don't. Even with landfills—the longer I take, the more toxins leak into the ground."

Ever slid away. "I should leave you alone."

"Please don't." Cygnet reached for her. She curled her crossed fists under chin. "I've—" He stopped. Would she think worse of him for admitting it? He was supposed to save the world. Emotion only mattered so far as it kept him from murdering humanity to save it. "I've been lonely."

Her forehead wrinkled and her nose scrunched. She had faint freckles. Cygnet had noted them, but they hadn't seemed important until they were—cute. "Don't the other databases, like, keep you company? Or don't you talk to people online or whatever?"

"No," he said. "I assumed people would be a distraction. Not that you are," he added quickly. "But when my creators told me that, I believed them." A gull landed on the sand and examined them with a beady-black eye. Its head tilted. Vacationers must have fed it, and it had come to tentatively beg. "They aren't like me. They're—insufficient." None had enough emotion to be true company.

"Why didn't they make another one of you, then?"

Cygnet drew small spirals in the sand. He'd never created art. Strange that he made the most primitive of symbols. Did it mean something or nothing at all? "I required a lot of rare-earth metals, time, and expense. They were also afraid that more than one AI like me would develop competing theories. We'd eventually have a rivalry which could result in a battle for supremacy." He paused. "My plans still exist. They could make me a companion."

Ever drew her fists into her sleeves. The gull pecked kelp, and far away, a sole loon bobbed on waves' gentle roll. "Why not a human?"

Cygnet had always carefully considered questions. Ever watched him like he could hand her instant answers about his singular blind spot. "I never said I was asexual until I told you because I never needed to think about it. But I'm—" This was the scariest part. What would she say? "I'm not aromantic. I want to be close with a special person. One person, I think." Polyamory or monogamy—that had never come up, either. "I want to share everything I can with them."

Ever picked up sand and sifted it through her fingers. Her nails were chipped and ragged. "I don't know what I am. You only like me because I'm here."

"That's not true." Maybe it was. But Ever had held that perfect shell for him.

"And you're made to help people?" She searched his face. "It helps that I'm mostly broken, too."

Maybe it did. But Ever had curled against him as the sun rose.

"I think we're alone in the same ways," Cygnet finally said. "And can I show you something? We have to go up to my house."

"I guess."

Ever trailed after him. He would have held her hand, but her fists stayed in her sleeves.

"They can't see this," he explained as he settled her on his couch with a warm blanket and turned on a monitor. "I've encrypted it. Would you watch it with me? It's short. The song's old but maybe you know it. My data says people still like it."

"Okay." Ever drew the word out, as if she were wary. Cygnet sat with her, but not too close. He couldn't presume. But he turned on "Bohemian Rhapsody." He didn't watch the crowd. He watched Ever.

She stared as those voices wove into one and soundlessly mouthed words Cygnet knew so well. Her eyes welled. When it ended, he leaned forward and flicked off the monitor. "Oh, Cygnet." Her voice was thick. "That was one of the most—" Ever's tears spilled over. "Do you have any more?"

Numbers failed him, and a beautiful uncertainty bloomed. Her heart beat like an echo and call. He could sink into its song.

Elizabeth Broadbent escaped the wilds of the Deep South for the Commonwealth of Virginia, where she lives with her three sons and husband. Her speculative fiction has appeared with, or is upcoming in, HyphenPunk, Tales to Terrify, Penumbric, If There's Anyone Left, and The Cafe Irreal. In summer of 2023, ELJ Edition published her novelette, Naked & Famous, about teenagers faking appearances of the South Carolina Lizardman. Her nonfiction has appeared in The Washington Post, Insider, and Time. Her Southern Gothic novella, Blood Cypress, is set for publication in early 2025 with Raw Dog Screaming Press.

Website: https://www.writerelizabethbroadbent.com

CRUSH DEPTH

BY BLAKE JESSOP

Merriweather spun the lock on her bathyscaphe's top hatch and made room for her new oceanographer. She avoided poking her head out, because the world above water was unbearably bright, and the weather extremely sunburn-ish. Merriweather was tall, freckled, and spent so much time underwater that she had to wear really dark goggles every time she went topside. Her bathyscaphe was technically indoors, but the submersible pen's roof was just a metal lattice thickly overgrown with vines and creepers, so patches of blinding sunlight leaked down to flutter on the ashcrete slips every time a breeze blew through.

A small, duffel-sized thump reverberated through the hull, followed by nothing else. Merriweather rose to full height, which was tall enough to poke her head out.

The pen was mercifully cool and relatively dark, but Merriweather still had to squint. Her bathyscaphe had been winched to the surface for loading, and its float was a massive off-white blob beside it. Somewhere in the green water below, skin divers with artificial gills were loading her cargo points with eutactic suspension crates. This was going to be Merriweather's first free-roam iron-fertilization run, and she was almost vibrating with excitement. No course, no schedule, just sailing until she saved the world.

There was another thump as someone fell awkwardly onto the hull. Merriweather reached out and caught a small but very firm hand.

"Careful, she rolls on the surface. Just crawl over here. I'll get your stuff."

Merriweather pawed around to grab the duffel by feel and dropped it down the hatch.

"Watch the float cables. I'm Sarah Merriweather."

"Otohime Sato," the oceanographer said, sitting awkwardly beside the hatch.

"Cool. You can just swing your legs in if that's easier. Watch your step."

"That will not be a problem."

Sato rolled up her pants and removed her legs. The prosthetics were beautiful twists of genetically modified bamboo. Merriweather cringed. She would have known her new crewmate had limb differences if she had bothered to read all her email, which she hadn't.

"Right. Sorry." Merriweather helped the smaller woman down into the pressure hull and tried to think of something to say that was less offensive. "On the bright side, you're not going to take up much space. Let me show you around."

THE TOUR TOOK ABOUT two minutes, because the bathyscaphe was only sixty feet long, and half of it was full of supplies, spare parts and ballast tanks. A pilot's couch at the front, near the big viewing bubble Merriweather used to steer. Cots amidships that could only fold down from the wall if there wasn't anyone sitting in front of a bank of screens and haptic computer interfaces. Long, neatly bundled cables carrying power from a hafnium-trigger power plant hidden under the floor, and fresh air from a liquid-breathing oxygenator whose intakes dotted the hull like cybernetic gills.

Sato was quiet during the tour, maneuvering easily on her palms. Merriweather had to move in a permanent crouch.

"Those are the main attractions. How much time have you spent in bathyscaphes?"

"You have a lot of plants," Sato said.

"They're good for the air. And I talk to them."

Sato raised her eyebrows, which were very fine and conveyed skepticism with delicate precision. The coms system beeped, and Merriweather said a silent prayer of thanks.

"Thank you, com system."

"Is anything wrong?" Sato said.

"No. Nothing's wrong. We're finished loading and they're about to drop us under the float. Get ready."

"How do I–"

The bathyscaphe jolted as the winch let go. They sank with a gentle wobble to take up the slack on the lines attaching them to the float, which was basically just a giant plastic lozenge filled with syntactic foam. Sato looked like she was going to be sick.

"Hey, it's okay. The wobbling is normal. So is talking to plants. That's what I do when I get nervous. Everything is fine."

The bathyscaphe settled into stillness while Merriweather tapped out an acknowledgement and lay down on the control couch. The bathyscaphe swayed as the screws kicked in, and they slowly descended beneath the surface like an airship sinking into clouds.

MERRIWEATHER TALKED. She couldn't help herself. She'd spent most of her career ferrying cargo to deep-sea stations, and rarely had passengers.

"Merriweather, are you alright? Are you nervous?"

"Not at all." Merriweather lay on her stomach to pilot the bathyscaphe, so she had to prop herself on one elbow and look over her shoulder to make eye contact.

"Do you talk to your plants this much?"

"Probably. What do you say, guys?"

The little pots of grass and herbs remained silent.

"Is that a substitute for watching where you're going?"

Merriweather glanced back out the front bubble. The water outside was the crystalline green of unworked jade.

"I know what I'm doing, okay? We're in open water, and according to inertial it's another twenty minutes before we get deep enough to snag on anything. Flying this thing is more like piloting a blimp than a jet fighter. You can take your time."

Sato shifted her cool gaze back to the oceanography screens. She had access to much higher definition pictures of their sonar track.

"Sato, relax. I have almost ten thousand hours in bathyscaphes. What about you?"

"Two," Sato mumbled.

Merriweather laughed.

"You're basically a virgin."

"I helped write the software that controls the iron-seeding nanomachine clouds. I got a PhD in oceanography as an *afterthought*."

"Sorry, sorry. I'm not trying to gatekeep being afraid of the water."

"I am not afraid of the water. I'm afraid of its density curve."

Merriweather looked over her shoulder again.

"What?"

Sato took a deep breath. Her brow knitted.

"Pressure. I am terrified of pressure accidents."

"Oh, okay. That's rational, but there's no need to be. I'm a 'hella good pilot, so we probably won't hit anything, and if the hull failed, it'd basically be like, *BLORT*."

She made squishy sounds and elaborated with her hands.

"Merriweather?"

Merriweather made more noises, laughing at how dumb they sounded. "Our hull is mostly sheets of graphene lattice – super strong but kind of brittle, so if we hit crush depth it's like, instant death. *Pthbt*. We'd get turned into protein paste. Nothing to worry about."

"Merriweather, I lost my legs in a pressure accident fifty minutes into my first drop."

Merriweather made a small hiccupping noise. There was a long pause.

"Shit," she said.

MERRIWEATHER LEANT ONE cheek on the forward observation bubble and the ocean's chill raised goose bumps on her forearms. They were 200 feet down and drifting slowly above what used to be a suburb. Somewhere in the far distance were the sunken towers of old New York.

Her nose was so close to the thermoplastic glass that her breath condensed along the curve. The water had cleared since the descent, and visibility was good enough to see the houses of an ancient tribe pass slowly by below her.

"It makes me nervous when we're in motion and you're not at the controls."

Sato was fidgeting back in bathyscaphe's waist. Merriweather heard her tapping at her screens with the nervous energy of a small fish.

"We're drifting at two knots. If anything goes wrong I'll have half an hour to get back on the couch. Let me know as soon as you find an iron concentration big enough to think about dropping our pods."

More silence.

"I don't understand how you can stare out at the old world for so long. It's dead, and still trying to kill us," Sato said.

Merriweather bristled. She thought it was beautiful and a little sad. Went to sleep imagining how living there had felt, because no one would ever feel whatever that was again. She tried to put these thoughts into words.

"I just like it, okay?"

Sato just shook her head and looked back at her instruments.

"This is hopeless," Sato said.

"I'll take us further toward the city center. The skyscrapers are metal, and there are a lot of cars."

"Too dangerous; we're losing light."

"I can do this in the dark."

A course change pinged on Merriweather's screen. She looked down.

Drop Anchor.

"Sato, I don't want to be rude but this is not how good co-workers communicate."

Another ping.

Drop Anchor, please.

Merriweather sighed and snaked her way aft to release the stern anchor. Sato squeezed out of the way to avoid touching her. Merriweather worked the hydraulic controls and turned back to her oceanographer.

"There's only one solution for work problems when you can't take a walk. Talk it out. It works with the plants. Tell me about yourself."

Sato looked pained, and so Merriweather plowed on. The bathyscaphe rocked as it took up slack on the anchor line.

"I'll go first. I usually run supplies to the permanent habitats down the coast toward Helen Bentley. I was always by myself unless I was ferrying crew or towing habitat bubbles, and talking into a headset really doesn't scratch the itch. I hope I'm not sounding too weird here, but it's really nice to have someone else onboard, and I'm excited about moving up to iron seeding. It feels like saving the world. It was pretty nice down here alone, but you end up talking to your plants, and-"

"I cannot imagine doing this alone," Sato said. Her voice was surprisingly rich, for such a small woman, but so soft Merriweather had to stop herself yelling, *what?*

"Yeah. Pretty lonely." Merriweather crawled back to her couch. She touched her fingertips to the sticks and felt the tug of the ocean on her anchors.

"So, you want to tell me what happened?"

The couch was designed so that Merriweather could rest her chin on it to avoid straining her neck. She didn't turn her head to avoid making Sato nervous.

"I'm not just a nanotech engineer; I am a cartographer. I was drafted into field duty because I wrote a bunch of the code we use to map ruins on the ocean floor. I didn't want to go, but the results of the first coast-wide iron seeding were incredibly positive, and they needed a lot more people."

There was a momentary increase in Sato's wattage. Merriweather heard something excited hidden in her voice. She turned from the exterior window. Sato sat with her hands pinched between what was left of her legs, black hair falling in front of her face.

"We were doing a cable drop into deep water. No float. I was crawling from the cabin back to my instruments when the accident happened."

"What went wrong?"

"Knit line failure. I heard a creak, looked over my shoulder at the pilot, and then the emergency bulkhead snapped shut on me. He did it. I don't know what he saw, or felt, or noticed, he just hit it. The seal was almost water-tight, even with my legs in it, and they started pulling us up as soon as the sensors caught the bulkhead closing."

"Jesus. Ouch. It's lucky your pilot was sharp."

"Almost as much as the door, but yes, he hit the emergency lock before the sensors registered a failure. I am not doing this because I love it. I'm down her because I have to be."

"Sorry, fuck. I didn't mean to trigger you. I just meant- what do I mean?"

"I'm honestly not sure what anything means to you. How can you be so cheerful down here? This isn't a cute little habitat full of plants and opportunity. It's incredibly dangerous."

"Hey, back off a little, okay? I'm not complicated. I like driving this bathyscaphe. I like my little garden. I like looking out the windows. This is my world, okay?"

"It's very small," Sato said.

~

NIGHT FELL FAST UNDERWATER. Merriweather flipped lights on as the water outside turned the kind of black the sky would be if there were no stars.

It was all Merriweather could do to keep her thoughts to herself. She wanted to talk to the plants. *Look guys, I think the engineer is freaking out, and I'm not sure how to fix her.*

Merriweather had felt genuinely hurt by the *small world* comment for a few minutes, but then kind of forgot why and decided to give the oceanographer another chance. What did it was the gentle thud of the bathyscaphe drifting against its anchor chains making Sato jump. Merriweather realized that she wasn't just being catty. She was terrified.

"Look," Merriweather said, losing her battle against silence. "I really want to enjoy this trip, so I've thought up a new strategy for communicating with you. The way I see it there's input lag, like when I move the bathyscaphe, so I'm just going to try to help you get comfortable as slowly as possible without scaring you. That may seem confusing, because every time the bathyscaphe's hull creaks you jump out of your skin with, like, no lag at all, but this is what I've got. I'm going to be nice to you around corners. Does that make sense?"

Sato looked up from her screens, and as Merriweather spoke her face contorted itself into a series of strong emotions. The last of them was surprise.

"Yes, that actually does make sense."

"Just roll with it. You know what's going to make you feel better?"

"I'm fine," Sato said, taking a deep breath.

"Soup. Soup works on everything. It's your first night down here, so I'll cook. Scooch."

"What?"

"Move, please."

Merriweather crawled by Sato, using one of her stumps as a hand hold, and the engineer was too surprised to get out of the way. There was a series of thumps as she mostly disappeared from view and rummaged around in the stores suspended in mesh sacks toward the bathyscaphe's stern. She emerged, improbably, with a single coconut. Sato laughed at the incongruity of it, and the sound was so pleasantly unexpected that Merriweather did, too.

"Okay, I'll heat water and you cut me some lemongrass. There are pruning scissors velcroed to the rack."

Sato diligently got the scissors, then stared at the rows of tiny pots. Snipped.

"That's spearmint. I want lemongrass. It looks like grass and smells like lemons. Just sniff around."

Merriweather simmered her broth, making a big production of cracking the coconut and adding tofu from a block kept in a cooler wedged against the hull. They ate, and the broth reflected the gentle blue light of the sonar return screens.

"How is it?"

"Very good," Sato said, then, after a while, and a little uncomfortably; "though my stomach feels slightly upset."

"You'll get used to the sway, but if you want to pick more spearmint, I'll make tea."

∼

ALL VERY DANGEROUS things became routine if you did them long enough. Merriweather talked to herself and Sato and the plants, and Sato listened. They spent a day cruising over what had once been a city called Newark, and finally got a strong iron return, only to discover that another bathyscaphe had gotten there first.

That led to a few exciting minutes of underwater email over the Janus modem and, after a little banter, the decision to press onward toward the city itself. Somewhere along the way, Merriweather said something that made Sato look up.

"Side note: I figured out what I meant," Merriweather said, picking up a conversation thread from so long ago that she wasn't sure if Sato would remember it. "I meant that I admire your old pilot. He just went for it. Figured out what was happening and made a great call. He died saving you. It's really pure."

"I already knew that was what you meant."

"Oh," Merriweather felt deflated. "I thought you'd be proud of me. Making and testing personal hypotheses."

"I am moderately impressed, but I also wish my pilot wasn't so enamored of the idea of dying beneath the sea."

Merriweather instantly felt like she was back at the beginning of a maze, with an entirely new problem to solve.

"Man, you can be hard to talk to."

"Really?" Sato said, deadpan.

"Wasn't there a story where this happened? Wasn't someone meant to leave some string for me to follow through the maze, or something?"

"I don't know what you're talking about."

"You being hard to reach," Merriweather said. "Mazes. Heroes with strings. Greeks?"

"Theseus and Ariadne. And it would only work if you'd gotten to the middle of the maze first."

Merriweather looked at Sato, and felt something tug at her like a deep water current.

"I think I did, though."

"That would make me the hairy minotaur."

Merriweather slapped her forehead with her palm.

～

SATO AND MERRIWEATHER'S COMPLEX, dangerous, world-rescuing work was also really boring most of the time, but Merriweather was overjoyed to have been let off the chain to sail wherever she wanted to. Honestly, it was more wherever Sato told her to after obsessively scrutinizing her instruments, but the important thing was that she was free to choose how they got there. She cruised ancient streets and dove very slowly between prelapserian steel towers, like a great whale looking for food.

For once, Sato left her instruments and come to look out at the drowned world.

"You're right. It is a little beautiful."

The high-rises swept from the sea floor into a green infinity above them.

"Yeah. I know we're not supposed to like the old world, but it's pretty cool-looking. I mean, it's hard not to look out at all this and feel like the world isn't worse. That we lost something we can't get back."

Sato was leaning on one hip. She ran a hand over her stumps.

"I understand what you mean."

"Oh, shit." Merriweather said. "That's not what I meant. I swear, Sato, I-"

"It's fine. I'm not serious."

"Oh god, really?"

Sato smiled, and absently patted Merriweather's shoulder on her way back to the sonar. Merriweather came to a further realization; she wasn't just getting used to the oceanographer's company, she was starting to enjoy it.

～

MERRIWEATHER PILOTED the bathyscaphe deftly through a maze of ancient spires. Their magnetic sensors only worked from reasonably close, so she had to drift delicately between old brownstone apartment buildings and make sudden shifts when high-rise towers emerged from the gloom.

"This patch is not ideal; too much high-carbon steel."

"So we go further downtown and see if it gets better."

"Too many obstructions. We should seed here."

"Oh come on. I can handle this. Let's take a few risks. Maybe we can find an opening to one of the subway tunnel systems."

Sato swiveled forward on her palms to lean over Merriweather and look through the bubble.

"That is not a terrible idea, but I don't know how we'd drop the nanoparticle canisters into such a small opening."

Sato had one hand supporting her weight and the other on Merriweather's back for balance. Merriweather got a good whiff of her. Washing wasn't easy in a submersible; you had to make do with sponge bathing using biodegradable towlettes. Sato smelled like sweat and cotton and lemongrass. Like some dish Merriweather hadn't had in a long time and didn't know she'd missed.

Merriweather turned her head and sniffed.

"I'm sorry," Sato said, immediately self-conscious.

"No, you actually smell pretty good," Merriweather thought.

Sato backed away from whatever was happening like a skittish animal. She went back to her screens and an iron scan popped up on Merriweather's screen.

"I didn't say that out loud, did I?"

"This is as good as it's going to get," Sato replied. "Iron concentrations are decent, but dispersed. I estimate sixty percent of the swarm would bite, and there isn't much phytoplankton here yet. It's a good spot."

"We can do better," Merriweather said. "Let's go downtown."

"It's too risky."

"Relax," Merriweather said. "We can do this."

WHEN MERRIWEATHER RAN the bathyscaphe aground, the hull made a bang so loud that Sato clapped her hands over her ears. The hull rocked fore and aft and something above them made a strange, wobbling twang. Like a sound effect from an old space fantasy, except real and fatally dangerous.

Before they creaked to a stop, Sato rushed from her station and latched onto Merriweather like a limpet.

"Sato, it's fine. We're fine. For now. We did not go *Pthbt*."

Sato just clung to her and shook.

∾

"Try the Janus."

Sato did. Tapping panels gave her something to do.

"Too many obstructions, no signal."

"I hope I didn't damage the intakes on the artificial gills."

Sato blanched. Merriweather wished she knew how to keep her monolog internal.

"Hey, I can still hear the centrifuge it uses to separate air from water. We're probably okay."

Sato squeezed her eyes shut. "I wish this deathtrap was big enough for a full electrolysis suite. Then you couldn't break it when you crash into things."

"Don't be mean to the bathyscaphe. She's doing her best."

"Then don't talk about things that might suffocate me."

Merriweather debated whether to tell her that the oxygenator breathed a lot better when they were moving, and that she was already topping up the atmosphere from onboard 02 tanks. She managed not to. A gentle alarm warned her that the carbon dioxide was rising, and Merriweather turned it off. The bottom line was that they were in terrible danger, it was just happening in very slow motion.

They would not, at least, run out of power. The hafnium-trigger power plant only had five grams of radioactive material in it, but it steadily chugged out electricity no matter how many things Merriweather asked it to do at once. It couldn't ramp up to give their screws a lot more power, because if they did that the reactor would become more dangerous than a nuclear bomb, but it would keep working forever. Merriweather liked that about her power source. At some point, someone working on an isomer-powered weapons program could have built a city-busting nuke, and figured out how to power spaceships and submarines instead. Drawing power slowly was actually *harder* than making it explode. Someone obsessive must have worked on that. Someone like Sato, probably.

"Merriweather?"

"Yeah?"

"Don't coddle me. I can see you turning alarms off."

"Okay, we're in trouble." Sato let out a moan. "But I can get us out of it."

"Have you ever done anything like this before?"

"Yes. No. Kind of. Not exactly this, but I've hit stuff before, and I'm good. I'm really good. Trust me."

"I don't know if I can," Sato said.

PILOTING the bathyscaphe was like trying to play a video game drunk. Everything Merriweather did took a painfully long time to translate itself from haptic input to hydraulic impetus to gentle drift in the water. It took almost three hours, but with a series of motions on the sticks as minute as plucking harp strings, she finally jostled them free.

When the bathyscaphe shook loose from the wreckage it was tangled in, the tether cables twanged with violent resonance against the hull. Sato let out a joyous little squeak before covering her mouth.

"Are we loose?"

"We're loose. I'm backing up."

In a confusion of relief, enthusiasm and embarrassment, Sato shook her fists in the air, them drummed her palms on the backs of Merriweather's thighs.

"You did it!"

"Yeah, I fuckin' did. And do that a little higher up, please."

Sato went silent, but didn't take her hands away.

MERRIWEATHER GOT them away from the skyscrapers as night fell, and dropped anchor in what must once have been a park. They both crawled amidships, exhausted.

"I'm too tired to stow the gear and set up the bunks," Merriweather said.

"It's procedure. It is not safe to sleep unsecured."

Merriweather pulled one of the foam liners out and laid it on the floor.

"What are you going to do? Climb up there and do it yourself?"

It was so outrageously insensitive that Sato could barely believe Merriweather had just said it.

"Seriously?" she said. Then said the word again, laughing.

"I didn't mean that. Or I did mean it but I didn't mean to be mean. Can you be angry at me for being a moron later? For now just lie down and sleep."

Sato could, and did.

~

MERRIWEATHER HAD ALREADY GOTTEN them underway when Sato finally woke up.

"What time is it?"

"I muted all the ship notifications so you could sleep."

Sato palmed her way forward and slid by Merriweather to perch herself in the bubble. An obstacle was sliding by to starboard; a faded sign in the shape of a badge, with the alphanumeric *I-87* almost hidden beneath a gently waving coat of algae.

"You were right, we should have dropped uptown. These old gas burners might work, though."

The hulks drifted by below them, like a rusted coral reef. They, and the asphalt they once drove on, were one of the reasons the world above could hardly breathe anymore. Headstones in a cemetery full of ancient sins.

"Not ideal; there's a lot of algae, and most of these models were built with aluminum. Iron rust is what phytoplankton eat. We need to feed them if we want them to clean the air."

Merriweather set the controls for a slow drift and crawled up to join Sato against the glass. There shouldn't have been enough room for both of them, but Sato didn't take up much space.

"You still think this is wonderful?" Sato asked.

"Yeah. Whoever drove these cars didn't try to kill me. I'm the one who hit an obstruction."

"I mean that the people who built all this are the ones who ruined the terrestrial habitat. They're the reason we're down here."

"I know."

"Then how can you love them?"

"I don't think I do. I just think this is beautiful."

"I do not understand."

"I'm a pilot. I love driving submersibles in general – the specific reasons I do it can change. They have changed."

"How?"

Merriweather struggled to figure out how to say it.

"I enjoy saving the world, but I could settle for you."

IT TOOK the entire rest of the day to sail far enough north to completely clear the megalopolis. Merriweather yawned.

"I think I'm done. I'll pull the bunks down."

Sato was already stretching on the foam they'd slept on the previous night.

"Scooch," Merriweather said, crawling past her.

"This is fine," Sato said. Merriweather sat beside her. The smell was back.

"Do you want me to-"

Sato reached up and pulled one of Merriweather's arms over her like a blanket.

MERRIWEATHER WOKE up with her face in Sato's hair. Sato rolled over, half asleep, and buried her nose in Merriweather's t-shirt. The Bathyscaphe smelled like sweat and polymer and a strange mixture of plants.

"Let me sleep," Sato mumbled. Just as Merriweather reached a decision on whether she would, she noticed something flashing on the sonar screens. She tapped at it groggily, and an alarm came to life.

They uncoiled from one another like snakes. Merriweather scrambled to the control couch on her stomach and hit the emergency lights. Shatteringly bright LEDs slashed through the gloom as she pulled back on her sticks to stop the drift. Skeletal structures loomed in front of the bathyscaphe. She had just gotten very, very lucky.

"The anchors didn't latch, and I forgot to turn the alarms back on. Are you okay?"

Sato didn't say anything.

"Sato?"

Sato was just staring at the screens. She shook her head and looked again.

"Are we okay? Are we safe?"

"Yeah, we're fine. What's wrong?"

"Nothing. I assume you can see some obstructions?"

"Lots of them."

"They're almost pure iron." Sato crawled forward, her voice full of excitement. "Angle the lights up."

Merriweather widened the cone of light, and a yawning skeleton loomed into view in front of them. A latticed metal rib cage soared above them, casting stark shadows in the silty water. Beneath it was row after row of iron behemoths overgrown with algae. Unseen beneath them, but making the magnetic sensor howl, was a gridwork of iron rail sidings.

"A train yard," Sato said with great satisfaction, rejoining Merriweather at the controls. "This is the best iron fertilization site imaginable. The first phytoplankton to smell out the rust we make are going to be the founders of an oxygen production dynasty."

"Triple nice. Fucking awesome."

"Merriweather?"

"Fantastic. I'm going to save the world. I'm– what?"

"Can you position us for drop, please?"

Merriweather teased the bathyscaphe upward, and let it drift very slowly forward.

"We can't miss."

Sato paused for a moment, then took Merriweather's hand.

"Let's plant a garden, then."

The bathyscaphe jolted as the payload dropped. The pods levered open like mechanical flowers, and clouds of tiny machines vanished toward the sidings like tendrils of smoke. Uncountable millions of little prayers, each made to feed the algae that fed the sky.

Blake Jessop is a Canadian author of sci-fi, fantasy and horror stories with a master's degree in creative writing from the University of Adelaide. His short fiction has been nominated for Aurora, Push-cart, Lambda, Locus, and Ignyte awards, and he has lectured about relevance of fiction and modern media for the departments of psychology and neuroscience at McGill University.

Speculative City: https://speculativecity.com/fiction/divide-zero/
Amazon Author Page: https://www.amazon.com/stores/author/B07BB7Z73N

SYNTHETIC DIVIDE
BY JOSEPH WELCH

I saw the room through two sets of eyes. There was a moment – not a long one – but a moment in which I was split between two perspectives. It was unnerving. My new, artificial body was seated back-to-back with my old, human body – which was good. It would've felt odd to watch myself watching myself. Then the moment ended, and I was looking through new eyes.

My limbs twitched and trembled while I acclimated to the control software. Self-diagnostic data, like power and audiovisual acuity levels, bordered my vision. I was used to using a HUD, technology that had long been able to interface with our brains, but this was a step further.

"Ms. Arakawa?" Dr. Hakeem Sidravani said. I focused on him, on his pristine white lab coat, and on his striking synthetic eyes. He still had the old models that looked like highly polished iridescent disks, which made it impossible to determine where he was looking. I found the antiquated tech somewhat baffling because of where he worked. I mean, we were surrounded by the cutting edge, but here he was. It was like cellphones, things that belonged in the past. Perhaps he was trying to make a statement? The rest of him was unremarkable. His shoulder-length hair was combed back and white as snow. His face was lined and tan with a slight sheen, like burnished copper, and he had an easy smile. "Ms. Arakawa, can you lift your right hand?"

I tried, and it took more effort than I would've expected. I looked down at my arm before looking back to him in confusion. "Is something wrong?" I asked.

He shook his head. "No, your body will take time to adapt to its new condition. In some ways, it's as if you're a newborn. Most people figure it out within a few days. Your recovery period is covered in the transition procedure."

I concentrated, and squeezed my right hand into a fist before relaxing it. I worked the arm around, and brought it to rest. He watched me run through a series of progressively more refined and controlled movements and, feeling a bit more confident, I stood. The urge struck me, and I couldn't resist. I turned to face what had, until minutes ago, been me.

The body wasn't dead. A heart beat in its chest and the lungs continued to draw air, but there was nothing behind the eyes. I found it disturbing and had to turn away.

"You needn't concern yourself with it," the doctor said, chuckling. "Rest assured, nothing will go to waste."

That was how I could afford this ridiculously expensive procedure – how many people could. My old body was the currency for the transition into a prosthetic body. All that was flesh and bone would go to medical centers to be parted out as needed. A tidy, equivalent exchange. And yet it bothered me in a way I couldn't articulate. It wasn't me anymore, but I still felt a claim, a lingering attachment. I shook my head. I had to move on.

"May I go?" I asked.

"Of course." He beamed a toothy grin at me. "Enjoy your new life, Mika."

~

"MIKA?" Darrin asked, his wise brown eyes catching a glint of sunlight, and bringing me back around from my wandering thoughts. It was as though the world had been out of focus until he uttered my name. The sudden buzz of the surrounding midday patrons' conversations in the street-side cafe made me wince. My brain could now distinguish each individual strand and process them in real time. I quickly set filters so that I was listening only to Darrin.

Out of habit, I'd ordered a coffee. It sat between us like a comment. I watched the separate particles of steam rise and curl, somewhat taken with the new level of granular detail.

"Sorry, you were saying?" I said.

"It's just... you've hardly said a word since we sat down. Are you feeling alright?"

Was I? I frowned. "This is all so overwhelming," I said.

"I can imagine. Though I personally prefer to keep the body God gave me."

"Oh, I see. Is this a sudden attack of religion?" I teased.

A faint smile crossed his lips. "You should know me well enough by now to answer that." He waved it away. "I just couldn't imagine... transitioning."

"Oh, come. Eternity isn't a little tempting?"

He leaned back in his chair, and his eyes drifted upward to the cloud-strewn, spring sky. "But how do you know? I mean, really know? You could just be a copy, some simulation of a person who used to exist." He gestured at my prosthetic body. "Technology's great and all, but I can't trust it that far."

I clasped my hands in my lap. He wasn't wrong, I had had the same fears. They're only reasonable, but I'd already committed. I had felt the moment of transfer from my human body to this, and there had been no lapse. The deeper philosophical stuff was all irrelevant anyway. If I was a copy, then there was no getting the original back. My sense of self sat in a digital braincase, as did all my memories. "I'm me. The only me I've ever known. Do I seem different to you?"

He furrowed his brow, and after a moment let out a measured sigh. "You're not exactly the same. Though I can't say just how."

"Hmm. I wonder." A slight breeze stimulated the dermal receptors on my bare arms. I'd opted for a natural human look, no plates or joints visible, nothing to indicate the mechanisms underneath. I closed my eyes and turned down my synthetic nerve sensitivity to prevent the looming sense of overload from so many dissonant inputs. It wasn't that the faux-skin covering made a difference; the sensors and feedback were an integral part of prosthetic design, not something dependent on the form of covering. They were supposed to work better than the real thing, give you a superhuman sensory experience – with all the latest enhancements authorized for civilians. "Look, Darrin, I need some time to process this. Perhaps we could meet again tomorrow?"

A look of disappointment crossed his face before he pulled his lips back into his gentle smile. He reached out, and put his mahogany-toned hand atop mine. "I'm here for you any time."

~

NIGHT WAS SETTLING IN, with the purpled and pink-tinged clouds highlighted by the setting sun. A light smattering of rain dotted the sliding door to my sad, narrow balcony. It really was more of a railing-edged ledge or an oversized window than an actual space. It fit in with the rest of my apartment. Small, compact, the bare minimum a person required, and yet it was still almost beyond my means. I supposed I could repurpose some of it now. I had no need for nourishment. A miniature fusion reactor powered by fuel pellets had replaced my heart, and would sustain me indefinitely. I wouldn't need the cookware or space for the storage of foodstuffs, but I would still need the shower. My body may not excrete anything anymore, but it accumulated dirt and particulate.

Redesigning my home to fit my new circumstances, however, wasn't pressing. I just wanted to sit and reflect. To acclimate myself. I attuned a jazz stream, and let the creative flow wash over me. The music hit me like a convergence, like the band members were just accidentally crafting the same song. I plopped down on my sleeping mat, and leaned against the sliding door. I closed my eyes, and shut off all the gauges and monitors that constantly flooded my vision. After a moment longer, I even shut off the jazz. I existed, hyper-aware of every fragment of my body and mind, but pulled within myself. It was intense and surreal, and too much. Perhaps I would get used to this new perspective in time, but for right now, I wanted to turn it down, to tune out.

I could simulate sleep, suspend my consciousness for set intervals, even dream, but somehow the thought of a program replicating sleep repelled me, and the loss of an actual physical need for it hit me hard. It just wasn't something I'd considered.

Others bemoaned the loss of food, but the transitioned could still taste, could still chew and swallow, and later dispose of the undigested waste. But eating was just a means to sustain myself. I never had derived the same level of joy some people experienced from a meal or even a dessert. That was one biological function I no longer need concern myself with. Sleep on the other hand... how would I spend that time? I would never tire, but rest was a gathering, a distillment. It reframed the day. And now it was gone.

I pulled up my chronometer. It had been only ten minutes since I had sat down. I opened my eyes, and got back to my feet. I needed to wander just now. I couldn't explain it. I wanted to move, to do something, and hanging around my apartment wasn't it. I'd never been much of a night owl. Even in college, where I spent many sleepless nights studying and cramming, ever worried about my academic performance, I never sought it out. When others were getting their release in the various parties and social gatherings, I was catching what sleep I could. But that life was over, and that me gone, replaced by this new version.

BETWEEN THE LIGHTS AND HOLO-ADVERTISEMENTS, the city was as bright as day, but the silvered tones banished all thoughts of nature. I would've thought the city would feel less busy now, but the only difference I noticed was a slight relaxation in dress. It's hard to feel any sense of individuality among so many, and perhaps I'd hoped for this, a bit of blending, a lessening of self.

A middle-aged woman in a conservative skirt-suit called out to me. "Excuse me, but have you heard about the recent surge in cyberbrain hacking? Your recent transition puts you at greater risk. The best source in news, the NHK can help you protect--" I waved away the hologram, which immediately attached itself to its next target. The Diet kept going back and forth on just what exactly defined private metrics, on what data were considered private, but the commercial lobbies had quite effectively pushed policy in their favor. It amounted to an annoyance, but more interminable than intolerable.

Other ads vied for my attention. Beckoning me to buy upgrades I didn't need or want. I wished I could shut them out, but the courts had ruled that companies had a right to advertise on public grounds.

People passed me by, absorbed in whatever private motives drove them, barely conscious of the others around them. Society has grown so impersonal that the distance between human beings can't be measured physically any more. Even if I reached out and touched someone in the passing throng, it wouldn't feel like contact. Although Darrin was an anachronism, obstinately refusing to become more than base flesh and bone, perhaps he had a point. Or maybe this is just the next step in our evolution, where we've moved beyond the physical realm. Children were becoming a novelty, and most people didn't exist outside the context of their 'net persona. But Darrin was also one of the few real, solid connections I had. And I cherished him for it.

A WEEK PASSED, and reality had taken on a sense of timelessness. Moments blended together, losing distinction. My internal chronometer was my only objective measure. I was anxious to return to work, to some semblance of normality. My recovery leave had overstayed its welcome, and I needed a grounding, but that would have to wait. Besides, my job wasn't especially important.

I was a quality assurance manager at a major electronics manufacturer, and the bulk of the work was conducted by my team. A few remote meetings and video check-ins were all it took to maintain my position. Technically, I didn't have to go into the plant, but I'd rather that than all this accursed indolence. At least today, I had something to do. I was meeting Darrin for lunch.

Restaurants were becoming a bit of a niche market as more people transitioned. But Darrin had a knack for picking some of the best. This one was a soba joint with a row of stools badly in need of mending along a bar and a handful of scarred, wooden tables for two. The room was long and narrow, with grease staining the wall and air. The heady aromas were just the thing to provide a sense of home and comfort. That, and the low-lighting added to the close, almost intimate atmosphere.

Darrin was sitting toward the back, and his face brightened when it alighted on me. "Mika," Darrin said, beckoning me back. He rose from his seat to pull out the opposing chair for me.

I smiled and pulled him into a familiar hug. We stood in the embrace for a long moment before breaking apart into our respective seats. A rotund man with a stained apron, bald head, pencil-thin moustache, and golden skin came bearing two steaming plates of noodles, looked at both of us, smiled a knowing smile, and set them down before us. I shot a look at Darrin, and was ready to object. After all, the superfluous food was beginning to make me feel self-conscious of my new condition.

"I know, miss," the rotund man said. "But sometimes it is necessary to indulge in unnecessary things." He bestowed us with another smile that if mishandled could very easily have been interpreted as condescending, but seemed somehow genuine and confidential.

Darrin placed his hand over mine. "It's fine." I was unsure whether he said it to me or to the man.

My next comment died on my lips, and I leaned back. I wasn't sure why the presence of food struck me so. The man receded, humming some tuneless melody to himself, and Darrin nodded to me. "And you wonder whether you've changed," Darrin said.

I felt a brief annoyance. "It's hard. Much more so than you'd imagine."
"Okay."

"No. I mean it. It's just... I feel lost, Darrin."

He took a contemplative bite and chewed for a maddeningly long time before swallowing and taking a sip of the cheap, green tea. "That's the catch, isn't it? This hyper-reality? All this more, and maybe we can't handle it." He paused. "Or, well, maybe we shouldn't try." He pointed at me with his chopsticks. "Why did you transition?"

I was taken aback. "I suppose... it was to avoid growing old, to avoid the loss that comes with age," I said.

"Hmph. That's straight out of the ads – or might as well be." He tapped the chopsticks on the table. "Anyway, I guess you accomplished that much."

I looked away, embarrassed. "I know, but millions of people have done the same."

"Well," he chuckled. "I don't particularly care about the millions."

Something in his look made me blush and took the heat out of the conversation.

He took a deep breath, and held it for a moment. "Anyway, would you take it back?" he eventually asked.

I shrugged, dodging his question. "I just... I really need you, Darrin. I need an anchor."

His chopsticks clacked against his plate and he leaned back in the chair. And did I detect a note of disgust or irritation in his expression? "Buyer's remorse?"

I looked down. "I just want to be happy," I said quietly.

"Such a simple request, isn't it?"

His words hit me hard. Was I being naive? It felt that way, like I was expecting this external change to touch every aspect of my being. But it also made me wonder, "Have I ever seemed happy?" I genuinely wanted to know.

He sighed, and drank his tea. "How can I answer that if you can't answer it yourself?" He hesitated. "Mika, you asked me whether I would ever choose to transition, and I told you then that I prefer to remain human. Even though most of my friends have transitioned." He frowned. "I believe that our limited existence is what compels us to achieve, to strive. You've abandoned that constraint. There's eternity before you, but no drive, no pressure to accomplish something meaningful before you die. I can't help but see the death of progress when I look at everyone who's chosen as you have."

"I should go." I stood and was on the verge of walking away, when he laid his hand upon my arm, stopping me.

"Mika," and there was real emotion coloring his words, "are you happy?"

I turned to him, and spent a long time studying his face, trying to salvage something of my former fondness for him, but the pity and disappointment lurking around his eyes dispelled any lingering sentiment. "I'm sorry, Darrin. I suppose I'm just another empty, ambitionless shell."

I saw the fleeting hurt pass through his eyes, and the frustration, before he released my arm and patted my shoulder. "Farewell, Mika. I truly enjoyed your company." His hand dropped away, and he gave me a sad smile and a solemn nod, then brushed past me. The finality of his words was unmistakable.

The rotund man, who had been watching the scene from the far end of the bar, sighed, threw down his cleaning rag and turned his back on me. I felt the urge, the compulsion, to leave, to flee this scene and retreat into myself. And yet, I couldn't. I collapsed back into the chair and stared at the door. I was reeling. What had happened?

My first impulse was to assume Darrin was the one who was being unreasonable. Had I really done anything so offensive? Then I tried to take his prospective. I was an affront, a perversion to him. I had rejected my humanity, and I couldn't even articulate my reasoning. And I realized that it was because I had none. No dreams or desires, no passion. So, I left the restaurant, without any particular destination in mind.

~

THE DAY PASSED INTO NIGHT, and the darkening gloom of heavy clouds promised rain. I had found my way back to my apartment complex, but I hadn't the will to enter. I simply stood there under the awning. What had I done, and how could I move forward?

I needed someone, some social contact. What I had failed to get from Darrin, something to recall me from the precipice my mind was teetering on. The impulse was so strong, I thought about accosting one of the passersby, or perhaps diving into the 'net. Some people lived their entire lives there, existing as digital avatars, but the inherent anonymity of cyber-space repulsed me. It conferred an almost godlike ability to be our own authors. All of it was fantasy and illusion, a carefully tailored facade. Even so, would they deign to engage? Somehow, I doubted it. And the bars and clubs held no promise, either. What I needed was something both imme-diate and lasting, not some hookup or casual encounter. Left without prospects, I entered the building, went to my apartment, and shut myself down until morning.

~

AWARENESS. It was like a switch suddenly clicked on. There was something quite disconcerting about software designed to toggle one's consciousness on and off. The thought that something might go wrong, that I could slip into permanent oblivion, terrified me.

Not that it was unheard of. There were stories, ones about other transitioned who flicked the switch off never to turn it back on, but that was akin to suicide, and if Darrin was right about my sacrifices, then they'd be sacrifices for naught. But I had to do something; I had to find some way to cope.

I opened a connection request to the counseling service Dr. Sidravani's secretary had given me, and after a moment of waiting, a window filled the center of my vision. The man who answered had electric-blue hair, shifting tribal-pattern tattoos crawling about his literally white face, and glowing crimson eyes. A rather extreme look.

He paused briefly, his features stationary as, I'm sure, he pulled up my info. I could identify the moment his focus shifted back to me. "Hello, Mika," he said. "Would you like to schedule a meeting?"

"I... yes. I think that would help."

"One will begin within the next few minutes. I'm sending you the connection information now." He smiled, and the window vanished to be replaced with a scroll of data, and a flashing "pending connection." I shifted it to my periphery.

I sighed, and stepped in front of the sliding glass door. It was early yet. The dark of night hadn't quite given up its hold to the light of day. Cars and people moved about below. It had the appearance of a choreographed dance with everyone moving to the same rhythm. No one looked at one another. It all seemed so cold and sterile. Clinical. It made me wish I was flesh and blood again: a warm body full of passion and hopes and fear. The pang of longing I felt now was deep and intense, like some living thing writhing about, trying to get free.

The prompt of an incoming call flashed, drawing my focus from the streets below, pulling me away from the depths of my own mind. I had almost forgotten that I was waiting on a session. I accepted, and the person who filled the screen was androgynous to the point that I couldn't tell what gender they were. Their purple hair with black tips was half-shaved on one side and their eyes were a piercing, glowing jade. Gauges decorated their ears, and their skin tone was a burnt sienna. "Mika?" they said. "Hello, I'm Karma. Pleased to meet you, how can I help?"

I hesitated. I was in need of a break from artificiality, and instead, I got this. Maybe I should have been numb to these extreme choices in style, and it was probably prejudice, but I could hardly take Karma seriously. "I'm sorry. I should go."

They smiled and their face was full of compassion. "Mika, whatever your reasons, you reached out. I'm here to listen, and maybe I can help, but I can only do that if you're willing to open yourself up. Please, trust me?"

They were being reasonable, and maybe I should be reasonable as well. I let the space between their words grow. I still wanted to end the call, but I needed this. Here was someone who would listen. But it hurt that this stranger was willing to make the offer that Darrin wouldn't, even if it was their job. "It's been a rough few days, I guess." I shrugged, feeling uncomfortable.

Karma nodded, their bangs falling across emerald eyes.

I worked to formulate what to reveal, weighing my words, then decided that if I really wanted something from this, I had to be honest. "I lost my only real friend, Darrin." I winced, what had happened between Darrin and me felt both painful and personal, yet I didn't stop. "He said some awful things, or, well, not really awful, but true, and now I feel aimless, like this... this transition was all a mistake. Like I have no one left, and now I don't know what to do, or who to turn to. It's all too much to take in. I'm not adjusting or finding a new balance, and I can't take it. I can't..." I felt as though I wanted to break into tears. Tears I could no longer cry.

Karma's face held a depth of understanding that seemed incongruous with their youthful appearance. "You're not alone, Mika. Many have these concerns in the first few weeks after transitioning. There's a reason you have an adjustment period: because it is a major life change, and it doesn't happen all at once or all the same. You are literally not the person you were. Technology's made amazing strides, but our brains and bodies have a hard time catching up. Talking can help, getting back into the things that brought us joy before, seeing friends, spending time with those we love, even the sense of purpose some if us get from work. You need to engage for others to engage with you."

"Joy?" That one word echoed what Darrin asked me and resonated within me. I wondered the same things I had in the diner, *Am I happy? Have I ever really been happy?* "What if nothing brings me joy?"

"Depression's not unheard of in those recently transitioned. We can try adjusting your simulated neurotransmitters and hormones to find an optimal balance. Would you like to explore that option?"

"I... I don't know what I want."

"Mika –"

I broke the connection. It was probably the wrong thing to do, but I had nothing more to say to Karma. If it was just an imbalance, then could adjusting my settings really change anything? Telling my brain that it was happy wouldn't fix the underlying problem. This had to be a solution from within.

KARMA HAD TRIGGERED several urgent care alerts, requesting that I come in. I ignored them all. I doubted they'd actually have me hauled in on critical mental health care.

I had also reached a decision. Karma said there were others like me, and surely some would feel as I did. I'd spent the past few days scouring the 'net for any hint of who they were and where I could find them. I figured that there, at last, I could make some real connections.

And I'd found them. This dissention from the trend of modern society was far from rare, and they were everywhere, even in Tokyo. The local group was called Synthetic Divide, and I was on my way to their meeting. They may not have the answers, but we all shared a common desire: to form personal connections with others.

I stepped through the door, and looked at the faces. They turned at my entrance.

A slight man with strong features stood to greet me. "You must be Mika. Welcome." He bowed formally.

I didn't feel elation. It was too soon to say whether I would find purpose or joy here, but as I bowed back and took a seat, I felt more hope than I'd expected. Here was old-fashioned, face-to-face, human interaction, and I glommed on to it immediately.

We talked and shared, until we receded into the night, off to whatever lives we were accustomed to. But the promise was there. We were connected. We were part of each other. And that thought left me with the beginnings of happiness.

Joseph Welch is a self-proclaimed nerd, with interests in SciFi, Fantasy, Anime and Manga. A lifelong Washingtonian, it all started for him back in '84 in Seattle, and he's fed himself on a steady diet of imagination and wonder since.

He thinks up his new worlds while running or playing piano and always has the help, perspective – and patience! – of his keen beta readers. Cooking, translating Japanese manga and computer programming fill his schedule. He is a senior at Ohio U. Other published works include "My Friend Princess" (2021) in Birds Have Teeth by Gypsum Sound Tales and "Written Upon One's Soul" (2022) in Phantom Thieves & Sagacious Scoundrels by JayHenge Publishing.

Amazon Author Page: https://www.amazon.com/stores/author/B0CC6VZNJN
Facbook: https://www.facebook.com/josephwelch84

TESTING DAY
BY D.M. RASCH

"What's the point? I won't qualify for anything," Flynn says, doing a useless about-face on the slidewalk moving them inexorably toward their future – or lack thereof, more like, they think – waiting to be decided at the Testing Center.

Honor, with characteristic empathy, turns to walk against the flow with them, close on their shoulder, not touching. It's the space she needs to hold at bay the tsunami of doubt, fear, and self-loathing rolling off her best friend in the world. A distance she can manage without it becoming part of her own experience.

"You're not finding out unless you actually make it inside, you know."

"Easy for you to say," Flynn sulks, stomping along the edge without a thought for the jam they may be causing. "You'll be drowning in opportunities with an empathy rating like yours. Not to mention that freaky talent you have for looking at any kind of mess or malfunction and lasering in on what's causing it before anyone else has a chance to even take a proper look. I'm such a Linear, I'll be lucky if I get an offer supervising recycling used 'bots."

"You know it's not 'easy for me to say,' Honor reminds this person who's known her since her overwhelmed and mainly mute childhood.

Before she learned to filter without shutting down – and advocate for herself – that is.

"You've been so preoccupied with how you *won't* qualify, you haven't even bothered with the pre-tests that might clue you into your strengths and where they best fit." A polite, but firm, smile from her clears a path for them, as travelers shift, like a school of fish, around the obstacle the two present.

Flynn shoots her a look, equal parts panic and daggers…then sighs in resignation when the only reaction from Honor is a raised eyebrow that dares them to deny it. Since it's obvious Honor isn't going to cooperate with any delay tactics – much less, a really satisfying argument – they pull another about-face to see the approach of the end of the walk. The Center looms over them in a manner they imagine to be pretty damned judgy.

A couple of bureaucratic-looking types, pads in hand, check in anxious applicants at the entrance. They embody the stuffy impression with (what seems to Flynn) to be fairly invasive once overs in the overlook department. Not to mention (again, in their opinion) unnecessarily personal questions. "Isn't the testing supposed to be inside?" they lean to whisper in Honor's ear.

"I have a feeling it's safe to assume *everything* today is a test," Honor mumbles under her breath.

"Great. Just great," Flynn grumbles, knowing Honor's *feelings* are never far off base.

NOTHING MUCH IMPROVES as the two are shuffled inside, Honor enduring the press of Flynn's arm against hers as they try not to get separated in the crowd. On top of the noise level and the random bumps of strangers' shoulders, it's a lot.

The crowd funnels into a second set of gatekeepers. This time, there are no questions. The holders of the all-knowing pads simply swipe the pad over each candidate's wrist to scan the ident chip. Apparently, Honor notices, information has been uploaded from the grilling they received at the doors, as the flow splits into 2 streams of shuffling students that pick up the pace as they step into a line moving left or right.

Though not really prone to getting "feelings"… Flynn senses the beginnings of a bad one creep into their gut.

"Uh, Honor," they leaned to Flynn's ear to be heard over the throng. "I think we're going to get separated up ahead."

"What?" [name Flynn] stops concentrating on the bodies too close around her to stand on her toes to get a better look at the split in the queue Flynn's nodding toward.

"Yeah, probably dividing us into Linears," they thump their chest with their free palm, "and Sensitives," they pronounce, bumping Honor's shoulder. "Saves 'em loads of time, I bet, not wasting the complex tests on us simple folk."

"Careful, you may not fit through the scanport, the size of that chip on your shoulder," Honor notices, with more familiarity than judgment. She's focusing on getting a good enough look at the sorting going on up ahead to decide for herself.

Turns out, chip or no chip, Flynn's not completely off base in their assessment. When they both arrive at the checkpoint, Honor is nodded to the queue on the right, Flynn to those forming a line on the left. Honor hesitates, eyes lowered. Flynn registers the silent "tag, you're it" and speaks up.

"Looks like that line," they say, nodding to the right, "isn't quite so long. Mind if I join my friend there?"

As if somehow sensing the invisible tether between them, the gatekeeper's impassive face softens around the edges. "I would if I could, candidate. Your profiles indicate your line. It's not up to me to change your course."

With a "what did I tell you?" lift of the eyebrow at Honor, and a "you can't blame a person for trying" shrug and grin at the gatekeeper, Flynn moves past to let the next candidate through to be scanned. Before heading for their queue, they stop in front of Honor and offer their hands, palms upward, knowing it's their turn to stop being a selfish arse and offer encouragement. Honor surprises them by slipping hers into theirs for the comfort of a quick, firm squeeze.

"Well, look at you, getting me in here today." They act surprised. Almost cheerful. "Guess I'm going to have to go through with it, now we've come this far. Now you can just focus on blowin' 'em all away on your side of the street while I try to dazzle 'em on mine. You don't have a thing to worry about, you know. Not a thing. I've got your back. Like always. We don't have to be in the same place for that."

Honor's face brightens. It's true. Sensory memories flash past her awareness of Flynn's flash of pain that brought her running when they'd crashed a lightboard in a sim with the safeties off, breaking their arm. The burn of shame when their period arrived, adding the confusing rush of hormones to equally burning questions they were having about their gender. Their frustration at trying to explain their inner conflict to their parents. And her ability to help them find words.

All the times, as well, that Flynn appeared on her doorstep when her parents interrogated her into tears about how she knew something they couldn't see or understand. Or when her more linear mother suggested she needed to "toughen up" or "deal with it if she was to get on in the world" when the physical and psychic noise of their home pushed her into hiding in her closet. Flynn had been the one to gift her filtering ear gels, allowing her to cope with the environment until her teachers sat her parents down to explain the enormous potential in her neurology. That, while different from their own, it would certainly allow her to "get on in the world." And more – with their support as her sensitivities matured.

Her eyes flick briefly up to Flynn's, sharing her belief with them.

"You're right. We always have. This'll be no different." Her shoulders straighten with their earlier confidence. "Go kick some ass," she says, knowing it will make them smile. "And I'll go *feel* some," she adds, going for the laugh. She's not disappointed. "See you on the other side."

"Yes. You. Will!" Still chuckling, Flynn trots off with exaggerated enthusiasm to join their line.

Turns out, they'd be seeing each other a bit sooner than either expected.

～

"Candidate! Get your head in the game! This isn't quantum theory." The Tester isn't wrong. Any other day and they'd have been the first finished with a simple physical coding test. Dexterity's their thing, nano-gelled fingers often flashing faster in v-space than their thoughts seemed to follow. The virtual pieces *always* fit together to create a working sim model that could be printed into reality.

Except this time.

They can't pin down the problem. Sure they're a bit distracted, wondering how it's going for Honor. The thing is, they can't tell. And that bothers the heck out of them. Even if she's kicking – or *feeling* – ass, and taking no names – they should be able to tell. Honor didn't filter with them. Ever.

When they botch the 3rd trial, the Tester taps them on the shoulder to indicate they should drop back into real space. Flynn wonders if this is it. If this is where they'll be deemed employable for nothing more than a long-term, make-work subsistence position.

"Candidate," the Tester muses, scrolling on their tablet, "explain to me how you made these ratings in school without being able to successfully complete a simple build? Is it nerves? It happens. But I don't see the indicators in your neuro ratings…."

That familiar burning shame creeps in between the cracks in their confidence. Not linear enough. And now, apparently not sensitive enough. And no words to express what that feels like. How much they miss Honor right now.

"Well, any thoughts?" The Tester's curious gaze isn't unkind. Just direct. When Flynn doesn't – apparently can't – respond, the look becomes downright probing. Then they ask, "What would be different if she were here right now?"

Shocked out of their wordless shame, Flynn hears words burst out before being aware of thinking them: "She makes me feel like I can fly."

~

IN THE SHIELDED space on the opposite side of the facility, the confidence Honor had regained is evaporating as quickly as the moisture in her stress-desert of a mouth.

"Let's try something a little more straightforward," the Tester soothes. "It's a stressful day – one of the most stressful, perhaps, in your life, so far."

Some empath, Honor thinks. This is nothing compared to the days before I realized that my sensitivities weren't defects. *Every* day was a stressful day, back then.

The Tester cocks her head with a knowing smile. "There you are. Thank you for dropping your shields. Pardon the insult. I do understand some of what you've been through. Most of us had a hard time getting the support we needed when we were younger. I couldn't hear or feel you and didn't want to push. You're entitled to your boundaries. And you've given us permission to test your abilities by being here. What do you say, ready to try again?"

Honor nods, reaching out for Flynn without thinking as she complies. She hopes they're sailing through whatever tests they're facing. Then she realizes she doesn't *know*. She's just hoping. Why can't she feel them? Then she recalls the huge relief she felt stepping into this room, the over-whelming noise of the public areas shutting down like a power outage. They must have these rooms shielded. Like the meditation rooms at school.

"Take a couple of breaths. Feel your feet on the floor. Your hands on your lap. Your chest and belly expanding. Releasing. When you feel solid and focused on these sensations, you can drop into v-space. We'll roll those sensory bits through again and you can tell me what you notice."

She tries to relax. To feel safe and solid. To focus. But each time she thinks she's there, begins to drop into v-space, she has the sensation of becoming unmoored from the anchor of her body and pulls back. Starts again with her breath. Gets frustrated at having to even think about it. She's done this thousands of times before with no effort at all. Now it's like she's a beginner all over again. Great.

Somewhere on the periphery, she's aware of a light knock, a burst of "noise" as the door opens, then quickly closes. She's aware of the ground solid beneath her feet. Feels her hands relax their tense grip on her thighs. Everything feels right for the first time since she set foot in this room.

Soft murmuring in the periphery, then she's joined in v-space by a familiar presence. Random bits of physical code start flying toward them, chaos in quantum-D. With the intention of finding an order, she begins to notice patterns of color, shape, speed, likenesses, differences – and qualities more ephemeral that challenge her perceptions.

As she notices each pattern, the pieces fly toward each other, as if by will. She knows it's not *her* will, though; but that of the familiar presence virtually pulling the bits, then the threads together, as more complex patterns emerge for her. The quantum becomes the virtual, something recognizable to the eye. Something capable of being realized and printed.

Something beautiful that can be shared. The process, itself, as well as the object. She feels the smile pulling at the corners of her mouth as she returns to real space.

"Well, that's unexpected," her Tester remarks, grinning at another standing beside Flynn, who is blinking as they fully return to the room, as well. "A new record, I'm thinking, for resolving that mess into anything at all – much less something so gorgeous."

"And utilitarian," Flynn adds, a hint of pride in their voice.

"And utilitarian," their Tester agrees, with a clap on their shoulder.

"You're excited," Honor speaks up with confidence to the Trainers. "Thinking, perhaps, it may be time to rethink the Testing protocol. What you could be missing by separating the groups."

"Yes," her Trainer laughs aloud. "No need for concern about your empathy rating, I see."

"And I was also considering that further individual training could benefit each of you. Build your confidence and ability to work alone. Or with others, when needed. A practical consideration. One that you'll no doubt resist right now." She glowers down at Flynn. "And that I'm sure you'll see the wisdom in as your careers progress. Starting here at the Center," they end with certainty.

"Here?" croaks Flynn. "With Honor ?"

"Most assuredly. Together. For now," Honor's Trainer adds gently." We have as much to learn from your collaboration as you do about your individual abilities. How's that sound?"

Her voice is warm and welcoming. Solid to Honor's senses. Full-body exhilarating to Flynn's.

"When do we start?" they ask, voices one.

D.M. Rasch writes feminist speculative fiction for LGBTQ+ young adults and adults, exploring where the social and political meet the personal. Her characters are often found doing their best in worlds that challenge them to become their best selves. Queer representation and reaching out to LGBTQ+ youth drive her writing, informed by her MFA in Creative Writing from Regis University and two bossy sister kittens who like to edit. She identifies as a genderqueer lesbian, currently writing and working (remotely) in the Denver, CO area as a creative mentor, coach, and editor in her business, Itinerant Creative Content & Coaching LLC.

Amazon: https://www.amazon.com/author/dmrasch
Linkedin: https://www.linkedin.com/in/deann-m-rasch/
Facebook: https://www.facebook.com/deannamrasch
Liminal Fiction: https://www.limfic.com/mbm-book-author/d-m-rasch/

THE LAST HUMAN HEART
BY J. SCOTT COATSWORTH

I run the lipstick over my still-human lips, staring at myself in the creased metal gas station bathroom mirror. The protective balm is a titanium blue, a radiant silver flecked with colors of the rainbow that accents the metallic skin of my cheekbones. Wrinkles line the edge of my lips where skin meets metal. *You're fucking perfect. Like a goddamned Monet.*

I snort. I used to care about such things once. Matching my clothes for a night at the clubs with Erik. Choosing our elaborate costumes with care — exposing a bit of muscled stomach or a flash of ass with our tight, waist-hugging jeans. Sometimes bringing another guy home with us for a threesome.

The memories are cracked and faded around the edges. The upload to my quantum brain did something to me, changed me into this Frankenstein of man and machine.

I would have made a hell of a scene on the club circuit.

Crash.

What the hell? Wary, I slip the little jar of the moisturizing lipstick, snagged from an old department store, back into my satchel and swing it over my shoulder. Inside my titanium rib cage, my human heart beats faster — too fast.

I grasp the sides of the old porcelain sink and breathe slowly, calming myself until my heart slows again. Then, silent as a cat, I pull the door open and peer outside through eyes I wasn't born with.

It's almost dark, the last bits of evening fleeing across the empty countryside.

Another noise, this time a long, drawn out squeal. My eyes whir and focus. There by the gas pumps.

I breathe a sigh of relief. *Just a scavenger bot.* Their kind rule the world now, traveling through the rubble and recovering materials on a schedule only they know, stockpiling them for humanity's return. I laugh bitterly at the thought.

I slip out of the bathroom to watch the little thing. It's a third the size of my own cyborg body, and it's working away at one of the old gas pumps, using a laser torch to cut it into pieces.

"They're not coming back." It's a whisper, and an admission. Something I don't like to think about for too long. *You're being morbid.* Erik would tell me that with a flash of his bleached white smile, before leaping at me and pinning me to the bed for a kiss.

I bite my lip with metallic teeth and sigh.

The scavenger stops and turns as if to look at me. I can feel it scanning me for parts. Then it whirs, a disappointed sigh, and turns back to its work.

I'm worthless. I laugh ruefully, a sound more like pistons firing than a human laugh. Even this little metallic vulture has no use for the likes of me.

I consult my map, painstakingly put together from bits and clues found on the neural web. Fifty years after the last human upload, it's a miracle the network survives at all. It's a broken, feeble thing, limited to small nodes here and there, but still… a testament to the Remainers like me who maintain it, the humans and machines who survived the climate and the last wars.

Like many of them, I wasn't "suitable for upload." One hazard of being an *early adopter.* I laugh harshly, pistons firing in my throat.

This insignificant speck of humanity's great accomplishments where I stand was once called Turlock, a tiny town in California's Central Valley. I wince. I know that name—a friend of mine once lived here. Did she upload, before the end?

The Sacramento trading station is less than a hundred miles away, if it still exists. The last time I'd been there was two decades ago. With luck, I'll be there in another day or so, and if I'm *really* lucky, they'll be able to replace my worn-out ticker with a new one.

My heart beats faster. I close my eyes and urge it to be calm, hoping they will have what I need. Otherwise this might be the end of the line. Still, I'm ready to go, if it comes to that. *Erik, I miss you.*

I set out at an easy pace, leaving the gas station and the scavenger bot behind. Soon I'm back on the highway, or what's left of it.

The full moon rides the clear sky overhead that's full of stars. Most of humanity's artificial lights are gone now, and once again the Milky Way reigns supreme.

A blistering hot wind slices at me from the south, as if pushing me toward my goal. I can sense the heat, but I only *feel* it on my exposed silver lips.

I remember cool nights in the summertime, lazy evenings at a rooftop party with friends in the City when the breezes blew off the Pacific. All of them dead and gone—They wouldn't recognize this world we Remainers have inherited.

How I miss wrapping those lips around things... *a Popsicle in the summertime as a kid. The sweet taste of a banana. Or Erik's...*

I derail that thought before it can overexcite my heart.

Erik uploaded fifty years ago. I wonder for the hundred-thousandth time what life inside the Core is like. Is he still *Erik?* Or has he become part of a hundred, a thousand other joined consciousnesses? Did he grow tired of it all at some point and self-delete? *Does he remember me?*

Broken, rusted-out cars litter the roadway. I don't look to see if there are any occupants inside. I've already seen too much death.

My steps are measured and even, powered by the solar energy I'd absorbed during the daytime while I rested during the worst of the heat.

Something skitters across the lanes ahead, pausing to stare at me.

I stop and stare back, my infrared vision filling in the outlines. It's a buck, a full-grown deer with an impressive rack of antlers as wide as my outstretched arms.

We stand there for a moment in absolute silence.

He's gorgeous. I haven't seen many animals on my travels—mostly smaller creatures, birds, squirrels, occasionally rats—in the hollowed-out remnants of the bigger cities. But nothing as magnificent as this.

I open my hand and shine a light on him. He's white, and his eyes glint red in the reflected glare.

He nods and sets off at a trot toward the far side of the highway.

I watch him go, recording the moment to play back later. *I wish I'd seen you in daylight.*

When he's swallowed up by the darkness, I continue on.

~

THE NEXT AFTERNOON finds me crouched in a culvert under the highway, waiting out the heat of the day after soaking up some sunlight in the cooler morning hours. They built my titanium body for hot days and chilly nights, and neither snow nor rain nor heat nor gloom of night could stop me.

I chuckle my mechanical laugh—I would have made a great mail carrier, instead of the fast food "technician" I'd been before the accident.

My human heart feels the strain of its long life. After more than eighty years, I've worn it out, and I need to conserve its resources if I want to reach my goal.

So I sit in the relative cool of the culvert, sipping on a bit of water that my remaining human parts still require for sustenance. Somewhere along the way tonight, I'll find some canned goods as well, cutting them open with my bare hands. It doesn't really matter what's inside—my augmented tongue and sensory nerves will convert the flavor into whatever I want it to be.

I sit back, remembering the taste of a medium-rare steak melting in my mouth. Or the fluffy buttery taste of mashed potatoes. I close my eyes and lose myself in a sensory dream of food.

Erik came home with me once for Thanksgiving in Vermont, back when it used to snow there. Mom had set out her holiday best, a spread that would have made Martha Stewart jealous. Cranberries, turkey, mashed potatoes and gravy, stuffing, green beans, apple and pumpkin pie, and a side plate of sushi—my father's one concession to mom's Japanese American heritage. Our little family holiday quirk.

In my mind I savor each dish, sinking into the fantasy, safe and warm again at home as snow falls on the red pines outside the dining room window.

I check the time. 2:59 PM.

There are worse ways to pass my time, and it does my heart good reliving those carefree days.

I set my alarm for sunset and lose myself in the languid heat and the smell of roasted turkey.

~

I SLIP out of the culvert as the sun falls behind the tawny hills on the horizon, a green flash lighting the sky. My heart beats at a steady pace.

Climbing back up onto the highway, I check the co-ordinates. With luck and a steady pace, I should reach the Trading Station by morning.

The stag crosses my mind again, that strange stare, beast to beast. There's so little out here for it to live on or in, no trees or shade or shelter from the blistering sun. Just grass. Lots and lots of grass. *Where did you go?*

Taking one measured step after another, I start on my way, timing them to the beating of my heart.

A heady sense of possibility fills my chest. It's strange, something I haven't felt in years. I've traveled the length of the continent, from New York to California. I've been to Alaska and as far south as the isthmus, where rising seas finally finished the work of the Panama Canal, severing North and South America. In a few short centuries, humankind accomplished what Nature had labored for eons to do.

An hour later, I get my first look at the towers of Sacramento. I haven't been here in decades, but it looks much the same as before. Its hulking skyscrapers and superscrapers look like bloody teeth in the infrared. Many are broken. Some still standing, others long since crashed back to the ground whence they came. They glow with stored heat, slowly bleeding it off into the atmosphere as the air cools.

Whence they came? I snort. I'm in rare form tonight—practically Shakespearian. Erik would have teased me endlessly for that.

I frown. He's been on my mind a lot lately. Mortality having her fun with me?

I flash back to nights in Shanghai, fighting with my metal brothers and sisters in the street-to-street combat of the last wars. Flashes of light and explosions as nano bombs fell into civilian neighborhoods, eating every-thing in their path—stone and brick, flesh and bone.

I shudder. I should delete those memories—they only bring me pain. And yet... *sometimes we need to remember the pain, so we don't repeat it. But we can't let it define us.*

Who said that? Erik? My father?

No. It was Cassie. My erstwhile traveling companion for a couple years after the upload. When all that remained in this empty, broken world were the bots and empty, broken cyborgs like Cassie and me.

She'd finally shut herself down two decades ago. *I'm tired of living, David.*

Pain leaches away some of my good will. Maybe she had it right. Maybe it's time for me, too, to give in to the inevitable. But I'm not quite ready yet, so I just keep moving.

Near morning, as I plod on toward my destination, the sky lightens, washing away the stars in the East. I'm passing a convoy of rusted-out semis when something catches my attention ahead, a glint in the night.

I blink, and it resolves into the white stag I'd seen the night before.

Hello, my new friend. I wait for it to trot off again, as bored with me as I am with myself.

This time, though, he approaches slowly, dipping his head and staring up at me. With his antlers, he's as tall as I am.

I pull a nutrient cube out of my pack, slowly so as not to frighten him, and hold it out in my palm. It's half sugar, so I am guessing he'll like it.

He sniffs at it, and then his pink tongue, lit by a soft glow from my metallic palm, flicks out to lick it up.

This close, I can see that he's gaunt, his ribs showing at his sides, his hide hanging limply from his neck. Still, he's a magnificent creature.

When he's finished the treat, he looks at me expectantly. Sighing, I pull out another cube. There are only a few left in my pack. If the Trading Station is still around, maybe they'll trade me for more. I don't need many, but there are things my remaining human parts require that sunlight and canned peaches can't provide.

He ignores the cube, his strangely green eyes meeting mine.

There's something in his eyes—a reflected image that I can almost make out...

. . .

"HE'S IN SHOCK." A man in a white coat is hovering over me as I'm wheeled down a long, sterile hallway.

"It was an accident. The car just went crazy, veering off the highway on its own. My crash foam activated, but his didn't." *Erik.*

I frown. He sounds worried. *I'm okay.* I try to say it, but no words come out.

"He's in awful shape, son." White coat again. A doctor. "We'll do what we can. Has he signed a waiver?"

"He's a pacifist. He'd never want that."

A long silence as we pass through a set of double doors that flap closed behind us.

"It may be the only way. Would you rather have him alive and conscripted or dead with his principles?"

A warm hand squeezes mine.

I want to say *It's okay, Erik. Let me go.* Nothing comes out. I feel woozy, disconnected. Something's broken in my chest, a dull pain radiating up my spine. *What's wrong with me?*

Erik's face swims into my field of vision. He looks horrible. There's blood on his forehead, and his eyes are puffy, like he's been crying. The blue lipstick he wore to the club is smeared across his cheek. "I can't lose him. Do what you have to." Then someone rips away his hand.

What's happening to me?

A minute later, a mask settles over my face, and the world fades away.

I SHAKE MY HEAD. I'd buried that memory so far down in my archives that I haven't accessed it in decades. *Why now?*

The deer stares at me.

"Erik?" It's an absurd thought. This poor creature is no more *Erik* than I'm still human. *And yet...*

It bows its head and turns away, trotting off between the hulks of the cars and semis on the highway.

"Wait!" I stumble after him, and my heart speeds up, pulsing in my chest. It's too dangerous, exerting myself like this, but I can't let him get away again. *Erik or no.*

I clear the last truck and look around wildly. There he is, just ahead of me, leaving the highway to cross a wild meadow, silvered by moonlight. The sky is bright with the approach of dawn.

I give chase, my heart pounding in my metal chest. I am pushing it too hard, and red warning lights flash in my head. *Danger.*

I don't care. *It's Erik.* It makes no sense, but I know it in my soul.

My metal feet trample the virgin grass of the meadow, following the stag's path as it trots toward a copse of trees.

No, not a copse. *A forest.*

I stop and stare.

The highway is gone. There are redwoods and pine trees, elm and oak and willow, as strange and motley a wood as I've ever seen in my human or cyborg life.

The old forests this far south are all dead, killed by heat and fire and beetle infestations. Only in the North do they still hold sway, in what used to be Alaska and the Yukon.

And yet here it is. *Mythago Wood.* A fairy tale from my childhood, made real. My heart slows just a little.

I set off after the stag, afraid I will lose it among the trees. It vanishes ahead of me behind the trunk of an enormous redwood.

I follow, fully enveloped now by the forest. The temperature has dropped a good twenty degrees from the highway, and a cool mist creeps along the ground, while silver moonlight traces the treetops above. What happened to morning?

There's rustling in the tree branches. I look up, meeting the eyes of a squirrel that chitters his displeasure at being disturbed.

Where's the stag? A flash of white between the tree trunks ahead catches my attention. I stumble after it, making my way over a tangle of leaves and roots.

I soon lose all track of direction. My navigation system seems to have gone haywire in this strange wood. Still, there's a beaten track in front of me, and another flash of white leads me onward.

I can feel the cool forest breeze on my skin.

God dammit, that's not possible. On my lips, sure, but not on my titanium shell—there are no nerve receptors there.

I hold my hand up. It shimmers in the morning light. Still metallic. And yet, I can *feel* the chill in the air.

I stumble along the faint track, chasing after the stag. *After Erik.*

Time loses all meaning. My heartbeat slows, steady in my chest. The trees close in around me, blocking out even the night sky.

I walk down a dark tunnel of tree trunks and slowly fluttering branches. Patches of golden fungus grow along the ground and between the gnarled roots of the trees, providing an eldritch glow. There are ash and alder and cottonwood, and many more I don't know the names of.

I soak it all in, feeling that sense of wonder and possibility return. It's been years… decades, even, since I've seen something beautiful and new. I take a deep breath, smelling the loamy soil of the wood, the piney scent of fir trees, the salty tang of the ocean. *What is this place?*

The tunnel ends abruptly, disgorging me into an open, moonlit space. I look up at the sky in confusion. It should be after eight, according to my internal chronometer, and yet somehow, in this strange forest, it's still night. A gibbous moon hangs over the clearing, lining the stag in argent.

The deer meets my gaze once more. We stare at each another across the open space, and something passes between us.

I can't explain it. A mix of joy and sorrow? A plea for forgiveness and a hope for redemption.

I nod, taking a deep breath of the cool air into the pumps which serve as my lungs.

The deer slips into the woods, vanishing from view.

Bright light blinds me.

Blinking, I look around. The sun is blazing above, and I'm in the middle of a junkyard. The strange wood is gone, replaced by piles of parts and furniture and other bric-à-brac stacked high everywhere like a modern-day version of that otherworldly forest.

"Can I help you?"

I look down. A scavenger rises on its treads to stand half my height, its bulbous head cocked sideways. I've never heard one of them speak before. A smiley emoji appears on its somewhat battered plas faceplate.

"I… I don't know." I stare at him. He's built for balance, not speed, rolling on a pair of metal treads, though they are missing a few chinks. His gray chassis has been beaten and patched repeatedly with plastic and metal in various colors, giving him a ragamuffin look. "You can talk."

The bot chuckles. "Kind of hard to do business with clients if you can't speak with them, am I right?" He bumps me collegially… I would have said *elbows me*, if he'd had any.

"I suppose so. What… who are you?"

"I'm the Collector."

"Where is this place?" I reach for the neural net, but there are no accessible nodes nearby.

A frowney emoji replaces the smiley one. "Ah, you came here through the wood, didn't you?"

I nod. "I suppose so. There was a forest—"

"Strangest thing. Comes and goes out of nowhere." A laughing emoji. "Brings me a lot of business."

I try to hurry him along. I have a schedule to keep, after all. "So this is…?"

"You're in what used to be upstate New York." He raises his skinny metal arms and does a little spin, kicking up a cloud of dust. "Welcome to the Junkyard."

New York? *How the hell did he bring me here?*

I look around in wonder. I've heard of this place. It's almost legendary, a graveyard of old tech, like Atlantis for us Remainers. In all my travels, I've never run across it—it's somehow fitting that I discovered it on the heels of a mythical stag. *It really does exist.*

"So what can I do for you?" The Collector's face plate lights up with a yellow question mark. "We have neural boards, capacitors, grapplers, flux stacks, quantum clips, power sinks and so much more." He waves the skinny double rods of his arms, pointing out one stack and then another. "What are you needing?" He raises himself up to my level, the question mark flashing, and a puff of steam or smoke erupts from his neck like a belch.

I stare at the strange little creature, trying to keep myself from laughing. He seems so… human. "I need a new heart."

"Oh, is that all?" His collapsing arms express his disappointment at my simple request. "This way, then." He spins around and rolls off through the piles at a surprisingly fast clip.

I follow him, veering past a stack of old treads—wondering why he hadn't replaced his clearly damaged ones with something better. He slips under a wide piece of scaffolding balanced neatly on two old server columns, and I duck to follow him.

"What kind of heart? We have 'em all. Positronic, animatronic, quantum, steam-pump, nuclear, electric, simple mechanical—"

"I need a human heart."

The Collector stops in his tracks and spins around, a yellow frowney emoji on its face. "You need a *what*?"

I sigh. "I need a human heart. My... old one has worn out, and it's not long for this world."

He rolls up to me and taps my metal chest. "May I see it?" He sounds almost reverent.

It's a strange request. It feels weirdly intimate, and dangerous to boot. He could pluck it out of me and kill me in an instant.

We stare at one another, in as much as one can engage in a staring contest with a *wow* emoji. I'm struck by the absurdity of the moment, but no one is laughing.

What do I have to lose? I'll be dead soon enough, anyway. "Sure."

I remember the stag I followed here. *Maybe Erik is waiting for me, somewhere out there.*

Nervously, I release the catch that keeps my chest plate closed, and it swings open, revealing my heart in all its glory. *Or gory?*

The Collector leans forward, tilting its head in a very human gesture. "You *were* human, once. I suspected, what with the lips and all... but of course it's rude to ask."

I nod. "Of course." My heart beats faster inside its metal enclosure, and I feel a little faint. It won't be long now.

The Collector backs up and stares at me, flashing red. A virtual blush? "Thank you for sharing it with me."

"Were... were you ever human?" He's right. It's one of those things you just don't ask a Remainer, but given the circumstances, I feel justified.

Sad face. "No, just a mech." He bows. "It's an honor to meet you. May I know your *before name*?"

"D-d-david." I stutter it out, the word unfamiliar on my tongue after all these years. *I used to be David.*

"You know you can replace that with something better. An artificial heart that will last you a couple hundred years, and make you faster and stronger, too."

I shake my head. "I don't want that. I've given up enough of my humanity already."

Thinking emoji flashes across his face. "Well, D-d-david, I think I have just the thing for you. Come with me." He spins on his treads and sets off again in a different direction.

I laugh. "Just David."

"What's that?" The Collector veers around a pile of old rubber tires that's three times taller than me.

"My name. It's just David. No extra d's." I close the chest plate and follow him, wondering how he got all this junk out here into the middle of nowhere. Wondering again how I got here.

There still are a few mysteries in this broken world of ours. "Have you always been here?"

He grunts. "Yes, but that depends on your definition of *here*." He waves his arms. "Here in New York for a while. Before that, I had a junkyard down in what used to be Georgia."

I consider that. "Are you—"

"I was created in Silicon Valley. One of the older scavenger models. They set me loose in St. Louis, after the city was all but emptied out by uploads." He stops to pick up an errant keyboard that had slipped off of a teetering pile of them, placing it back on top with the agility of a ballerina.

Just ahead, past a pair of clear plas bins filled with a stunning variety of cords and cables like a nest of vipers, there's a little cottage. The bins are topped off by an old rusting car bumper, making a grand columned entrance to the courtyard in front of the little house.

It stands out in the Junkyard's midst, both for its surprising country charm—it's made of bricks with bright red trim—and for its lack of a single bit of visible tech or tech debris. The yard around it is trimmed in rose bushes, all beautifully in bloom. "You live here?"

"The philosophers have been debating that question for centuries."

I laugh again, pleased to be in the company of another sentient being. "The roses are beautiful."

"A personal hobby." He pulls open the door and gestures me inside. "This is where I keep my most precious treasures."

I step in and adjust my eyes to the interior.

It's nothing like the outside. Jam-packed with tech, in fact. In one corner, a charging station awaits the home's owner, three solid green concentric circles glowing on the wall. I wonder if he dreams while he recharges? I've never been able to talk to a scavenger before.

Shelves line the walls, covered with things that beep and blink and *whir*, and a cold case occupies half of one wall, under a clear double-paned glass window.

In another corner, an adjustable metal chair is plugged into a bank of quantum servers via an array of cables. I've seen its like before, when the military called me in for a tune-up or upgrade. I raise an eyebrow. Or I would have, if I'd still had them.

"Cables are more reliable than ai-fi." The Collector opens the cold case and rummages around inside. "I know I put it in here somewhere." He takes out a silver metal canister, then a yellow sphere that pulses with golden light. "Can't let that get too warm." The sphere goes back into the case. "Aha!" He pulls out something square, trailing a cascade of cold fog. "I present to you the last human heart." He holds it up to me like a proud parent showing off his only child.

I take it in trembling hands. The box is metal framed, but the plas window lets me peer at the organ inside. Blue lights run around the edge in steady succession. It's a stasis container, capable of keeping its contents in perfect shape for years. Decades, even. "It's beautiful." I run my hand across the plas, wishing I could *feel* the cold. "But you said it's 'the last' one?"

The dollar symbol appears on his face plate. "I can't know that for sure. But I'd be a poor salesman if I didn't use every trick to drive up my price, wouldn't I?" He swiveled to look at the cold case. "And it *is* the last one I have. Don't get much call for them, these days. Plus, the supply has dwindled down to nothing." The tongue emoji.

I nod. "So what is your price?"

"Ah, right to the game. I like that. Direct."

"Thanks." I hand back the heart and he places it in the cold case again, closing the lid. "So, the price? I have a number of things I've gathered during my travels that might interest a collector like you—"

"Your heart." He stares at my chest with googly eyes.

I laugh despite myself. "Well, of course. It's no good to me now anyhow." Though the thought of leaving one of the few remaining original parts of myself behind has an unexpected sting. "I... I can do that." I'd never given it much thought, but now that it's time... "Is that it?"

A neutral face emoji replaces the enormous eyes. He's holding this one close to the vest.

It's gonna hurt.

"And your human memories."

I gasp. *Those are private, mine and mine alone.* Erik, my childhood... my life before the accident. "I can't give those up. I... those more important to me than a new heart."

I turn to go, the weight of failure already crushing me. Maybe he can send me back to California. Or maybe there's another trading station closer. There used to be one up in Albany. My navigation is still glitched, but I can find it.

Maybe I'll trade it out for a mechanical heart, after all.

"Wait."

I turn to see the collector lower himself down to the ground, a pleading emoji on his screen. 'I wouldn't take them from you. Just make a copy."

"What for?" *Damn my lack of eyebrows.*

"To feel what it's like to be human."

I stare at him for a long time.

He's never felt the thrill of a cold wave splashing across his sandy toes. Never tasted a Thanksgiving dinner. What was it like to know you were created to be inferior, to be a servant to your master? A Pinocchio forever trapped in your wooden form?

At least *I* have my memories. I *lived* them. I was made from flesh and bone before the accident. In some fundamental way, I *am* still human, despite my metal skin and my quantum brain.

Not that I'm so sure any more about the superiority of homo sapiens. Look what a mess we'd made of the world. I take a deep breath. "Just a copy?"

"Yes." He is absolutely still as the moment stretches out between us, the air sparkling with tension.

It's a gift, really. To share my time with Erik with someone else—the chance for my memories of him to go on, even after I expire.

A new thought strikes me. "This is what you really collect, isn't it? Memories? The rest is just *stuff*?"

The Collector nods, a very human gesture, and his face goes blank. "I always wanted to be real."

That hits a little too close to home. *Pinocchio, for sure. And I can be his Geppetto.* "All right, I'll do it." I frown. "But you *are* real. Don't ever let anyone tell you you're not." I'm not sure if I am talking to him or to myself.

The Collector spins around again on his treads, emitting a happy piercing tone. "Thank you! You won't regret it."

I'm already starting to. Still, his happiness and antics are infectious—it's good to have company again, even if it's in the form of a crazy little scavenger robot. "What now?"

The Collector's treads meet the floor, and he points at the chair. "Just take a seat, and we'll get started."

I settle myself awkwardly into the chair. It's been a long time since I sat in one of these.

My mind flashes back to a field hospital in Beijing, when I'd lost the rest of my right leg. The brutal efficiency of the med mech as it replaced it with a titanium version custom printed for me. The howling pain subsiding as it blocked the nerve and gave me a powerful tranquilizer.

"You comfortable?" The Collector's voice is a world away from that stone-cold mech, in space, time, and temperament.

"Yeah. Just a little nervous." I'm not sure why, but I trust him.

"This won't hurt." He hooks a feeder line up to one of the ports in my neck, and liquid flows into me.

I analyze it casually. It is warm and full of nutrients. And something else.

"This will make you feel fantastic for a bit and take away any pain."

My worries slip away, and I'm floating on air as warmth suffuses me. I can't remember feeling so... happy. So whole. Not in a long time. *This is some good shit.*

"We'll copy the memories first. It's good to have a back-up ... just in case."

"In case of what?" I try to feel worried but can only work my way up to mildly concerned.

"There's danger in every choice we make."

I nod. *That sounds right.* I drift in a fog as my memories seep out of my head into the Collector's data core. The walls of the cottage bow inward and then snap back out.

The Collector looks over me, his worried face on. "Everything okay in there?"

I nodded. "I'm good. Great." Something *is* wrong, though. *My heart.* It's beating irregularly, sending me distress signals. I frown. "My heart is funny." I frown, trying to work that one out. *How can a heart be funny?*

The Collector looks at something just outside my field of view. He leans over me, frowney face on. "You're having a myocardial infarction. I have to change out your heart, now. You're going to go dark for a few minutes." He puts a metal claw on my cheek in a curiously intimate gesture. "Don't worry. I'll bring you back."

"Back from where?" The pain in my chest amps up, and I buck in the chair.

Myocardial infarction. A heart attack.

I'm dying. My heart is giving up on me at last. His hand grips mine, warm like Erik's. Or is it Erik?

Pain courses through me, and then regret. *I'm not ready. I'm not done yet.*

The Collector reaches into my chest. I watch through a pain-filled haze as he does something in there. Then he lifts my heart out in his hands. It pulses, once, twice, three times.

My world goes black.

～

I AWAKEN IN A WHITE WORLD. The pain is gone.

Crystals like snow form all around me, dividing and recombining in a frenzy of activity. I have no form. Just another snowflake in the blizzard, tossed about by the wind. *Is this heaven?*

Slowly it comes back to me.

DAVID COLLIER. Twenty-four. Injured in a car accident.

Erik hovers above me.

"They're going to give you a mech suit. They can replace your damaged organs. Make you whole again." His hand squeezes mine. "I'm sorry, *cuddlebear*. It's the only way."

No. I try to shake my head. *I don't want to be a mech.*

No one can hear me. *Erik, let me go. I don't want this!*

His hand releases mine.

Don't let them do this!

They wheel me into surgery, and someone lowers a mask over my face as I scream inside. *I don't want this!* But no one hears me as the anesthesia fogs my mind.

I OPEN my eyes in the foggy *now*.

The "snow" has subsided, and I'm standing on a wide, white plain of it, hills fading off into the distance. There is no sky—just white, roiling clouds a few feet above my head.

There's a patch of something darker on the horizon, outlined against the snow. I squint, trying to make it out. Whatever it is, it's approaching at a rapid pace. As it gets closer, antlers take form out of the whiteness. I blink in surprise.

The stag trots right up to me, its snout mere inches from my face, a puff of warm breath fogging my lenses.

It stares at me, head cocked sideways. It looks healthier, its ribcage filled out, its fur now clean and white instead of dirty and mangy.

I reach out and touch its head between its antlers. It's soft as rabbit's fur. "What are you?"

The stag steps back and shifts, shrinking as I watch in astonishment. It splits in two, sinew and muscle and bone ripping apart.

If I still had a heart, it would be hammering in my chest.

Each of the shapes flows upward, taking on new solidity and form.

The first one becomes Erik, flesh flowing smoothly over bone. I recognize his body—I knew it as intimately as my own, once.

He stands naked before me, as beautiful as the last night I saw him. Not muscular, not a model. Just… Erik.

His face takes on human form. He looks sad.

Sad for me.

And the other shape…

I step backward in shock, kicking up a bunch of the snow-that-isn't snow.

It's me. "What the hell?"

Other David smiles. It's a weak smile, tinged with sadness. "Hello, David."

I look back and forth from one to the other in alarm. *Is this a dream? This must be a dream.*

Eric closes the distance between us and gives me a hug. "This isn't a dream. Not like you mean."

I close my eyes. I can feel him. Like, actually *feel* his hug around my metal body. *That's not possible.* Still, his arms are solid on my back, his breath warm on my cold, hard shoulder.

Tears come out of my eyes and course down my cheeks. *Not possible.*

I snort. *I may have to adjust my parameters for possible.* "What is this place?"

Erik lets me go.

My other self squeezes his shoulder. "We call it the in-between. Humankind has many names for it. Purgatory. The Pearly Gates. The abyss. The great waiting room in the sky. It's a waystation between the reality we know and what comes next."

It's surreal, talking to myself. "So what comes after this?"

Other David smiles and takes Erik's hand. "It's not like any of us imagined."

That's cryptic. "Why am I here? Am I dead?" I look into David's brown, human eyes. "Why are there two of us?"

They glance at each other, and other David nods.

"This… it's hard for me to tell you." Erik squeezes other David's hand, and I tear up again. We were beautiful together, even more so than I knew, back then. "You're not David."

"Of course I am." *What the hell?* "I remember everything... when I was a kid, playing in the back yard under the oleander bushes. Meeting you in that run-down bar in the City. The accident..." Pain sears my consciousness.

"All of that's true." Eric's green eyes meet mine. "You have David's memories."

I don't like where this is going. "Then what?"

"You're not the *original* me." Other David's eyes are wet now, too, and his words are halting. "That night... when we were in the accident..." His voice cracks. "I died, David. On the operating table. When they transferred all my memories into your brain."

I stare at him in shock. "But they told me... they said they transferred my consciousness... our consciousness into the mech suit's mind too."

"*Copied.* And it's a beautiful copy." Other David steps up and touches my cheek, hand warm against my metal skin. "You *are* me. In every detail except one."

I look at him, and then at Erik. *This can't be real.*

Erik nods. "I am so sorry, David. I didn't know when I gave them the okay. I thought..."

"That I would still be me." Of course it made sense. Who were human beings to think they could capture the soul in a bottle?

Erik's lip trembles. "Yes."

I take a deep breath and exhale. "So why am I here? *How* am I here?" I look around at Purgatory. "Am I dead?"

Another exchanged look between them. "We don't know. We've watched you for a long time." Erik scratches the back of his neck, a gesture that's achingly familiar.

He's still so beautiful, his green eyes piercing mine. I wish I could kiss him, but he doesn't belong to this me.

"Then the last few nights... something shifted."

"My heart." I touch my metal chest.

"We think so."

I take it in, a bitter pill that leaves a rancid taste in my mouth. I've been living someone else's life. My soul feels sick—if I even have one. "It was all a lie."

Erik shakes his head emphatically. "No. It wasn't." He sighs. "Maybe it was, at first. But the memories you've made since—far more than those first twenty-four years… those are yours and yours alone."

Other David nods. "You can't see it. But you've become so much more than I ever was. From those children you saved in Beijing, to all the amazing things you've seen as you have crisscrossed the world… those belong to you, and you alone."

I shiver. *It's too much.* "What about you?" I stare at Erik, lashing out. "You uploaded to the Core. I saw it. You left me after they sent me to war." I poke him in the chest, hard. "Then you uploaded. How is that any more real than this?"

Erik's face goes gray as ash. "I didn't *leave* you. They wouldn't let us be together."

I stare at him. "What? They told me…"

"That I found someone else? That I didn't want to hear from you anymore?"

I nod dumbly. *Jesus fucking Christ, I am such an idiot.*

"It was a lie, to get you to accept your new life." Erik sighs. "The new life I consigned you to, without thinking. Without knowing what it meant. You… David told me, when I found him again. You didn't want *this*." He gestures at my robotic form.

I remember waking up in my new body. Screaming. Raging at the doctors, the nurses, the General. Until he simply shut off my brain for a couple days. I learned quickly not to complain.

"You're right, though. The copy of me in the Core is no more the original *me* than this one is *you*. But he's no less real, for all that."

The world begins to darken, the "clouds" descending.

"What's happening?" I feel thinner. Hollow.

"You're waking up." Erik leaps forward to hug me again. "This is the last time we'll see you, I think. I wanted to apologize, and tell you that you *are* real, David. Real to me. Real to the rest of the world."

My other self joins him, wrapping his arms around the two of us. As the waiting place fades away, other David whispers into my ear. "You have so much more to do. Take his heart. The other Remainers need you."

The blizzard fades away, and they're gone. Only their warmth on my skin remains.

I open my eyes.

"All done." The Collector stares down at me, his worried emoji on again. He taps my metal forehead. "Everything okay in there?"

I sit up slowly and look inside my chest. The new heart is there, no longer still. It beats strongly, health flowing through my veins and conduits once more. "Yes. I feel… good. Better than good, actually." I look around. "Did I… say anything while I was under?"

"Nope. Calm as the grave."

I shudder—a little too close to the truth. I close the chest panel and latch my new heart safely inside.

The Collector puts my old one in the stasis box and reactivates it.

"Take good care of that."

He nods. "One of my greatest treasures. The memory copy went well." He bows and then jumps up and spins around. "I sampled them. So much beauty. Your childhood dog Max, your lover Erik… your memories made me happy."

I blush. "Not *my* memories."

"Pardon?" Question mark.

"Never mind. They're yours now. Enjoy them."

Take his heart. What did my other self mean? "Hey, did the stasis box have any information about the donor? A name, maybe?"

The Collector picks it up and stares at it, turning it over. "No. But there's an experience file if you want it? I already have a copy."

"A full?"

"No. Just a few identifiers."

My pulse quickens. "Yes, please."

The Collector picks up a tiny silver mem-cap and plugs it into one of my ports. "There you go."

The first memory floods my brain, and I stare at myself through another person's eyes.

I love you, Erik. The first time I ever said it to him. Other David is grinning, dripping wet. The rain is raging, thunder shaking the sky, and we're huddled under the metal struts of the Eiffel Tower.

I race to another memory.

Me again. I stare at myself across the bar, thinking, *What a cutie. I'd love to fuck that…* Then the *me* in the bar turns to look at Erik and flashes him the goddamned sexiest smile I've ever seen.

I flick from memory to memory. They're all of me, each and every one. *Take his heart.*

I open my eyes. "Take his heart."

"Pardon?" The question mark flashes across the Collector's face plate again.

"Nothing." I touch my hand to my chest. Inside, Erik's heart beats steadily, strongly giving me a new lease on life. *He's with me.*

I close my eyes and see them together again. Erik and David. All this time I was worried about him. Brokenhearted that I'd never see him again. Afraid that he was all by himself in the core.

He isn't alone. He has David.

Now I'm not alone either. "Thank you. You have no idea what you have given to me."

The Collector snorts "I have *some* idea. And you made me a fair trade."

"Have you always wanted to be human?" I search his visor, wishing he had eyes I could look into.

The Collector was silent a moment. "Yes," he said at last. "It's just—"

"I know. But we never will be."

The question mark flashes.

"We'll never be *them*. But that's okay. What we are now… it's enough." I disconnect myself from the feeder line and stand, stretching my titanium arms. I find my satchel and pull out the blue lip balm, spreading it nimbly across my lips.

"Would you stay for the night? I'd love to have someone to talk with." A quizzical emoji lights up the Collector's face.

I nod. Once, a proposition like that would have led to a lot more than talking. Now companionship is what I crave. "I'd like that too."

A new sense of purpose fills me. There's an entire world full of broken people like us out there, wandering, lost, pining for something lost. Some started out as human, and some never were. *It's time for all of us to become something new. Starting with me.*

I'm not David. Not really. I never was. David was a twenty-four-year-old gay man who died young, after a tragic accident, in a world that no longer exists.

I'm someone new, part David, part Erik, and part everything that has happened since.

I'm Darrik. I laugh. *I like the sound of that.*

My heart—the last human heart—beats in happy agreement.

Scott lives with his husband Mark in a yellow bungalow in Sacramento. He was indoctrinated into fantasy and sci fi by his mother at the tender age of nine. He devoured her library, but as he grew up, he wondered where all the people like him were. He decided that if there weren't queer characters in his favorite genres, he would remake them to his own ends.

A Rainbow Award winning author, he runs Queer Sci Fi, QueeRomance Ink, and Other Worlds Ink with Mark, sites that celebrate fiction reflecting queer reality, and is the committee chair for the Indie Authors Committee at the Science Fiction and Fantasy Writers of America (SFWA).

Website: https://www.jscottcoatsworth.com
Facebook Personal: https://www.facebook.com/jscottcoatsworth
Facebook Page: https://www.facebook.com/jscottcoatsworthauthor/
Mastodon: https://mastodon.lol/@jscottcoatsworth
Liminal Fiction: https://www.limfic.com/mbm-book-author/j-scott-coatsworth/

FROM THE DUNES TO THE STARS

BY CHRISTOPHER R. MUSCATO

"You need to tell them!"

"Please sign here, sir."

"Taderfit, cooooooome onnnn- it will be fine."

"Thank you for your business," Taderfit bowed.

"Taderfit…"

"For the love of stars, Bakhta!" Taderfit exclaimed, switching from Arabic to Tamazight now that the customer had returned to his shop. She swung her holopad at her friend, who ducked out of the way. "I have deliveries to make! So do you!"

"See, that! That right there!" Bakhta jabbed a finger towards Taderfit's nose. "That work ethic, that commitment! That's exactly why you'd be a great captain!"

Taderfit rolled her eyes.

"If I were captain, Bakhta, you can be sure that your lazy bum would be marooned faster than you can say Hellas Planitia."

"So you admit that you'd make a great captain!"

Again, Taderfit rolled her eyes. But this time, she was clearly less committed to that universal gesture of annoyance. In its first recitation, Taderfit had punctuated that rolling her eyes with the anguished upward sweep of the hand. By the second recitation, however, as she rolled her eyes she turned her head, looking down and kicking at the sand.

Bakhta smiled quietly to herself, knowing that she was right, knowing that Taderfit knew she was right.

"You know I want to," Taderfit conceded, fidgeting with the holopad, the delivery schedule still flashing on its surface. "But you know I can't. I... I just-"

Bakhta's hand pressed gently on Taderfit's shoulder.

"Think about it. I know it's tough, but they'll come around."

WITH BAKHTA OFF on her own delivery route, Taderfit was able to complete her remaining tasks with little distraction. Soon, the ship had been emptied of its contents and Taderfit was snuggly fitted into the cockpit, flipping switches and counting sequences of lights. The engine rumbled and as she felt that familiar embrace of gravitational forces, she glanced out her window at the shrinking expanse of golden browns below her, the vast sea of sand in its deceptive lifelessness set against the turquoise churning of life-giving water, a study in contrasts united by motifs of swirling hues.

The continent shrank, and shrank, and Taderfit's glance shifted ahead to another vast sea, this one black and still, unfathomable in its depth and breadth, a desert of nothingness that sparkled with white-hot diamonds burning trillions of miles beyond. Some of these twinkling lights began to grow brighter, and as her console blinked to indicate she had reached the level of low Earth orbit, one star grew larger and larger, light reflecting off an ochre surface.

"Home sweet home," Taderfit sighed, leaning on the steering column and pulling her craft into dock with the red-hued revolving satellite that was her family's ship.

"Taderfit, how were your deliveries?" Taderfit's father greeted her at the airlock with a hug as he snatched her holopad and started scanning through it.

"Mr. Naciri needs double shipments for his bazaar tent of ginger, turmeric, and argan oil before Yennayer," Taderfit answered, removing her sandals and sliding into her house slippers, hanging her cloak on the door. "He says he'll throw in a cart of kilims for the inconvenience."

"He should've made that order a month ago," her father grumbled. "Anything else?"

"Abdul El-Baz said the durum wasn't the right quality for his couscous."

"That's between him and the wheat farmers, we just deliver," her father grumbled again. He turned to leave, but paused long enough to give his daughter a kiss on the forehead before rambling towards the stockroom in his agitated gate. "Good work Taderfit. Grandma is in the kitchen- go get something to eat."

Taderfit swung her arms, loose robes billowing with the practiced motion of the reluctant, before clapping her hands, nodding to herself, and making her way into the ship's kitchen. As she pulled aside the fabric curtain, her senses were immediately plunged into the comforts of home, of nostalgia, of times when you didn't have a pressing matter to discuss with your family that you knew would break their hearts but you just had to do it. Eventually.

"Taderfit!" Her mother's mother clapped, the coarse and weathered voice dancing through the curling steam rising from pots of stew and couscous, carrying over simmering vegetables and the rattling kiskas in the corner. "Good timing! Come and taste my tfaya, it is missing something."

Taderfit did as instructed, sniffing and then sampling the garnish, rolling it across her palate. The onions were perfectly caramelized, the cinnamon noticeable but not overpowering, the saffron quiet but efficient, the ginger biting.

"You usually add orange flower water to tone down the ginger," Taderfit observed. Her grandmother popped off her stool wagging a finger in the air, disappeared behind a colorful curtain into the pantry, and reemerged a second later with the small bottle in her hands. She tipped several drops into the pot, stirred it, and took a deep inhale, eyes closed in concentration.

"Ah yes. Yes, that was it."

She opened her eyes, beaming.

"My Taderfit! What would I do without you? Come and sit while I cook, tell me about your day."

Taderfit did as instructed, taking the stool she had taken a thousand times, telling her grandmother about her deliveries, gossiping about friends and the other families of their tribe, sampling this recipe and that sauce, sneaking a few cookies that were supposed to be saved until after dinner, laughing and joking and thinking and cooking.

In the time that passed, the family ship continued to revolve, performing its circular dance through space at low orbit around the great blue marble ever present beyond their windows. Several more vessels docked at the hangars, and soon the hallways were filled with the sounds of her rambunctious twin brothers banging through the halls, her mother chasing down her youngest sister as she tried to force the protesting girl into the new formal robes they had just purchased for Yennayer, uncles and aunts and cousins shouting their hellos and asking where to put the side-dishes they brought or if someone could help them unload the cargo from the farms into the stock rooms. With the holiday approaching, there were more orders than usual, so families like theirs were constantly busy in transporting foods from low-orbit farming stations to the people on the surface below.

"Ah, Umaler! You look so lovely," Grandmother clapped her hands as the 12-year-old girl was marched through the curtain into the kitchen, Taderfit's mother clasping the girl's shoulders. Umaler scowled from under the vibrant red and white fabric of the ceremony kaftan, with its gold thread and silver baubles and layers of beaded jewelry.

"Taderfit's kaftan isn't this formal," the young girl complained. Taderfit laughed, adjusting her sister's robes and jewelry.

"It was the Yennayer that I got my siyala," she thumbed her sister's chin.

"Exactly, the tattoo mistress is traveling a great distance this year," their mother said. "It's a big year for you."

Umaler looked at her sister, then her mother, then her grandmother, a thin line flanked by fine dots ornamenting each chin from the youthful to the aged, and with the sigh of the defeated her shoulders dropped in surrender.

"Come, let's eat!" Their father's voice saved Umaler from need to wear this outfit any longer and she scampered off to go change. Taderfit laughed, watching her sister, remembering herself at that age, many tattoos ago. She was 20 now, the eldest child in her family. Set to inherit the family business. Pushing down the aching in her chest, she started to bring food to the table.

During such a busy time, it was only once every other week that the entire family gathered together for dinner so there was a lot of gossip to catch up on as they settled onto colorful cushions around the table. Taderfit's youngest cousin would be getting his first haircut during Yennayer, and her aunts swooned and cooed over the locks about to be trimmed. Her uncle and father vowed not to talk about the family business over dinner and broke that promise almost immediately, complaining about the farmers who did not provide enough supplies or the clients who couldn't keep their own orders straight. Several cousins talked mechanics and the work they were doing to improve their vessels, from specs for nanotech to the newest innovations in thrusters that could be retrofitted onto the revolving family ships. And eventually, they all started to talk about the move.

"We should be in the next quadrant a week after Yennayer," her father proposed, scanning his holopad between bites of pastilla, crumbs of the flaky delicacy drifting through the hologram display.

"A week! What is your rush?" An uncle complained, pointing out that the farms in that quadrant wouldn't have their first crops ready for delivery until at least two weeks after Yennayer. Taderfit's eyes shifted to the table, fork absentmindedly chasing a pea across her plate.

"Did you hear about the Lmrabet boy?" An aunt whispered. Taderfit's ears perked up and she glanced quietly in the direction of the gossip.

"Yes," Taderfit's mother sighed, her voice dripping with sadness for that poor family. "Can you imagine? Already leaving the family ship to start his own, and he's not even married. Who's going to help him run that big empty ship? And orbiting Mars! So far away! What a pity."

Taderfit's eyes fell back to her plate.

~

"Meddur Lmrabet, you are a fool!" Bakhta waved a fist in frustration.

"What? The Bride of Anzar is a great name for a ship," the young man on the screen shook his head, disappointed in his friends' lack of vision.

"Nobody is going to do business with us!" Bakhta threw a hand in the air with such vigor that she dropped her holopad. As she scrambled to pick it up, holding it upside down, she gestured at the third face hovering in the conversation. "Tell him, Taderfit."

"There's a reason most families use their name for the business and the family ship," Taderfit replied, voice quiet as she reclined in the corner of her room, hugging a cushion with zig-zagging motifs stitched across it. "A name shows that you're working with a tribe, and a family, and your business has legitimacy from that."

"Well, from the way my parents reacted, I don't think we'll get to use their name," Meddur frowned. Bakhta nodded, brow heavy.

"My family is being more supportive, but we still can't associate our new ship with theirs since I'm choosing to leave, without being married and without their approval."

"So, we need our own name!" Meddur's voice escalated as the fires of passion for this new endeavor burned within him. "There are more than enough families working Earth orbit, but now the terraforming process is beginning on Mars! The first farms are already in orbit to provide for the terraforming crews, and soon colonists will be arriving. We'll be among the first ships out there, so we'll prove our legitimacy that way, by being ready for the next wave of space colonization. Come on Taderfit, wasn't it your grandmother who helped lead the first generation of Imazighen into orbit? Where would we be without her boldness?"

"Grandma Tafrara," Bakhta whispered, eyes closed in reverence. "From the dunes to the stars."

"And in honor of that legacy, I think we should choose a ship name that celebrates our Earthly heritage, like The Bride of Anzar!"

"Meddur, I swear if you say that name one more time…"

Taderfit sat in silence while her friends continued the debate, glancing around her room, taking in its soft carpets, its colorful tapestries covering each wall, the flowing curtains and cushions and blankets and all those comforts of home. The walls, pressing in a little tighter every day. She looked out the window at the vast, dark desert beyond, infinite freedom set with white-hot diamonds.

〜

"Biodiversity," Taderfit laughed, making sure to clearly annunciate the word her sister had been trying to say.

"Bido- yeah, that," Umaler nodded, face serious as she looked out the window at the world far below. "That's what we're studying. Teacher said that by moving our farming into orbit, humanity could let the animals and plants grow back in all those places. That's a lot of habitats. Even the desert is an ecosystem, did you know that?"

"That's right," Taderfit said, glad that her sister's teacher was a good one this year. "And our ancestors knew this better than anyone. They were the first to live on that desert, to make it a home."

"Why would they live there?" Umaler asked as she peered out the ship's window, scanning the vast patchwork of browns and yellows and gold stretching across the continent like a barren quilt. Every now and then, a shimmer of light would reveal some of the massive solar farms now covering that desert.

"Why do we live in the stars?" A voice came from behind them, cool and steady.

"Ziri's right, it's just what we do," came the other voice, energetic and warm. "Hey Taderfit, can I steer?"

"No, Azenzêr, you cannot," Taderfit swatted her brother's hand away from the control panel. "You two go and strap in, we're about to make our approach."

Taderfit smiled to herself as she heard the racing of feet, the pushing and shoving of her 14-year-old brothers, Ziri and Azenzêr, light of the moon and sun, night and day, thoughtfulness and impulse, constantly encouraging each other in a perpetual cycle of mischief. She leaned on the steering column and the ship tilted towards the revolving space station looming ahead, this great spinning greenhouse one of the many farms sharing Earth's orbit.

Having docked and unloaded, Taderfit pulled up the order sheets and began conferring with the farmers, the Mehrgarh clan, in this case. Taderfit's father was completing business with another farm and would be on his way soon, but in the meantime Taderfit provided the farmers with the orders made by merchants back on Earth as her brothers busied themselves in the task of preparing and loading the cargo (while making time to flex their muscles in front of the Mehrgarh girls). Umaler stayed at Taderfit's side, watching her sister negotiate prices and tour the greenhouse with the farmers to inspect crops and sample the products.

"This one," Taderfit rubbed the cumin powder between her fingers, tapping it on the tip of her tongue. The seeds had been roasted perfectly before grounding, the sensation was warm and earthy and just slightly sweet. The farmer beamed, for Taderfit's taste for quality was legendary among those who grew spices and herbs, and if she endorsed it then he knew it would sell.

"It will be a shame to see you go, Taderfit," he mentioned as they exchanged holopads, each signing the others to confirm the transaction.

"Don't worry Mr. Mehrgarh, we'll be back in a few cycles. We're just rotating quadrants."

"Yes, but I meant your relocation to the Mars orbit."

Taderfit froze.

"Your friends Meddur and Bakhta stopped by just this morning to discuss the business of your new ship. I must say, it is a risky thing you are doing, but knowing that you are a part of the endeavor makes me feel that I can trust their judgement. You may let your friends know that I will be happy to use your new ship for Earth-to-Mars transport."

"Th-thank you, sir," Taderfit mumbled, turning as quickly as decorum would allow before Umaler could ask any questions and praying that the girl had been too distracted by the farm to have noticed the conversation. But as she turned, it was not Umaler who met her gaze, eyes wide in confusion.

"Taderfit?" Her father whispered, jaw hanging open.

～

"GRANDMOTHER WON'T SEE YOU?" Umaler asked, hands behind her back as she swayed in small steps, eyes down and toeing the rug with her slippers. The flight from the Mehrgarh farm back to the family ship had been tense, and the conversations that erupted upon arriving far worse.

"No," Taderfit replied quietly. "She won't."

"Will you still be there for Yennayer when I get my siyala?"

Taderfit stopped packing and set down her bags. With a few steps she was across the small room with both arms wrapped around her sister.

"Of course, Umaler, of course. I wouldn't miss it. And you know, I'll still come back and visit you all the time, okay?"

"I don't understand why you have to go," Umaler pouted. Taderfit ran a hand over her head.

"You heard Grandmother. I don't think I have much choice. If I'm going to abandon the family I might as well just go."

"I meant why you have to go to Mars."

Taderfit pulled some pillows from her bed and set them on the floor, nestling onto one and patting the other. Umaler joined Taderfit on the floor, leaning against the wall.

"Do you remember what I told you today, about our ancestors and the desert?" Taderfit asked. Umaler thought for a moment, and nodded.

"I said the desert was an ecosystem, and you said our ancestors lived there."

"That's right," Taderfit nodded. "The desert is unforgiving and harsh, but they lived with it in harmony. Space is even harsher, but our people made it a home too. Earth orbit is getting crowded, too crowded for many more of our ships. But Mars colonization is just beginning. The colonists will need ships to transport supplies back and forth from Earth to Mars, to transport supplies from the farms and stations to the surface, and who better to do that than our people, we who navigated the great deserts, who were the first to move entirely into orbit, who have always been connected to the vast spaces that others see as uninhabitable? For humanity to thrive in the stars, we have to see it all as an ecosystem, an environment, a space of nature we can live with in harmony. I can help be a part of that."

Umaler nodded, face serious as she listened.

"Are you mad at Grandmother?" She asked at last. Taderfit sighed.

"No, I'm not."

She was still a moment, then she went to her desk and retrieved a small cube. She sat back down and handed the cube to Umaler, and the younger girl turned it over with wide eyes. Flickering within the translucent object was a moving image of a young woman, draped in a flag of four colors under a large red letter. Written across the surface of the cube, in Tifinagh, were the words, the rallying cry of that generation, "From the Dunes to the Stars".

"Is this…Grandmother?" Umaler whispered. Taderfit nodded, and pointed at the four stripes of the flag around the shoulders of the woman in the holo-cube, this much younger version of their grandmother.

"Blue for the sea, green for the Tell mountains, yellow for the Sahara, and black," Taderfit glanced out the window. "Black for space. This flag represents freedom for our people, that's what the red Yaz symbolizes in the middle, and the colors indicate harmony with nature. When Grandmother was young, at the onset of space travel, she helped lead the first of our people to orbit, as a way to preserve our culture and move it beyond Earth. She used to talk about her dreams of moving closer to the stars. Her stories, the ones she told me when I was younger, they're what inspired me to do this, to help establish the Mars orbit."

"Then why is she so upset about you leaving?" Umaler asked, still transfixed by the woman in the cube. Taderfit shrugged.

"Family is complicated, Umaler."

A light on Taderfit's communicator began to blink.

"I've got to finish packing. Bakhta and Meddur will be here soon to pick me up. I promise I'll be there for Yennayer."

"At least try to fix things before you go," Umaler mumbled, and Taderfit wrapped her in a big hug.

Taderfit quickly finished packing and, heeding her sister's words, roamed the ship in search of reconciliation. It was quiet, unnaturally so. The family rooms were empty, the hallways that normally echoed with laughter were silent, and even the kitchen had gone dormant. Taderfit poked her head into the workroom and sure enough found her father, tinkering at the 3D printer they used to create spare parts for the engines.

"I'm sorry I didn't tell you," Taderfit said quietly as she entered the room. Her father was still, back towards her. Then his shoulders fell.

"Your eyes have always been on the stars, Taderfit. You are very good at this business, and I had hoped you would take over this ship one day, but inside, I knew…I always knew…"

He turned and Taderfit felt her breath catch in her throat as she saw the glistening in the corners of her eyes.

"You will not be happy inheriting my ship, your mother's ship, your grandmother's ship. You were always meant for your own."

He spoke with eyes locked on hers and chin held high, though his hands trembled and his shoulders shook. In gentle strides, Taderfit crossed the room and hugged him.

It was several minutes before the embrace was broken.

"Do you know where I can find Grandmother?" Taderfit asked, now helping her father assemble the pieces he had been printing. "She wasn't in the kitchen or her room."

"She's with your mother," he answered softly. "She will need time to process this, Taderfit. In her mind, everything she did was to establish a home, a safe home, not just for her daughter but for Umaler, and Azenzêr, and Ziri, and you."

That night, as Taderfit slept under the few blankets she had brought to her new ship, surrounded by only a few bags of possessions, she wept.

Over the next few weeks, Taderfit worked with her friends to set up their ship, meeting with farmers in Earth orbit and merchants on the surface, as well as captains of the terraforming fleets and colony magistrates. The demand for transportation ships proved to be high, and it was not long before they had orders scrolling over their holopads and cargo overflowing their hull. And still, the ship seemed empty.

"My family ship had tapestries on every wall, carpets on every floor, cushions and tables and lamps," Taderfit observed as she and Bakhta discussed the issue. "All the comforts of a home."

"Mine too," Bakhta looked around their ship, barren metal walls and floors, decorated with all the sterility of space.

"Maybe we can pick up some things from the bazaar while we're on planet for Yennayer," Meddur offered, sitting on the floor beside them. "We're already doing better than I thought so we have money for some things."

"Of course," he added with a wink at Taderfit, "it's up to you, captain."

Bakhta cheered and Taderfit buried her face in her hands, blushing.

"Alright, alright," she said, waving off the laughs of her friends.

"How are things with the family?" Bakhta asked after a minute.

"My mom is coming around, and I got to explain everything to my brothers," Taderfit sighed. "But my grandmother still won't talk to me."

"I'm sorry," Bakhta hugged her friend.

"It's okay," Taderfit wiped an eye. "It's time to focus on the future. On our future."

Finally, the day of Yennayer arrived. Even with so many of the Imazighen scattered throughout Earth's orbit, holidays like this were still best celebrated on the surface. Taderfit and her friends had taken one of their smaller vessels down the night before, leaving the business ship revolving in orbit, and landed on the vast golden sea of sand among the other ships of her tribe. All three of the friends dressed in clothes appropriate for the occasion, although they were all somewhat quiet that morning. Yennayer was a time for joy and celebration and family, and although they were excited for the adventure ahead of them, the uncomfortable relationships with their families hung like a cloud over their heads. Thus, it was a surprise when a beeping signaled that somebody was outside their door. Together, the three friends opened the hatch to find an old woman, weathered and wise as the Tell Atlas, hands tucked inside colorful and lively robes.

"Grandmother?" Taderfit sputtered.

"Miss Tafrara, an honor," Meddur bowed his head.

"We'll let you talk," Bakhta pulled Meddur back into the ship. Taderfit watched her friends scuttle inside, then turned. Her grandmother was eyeing the ship, eyebrows furrowed. Taderfit's mouth was dry, as if she'd been wandering the desert for days, her throat suddenly parched and her words turning to dust on her tongue.

"Grandmother…" She managed to say again, voice hoarse, and she realized there were tears welling her eyes, tears of joy at seeing her grandmother, of anger and frustration at the lack of support, confusion at the sudden unannounced appearance.

"I am not happy that you are choosing to leave your family home," her grandmother began, eyes still on the ship. She was quiet a moment. "My mother never spoke to me again when I left for Earth orbit. She said my boldness was a shame. But I am proud of you, Taderfit."

Her grandmother's eyes fell to meet Taderfit's, and Taderfit saw the welling of tears within them too. Slowly, her grandmother extended a hand. In it, there was a glowing cube with an image of a young woman.

"Umaler gave this to me. I thought I lost it years ago; where did you find it?" She asked.

"I've had it ever since you told me your story," Taderfit admitted. She paused, and then all the emotions and feelings and frustrations and love burst forth. "I'm sorry, Grandmother! I have to do this, to stretch my world, to reach for the stars! Like you did!"

"My Taderfit, what will I do without you?" Grandmother grabbed Taderfit's hands and smiled, eyes heavy with sorrow, with pride.

"I started our family ship, I went to orbit so that our family could be free, truly a free people," she patted Taderfit's hands. "I seem to have forgotten that. Take it with you, Taderfit. That that spirit closer to the stars."

"Thank you, Grandmother. I'll take everything you ever taught me, every lesson, every recipe, all of it."

"Well, first you must remember that Yennayer is a time for family!"

With that, Grandmother waved her hand and the rest of Taderfit's family appeared, aunts and uncles and siblings smiling and waving, carrying in their arms blankets and rugs, cushions and curtains, pots and pans and lamps. Her parents held her hands, regarding her as a woman. Her brothers bristled in rambunctious joy. Umaler, dressed in her formal kaftan and ready to make her entrance into womanhood within the tribe, beamed in admiration of her brave big sister. As the family flooded into the small vessel, filling it with small treasures and comforts, Bakhta and Meddur were embraced as well, as family, as business partners of the tribe, as equals. Finally, crowded within the small space, Taderfit's grandmother bestowed her final gifts.

"My orange flower water," she said with a wink as she handed Taderfit the bottle. "And this, for you to wear proudly among our people today."

From her robes she withdrew a large sheet, old, weathered, but cared for over the years with affection, and wrapped it around Taderfit's shoulders. Taderfit felt her cheeks burn, her eyes swell with pride as she traced the four stripes of color, the large red letter in the middle.

"Thank you," she whispered.

"For Taderfit!" Bakhta cheered, raising a cup, and others merrily followed suit. "From the dunes to the stars!"

Christopher R. Muscato is a writer from Colorado, USA. He is the former writer-in-residence of the High Plains Library District and a graduate of the Terra.do climate activism fellowship.

X: https://www.twitter.com/ChrisRMuscato

ABOUT OTHER WORLDS INK

Other Worlds Ink (OWI) is the brainchild of author J. Scott Coatsworth and his husband Mark D. Guzman. It's part publisher, part blog tour company, and part author support organization.

We publish the annual Queer Sci Fi flash fiction anthologies, many of Scott's books, and we're now branching out to other things, including this anthology.

We are dedicated to making the world better, now and in the future.

OTHER BOOKS FROM OWI

Queer Sci Fi Flash Fiction Anthologies

Ink | Clarity | Rise

———

Writers Save the World Anthologies

Fix the World | Save the World | Transform the World

———

J. Scott Coatsworth's Works

Liminal Sky: Ariadne Cycle

The Stark Divide | The Rising Tide | The Shoreless Sea

Liminal Sky: Redemption Cycle

Dropnauts

Liminal Sky: Oberon Cycle

Skythane | Lander | Ithani

Other Sci Fi/Fantasy

The Autumn Lands | Cailleadhama | Firedrake | The Great North | Homecoming |
The Last Run | Wonderland

Short Story Collections

Spells & Stardust | Tangents & Tachyons | Androids & Aliens | Love & Limitations

Contemporary/Magical Realism

Between the Lines | I Only Want to Be With You | Flames | The River City

Chronicles | Slow Thaw

99¢ Shorts

The Emp Test

Audiobooks

Cailleadhama | The Autumn Lands | The River City Chronicles | Dropnauts |
Skythane | Lander (2024)